THE
THESEUS
PARADOX

ABOUT THE AUTHOR

A former Scotland Yard investigator with twenty years' policing experience, including counter-terror operations and organised crime, David Videcette has worked as a Metropolitan Police detective on a wealth of infamous cases. He currently consults on security operations for high-net-worth individuals and is an expert media commentator on crime, terrorism, extremism and the London 7/7 bombings.

To find out more about David and subscribe for updates, visit: www.DavidVidecette.com

THE
THESEUS
PARADOX

What if London's 7/7 bombings were the greatest
criminal deception of our time?

DAVID VIDECETTE

The first title in the
DETECTIVE INSPECTOR
JAKE FLANNAGAN SERIES

The Theseus Paradox

Published by Videcette Limited

Copyright © Videcette Limited 2015

ISBN: 978 0 99342 631 5

Typesetting and proofreading by www.tenthousand.co.uk

Find out more about the author and his upcoming titles at:
www.DavidVidecette.com

FOREWORD

I went out to work on 7 July 2005, and two weeks later I came home wearing the same clothes and with fifty-six people dead.

The quest for the truth about the London bombings took years to unravel. Thousands of men and women played their parts in helping to unravel that truth, some of which was presented to a public enquiry. Yet, despite years and years of painstaking work, I still feel that we only ever scratched the surface of what *really* went on.

I was not a victim of the bombings, but in many ways my life was altered forever by that day too, along with a large proportion of the people I worked with on Operation Theseus. What started off as a normal day at work within the Anti-Terrorist Branch turned into a nightmare that still haunts me and many others.

The story you are about to read is fictional and so are the characters within it. I have drawn upon open-source research conducted over the last decade.

Angie, John and Nev – thank you for the confidence you had in me.

To Teena Lyons for her advice and to Caroline Sephton, without whom I could never have created this book. Caroline has helped me to understand myself and make sense of the things that have taken place.

Lisa, without your unwavering support, I'd not be here today.

And to my girls whom I love dearly – this is for you.

I can't tell you the truth, but I can tell you a story. This is what happened during London's summer of terror…

1

'I can't tell you the truth, but I can tell you a story...'

It was dark and still, the new moon barely visible to the naked eye.

Within hours, the sight of the bus's twisted metal skeleton and the odour of the charred fibreglass shards ripped from its body would take full control of his senses, but for now all Jake could smell was the scent of the pollen that hung in the air after the long hot day.

'And the host city for the 2012 Olympic Games... is... LONN-DONN!' blared the news from the car's radio, startling him. He reached for the volume control.

The female newsreader's voice continued quietly, almost inaudibly, '...Following a nail-biting vote between Paris and London, shares of British construction companies rocketed with yesterday's announcement that London would be the chosen venue for the 2012 Olympic Games. Mortgage lenders predicted property prices in the capital would soar, following an eighteen-month race that hinged on a knife-edge in the final voting stages...'

It was time. He could wait no longer.

Jake got out of the unmarked car, deadening the jangle from his keys as he made his way swiftly to the right property.

The rough red brick pulled at the skin of his arm through his baggy DKNY sweater as he clambered up, over and into the rear garden of an ordinary-looking, small, three-bedroomed Victorian home.

He crouched in the darkness of a large bush, looking for lights or movement on either floor of the mid-terrace.

Nothing.

All remained quiet on the sleepy, West Yorkshire street.

The shed and wheelie bins offered him scant protection as he sprinted up the garden toward the shabby back door. Standing as close to it as possible, he grabbed the faux-gold handle and tugged hard.

It was locked. Through the window he could see the key on the other side of the door. There was no time to mess about. With a quick swing from the hip, he slammed his jumper-covered elbow into a small pane of glass in the upper half. It broke easily with just a little thud – with practice, most windows did.

Jake was wearing two pairs of surgical gloves. He was well aware that sweaty hands meant fingerprint-ridge detail could travel through a single pair.

The entry was not an authorised one. He knew that at this stage he was on his own. The boss was going to take some placating, but only if Jake actually got round to telling anyone about his actions.

Normally, this sort of thing was just kept at a discrete level between line managers and operatives; only made 'official' if something was found. In those cases, retrospective steps would then be taken to give the impression that all was above board and legal.

This time, though, Jake hadn't even told Helen in advance.

He knew there was something big going on here, even if he couldn't convince the bosses yet.

Ten minutes earlier, he'd seen Wasim put a rucksack into the small blue car at the front of the terraced house – same time, same routine as the previous day. Only something had gone wrong the day before. Wasim's pregnant wife had come running out of the house and grabbed her husband. She'd been holding her stomach. Wasim had gone back inside. Then both of them had gone straight to the hospital.

Jake now knew that Salma, Wasim's wife, had experienced serious complications with her pregnancy, which had led to the loss of their unborn child. He had watched Wasim type a flurry of text messages shortly after Salma had grabbed him in the street. Major plans had clearly been altered yesterday. Jake could put in a RIPA request to see the content of those text messages, but it might take some weeks to get the stuff back from the mobile-phone company, depending on who the service provider was. Some were quicker than others. He could also ask the Security Service, but getting them to share it might be hard work.

Jake had picked the easy route this morning; the good old-fashioned way: get in, have a look around… and get out.

He was inside. He moved to the front of the house and stood in the small kitchen, surveying the jaundiced Formica units. What had Wasim been doing in here before he left? Jake had a quick scout around; everything looked normal – neat and tidy, nothing out of place.

As he bent down to begin scrabbling around in the kitchen cupboards, he saw it: two brown marks on the white linoleum floor in front of the washing machine.

All washing machines leaked water after a certain amount of time. It would run down and collect on the legs and feet, turning them rusty. When you pulled a unit out from the wall, the feet would inevitably leave marks on the floor, as per Dr Edmond Locard's exchange principle: 'Every contact leaves a trace'.

Jake touched the marks on the lino. They were wet. The machine had definitely been moved that morning. Before 0300 hours? Why?

He wrestled the machine away from the wall. A pipe was loose at the back. Taking out a kit from his pocket, he wiped the inside of the pipe with a cotton bud, then placed the cotton bud inside the vial.

He shook it. The entire vial turned brown instantly.

It was positive for HMTD. Hexamethylene triperoxide diamine – a highly explosive organic compound that lent itself well to acting as an initiator.

Wasim had a bomb.

2

Jake had to stop him. Where was he headed? Wasim had left the house only minutes earlier. Surely he'd be relatively easy to spot at this time in the morning? He retraced his steps out through the back door and over the wall. Back in the Audi, he tried calling Helen on his mobile, but he couldn't get a signal.

Wasim and his Nissan Micra had gone right at the main road that morning. Making an educated guess, Jake copied Wasim's lead – accelerating hard in the direction of Leeds. Houses and trees slipped by as he sped down the road; there was no sign of the blue Micra anywhere.

He shouldn't be here. He had broken into a house without permission. And now he was going to have to confess everything to his line manager with no proof but a swab test.

This was going to take a lot of report writing to justify. It was potentially job threatening. But no one had seen him. He didn't have to tell anyone – and it wouldn't be the first time. Maybe it was a good job he hadn't been able to get a phone signal earlier? Jake made the decision not to call in and explain what he'd done. Not yet anyway.

On the approach to Leeds city centre, he realised that he had managed to make it all the way there without seeing another car. It wasn't like London; this place went to sleep. He decided to double back and retrace his route.

As he made his way back along the dual carriageway, there it was – the Nissan Micra passing him, going in the other direction.

4

Wasim was no longer alone in the car. There were three of them. Wasim had clearly made a detour to pick the other two up.

Jake floored the accelerator in the A4, knowing that the next junction was about two miles up ahead. The broken white dashes on the grey tarmac appeared to merge into one solid lane line, and the wind produced a high-pitched, tea-kettle whistling noise as it slipped past his car.

Jake turned back on himself at the roundabout, tyres screeching, and joined the opposite carriageway – now heading in the same direction as the Micra.

The road led directly to the M1 motorway. The 1.8-litre turbo engine roared as he pushed the Audi to its full capacity, trying desperately to close the distance between himself and Wasim. The speedometer hit 145 mph.

He was now back at the exact point he'd seen their car two minutes ago. His heart rate and adrenaline levels were climbing exponentially; they couldn't be that far ahead of him. There was only one more exit at which they could pull off before they would hit the M1 going south.

He saw the tail lights of the Micra pass the final slip road without turning off.

They'd stayed on.

They were heading south toward London.

London? Why would they be travelling toward London?

Jake felt a sudden surge of panic.

He needed help. There was a radio in his vehicle but it was a Metropolitan Police surveillance one. It used a frequency not monitored by the West Yorkshire force; it was worse than useless to him here.

Instead, he grabbed his mobile and called 999, a more efficient route to get help when operating outside of his own area.

'Hello, emergency, which service please?' asked the female operator.

Jake knew there was no point outlining any details to the BT-employed operator. Information was only recorded after the call was switched to the relevant emergency service – any explanation right now only served to delay that process.

'Police, police, I need police!' Jake heard a note of fear beginning to rise in his own voice as he spoke.

'Police, thank you.'

There was a pause as the system traced which area he was calling from and connected him to the right control room.

'West Yorkshire Police, how can I help?'

Jake almost cheered when he heard the police call handler, relief washing over him.

'I'm Detective Inspector Jake Flannagan of the Metropolitan Police Service Anti-Terrorist Branch, SO13. I require urgent assistance, M1, southbound.' Jake paused, awaiting a reply.

But there was none.

'Hello? Hello, can you hear me?' Jake shouted into the handset.

There was no response.

He wrenched the phone from his ear and looked at the handset. The screen was blank. His battery was dead. How much of the call had the call handler heard? Had they heard any of it at all?

Jake was now travelling right behind the Micra. He could see Wasim looking at him in his rear-view mirror. They knew he was there. Jake had slowed from 145 mph to 65 mph and pulled in behind them. He might be in an unmarked car, but on a deserted motorway at this time in the morning there was no disguising that sort of driving behaviour.

Leaning across to the passenger side, he rooted around with his left hand in the glove compartment for his charger, before hunting in the passenger footwell. Where the hell was it?

It was decision time. What if they were delivering a bomb?

He had to stop them.

Abandoning the one-handed search for his missing charger, he dropped the dead Nokia phone onto the passenger seat beside him. It slid across the black leather and disappeared down the side.

His cover was blown, he couldn't communicate with anyone and he was all out of options. Except for one.

He switched on his emergency vehicle equipment. The headlights of his car began to flash alternately, the two-tone siren wailed and the covert blue lights hidden behind his Audi's front grille began to pulse onto the Micra in front of him.

Focussing his eyes properly back on the road, he spotted two small objects hurtling at speed from the direction of the Micra. What were they? Bottles?

Before he had time to wonder what was happening, there was a flash of white in front of him so dazzling that everything in his peripheral vision turned pitch black. The incandescent glare almost seared the back of his retinas, forcing him to close his eyes, before it faded with a yellow glow.

He opened his eyes again for a split second.

He could see hundreds of tiny flakes fluttering past and wondered if he were being shaken around inside a snow globe.

As the flakes hit his face and body, he realised that they were actually miniscule fragments of glass flying through the air as his vehicle rolled over and his windows shattered.

Jake's ears were ringing. He'd stopped moving. He could smell battery acid and there was a funny taste in his mouth. Was it coolant from the engine? He touched his head – blood. He was upside down, or the car was upside down – or both. The seat belt had locked tightly across him, thankfully – absorbing his body's independent inertia. His ribcage and pelvis were bruised where the webbing had spread its stopping force.

Whatever they'd thrown from their car had exploded in front of him. He felt something sharp and spiky beneath him; metal pins digging into his flesh. He lifted his arm. Nail bombs? Jake knew that nail bombs didn't kill through concussion; they killed by the blast effect of metal tearing tissue.

He needed to stop them, needed to tell someone. The fire brigade, the paramedics, police – they would come for him now. Someone would find him.

Wasim and his friends would be stopped.

If only they'd listened to him sixteen months ago – even ten days ago.

It would all be OK now though – when they arrived to help him.

He lost consciousness.

3

16 MONTHS PREVIOUSLY
Saturday
28 February 2004
1825 hours
Crawley, West Sussex

Sleet hammered down on the front door of the house they were watching, like an angry man with thousands of tiny fingers – the fingers exploding as they hit the panes of glass.

It was bitter; Jake was glad to be inside.

The flat in which Jake had set up camp belonged to an elderly lady who was not in great health. She'd been staying with her daughter for the past few months and the place had been sitting there empty. Jake had found it as he'd wandered through the estate a few weeks earlier. The sheer amount of post hanging from the letterbox and the stale milk outside gave away that the occupant was either dead or absent long term. A few phone calls to the local council quickly revealed that the old girl was unlikely to return for some months. That's how observation points were found – basic common sense and asking questions of the right people. But you had to be sensible about whom you questioned and what you asked.

After introducing himself on the phone, Jake had picked the keys up from the old woman's daughter. He'd told her that he was a police officer, but not that he was a detective inspector with the Anti-Terrorist Branch. She'd asked what it was that he wanted the flat for and Jake had given her the usual cover story about targeting some local teenagers dealing cannabis to schoolchildren down the street. He 'needed to borrow the place to catch them in the act'. She was very keen to help – as

8

most socially responsible citizens were when they'd been spun the tale – and she'd handed over the keys easily. Jake would reward her with several bunches of flowers and pay the utility bills when they'd no more use for the place – but that could be anything up to a year in some cases.

Jake often wondered why people never questioned his local-bobby-on-the-beat impersonation. He wasn't in uniform and didn't drive a Vauxhall Astra. The expensive suit and high-powered, top-of-the-range Audi were a bit of a giveaway.

He was sat in the flat with Paul Deacon, a junior detective on his team. Paul was fairly new but Jake liked him already. He could see some of himself in Paul – a reminder of the Jake from nearly sixteen years ago, when he'd originally joined the force.

Jake had been twenty when he'd joined the Met. He'd worked across various covert and specialist units during his career but it was only once he was selected for the Anti-Terrorist Branch – 'the Branch' as they called it – that he felt he'd found a true home for his skills and expertise.

When he'd started, there had been just sixty detective constables on the Branch; a tiny team in comparison to other police units, but those selected were always the very best in their field. Jake had been immensely proud when he'd got the nod to apply.

Funding to combat terrorism had all but dried up following the IRA ceasefire. Then 9/11 kick-started the machine again and the Branch began growing rapidly in size, with the threat, as if from nowhere, that Islamic fundamentalism was now said to pose.

Jake had been asked to help out on Operation Crevice. The police had been briefed intensely by the Security Service about a group of al-Qaeda operatives in the south of England – the group that Jake and Paul, crouched in the old lady's flat, were now watching.

Things were hotting up and the Branch was running out of people. 'Short on sleep and long on memory' was the official motto on their coat of arms. With two kids and a failed marriage under his belt, Jake knew this only too well.

Claire, Jake's current girlfriend, worked at the Security Service. She had convinced Jake that the group they were tracking on Operation Crevice were serious and had a credible attack plan that was linked to dangerous factions back in Pakistan.

The Security Service believed that these men were plotting to deploy explosives made from fertiliser at various locations across the country, including nightclubs and shopping centres – Bluewater being just one of them.

So the Security Service would supply the intelligence about the attack plan and who was involved, while the police's Anti-Terrorist Branch were there to collect anything that could be used as evidence in a traditional court of law.

Jake had worked hard to get this observation point up and running – getting the right paperwork completed and signed up, getting his team fully briefed, fitting the cameras and listening devices. He couldn't understand why many of the Security Service appeared not to have the slightest idea what the police did and how evidence was collected and presented in court.

Fresh from fantastic universities, the Security Service's graduates were trained to look at intelligence and produce reports, but Jake always thought that their lack of real-world investigative skills gave them a very one-dimensional view of what they were looking at. He resented the fact that they had primacy for all terrorism investigations whilst the police ate the crumbs from their hand.

The house they were watching was several hundred yards up the street from the flat they now sat in. Jake had requested a clear view of the road and the front door of the property. The recently planted, covert cameras beamed back images onto a dish sat on their flat's balcony, which meant that they could watch any comings or goings from relative safety, whilst warm and dry.

Jake and Paul sat in the lounge; several small TV monitors were dotted across the elderly lady's nest of tables. They sipped their tea out of what were probably her best cups; tiny little china vessels adorned with pink roses and dainty handles.

The radio crackled into life. 'Permission 6-1.'

Jake picked up the black hand-held radio. 'Go, go!' he said, authorising 6-1 to speak.

The reply came loud and clear. 'Silver Honda Accord moving up the street toward the target address.'

Jake gripped the radio and pressed the talk button in reply. 'Contact OP,' he said,

'OP now has the eye.'

The silver Honda stopped and parked directly outside the suburban house they were interested in. One of the monitors on the old woman's nest of tables showed two Asian men climbing out of the vehicle and heading toward their target's front door. They looked to be in their twenties and were both wearing tracksuits.

'All units from OP. Silver car has parked outside the target address. Two Asian males, mid-twenties wearing tracksuits, are out of the car and into the target address,' Jake said into the radio.

'Did anyone get the index?' Jake asked the rest of the surveillance team via the radio. He was wondering who the hell owned this car and what it was doing there.

'Permission 4-2,' the radio chimed again.

'Go, go,' replied Jake.

'The Honda index comes back to an address in Leeds, I just ran it on the PNC and Intel via reserve. Don't know anything about it. It's new to us.'

'Received,' said Jake. This was odd. He had a bad feeling about finding new people this far into the investigation. He asked for the keeper's address and scribbled it down.

The two men were now inside the house; Jake could just about hear them on the listening devices that had been planted inside. These Asian guys sounded different – Yorkshire accents.

Jake handed his headset to Paul. 'Make sure you listen to exactly what they say. I want to know what the fuck they're doing this far south.'

Jake used his mobile to call Claire. No point in using the official Security Service channels at a moment like this. It would take hours and this could be important.

11

'Claire? It's Jake. Are you at work?' he asked.

'No – night off. What's up?' she asked blearily.

Jake could tell from her voice that he had just woken her up. It was barely 2000 hours. Why was she asleep?

'I need some checks on a car and an address. A new motor just turned up here in Crawley.'

'OK – will call the office. Give me the intel.'

Jake handed over the details then turned his attention back to Paul, who was still listening to the conversation inside the house on his headphones.

'What's going on?'

'Not really sure. They seem to be talking about money. Don't think it's anything important.'

Jake took the headphones and listened intently. He could hear one of the tracksuited visitors speaking in a broad West Yorkshire dialect interspersed with the occasional Pakistani inflection: 'Well, I'm not looking to come back. The brothers can do what they want when I am gone. Use my name and get the money. You can use that how you fancy, doesn't bother me. Can you get me there?'

'Of course I can get you there. But it's just a question of cost. It's gonna be three thousand. That's for my amir, not me.'

His phone vibrated in his pocket. It was Claire. He handed the headphones back to Paul.

'I checked it out. They're fresh. Nothing known about the car or the address,' she said. 'What are they doing there?'

'No idea. Just had a listen myself and something's not right,' he replied.

'They're probably just nobodies. Put it through properly in the morning, Jake, and we'll confirm things fully,' said Claire, before ending the call abruptly.

'I think they're leaving, guv – the two Yorkshire lads,' said Paul. 'They're saying their goodbyes.'

'Shit!' said Jake.

4

'All units from OP. We're going to go with the Honda and the two guys in it, I want to put these two blokes to bed tonight,' called Jake into the radio. 'Paul will stay at the OP. I'll catch you up after you're off the plot.'

Jake thought of himself as a very good decision-maker, yet this part of the job often caused him problems. The brass would want to run everything past the Security Service to make sure they weren't stepping on any toes. But that took time, time that was not on the side of someone who had to make a swift call on the ground on a dark and windswept night.

Jake cared little for office politics. Criticism was a constant in the job – although it mainly fell on those who had nothing to show for a bad decision. Jake went by the rule 'nothing ventured, nothing gained' – or at least he prayed that would be the case tonight.

He had decided to follow the Honda, wherever it might go – even if it went to Yorkshire. In an ideal world you actually needed authority for that, but he decided he would worry about it in the morning.

'Received 4-2.'

'6-1.'

'7-6.'

'8-4.'

'2-3.'

'3-5.'

Each member of the surveillance team called out their numbers to acknowledge the command and that they were aware what they were to do next – follow the Honda and see where it went.

Most of the surveillance team were in cars. Except that was for 4-2. He was the poor guy on a motorbike in the rain. It was a role Jake had done many times and loved. Being of average height and weight, with blue eyes that missed nothing, he was a natural at surveillance and blended easily into a crowd. Then there was the added buzz of being allowed to do 190 mph legally. Yet it could also be a bloody killer, being stuck outside on a bike in all weathers – especially on a night like tonight.

Jake watched on the monitor as the two Asian men with Yorkshire accents hugged the head of the group at the door and walked toward their car.

'All units wait... Two males into the car from target address...'

'Honda is off, off, off, toward the station!'

'Contact contact 7-6. Vehicle is 40 mph toward Crawley on A23.' The surveillance team had picked up the Honda and were now following it.

Automatic Number Plate Recognition cameras dotted around some suburban areas could give you a rough route, after the fact – but you could never tell where a vehicle had stopped, for how long or the actual address that it had been visiting.

Just knowing who the car was registered to didn't actually identify who these two men were either. You needed full-blown, full-on surveillance for that. You needed photos, addresses they visited, the credit-card number they used when they paid for petrol – but most of all you needed to know where they slept at night. That's how you identified people. You 'put them to bed'.

Jake had made a judgement call on the Honda. He would call it in to the Yard after they had garnered more information about these guys and what was going on. It was no good trying to explain a hunch to a senior manager – not unless they trusted your judgement implicitly. Jake knew which senior officer was on call tonight. He knew they would be one of the tougher ones to convince. Better to get forgiveness than permission in these circumstances.

If he gained nothing, nothing was lost in getting a bollocking. If he turned up something worthy, something of note – then hopefully permission would be given retrospectively, so that what he'd found was 'evidential'.

Jake told Paul to keep an eye on the address and to let him know by phone if there were any developments.

'When will you pick me up?' asked Paul.

'I don't fucking know, do I? You'll be all right. Don't open the door to anyone and if anyone asks for me, I'm down at McDonalds. Speak later.'

Jake knew Paul would be OK. He was learning the ropes; this was how it worked.

Jake ran down the stairs to the blue Audi A4 tucked into the garages at the bottom. The team were now out of range of his police radio but he managed to get through on his mobile to one of the guys tailing the Honda.

'Where are you?' he asked.

'We're clockwise on the M25,' was the response. 'They're doing eighty-five, not hanging about.'

Jake put the Audi into gear and pulled off slowly and silently. Half a mile down the road he hit the accelerator hard. Even after all these years he still relished this part of the job. Red light after red light was despatched with ease, despite it being a busy Saturday night traffic-wise. Driving fast outside London was a breeze – wide roads, dual carriageways and few pedestrians. When he reached the M23 he floored the Audi's accelerator. It always took longer than you expected to catch the rest of the team from behind – even at top speed. Sometimes you never would.

5

The meeting room on the fifteenth floor could seat forty people, yet today it held just four. They were sat on opposite sides of the large, rectangular pine table, like two opposing teams going head to head.

The Anti-Terrorist Branch was unlike most police command units – there was no autonomy for the officer; everything had to be actioned and signed off by some bigwig up the food chain who was at least two ranks above you. For Jake, that meant at least superintendent level and discussion after discussion in meeting after meeting. Jake hated that side of his job. If something needed doing he was used to getting on and doing it.

But not at the Branch.

Sat opposite Jake in the Battle of the Meeting Room were his big boss, Chief Superintendent Malcolm Denswood, and a minute taker. Sat on Jake's left was his immediate boss, Detective Chief Inspector Helen Brookes.

'OK, Jake – what's this about?' Malcolm Denswood began the meeting.

Denswood was six feet tall and slim, with dark receding hair and edging slowly toward his middle fifties. He was an intelligent guy who knew his strengths and weaknesses and was often good-humoured – but if you got on the wrong side of him, you were finished at the Branch. He was a very private character; work and home didn't mix. A product of the Police

16

Staff College at Bramshill, Jake thought he fitted the pattern of their typical output like a clone – he never swore, never raised his voice and was very careful with the words he used. It was rare for Denswood to look outside the box or do things differently. Jake knew this wasn't going to be easy.

'Sir, I know you're keen to conclude Operation Crevice, but I think we may have missed some things up in West Yorkshire. I've gone back over the files. Remember those guys we saw back in February 2004 on surveillance in Crawley, the ones from Leeds? The ones I followed back up north and you bollocked me about?'

'I do remember, Jake, yes…'

'Well, sir, I've been looking at the intel we collected and I've done some cross-checking.'

'Jake, we had this conversation last March when I found out what you'd done. I told you back then what my feelings were about it. Anyway – we actioned all that stuff out. The Security Service said the conversation was benign and that was the end of it.'

'But the actions were never followed up. They were written off. We, the police, never even spoke to these guys. It's obvious why we never did that; obvious to anyone who knows anything about the Security Service that is… My point is, sir, that that conversation wasn't benign. They were talking about going and fighting in Afghanistan – about not coming back. They were talking about a suicide mission. They *were* talking about finance, as the Security Service said, but in a totally different context to what they meant.'

'So what do you want, Jake? What are you proposing?'

'I think there's a job in those guys – they're at it – we *should* be doing something about it. We shouldn't just be leaving it like this… My team are a bit light on work, we have the capacity. It's a criminal investigation and not a totally proactive fishing expedition – it's in our ballpark. It should be ours to crack on with.'

'Jake – you know it doesn't work like that. I hear you. But we cannot lead. I'll speak to the Security Service and ask. If they say it's OK, we'll talk about it again. In the meantime lay off any unauthorised intel work you're doing on them please.

I know what you're like. I've got a few little things I can throw your way to keep you busy without that anyway. I'll pass them through to Helen to give to you.'

'The job's ready to go, guv – I've done loads already!'

Jake had visited Leeds twice and gathered enough material to carry out surveillance and full-time observations on the Honda driver's home. He was damned if it was all going to go to waste.

'You heard what I said, Jake. No more unauthorised work!'

Malcolm Denswood and the minute taker got up and left the meeting room.

Helen remained seated. She looked concerned.

There was silence between them until they both knew that Denswood was out of earshot.

'This isn't right, Helen,' said Jake with a slight sigh as he stared out of the window.

Jake liked having a female boss – Helen was one of the few people who could criticise him without making him angry. He respected her; she knew her stuff and had shown she could cut it with the best. She also knew that Jake's methods were often unconventional and sometimes even illegal, but that he got results. She chose not to interfere or ask too many questions about how he did things – it was safer for them both. But this time his actions might impact upon both of their jobs.

'You have got to let this go, Jake. We're both going to end up in trouble if you don't. This whole Leeds stuff has got to stop. I know you've been up there recently – I've seen your Amex statement – the hotels, the food expenses on it – not to mention the bar bills! If Denswood asks me, I can't honestly say that any of that was authorised, Jake.'

Jake was disheartened. He'd often felt that he'd been held back in his career by other men, yet he'd experienced none of that with Helen. They'd quickly struck up a strong working relationship when he'd joined the Anti-Terrorist Branch. She'd become one of Jake's strongest, and perhaps most powerful, allies. Not only was she a woman *and* tipped for promotion, but she regularly deflected any backbiting that headed Jake's way. Yet here she was just adding to his frustration.

'But I was working on two people who appeared on our plot, Helen. They went into an address and spent time with suspects who have now been charged with terrorism; suspects who were making a bomb to blow people up,' he replied. 'Those guys from Leeds *must* be at it. The only reason we're not working on them is that the Security Service are calling the shots and making us hold off. This is a stupid way of doing things! Have you read what those Leeds guys were saying back in Feb 2004, in Crawley, Helen? What the probe picked up? The Service says "they were just talking about finance". Bullshit were they *just* talking about that!

'One of the Leeds guys was asking to go on a one-way trip to Afghanistan – a bloody suicide mission. They talked about using his name and details to scam banks and credit cards when he was gone, because both parties knew he wasn't going to come back again!

'Yes it was finance and fraud – but within the context of a conversation where the fuckwit wants to go and blow himself up abroad, probably killing US and UK service personnel in the process. That's terrorism, that's a crime, that's a police matter – and we have the evidence.

'It's crazy to think that *we* – the police – can't act on that because it's not the right thing to do for... *national-security* reasons. I mean, how does it protect anyone in our nation? Letting these guys go and do that?'

Jake could feel himself getting angry. He was determined that this wasn't going to be dropped – incensed that anyone would even think of doing such a thing.

His boss was usually unwavering in her support of him – continually fighting his corner and providing that extra emotional engagement that the boy in him constantly craved. Today, he felt ungrateful; his tone showed none of the usual respect for Helen and Helen's rank.

She took a deep breath. Jake could sense immediately that this wasn't a good sign.

'Look, Jake, the Security Service have the whole picture. They know how these guys fit into that picture. Taking them out of the game might interfere with some other job that's being worked on somewhere else – that's why it works this way. Leave it alone. Let the Service get on with it. No more trips to Leeds.'

'But…' Jake trailed off as Helen's hands motioned for him to drop it.

Jake had pushed it as far as he could go. He knew he was in serious danger of jeopardising his current position and maybe even Helen's promotion too. There was no use in him banging his head against a brick wall.

'Maybe you need some time off, Jake?'

'Do I? Why?' Jake was surprised by her question.

'Maybe – if I'm honest with you, Jake – I'm a little worried about you. You've lost your mother *and* grandmother recently. On top of that you walked out on your wife and kids…'

Jake could tell Helen wasn't finished.

'…and you know I'm not one to plug into the rumour mill, but… upper management are asking me questions about what they're hearing.'

'Like what?' Jake asked a little worriedly.

'"Is he drinking too much?", "What's the truth in all this talk about dalliances with female colleagues?", "If he's out on the lash all the time, can he be trusted?", "Are we OK with his vetting?" – you know what this place is like…'

'What the hell has my vetting got to do with it?'

'If you're drinking too much that *could* be an issue for the vetting office, Jake. If you're enjoying *too* much pillow talk with *too* many strange women it *could* be an issue for the vetting office… *Semper Occultus.*'

Semper Occultus was Latin for 'Always Secret' – the Security Service motto. Vetting was about ensuring that you knew who your people outside of work were, about what they got up to. That they didn't participate in risky behaviour such as taking drugs or attending swingers' parties; that they were at the lowest risk of possible compromise; that they couldn't be blackmailed easily.

'I don't need to tell you this stuff, do I? Reputation is a big thing here, Jake.' Helen sounded slightly annoyed.

'Helen – you know what this place is like. According to rumours I've slept with every woman here, including you…

and we both know that rumour isn't true, don't we? So why should the rest of it be?'

'Yes, I'd heard that one doing the rounds as well…' she said, unamused. 'Look, aside from the rumours, I know things are tough for you right now. I've seen you out drinking, flirting, messing about with the girls from the MIR. I know that stuff is all likely a symptom of what's been going on in your private life, but – it keeps these rumours going, Jake. These are all things that *could* be an issue with vetting if we have a mistake or a problem arises that they can hang that stuff on. You've got to be careful.'

'Fair point, I hear you. I appreciate you mentioning it. None of it's a problem, honestly…' Jake sounded like he was trying to convince himself as well as Helen.

The truth was he didn't really know if his behaviour *was* a problem. There was the odd strange woman and he was drinking most nights. But everyone drank, didn't they? All warm-blooded men needed a bit of female attention some-times, didn't they?

'Yes, maybe I should take some time off,' he acquiesced. 'Just a few days, but might be longer. That OK?'

'No problem. What are you going to do? Where will you be if we need you?'

'Going to pop to Manchester. Pal of mine is having a tough time at home – be good to see him and check out the night-life…' He winked at her and smiled. 'Plus it will put some distance between me and this Leeds stuff, I think.'

'Great idea, Jake. Just slow down a bit on the old drinking. I know it's hard with everything that's gone on. Take the car with you, just in case we need you back quickly,' she replied as she got up and made her exit.

Jake sat in silence, alone in the meeting room. His mind wandered.

Leeds was only forty miles from Manchester. Thirty-odd minutes if you put your foot down.

6

Jake awoke wearing a flimsy green cotton robe. He was lying in a hospital bed. He touched his head and found there was a dressing on the front of it. He hobbled to the nurses' station. They were all watching the news on TV, engrossed in it; they hadn't even seen him get up. Walking round to the rear of the counter he could make out the large, rolling Sky News headlines on the screen, which read: 'London Terror Attacks'.

His heart felt like it had stopped beating. His chest hurt.

'No. Please. NO!'

An attractive blonde nurse with freckles looked up at him and smiled.

'You're awake. How are you feeling?' she asked in a broad Yorkshire accent.

'I feel like shit. Where am I and what happened?' asked Jake groggily.

A young male nurse came over to steady him. He walked Jake back to his bed, sat him down and gave him some water. 'Hello, sir. Feeling better after your accident?' he asked.

Jake realised the confusion on his face was evident, because the male nurse took pity on him. 'You had a car accident... a nasty one. You hit the central reservation on the M1 in your car. Do you remember?'

'They threw something at me – it exploded in the road...' Jake tailed off.

'Who threw something at you? No, I overheard the paramedics talking – the police said there was no other car involved,' said the male nurse. He handed Jake a couple of painkillers and went on his way.

Jake got up gingerly. Next to his bed he found a locker containing a property bag full of his tattered, ripped clothes. Hidden amongst them he spotted his warrant card and sighed with relief. It was always grief with a capital 'G' if anyone lost theirs.

Just as importantly, both his police credit card and his personal debit card were intact and tucked safely inside, meaning he had ready access to escape funds.

He scooped up his belongings, looking for a nearby toilet in which to change, but found that his clothes were in pieces, cut by the hospital when he'd been unconscious. He beckoned the male nurse back over, who kindly found him some charity hand-me-down baggy jeans and a Def Leppard T-shirt. At least they were clean and in one piece. The hospital staff were used to sorting out people who found themselves in an unfortunate position with no clothing – but not usually ones who'd been chasing cars full of nail bombs down the M1.

At reception he requested to be released from the hospital's care. The female nurse with the freckles and broad Yorkshire accent he'd met earlier pushed some forms toward him. Jake signed his discharge documents.

There was a mirror on the wall behind the nurse. Jake caught his reflection. He looked awful.

'We informed your next of kin you were here, Mr Flannagan. The police gave us the contact details. Your wife I believe it was…'

'Ex-wife. She divorced me. Too many nights away from home, waking up in strange beds…'

'You wake up in hospital beds often?'

Jake gave her a wry smile.

The truth was that Jake had walked out on his wife. There had been no one else at the time. He'd been married five years – Stephanie, the kind of woman everyone referred to as a 'lovely lady'. Yet he couldn't go back; he didn't have a time machine.

And deep down he wanted to believe that he'd made the right decision.

They'd had two girls together, but both the kids and Jake's job had put so much space between them that he began to feel he barely knew her. He was away most weeks with work. There was no time for 'them' any more. Jake felt unwanted. Unloved. Unneeded.

One day, whilst Jake had been away working, his mother had called.

'I've got cancer, Jake. They've given me two years – we'll just have to make the most of it,' she'd said.

Jake carried on working. Six weeks later his mother could barely talk as she lay in a hospice bed riddled with the disease. Then she was gone, gone forever; gone faster than it took the tears to roll down his face.

Life was so short.

Two-point-four children, two cars, mowing the lawn on a Sunday, unkempt bikini lines, sex with the lights off, spag Bol on a Monday, Saturdays spent shopping.

Did his mother die before she realised that it was all humdrum, pointless nonsense? Did he really want all that for the next thirty or forty years? That normality? That sort of routine?

Jake felt you only got one shot at life. He was of the belief that every day should be an exciting journey spent feeling good about yourself.

Was Stephanie really what he wanted? Had she really wanted him? He loved his two girls dearly, and he loved Stephanie – but had he done all the things he wanted to do?

He remembered the countless arguments; being ignored and made to feel shitty because he forgot to buy some pasta at the supermarket and got a Mars Bar instead.

What was the point of feeling shitty all the time? Feeling like you were second best? Inferior?

He'd walked out one day. Said he needed a break – time to sort his head out. He'd spent several weeks inside a bottle of whisky.

But sometimes, just sometimes, at the end of the day, Jake looked at the four walls that surrounded him and wondered if homemade spaghetti Bolognese on a Monday night might have been the better option.

On days like those, he'd have liked a bit of normal.

Two years later and he was still trying to figure it out – an attractive nurse with a good figure made it no easier.

'Mr Flannagan, you shouldn't really be leaving the hospital,' said the nurse. 'You've had a very nasty bang to the head.'

'I can't stay. There are things to do,' replied Jake.

She gave him his prescribed pain medications, guessing he wouldn't be hanging around waiting for a discharge prescription and made him promise to get his stitches removed in a week or so. Jake nodded in agreement, knowing full well he'd end up doing it himself, as always.

He made it out to the car park in a daze before realising he didn't actually know which hospital he'd been in. The sign outside put him straight. He had no phone and no car – he had to contact the office. It was only a five-minute walk into the city centre; he needed to clear his head and decided to aim for Millgarth police station, next to the bus depot and markets.

1

Millgarth police station looked like it should be a multi-storey car park from the outside. Architecturally speaking it was not one of the prettiest buildings Leeds had to offer. Jake had visited a couple of times whilst he'd been working up north; red brick with a nasty, bare-concrete staircase at the front, and few windows.

The place had a lot to answer for. West Yorkshire Police had orchestrated the Yorkshire Ripper enquiry there during the late seventies and early eighties. The enquiry had missed the culprit himself, Peter Sutcliffe, for many years – despite him being named during the investigation and interviewed nine times.

Jake made his way swiftly across the car park. Regardless of his injuries, he didn't hang around; the place was well known for being infested with rats the size of small dogs. He was buzzed in and made his way up to the small front desk. He asked the officer manning reception for a phone to call the Anti-Terrorist Branch Reserve Room. The officer looked quizzically at his Def Leppard T-shirt and checked his ID before ushering him into his office.

Jake made the call back to London. 'DI Flannagan calling. What's happened?' he asked, without waiting to hear who was on the other end of the line.

'Sir – heard about your accident. Are you OK?' asked the officer manning the phones.

'I'm fine, fine,' Jake lied. 'What's gone on?'

26

'There's been a terrorist attack. Four separate explosions – suicide bombers possibly – all at separate sites. Three Tube trains and a bus – large number of people dead and wounded.'

'Who's in charge down there?' asked Jake.

'Well, sir – it's all a bit patchy at the moment. As you know, everyone and his wife was up in Scotland for the G8 summit. Tony Blair is flying back later today with two of our superintendents on the same flight. All of our cars are up there. Personnel and vehicles are on their way back but won't get here until later tonight. You're not exactly flavour of the month for writing the Audi off, sir…'

'I'll sort that out. Where's DCI Helen Brookes?'

'She's at the scene of the bus bombing in Tavistock Square.'

'I need her mobile number. I lost my phone in the accident.' Jake took down the number and ended the call.

He turned to the station officer who'd clearly been listening intently to the call. This was no place to have a private conversation, thought Jake.

His head was still fuzzy; he needed to know the circumstances behind the crash.

'I had a car accident on the M1 early this morning,' he told the uniformed Millgarth officer. 'I've been in hospital. Who would have dealt with that?'

'I'd imagine the traffic department. Let me have a look on the system for you.'

Jake watched as the officer called up the incident log on his PC.

'Here you are, sir. Would you like to check the log yourself?' Jake sat down at the computer and read:

0433 hours: Caller has found an Audi A4 overturned on the motorway. Driver unconscious but breathing. Ambulance called.

0443 hours: Vehicle registration check shows car as Metropolitan Police vehicle: Met Control Room to be contacted.

0445 hours: Met Police Central Command and Control say vehicle is used by SO13 Anti-Terrorist Branch. They will ask them to contact West Yorkshire Police.

0455 hours: West Yorkshire Police traffic department on scene and dealing. Officer says simple accident, no other vehicle involved. Driver hit central reservation. Ambulance required.

0505 hours: Ambulance on scene. Male driver (believed to be Detective Inspector Jake Flannagan of Metropolitan Police) is en route to Leeds General Infirmary.

0630 hours: Leeds General Infirmary states Inspector Flannagan's injuries are minor and not life-threatening. Officer remains unconscious. Met Police informed of officer's condition. Met Police advise DI Flannagan has next-of-kin emergency-contact details recorded on file as wife, Stephanie Flannagan. Telephone number provided to hospital.

Jake's felt slightly sick as he realised that he was lucky to be alive.

The stitches running across his arms and down his back were now beginning to bite into him. He needed to find somewhere comfortable to lie down; somewhere he could use the phone in private.

8

Jake lay down on the hotel bed's quilted, maroon counterpane and called his boss's mobile. He was glad of the privacy.

'DCI Helen Brookes.'

'Helen, it's Jake…'

'Jesus, great time to write the car off, Jake! We were worried sick. What the hell were you doing?' Helen sounded more than a little upset.

'Helen, I think I know who did this.'

'Did what?'

'The bombings!' Jake knew this was going to be difficult to explain.

'Who? Not that lot from Leeds that the Security Service told you to leave alone? You were supposed to be visiting friends up there in Manchester. Don't tell me you were working up there without permission, Jake! How did the car get written off?'

'Helen. I need to explain some stuff to you…'

'Jake, before you say any more, think carefully. Do you know what's happened down here?' Helen was always shrewd with what she shared with anyone.

'I know what's happened. That was no ordinary accident I had…'

She interrupted him. 'I hear they found lots of nails on the road near your car, Jake – not to mention the ones stuck in your body from where you overturned the car. They said you had a blowout on the front tyres from the nails. That *is* how

29

it happened isn't it, Jake? That *is* what you were going to tell me, *isn't it?* I need you back in London today, Jake. Tavistock Square. Please do not tell me about anything you've been up to in Leeds – OK?'

The line went dead. She'd hung up.

Jake lay on the bed of his hotel room, looking at the ceiling. It hurt to move. He'd been told that his line manager would not support him in claiming anything other than a simple car accident. It meant he couldn't retrospectively get permission on the forced-entry job up at the house in Dewsbury. What a fucking mess.

It was time to go and face the music back down south. He checked out, making sure to pay with his own debit card and not police funds. He was not here officially. He'd been told that. His head throbbed and the painful bruising across his torso gnawed at him as he walked the short distance to the train station.

The train was packed with holidaymakers. The carriage was noisy as it trundled and jerked its way toward London. Jake read a couple of dog-eared newspapers he found in the luggage rack. Between the din of the excitable tourists unaware of the mess that awaited them in the capital, and the roar of the tracks beneath him, Jake knew there was no point trying to make polite conversation with anyone. They'd be lucky if they reached London before the rail network was shut down completely, he thought.

9

It was bedlam. Much of the ticket hall and waiting area was being used as a makeshift field hospital to treat casualties. Train services were being cancelled left, right and centre. The Tube was closed. Jake knew he had to make his way over to the site of the bus bombing in Tavistock Square and was torn between that and helping the walking wounded. Outside, it was chillingly quiet. There was little traffic apart from the occasional wail of emergency-service sirens as response vehicles tore past.

Jake trudged past Euston station. When he reached the square, it was cordoned off. They'd already erected huge barriers made from scaffolding and wood to prevent people from getting close to the scene. Jake flashed his warrant card and the uniformed police officer on the outer cordon allowed Jake entry to the street. At the inner cordon Jake met an officer that he knew from the Branch. He allowed Jake through, despite the Def Leppard T-shirt.

Anti-Terrorist Branch officers were knelt down in a line in the road behind what was left of a red double-decker bus. They wore pale blue, disposable boiler suits and blue gloves to ensure that they wouldn't contaminate the scene.

The temperature was in the upper seventies Fahrenheit and humidity was touching ninety-five per cent. They must be sweltering inside those coveralls, thought Jake.

This was standard Branch stuff. You got sent on a bomb course. They'd blow up a car. You watched. Then you picked up the pieces. You learned fast. You'd pick up every tiny fragment that you could find and pass it back to your team leader. It would get sorted into 'plastics', 'metals', 'glass' and 'others', there and then. The fragments and parts would eventually be assembled to build up a picture of the explosion. Very early on, officers picking up the tiny pieces could often get an idea of what the bomb consisted of by the spread and type of debris. This was very different from the course though; they had both blood and body parts to contend with.

He spotted Helen stood on some steps surveying the scene. She waved and came over to greet him. Tall and slim, she was wearing her favoured, trademark outfit of an expensive black trouser suit with a white blouse underneath. Her long dark hair was swept up into a chignon.

'How are you doing? How's your head?' Helen looked sombre. Her mood was different from when they had spoken on the phone earlier.

'I'm OK. How many dead?' asked Jake.

'We think fourteen here. Difficult to say right now; not all the bodies are in one piece. We think one of them is the bomber himself.' Helen ushered Jake back out through the inner cordon. She led him to the foyer of a nearby hotel that had been completely taken over by the Branch and their exhibits function.

'We've found some identification that belongs to a guy from Leeds at the scene, Jake. The ID was loose – not near any of the bodies. It's like it was dropped deliberately. I'm told that there are Leeds IDs found in similar circumstances at all of the other scenes too.'

'Shit.' Jake sighed and placed his head in his hands. If only he'd been able to stop their car.

'Who are they, Jake?' asked Helen.

'A primary-school teacher and some of his friends. Two of them came up in Operation Crevice in Crawley sixteen months ago. We followed them back to Leeds – you remember? We talked about it again last Monday with Denswood?'

'Why were you up there? Why now?' demanded Helen.

'I went up to Manchester to see my friend, like I said I would. Then I thought I'd just have a little trip across the Pennines – see what they were up to. Straight away I could tell there was something weird going on. They were using anti-surveillance in everything they did… it was just a hunch really, intuition.'

Helen grimaced. 'We've got to keep this quiet, at least for now. You had no authority to be up there. We'd both be up shit creek if this got out. Who else knows you were snooping around up there?' she asked.

'No one.'

'OK, it never happened – you know nothing more than the Security Service have told you. They are the lead. Not you!'

'But, Helen, I was so close this morning…'

'Not close enough, Jake. What am I supposed to say? "A rogue cop saw this coming but didn't tell anyone"? The Security Service has primacy. They call the shots. You were told to lay off. How do you know that your snooping around didn't provoke this?'

'Oh for goodness sake, Helen! Give it a rest!'

They might be great colleagues and good friends, but Jake wasn't about to take that sort of comment lying down. 'There's something not right, Helen! You've only got to look at the transcript of the conversation they had with the Crawley lot. What were the Security Service thinking when they assessed it? Those guys were up to their ears in it. The whole thing stinks!'

'We can't say anything, Jake. You know how it will be made to look in the media, don't you? This is the Security Service's fuck up – not ours. If we say anything, this becomes our mess. It's theirs. They decided not to do anything, or to let him run – for whatever stupid reason that was. It's their reason and their mess. I don't want to talk about it again. You let them lead. Understood?'

A part of Jake knew that Helen was speaking sense. On the other hand, a part of Jake was immune to sense in all its forms, because often he ran purely on instinct.

'OK,' he replied reluctantly. 'So where do you want me?' he asked, gesturing toward the bomb site.

'The scenes are being dealt with. They're difficult because of the bodies.'

'I saw the seagulls waiting for their opportunity when I went in a minute ago…' He winced.

'Yeah, the rats down in the tunnels are causing the same problems.' Helen shook her head. 'Awful, just awful.'

'Any idea of the total numbers dead and wounded yet?'

Jake had seen speculation on the rolling news whilst in hospital, but he'd not really been in a state to absorb much of it.

'Information is sketchy, Jake – we've no fixed idea at the moment. There's still a lot of confusion… we were told six explosions on the Tube to start with, not three. The trains were between stations when the bombs went off and casualties were all over the place; people emerging from both stops. We weren't sure at first if there'd been an explosion at each one. We've got officers constantly in contact with all the hospitals, but more and more injured are turning up, reporting every hour… We're pretty sure there are at least fifty dead – maybe a thousand walking wounded.'

'What sort of explosive was used?'

'We don't know, yet… Look, all this Leeds photo identification we've been finding – it was dropped in plastic bags away from the blast seat – far enough away to remain intact. We've got gym memberships, student cards and driving licences – and on top of that we've got your West Yorkshire exploits and suspicions.

'I'm pretty sure we're going to need you back up north. Take a right-hand man with you; I want you to be the forward-planning party for anything we get up there. I don't know when that will be, but once the decision is made, I want you to be ready to roll on Operation Theseus.'

Jake nodded. He was pleased. Helen was placing her trust back in him.

'Operation Theseus?' he asked.

'Yep. They've randomly assigned us a name for this job already. Theseus. Firstly a tragic Greek myth, and secondly a failed World War II mission.'

'Jesus. Is this the third time lucky or what?'

'Well, with your antics we're sure to be doomed from the start,' replied Helen. 'Get to the Yard, Jake. Get a new car. Take whoever you want with you. Keep a low profile up there for the time being... and no maverick decision-making of your own. Everything comes through me. OK?'

Jake tried to hide the rueful look on his face. He hoped Helen had not seen it. 'Of course, guv'nor.'

Promotion above the rank of inspector was more about whom you knew and how well you toed the party line. Jake knew he was never going any higher than inspector because the only line he ever toed was on the athletics track, crouched in the hundred-metres blocks, waiting for the starter's gun.

10

Thursday
7 July 2005
1822 hours
New Scotland Yard, Westminster, London

Jake arrived on the sixteenth floor, home of the Anti-Terrorist Branch Reserve Room. The room was filled with an assortment of computer terminals and was the single point of focus for people requiring anything from a check on the Police National Computer through to a team of people 'on the hurry up'.

Welcome to Roley's empire, thought Jake as he walked up to the little cashier-style window. Roley ran the Reserve Room and held all the power when it came to owning and allocating resources. You never upset Roley. If you did, you'd end up bottom of the pile for anything that he might be able to push in your direction. If you wanted a car, Roley held a pool of cars. If you wanted a pen, Roley had a box of pens. But of course Roley was the one who decided whether you got the basic or the super-deluxe model.

Roley looked up from his desk on the other side of the small window as Jake peered through.

'Alwight son?' This was his favourite greeting.

'Head's a bit sore but I'll live – I need a new car and a new phone.'

Roley chucked a bound book with a blue plastic cover through the hatch at him. It had a set of car keys in it. Jake looked at the front of the book to see what sort of car it was – a BMW 3 Series. Fine. The blue cover meant the car had been fitted with blue lights and two tones. Extras would include a radio, bigger batteries to run the extra electrical equipment and upgraded brakes, if he was lucky. He'd driven many a vehicle fast, then experienced the all-encompassing fear that came from hitting the brake pedal at 100 mph to be met with the dreaded smell of burning.

'Try not to write this one off, son,' Roley said with a smile. 'Phones are with Maggie in the office.'

Jake walked down the corridor and into the concrete stairwell. Maggie's office was on the floor below.

She was a cantankerous civvy in her sixties with a nasty, old-fashioned perm. Civilian employees – those who'd come from outside the force – were deemed the lowest in the gene pool at Scotland Yard. Maggie ran the stationery store and ordered anything that needed ordering – provided you had filled out the right form, in the right way, with the right coloured pen, in triplicate, with the right authorisation signature. She was a stickler for the rules. She made Jake's blood boil.

'Take one pen – not the whole damn box!' she was shouting at a DC, as Jake walked into the office.

Jake hated anyone's rules. He hated Maggie's rules more than most.

As he walked over to her desk, he noticed that she was sporting her favourite orange woollen cardigan that everyone said smelled of mothballs.

'Hello, Maggie – how are you?' Jake forced a cheery smile just for her benefit.

She didn't reply. That wasn't unusual.

'That's a nasty bump on your head,' she said eventually, looking up over the top of her half-rimmed glasses at him.

'Car accident this morning, lost my work phone… I need a new one, please.'

'I can only do exchanges. You know that. If it's been lost, I need a superintendent to authorise it before giving you another one.'

'Malcolm Denswood authorised it – said he was going to call you as he can't get in to sign the form right this second. It's a bit on the busy side out there as you might know, Maggie… He's not rung you?'

All of that was lies, except the part about it being busy – but he coupled it with his best confused-looking face, which he hoped would do the trick.

She shoved a new, boxed Nokia phone and a pile of lost property forms at him.

'I need the forms done now!' she barked.

Jake looked down at the paperwork Maggie had handed him. The forms were going to take ages! There were dead bodies lying on London's streets and in its Tube system and this civilian clerk wanted an hour's worth of paperwork filling in? He waited until she was distracted by another officer and then departed quietly with his haul. He dropped the blank forms into a waste-paper bin outside her office as he made his way to the lift. He prayed that he didn't have to wait fifteen minutes for one travelling down to the basement.

The basement area of New Scotland Yard was one huge underground car park. Always jammed full of vehicles, it could often take half an hour just to get out of there. Today there were hardly any vehicles to contend with. The whole of the Yard were at the scenes, rushing home from annual leave or returning from the G8 summit up in Scotland. Jake found the silver BMW easily and sat in the car looking at a Branch team list that he'd picked up from the reserve office. It detailed all the officers' names and phone numbers on it. Jake already knew whom he was going to call – someone he could bounce stuff off and whom he knew he could trust.

He skimmed through the list until he spotted the name he was looking for... Detective Sergeant Leonard Sandringham.

A career detective with more than twenty-five years of service under his belt, Lenny was a hard-working copper; one of the best Jake had ever worked with.

They'd met when Lenny had been on the Area Crime Squad and Jake had been working on an operation involving the importation of drugs and stolen cars. They'd quickly become friends and not long after had both ended up working at the Branch, albeit on different teams.

A slim, dapper silver fox in a tweed jacket, Lenny had two grown-up daughters and a long-suffering wife whom he adored. The day job had changed considerably during Lenny's lifetime of policing – but his tales of noble cause corruption from earlier years on the force could still entertain.

Jake plugged in the number listed and found that Lenny was currently on his way back from a camping trip in Devon. He'd cut it short after hearing the news about the attacks.

They exchanged the usual pleasantries.

'Have you got any plans for the next month, Len?'

11

Jake parked the BMW on double yellow lines. He needed some fresh clothes. The Def Leppard T-shirt and baggy jeans had to go.

Upstairs in his flat, he grabbed a holdall off the top of the wardrobe and started to pack.

The place was baking. It had been shut up and neglected for almost a fortnight. The spider plant in the bathroom looked close to death; unwashed teacups in the sink had grown mould.

Jake looked out through the sash window. There was no sign of Ted on the extension's corrugated iron roof.

The flat sat in a row of severely neglected Victorian properties that housed retail space down at street level. The buildings, though distinguished in their time, had faded as they'd fallen into disrepair. The place had been his grandmother's until she'd passed away six months previously. It was like being in a time warp with its carpet of dark brown and orange swirls and its avocado bathroom suite.

After his grandmother had died, he'd moved in to look after the damn cat, Edwina. Jake had renamed her Ted.

Both his grandparents had grown up in Whitechapel, both of Irish heritage. Jake remembered the stories they'd tell of how their families fled in the 1850s; the hatred for the English landowners who'd ignored the potato famine and continued to export nearly all of Ireland's grain – creating a catastrophic situation out of a mere crisis.

The Irish had flocked to the cheap accommodation in the slums of Whitechapel, with its thousands of prostitutes, numerous whorehouses and Jack the Ripper. His great-grandfather had worked in Whitechapel's filthy slaughter-houses and butchers. Yet Jake's grandmother had always joked that Whitechapel was still like living in a palace after you'd been reduced to sharing accommodation with your own live-stock back in Ireland.

Jake sometimes wondered if his love of bacon was in his DNA.

'Ted, Ted!' Jake shouted as he leaned out of the window and banged the side of the cat-food tin with a knife. Ted was coming back less and less lately; he was sure someone else was feeding her. Like all the women in his life, this feline had grown weary of being left on her own for long periods.

'Ted, you little shit, where are you?' he shouted wearily.

He could hear the steady hum of the traffic. Car after car used the side street to try and dodge the gridlocked traffic at-tempting to head out of the city along the main road.

It was still scorching outside. The rusty, corrugated iron roof below radiated heat into his face; it felt as though he were being slapped across the face by a sizzling frying pan.

He closed the window and picked up his bag containing two of everything. It was time to leave. Ted would have to fend for herself again.

He had a lot of driving to do – the M25 to Surrey to collect Lenny and his bags, and then back up to Leeds.

12

The four of them stood on the edge of the dance floor – Lenny, Jake and the two new DCs he'd requested. The place was packed and the music thumped. Friday-night revellers wore short skirts and T-shirts, but Jake and his team were dressed like City boys in their suits and stood out a mile.

Jake had spent a long day hard at work – putting together the start of the research packages in a small office he'd found for the team to use at Millgarth police station. Tonight it was time for a drink; he needed it after the couple of days he'd just had.

'Did you hear what the Mayor of London announced today?' asked Lenny loudly above the pulsating dance track. Jake was only half-listening to the conversation. Watching the dance floor and enjoying his drink were less taxing options right now. The two DCs shook their heads. 'He's pledged free tickets to the Olympics for those seriously injured in the bomb blasts,' continued Lenny.

Jake excused himself from a discussion about who'd pay for this initiative and made his way to the bar. He ordered a round of beers and a round of translucent shots in a variety of lurid colours. They looked foul, but he didn't really care.

The bar was the swankiest that Leeds had to offer. They'd been told 'members only' at the door, but this wasn't London. Their warrant cards still got them into places. London door staff had become hostile toward police officers 'briefing it' to

42

get in – the warrant card was often referred to as 'ya brief'. Outside of London they were far more welcome. It was usually accepted that officers weren't going to cause a fight and would probably help staff out if there was trouble.

On his way back to the group, Jake spotted the Leeds football chairman, Ken Bates, in a shaded corner. He looked like Father Christmas in NHS glasses, yet the ladies appeared keen on him.

The beer was cold, and already Jake was forgetting about the last few days. He needed to forget. Alcohol made him forget. Enough of it and he would almost forget that he'd been so close to stopping Wasim, about the body parts strewn across Tavistock Square.

Life had felt hollow since he'd left his wife. Work was all he had, but at times like these even that made him feel lifeless inside. Jake missed his daughters and they were growing up so fast. All he managed of late was a daily phone call with each of them before bed – if he wasn't doing something at work that prevented it. Claire was barely ever available and the pressures of both their jobs seemed to preclude them from conducting a 'nice, normal' relationship.

Their phone calls were often the prelude to his drinking, the drinking made him crave attention and the cravings and loneliness made him long to be close to a woman – any woman.

Jake and his team downed more beer, incredulous that it was half the price of a London pint – even in this place, on the most expensive street Leeds had to offer. The alcohol was having its effect. Jake was now ready to take on the world. Not the world he took on by day; the world he inhabited by night. A world that had no problems, no terrorists, no high-ranking bullies warning him off, no ex-partners screaming at him for money, no girlfriends arguing about when they could or couldn't spend time with him.

'So how did you write that car off, guv? Tell us, we're dying to know.' DC James said, licking the overspill of beer off his hand.

'Loose lips sink ships. If I thought you needed to know, you'd know.' Jake winked and laughed as he said it. It was enough to convey the message that he'd been up to no good and to not ask again.

'Anyway, that's work. You know I don't talk about work when we're not at work. You're guilty, DC James. I sentence you to buy more beer. Go! Buy me beer.'

As Jake pushed James toward the bar, he spotted a familiar-looking brunette in a black rah-rah skirt out of the corner of his eye. She wore a black vest top and blue high-heeled sandals. Her chin-length bob was chestnut brown and wavy, identical to Claire's – and, from a distance, her dainty facial features looked uncannily reminiscent of his girlfriend's.

He did a double take, fixing his gaze on her to check again who it was. She returned the attention she was getting with a huge grin in his direction.

His heart sank. No, it wasn't Claire.

She continued to smile back at him. There was no denying that she was very attractive indeed... and that she was interested in him.

Jake wiggled his hips in time to the music and the brunette laughed back at him. With their eyes directly on each other, she joined in the dance from the other side of the room. Stuart chuckled at the scene before him. 'It's like shooting gazelle with an elephant gun in here, guv – the women are gagging for it!'

Jake turned away and ignored her, mid dance.

'She wants you, Jake. What are you doing?' asked Stuart, bewildered.

'I'm unavailable,' replied Jake, shrugging. 'Anyway, we're supposed to be keeping a low profile up here and I've been spotted by Dennis Wise already...' Jake pointed out the former footballer, who was watching them. 'Our cover is blown.'

James had returned from the bar with more drinks. He burst out laughing when he saw the familiar figure looking at them.

They drank.

The DJ segued into another track. Jake recognised it as the same song that had been playing on the radio when he hit top speed heading south on the M1 the previous day. His mood darkened. The sudden realisation of what had happened to all of the people on their way to work that morning brought him crashing back down to earth.

The drink always did that to him. Made him totally forget where he was, who he was, the situation he was in. Then something would happen and he would be standing back there in the present, angry at the world.

He downed his pint. It didn't taste great after the numerous fruit-flavoured shots still coating his mouth. His arm wobbled slightly as he put down his glass.

'I'm done with this shit tonight. I'm going.'

As Jake walked past the bar on the way to the exit, the song was still playing.

His head was spinning and the bright lights from the dance floor hindered his vision. Was he drunk? What was he doing here? The brunette was no longer dancing across the room. Why had he come to Leeds? 'Angels on the Subway'... Was that the song?

He'd had the chance to change things yesterday. He'd messed it up. His phone wasn't charged. How had that happened? If he'd been able to communicate with the call handler, would all those people now be dead?

If he hadn't been looking at his handset, would he have been able to avoid the nail bomb?

Had he been drunk the night before? Forgotten to charge his phone? Fuck the drink. He hadn't seen his daughters in two months; couldn't remember the last day he'd had off to spend with Claire. He'd been too busy at work. Had he been drunk the night before he told his ex-wife it was over? Forgotten what marriage was like because he'd been too busy at work to try? Drowned himself in drink because he was too scared to be a father – agonising over when he would get the chance to do the growing up he needed to do himself?

This song was driving him crazy. The Angel. That was near King's Cross. *The* King's Cross – scene of one of the bombs.

'Hello,' he heard a female voice call across at him. Jake looked up. It was the brunette in the black rah-rah skirt. She was heading toward him. He wished it was Claire. He needed her there; needed her to make him feel better.

45

Before he had a chance to reply she'd grabbed him at the shoulders – and, reaching up, began kissing him passionately on the lips.

She tasted of stale beer, of cigarettes.

He suddenly saw black smoke. He pulled away. Looked at her. But there was nothing. There was no smoke.

Did he really want to be with this woman? His drunkenness was making him confused. She grabbed his hand and smiled conspiratorially, leading him past the bar toward the toilets. There were no words but they both knew where they were headed and why. They slid into a cubicle and she locked the door behind them.

Once the door was secure, she faced him, kissed him, un-zipped his flies, then turned her back and bent over the toilet, pulling up her skirt as she did so. She looked exactly like Claire from behind. He yanked aside the black thong underneath. Then he was inside her.

What was he doing here? He hated himself. He hated that he was drunk. Again. Using anonymous sex as a conduit to feel something, anything.

He had hold of fistfuls of her hair as he drove into her from behind. He was being overly rough. She was screaming, 'Harder, faster!'

It was angry sex. The fury in Jake welled to the surface. He didn't understand it. Bitterness coursed through him.

He began swearing at her, 'Fucking dirty bitch!'

Jake was lost. Who was he? Who was this girl? Why was he taking his anger out on Claire's Yorkshire lookalike in a piss-stained cubicle? She probably would have fucked any man that had shown her the slightest bit of attention in that club – he was just in the wrong place, at the wrong time.

Maybe he should have listened to Helen's words of warning? He stopped. Pulled out.

The girl turned and looked at him, confused.

'What the fuck did you stop for?' she shouted.

Jake did up his flies.

'I'm sorry,' he said as he left the cubicle.

'Come back here, you stupid wanker!' she called after him, slurring her words.

Drunken sex with a drunken stranger wasn't the answer to his problems tonight.

He hated himself. Helen was right.

He had to get out of the place.

13

Tuesday
12 July 2005
0545 hours
Holbeck, Leeds, West Yorkshire

'Just tell me what's happened to my fucking brother! Where the fuck is he? Why the fuck do you want to come in here and search our house?'

Karim Rahman edged closer to Jake as his anger built, so that they were almost nose to nose. Jake could feel the spittle hit his face as Karim shouted in it.

Karim was the elder brother of Asif Rahman, the eighteen-year-old suspected of blowing himself up on the number thirty bus in Tavistock Square.

Jake stepped backwards – there were times for fighting and there were times when physical confrontation just made things worse.

They were standing in the living room of the terraced family home in Holbeck. Karim was waving his arms about animatedly as he squared up to Jake. Karim's mother was sat at a table in the corner sobbing, whilst his father – a dark-skinned Pakistani man in his sixties with white hair and a white beard – shouted at the top of his voice at a uniformed police officer in the kitchen.

'Bloody police! You bloody… you bloody come round here… we report our son missing and you do nothing. Then you come round here and want to search our house… you bloody fuck off!'

When Asif had failed to return from a trip to London the previous week with his friend Wasim, Mr Rahman had called the police and reported his son missing.

The whole family had just been dragged out of their beds by a firearms team who'd smashed open the front door. Mr Rahman was wearing a pair of beige cotton pyjama bottoms and a white T-shirt.

'What are you fucking gonna do to us?' Karim shouted in Jake's face.

Attitude breeds attitude. It was easy to get caught up in the heat of the moment, easy to rise to their level of anger – most people would get angry at police with guns running up and down their stairs and shouting at them at 0500 hours. It was easy to feed off the adrenalin pumping around everyone's veins at this intrusion. None of that would help matters though.

Jake took another step back from Karim and raised his hands in front of him.

'Please calm down. I can explain. Please sit down in the chair.'

Jake spoke in a low, composed voice. Karim wouldn't be able to hear what was being said if he kept shouting at Jake. It was a tactic Jake had used many times before – get them to come down to your level – a calmer level.

'I don't want to fucking sit,' Karim retorted – but the shout had gone from his voice.

'I can explain to all of you... May I sit down?' Jake turned to ask Karim's father who was now silent and looking at him from the kitchen.

Karim's father nodded. It was important that the head of the house allowed him to sit.

Jake perched on the grey L-shaped sofa. Karim sat down two seats along from him. Jake noticed that he was wearing an England cricket tracksuit. There was silence in the room.

Jake paused for moment to check he had their full attention and began, properly this time. 'As you know, a number of people have died in London as a result of four explosions. At this stage we cannot confirm that Asif is one of them. What we *do* know is that identification belonging to Asif was found at the scene of the bus bombing in Tavistock Square. We are investigating the possibility that he was involved in the bombing. That's why we are here; that's why we have a search warrant.'

The room was silent.

'No. Not my boy. He wouldn't do anything like that… He's a good boy!' Karim's mother said from the table. Tears rolled down her face as she spoke.

Jake already knew that the attacks had been undertaken by suicide bombers. Witnesses had described men on the Tube and the man on the bus as 'exploding'. Jake already knew that Wasim had had explosives in the washing-machine pipe at his house; he already knew that the bus bomber had blown himself into a number of different pieces. He was convinced that the DNA sample they would take from Asif's toothbrush – or from one of the hairs they would take from his hairbrush – would match the DNA on the fragments of body, the two stray arms and two stray legs that had been found in the square – but this wasn't the time to talk about his opinion. He was dealing with facts.

'We don't know yet that he was definitely involved. We do not know if he is alive or dead. But we are going to search this property to try and help us ascertain if he was, or was not, involved.'

Jake waited for a response.

'So what? So what if his identification was there? He might be injured in a hospital somewhere. Are you searching *all* of the homes of the people hurt?' Karim responded.

It was a fair question. Jake thought about it for a moment. There were so many things to consider here – one of them was that Karim could be involved, as could the mother and father. Revealing information about what police knew and didn't know had to be controlled.

'We found identification from three other Leeds-based people, a different set of identification, one at each of the bomb scenes in London. We are searching their homes at this moment too… The other three people are the ones you say Asif went to London with.'

'It's that fucking Wasim, isn't it? That cunt! That fucking cunt! I fucking knew it… You think my brother martyred himself, don't you? That he's a suicide bomber?' Karim punched the sofa repeatedly, in sheer anger.

Karim's mother started to wail loudly and rock in her chair.

Strike while the iron is hot, Jake. Don't wait. Use the anger, Jake's inner voice said.

'Why do you say that, Karim? Why do you say it's something to do with Wasim?' asked Jake.

'Look at the age difference. My brother is just a kid – eighteen. Anything he's done, he's done for Wasim. He has some fucking spell over Asif with his stupid jihadi war stories. He's a cunt. His fucking family are going to pay for this,' Karim said through gritted teeth. 'I've been to see Wasim's brother – we almost had a fight. His brother reckons he don't know where he is either... They were supposed to go to London on the sixth, but that got called off at the last minute. Car trouble, Asif said. They went on the seventh instead...'

Jake saw Karim look at his dad. The pair made eye contact. It was subtle. There was a slight nod from Asif's father.

Karim stood up.

'Come... I found some stuff in my brother's bedroom... It might help you find out what's happened to him.'

Jake stood up alongside Karim. 'OK, show me,' he replied.

14

Karim led Jake upstairs and into a small box room at the front of the house. It contained a single bed. At the foot of the bed was a narrow wardrobe.

The room was immaculate – like the rest of the house. On top of a light green bedspread sat two mobile phones and a piece of paper.

'I found those on top of his wardrobe over the weekend – I've not seen them before.'

Karim pointed at two grey Nokia handsets and the sheet of paper. Jake was careful not to touch them with his bare hands; he left them lying on the bed.

'Who's handled the phones and the piece of paper other than you, Karim?'

'No one – just me. I've called the two numbers on that note and some of the numbers from the phones to ask if they know anything – if they know where my brother is.' Karim stared off into the air. He began to cry silent tears.

'What have these people said to you?'

Karim wiped his cheeks with the cuff of his tracksuit. There was a pause while he inhaled and composed himself.

'The one with the name Shaggy against it – he says he lives in Sheffield and reckons he don't know my brother. He hung up on me. The Shahid guy says he knows my brother from the mosque but doesn't know where he is... Thing is, right, that's my brother's handwriting on that piece of paper. I've never heard of these people; never heard him talk about them... Who the fuck *are* they?

'Same with the phones – I've called some of the numbers stored in the contacts... same story. People I've never heard of... One of them says he's in Egypt, says he don't know my brother, but that he knows Wasim. Says he rented a flat to him in Leeds. I've been round there, but there's no answer...'

Jake remembered the morning of 7 July – he'd seen Wasim leave his Dewsbury home. He'd driven toward Leeds. Jake had lost sight of him but he'd been somewhere – why would Wasim rent a flat in Leeds when he had a house in Dewsbury?

'Karim, I need the address of this flat. I need you to show me where it is.'

Jake motioned for Karim to lead the way back down the stairs. Karim went to speak with his father, who was in the kitchen. Jake caught snatches of Urdu. His father nodded at whatever Karim had said to him then followed his son out into the hallway.

'He will take you – you find who did this to my boy. He was just bloody eighteen, you know,' Karim's father said to Jake.

'Thank you. I will find who did this. I promise you.' Jake nodded at Mr Rahman who appeared to be coming to the realisation that he might never see his son again. 'Is there anything else I need to know?'

Mrs Rahman stood up from the table and tried to speak through her sobs. 'My son – he come back from Pakistan... from wedding... February... He so thin. He always sick. I buy him new clothes... old ones too big for him... his hair, it was lighter, blonde at the front... not my boy,' she said as her grief turned to wails. Jake could hardly understand her through the tears.

He thanked the Rahmans for their help and grabbed Lenny as they left the house with Karim.

15

Tuesday
12 July 2005
0630 hours
Holbeck, Leeds, West Yorkshire

Karim's road had been blocked off to the public at either end, to stop the press taking photos.

This place was alien to Jake. The houses were packed in rows back to back. Jake was used to seeing houses with front gardens and rear gardens, but here there were neither – two houses sandwiched together, pavement, road, then two houses sandwiched together, repeated over and over, row after row.

Karim sat in the passenger seat of the BMW as Jake turned the ignition.

'They're talking of flattening this whole place and building new homes here, flash apartments and all that. Be better than this slum, maybe even make some jobs too,' Karim said as they drove into Leeds.

Karim directed Jake to the north-west side of the city, close to the university. They drove into a road called Victoria Park and began climbing a hill. After about two hundred yards, they passed a modern-looking mosque on the right-hand side.

'That place there... number twenty-two.' Karim pointed to a 1980s development directly opposite the mosque.

Jake stopped the car halfway up the hill.

'I came here yesterday – there was no answer,' said Karim.

'Wait here...' Jake got out of the car and walked back in the direction Karim had pointed.

A block of flats, on several different levels, zigzagged up the hill. Eventually Jake found number twenty-two – it had two doors, both red. Jake looked to see which entrance had the hinges visible on the outside – the back door. It would open outwards – and would be the hardest work to smash in.

To one side of the flat, a row of windows was hidden slightly by box hedges. Jake noticed that the leaves nearest the windows were a different colour to the rest of hedge – sickly and yellowed, and some areas were even turning brown.

Jake tried to look into the window directly behind the most decayed area of foliage. There was a net curtain obscuring his view. He rapped hard on the window and waited.

No response.

Jake looked at his watch. It was 0645 hours. He needed a search warrant. It would take an hour to complete the requisite paperwork and then the courts didn't open until 1000 hours. That was way too long in these circumstances. He had to make other plans.

16

'I swear by almighty God that the content of this, my information, is true to the best of my knowledge and belief.' Jake
stood with a copy of the Bible in his left hand; his right hand
was held up like a Native American Indian from a Spaghetti
Western.

The magistrate was a slim, spindly woman in her fifties with
rollers in her hair. She had been trying to get ready for work
when Jake had arrived. She sported a silk paisley dressing gown
with a set of pastel pyjamas underneath.

They stood in the dining room of her detached house in an
affluent suburb on the outskirts of Leeds. A Jack Russell dog
sat at Jake's feet, looking up expectantly at him and panting.

Jake always found out-of-hours, urgent search-warrant
applications amusing. Each force area had a rota of on-call
magistrates. Mrs Jackson was on the list for today.

Completing the paperwork in record time, Jake had briefly
outlined the events in London from the previous Thursday
and the circumstances of his morning so far. Then he'd driven
to Mrs Jackson's house as fast as humanly possible. It was rare
that a search-warrant application was declined, but not unknown – and police couldn't legally enter the property without
one. This one was vital and desperately pressing. Jake mentally
crossed his fingers and watched the pendulum of Mrs Jackson's
carriage clock swing to and fro as it sat on the mantelpiece, the
minutes ticking away.

'Thank you, Inspector – is there anyone inside this address at the moment?' asked Mrs Jackson, sitting down at the table with a cup of coffee.

'Not that we are aware of, ma'am. I've knocked there this morning – there's no reply. We've called in our bomb-disposal experts,' Jake said as he placed the Bible down on the polished dark wood table.

'Sit down, Inspector – please.' Mrs Jackson pointed at the chair closest to him.

The Jack Russell jumped excitedly at his legs as Jake pulled out the chair and sat down.

'Do you *really* think there's a bomb in there?' Mrs Jackson's eyes were as wide as saucers.

'We don't know. There's something very odd about the rental of this premises; it's not like the other warrants we executed this morning – they were family homes with people living inside. This is different. The bushes are dead or discoloured outside the windows of the flat. I think it's down to some form of chemical that's been used inside there – we need to expect the worse.' Jake attempted to smile reassuringly at her as he finished his explanation.

His mobile started to vibrate. It was Lenny calling – Jake had left him on guard outside the suspect property.

Jake looked at Mrs Jackson and she nodded to indicate that she was happy for him to take the call. A little bit of court etiquette went a long way, even in a magistrate's home.

'Lenny... you OK?'

'Everything's fine. No movement at number twenty-two. Everyone's here. I've got ten uniform from West Yorks and EXPO have just arrived. We're ready to rumble. You got the warrant for this place?' he asked.

EXPO stood for explosives officer. In London they were police officers; up here the West Yorkshire force usually had to organise for a team from the Army to come in. Jake had planned ahead for this eventuality with two EXPO officers from the Met ready on standby. They'd arrived in Leeds on Sunday and had been waiting for the call.

'The magistrate hasn't authorised the warrant yet, Lenny…'
Jake looked at Mrs Jackson as he spoke.

Mrs Jackson picked up the pen, signed at the bottom of the search warrant and nodded her head.

'She's authorised it now – start evacuating the premises nearby, get the roads shut off. I'll be there in twenty minutes.'

17

Tuesday
12 July 2005
0915 hours
Victoria Park, Leeds, West Yorkshire

Jake briefed the EXPO as they walked around the exterior of the flat. They'd knocked on the windows and doors several times to no avail – the place appeared to be empty. Geoff Wilson was an ex-Army ordnance expert approaching retirement with just six months left in the job. He was staying at the same hotel as Jake in Leeds city centre – they'd met and shared a few beers at the hotel bar the previous night.

'I don't think we should use either of the doors as a point of entry. We'll go through the window – just in case they've wired it up for us. You happy with the guy that showed you this place? It could be a set-up, Jake,' said Geoff.

'I can't double-check everything that he's said right now, Geoff, but my gut feeling is he's telling the truth – it's unlikely to be a set-up in my opinion. We've evacuated everyone in the rest of the complex as a precaution anyway.'

'What do you know about the internal layout of the premises, Jake?'

'I understand the neighbours have told my DS that it's a two-bedroomed flat. Six separate rooms in total, including an entrance hall. The area where the garden door is – that's the living area. The area where the bushes have died by the window are bedrooms.'

'OK, we'll break the living-room window with the robot just in case you're wrong about your man. We can use the cameras on the robot's arm to have a good look and check that it's safe before we

59

get too close ourselves. If he is leading us into a trap, I don't fancy being nearby should the whole place go up.' Geoff winked at him.

Jake smiled. 'OK – good advice.'

Jake had seen the robots in action once before – they were remote-controlled vehicles that looked like small tanks.

Jake thought back to his explosive-device training. The four main parts of a bomb operated in a specific order to detonate in a controlled way on command. The power source, a trigger, an initiator and the main charge.

Jake knew all too well that in suicide missions the trigger was the suicide bomber, who simply connected up the power source to the initiator or fuse – basically like that on a stick of dynamite.

More sophisticated devices involved a remote trigger for the initiator. Sometimes these triggers could be physical – as simple as someone opening a door. Outside this flat now, Jake knew they had to be careful not to start that chain reaction – and be far enough away to survive a blast if they did.

Jake and Geoff walked the hundred yards back to the outer cordon where the EXPO van was parked.

In the back of the large, Luton-bodied Ford Transit van sat two robots – one designed for small spaces and the other designed for bigger, heavier, more robust work. It had taken about an hour for Geoff and his co-pilot, Mike, to set the robots up and check that they were working correctly.

The unmarked van also contained a small desk with three screens above it. On the desk were two joysticks and a computer. One joystick controlled the movement of the robot's caterpillar tracks and its direction; the other controlled the robotic arm.

Geoff and Jake watched the screens silently, as Mike began moving the larger of the two robots toward the flat. It edged up the hill and down the concrete path toward the red door. Tape on the path showed the route that Geoff had painstakingly marked out that morning for the robot to follow.

As it reached the window, the robot turned slightly to find a better angle. It needed to line itself up with the glass that it was programmed to break.

'Here goes...' said Mike.

He pushed the joystick forward and the robot suddenly lurched toward the flat.

Jake held his breath, willing against any sort of detonation.

A long, rigid, spiked arm, which held a diamond point at its tip, rammed against the window like a lance as the robot drove directly at it. The camera on the robot jolted and wobbled as the spike made contact with the glass.

They could hear it breaking. Geoff looked skyward and smiled.

Several large triangles of glass hit the concrete and appeared on the video screen in the van.

Geoff asked Mike to stop for a moment so that they could assess the situation.

The top camera panned over the entire window. It was like a starburst from the point of impact; large triangular shapes of glass separating from each other, getting bigger as the crack moved toward the edges of the pane.

But the window was double-glazed; there were two panes of glass. Only one had broken.

Geoff groaned.

'You little fucker... Let's have another go,' said Mike as he pulled the joystick back toward him and pushed it away again.

Jake braced himself once again for the noise and force of a potential blast.

The lance's spike went cleanly through the second sheet of glass and into the flat.

'Gotcha,' said Mike, as he reversed the robot backwards.

Jake's sigh of relief was audible.

'No explosions, good. Maybe your man was being straight? Let's have a look inside then,' said Geoff, as he began using the other joystick to move the mechanical arm on the robot.

The arm moved up and toward the hole in the glass before pushing through and widening the aperture. There was a slight tangle with the net curtains, which had somehow been secured very firmly and snugly to the window frame, then suddenly Jake could see inside the flat – the screen on the wall of the van showing him in full colour the state of the living room.

'Jesus!' Jake exclaimed.

18

The walls were regulation magnolia. A red patterned sofa sat on what appeared to be a blue and red carpet. Jake couldn't really tell – mainly because the floor looked like a rubbish dump. There were bin bags full of stuff, boxes for mobile phones, rucksacks, plates with some odd-looking brown substance on them. Things were just strewn everywhere. It was a gigantic mess. A kitchen area off to the right of the living room looked just as bad.

Jake was gobsmacked. This was an absolute treasure trove of evidence just waiting for them.

'Wow. That's going to take some work, Jake. We'll have to take it slow – take it out piece by piece, item by item; each thing is a potential explosive risk.'

Jake felt both elated and disappointed. He needed to know exactly what this place was.

Lenny appeared at the back of the van. 'Guv, found a witness as we were evacuating, says there was a group of men who rented number twenty-two – Asian guys, in and out all the time – says they were a pain in the arse with their hours. She saw them at about three thirty or four a.m. on the morning of the seventh. Reckons they were loading rucksacks into a small blue car. I think we've got the right place.'

'Good work, Lenny. Get a written statement off of her, will you?'

Lenny smiled, nodded and walked away from the van.

'Geoff, how long before we can get an investigation team inside that flat?' Jake asked.

'I don't know. We'll need to check it's safe. Then we'll need the police photographer here to document everything. Then that ton of stuff in there will need to be removed and processed… I tell you what, rather them than me in that small place with a load of explosives equipment! I wouldn't fancy storing and assembling all the different bomb parts side by side. What if it all went up in one go? What sort of idiot assembles all three parts of a bomb in one tiny flat?' Geoff shook his head in disbelief and went off muttering to himself about the danger of explosives.

Jake needed a coffee, maybe even something a bit stronger. There was a lot to take in. He was shocked by how much stuff was in there. Almost too much.

He brought back three paper cups of double espresso from a small café around the corner. He'd also treated Geoff, Mike and himself to a bacon roll each. Jake was starving. It had been a long day already. Up at 0400 hours, briefing the search teams at 0445 hours. He'd not slept much the previous night anyway; he never did the night before a job, and this was probably the highest-profile one he'd done.

Geoff and Mike were stood behind the EXPO van, finishing up their rolls.

'I'll get an exhibits team here; you'll have to work with them. I want a photographer in there today – and maybe a sample of the brown substance from the plates that we saw on the floor.' Jake sipped the hot coffee as he reeled off his requests. He was desperate to get started.

'You can photograph from the window, mate, fine, but I'm going to have to clear a path inside through everything that's on the floor. We need to be able to move around inside safely before I can let anyone in there. The place could be full of explosives.'

'How long? Just give me an idea of how long,' said Jake.

'Two or three days, all being well – assuming that we don't find any viable devices as we clear the path. Your photographer can do some initial photos from the window – I'm not having anyone blown up on my watch,' said Geoff sternly.

19

Thursday
14 July 2005
0330 hours
Dewsbury, West Yorkshire

The night was humid. They'd wound down the windows on the car to let in some air. Clouds that had locked in the day's heat at sunset were now blocking out the light from the moon and there were very few street lights actually working in the dark, familiar cul-de-sac. The few that were gave off an eerie yellow glow in their immediate vicinity only.

It was the third night in a row that Jake and Lenny had been sat in the BMW together. They'd decided against looking for an observation point in any of the houses. It was too risky; everyone knew everyone else in the street. It was bound to get out and back to their target – Wasim's wife, Salma.

They still had to have good vision though, so the BMW was the next best thing. Sitting in it hour after hour meant that they could ensure the street was clear and safe for the walker to go in. The walker was a West Yorkshire officer together with his dog Spike, a white West Highland terrier. Spike wasn't specially trained and had no security or counter-terror skills; he was a prop and he belonged personally to John the police officer. Spike was the reason John was walking around the streets at 0330 hours – at least that was the cover story if anyone stopped to ask. Even Spike thought that was the real reason; they were just out playing ball, weren't they?

Anyone looking at the bloke and his dog in the street, as John kicked the tennis ball lightly along the ground, would most likely think the same.

Spike was a natural. He hadn't needed to practise his role on repeat for the past seven days like his owner had. John had stood at the side of an identical red Honda Civic upwards of a hundred times. He'd spent two days learning every inch of the underneath of the chassis to find exactly the right place to attach 'the lump'.

The lump was a small magnetic metal box that held a tracking device. It could tell you the car's exact location at all times and how long the vehicle had been there. Best of all, it could do it all on its own. In remote mode you could even program it to send text messages to you to say it was moving. When it did, you could then log on to a specially configured laptop and watch its movements live on the computer from wherever you were located.

The dummy Civic, which John had been memorising every inch of over the past seven days, was identical to the one that Wasim's wife drove; identical to the one she'd been using ever since the bombings in London. It was too early to say if Salma Khan was involved in the atrocity or not. Had she hidden things? Perhaps more explosives? 'Keep tabs on her, just in case,' Denswood had said. 'Know where she goes.'

The risk was that if she *were* involved in the bombings, she might well be surveillance aware. With cars and people following her all the time, she'd be likely to spot them eventually and change her behaviour.

So rather than tailing her day and night on foot themselves, they were putting a high-tech lump on her Honda Civic to track her movements.

Jake had tried to source the exact equivalent of Salma Khan's red Civic himself through the car-trade magazines, but he'd been unsuccessful. There was no time to waste and it was a hurdle that was beginning to get in the way of the investigation – so he'd turned to long-time informant and notorious bad boy Zarshad Ali.

20

Jake had known Zarshad Ali for the past five years – since his days on the Organised Crime Group.

Zarshad had been a key informant of his on a major car-ringing investigation.

The tentacles of the network Jake had been investigating stretched across Europe, the Baltics and Russia. Zarshad had been in charge of locating particular models of UK-based cars that the gang wanted to steal. He'd fronted up as a used-car dealer, trading from his council flat in Chelsea – when really he was a high-tech, vehicle-theft expert living the high life off the lucrative proceeds of his activities.

Stolen cars had simply been a commodity for the gang; a low-risk cash cow for financing other illicit activities. Zarshad had been a small part of it, but an invaluable source of information to Jake.

When they'd been struggling to source an identical car to practise with up in West Yorkshire, Zarshad had been the name that had immediately leapt into Jake's head.

The phone call a week ago had been short and sweet. The best type for an informant handler in Jake's book.

'Zarshad, it's Jake. You OK?'

'Yes, guv'nor – what's up?' Zarshad had sounded surprised by Jake's call.

'Nothing's up. I need a car, need you to locate one for me urgently. But I want a legit car with full UK paperwork, not nicked. You're not authorised to steal one – do you understand?'

Registered informants could be authorised by the police to break the law. You had to be crystal clear with them what you wanted, otherwise it could quickly end in tears.

'Course I understand, guv'nor. What car you after?'

'I need a 2001 Honda Civic, five door, 1.6i VTEC SE.'

'Fuck me – that's a bit specific, ain't it? That's the sort of order I get off the bad boys when they have dodgy paperwork for a motor. What do you want that for?'

Car manufacturers made minor changes to their model line-ups. You had to get the exact same type and year of car, otherwise the chances were that the spot in which you wanted to place the lump might not be there, or would be filled with a bracket you weren't expecting.

Jake ignored Zarshad's request for information about why he needed the car. 'Look, I need it by the end of this week. There's £500 in it for you, plus the cost of the car.'

'End of the fucking week! That's two days away… you must be having a fuckin' giraffe?'

'Do you want me to give the five hundred quid to someone else, Zarshad?'

'Nah, nah, nah. Alright. Leave it with me.'

Zarshad had come up trumps and had an identical car by the following morning. It had cost the Branch £5,000, plus Zarshad's £500. The practice model was now safely back in a secure garage at West Yorkshire Police HQ in Wakefield, where John the walker had spent hours practising fitting the lump on it, in readiness for the real thing.

'Looks good. Coast is clear. You're good to go – OP over,' Jake spoke into a radio mike in his hand. The lead from the mike led up the inside of his jumper sleeve to a hidden radio unit in a special covert harness on his body.

'Received. I'm go, go, go now,' John said into an identical radio unit several streets away. The message reverberated in Jake's covert earpiece.

John and Spike came into view as they rounded the corner from the top of the road. Both seemed at ease. The street was clear. It was looking good.

John deliberately kicked the tennis ball underneath Salma's red Civic. Spike went bounding after it but waited by the driver's door, unable to squeeze his body underneath. It was perfect – unlike the last two nights. The first night a taxi had pulled up in the cul-de-sac delivering someone home from a late night out. The second night someone had switched on a light in the house as John walked up to the car.

Everything had to look exactly right or the risk of compromising the whole job was too great. It all had to appear completely natural and fluid. Tonight, third time lucky, it did.

John lay down next to the car. He was fitting the lump, but for the benefit of anyone else who might be watching, he was getting Spike's ball.

Jake's heart was pumping so hard he thought his head was going to explode. This was the riskiest bit. John was at his most exposed. This was the point during a job at which, if it went wrong, they were fucked. They might be dealing with killers, mass murderers even, who might have guns.

It took seconds but it felt like minutes before John stood up and held Spike's ball aloft for show, just in case someone was watching. Spike bounced up and down, clearly excited that his owner had managed to get it. John threw the ball and walked away from the car, whispering into his microphone, 'It's on. All good. Repeat, it is on. Going back to my van. Stand down, stand down.'

'Fucking good job. Well done!' said Jake into the radio.

'Top man,' Lenny said to Jake, as Jake started the car and pulled away.

'She's ours now, whatever she does – she's fucking ours to watch,' said Jake jubilantly.

21

It had been a long week of unsociable hours and the hard work was only just beginning. Jake stifled a yawn as he read out to Lenny the latest forensic update from Scotland Yard: 'Preliminary tests indicate that some form of explosive compound has been found at the flat in Victoria Park, though at this stage we are unable to identify what the chemical make-up of the compound is or how it has been manufactured. It is however accepted, given what has been found inside so far, that the flat has been used to at least partially manufacture this explosive compound and that the construction of improvised explosive devices was carried out there...'

'So it's the bomb factory? Good job!' Lenny looked pleased with himself.

'It's a place they used to make some sort of explosive, Lenny. I don't think it's the icing on the cake, myself. In fact, I'm not even certain we have the ingredients for the cake sorted yet. Don't get too excited,' Jake cautioned.

Lenny said nothing.

They were sitting in Dudley Hill police station in Bradford. The latest developments in the case meant the Yard had decided it needed a long-term investigation team up in West Yorkshire. Bradford was to be their far less glamorous base from here on in. The Dudley Hill building was newer, but it meant they were now located in the middle of nowhere, not in a city centre. It also meant they were having to fight for desk space with West Yorkshire's homicide team.

'So how are we doing with the other stuff, Len?' asked Jake.

'Well, the searches of the houses are well underway. We've taken mobile phones and computers belonging to the suspected bombers – and clothing from their wardrobes is being tested for explosive residue. We're also expecting to match fibres to the Victoria Park flat.'

It remained slow going up in West Yorkshire. They were still taking things out of the Victoria Park address one by one, photographing them, and then packaging them up to send down to London for DNA and fingerprint testing. They'd carried out several small controlled explosions on material from inside the flat – stuff so volatile that they couldn't move it safely. In total they were searching six residential homes up in West Yorkshire, plus the Victoria Park flat.

What's the other news from London?' asked Lenny.

'I spoke to Helen. The bomb scenes down there are almost finished with from a forensics point of view. The streets and underground tunnels have been cleared of dead bodies, limbs, organs and debris. We're left with four separate bomb scenes with four suicide bombers carrying rucksack bombs; a death toll of fifty-two people not including the bombers themselves, plus hundreds more injured. And they've found a car at Luton Central railway station that they travelled south in, containing fifteen incendiary devices. They're calling it the largest criminal investigation ever undertaken.'

Jake had been told that upwards of two thousand staff had been subsumed by the enquiry back in the Major Incident Room in London, and half of the fourteenth floor of New Scotland Yard had been allocated to it. The scale of it was colossal.

Jake wasn't going home for some time, he knew that much for sure. He hoped Ted would be all right.

'How's it going with that witness, Lenny? The old girl you spoke to on Tuesday up at Victoria Park?' asked Jake.

'She's a bit on the woolly side. She says she saw some men acting strangely. But from what she's told me, I'm still not sure if it was strange or if it was just very annoying for her at the time. It's tough to get any sharp detail out of her because none of what she saw seemed that important when it actually happened. Five days later and she's not sure if she's seen four or six men, one or two cars, maybe even a woman?'

As a good investigator, Jake knew that not everything witnesses saw could be relied upon – it needed corroboration. Nonetheless, it was possible, a maybe. Maybe the old woman was right. Maybe there *were* others who had helped the bombers.

22

Sunday
17 July 2005
2036 hours
Longthorne Oak Hotel, central Leeds, West Yorkshire

Jake's phone vibrated. He glanced down at the Nokia handset. Claire's mobile number lit up the small screen.

'Hi, how are you?' he asked.

'Not too bad.' She sounded edgy. 'We need to meet.'

'You OK? What's up?'

'Can't tell you by phone – in person only.'

'I can't get away, Claire – it's manic up here. Why can't you tell me by phone? It'll have to wait at least a few days unless you can come up here?'

A million thoughts ran through Jake's head. Was she pregnant? Was it his? Was it work? Did she have an STI that she needed to tell him about? Had she heard about his big mistake in the club that night? Was she seeing someone else? It was odd that she wouldn't even speak to him via mobile.

'Look – I'll be on the first train up to Leeds tomorrow morning. I'll text you the ETA. Pick me up from the station.'

She hung up.

Jake was worried.

23

Leeds was awake. 'Loiners' – as Jake had learned they were called after the Yorkshire dialect for lanes – were busying the streets, running for trains, walking to offices.

The air was humid and made Jake feel sleepy; he'd been up worrying most of the night about what Claire was so anxious to speak to him about. When the alarm finally went off, he'd almost wanted to roll over and hit the snooze button. Nevertheless, he was looking forward to seeing her.

As he waited in the busy concourse area, he spotted her bejewelled pumps wending their way toward him in the early-morning haze. There was a half-smile on her face as she acknowledged him, but just watching her posture as she walked from the platform, he could tell she was tense and drawn.

Jake had first met Claire back in 1990 whilst they were both studying at Lancaster University. He had managed to scrape through his A levels and was doing politics and law. He'd noticed Claire on the campus a few times, but their social circles and courses were different and they hadn't spoken. She was studying psychology and computing.

Every year there was an annual sports competition between Lancaster University and the University of York – the Roses Tournament. Jake was a handy sprinter. His stocky build gave him an explosive strength that was difficult to match. Claire

73

was a decent distance runner and they'd got talking on the field during their warm-ups.

There had been a lot of drinking after the Lancaster team had won the tournament. Jake had found himself drawn to Claire. Yes, she was slim and good-looking – with a trim, athletic figure – but there was more to her. She had a depth to her personality that attracted Jake in a way that he hadn't experienced with previous girlfriends. Jake could tie most girls up in knots with his wit but Claire always had a fast comeback. Just as sharp and just as funny.

During the heavy night of celebratory drinking, Jake found out that Claire had been seeing someone from her campus – she called him her 'almost boyfriend' because she had feelings for him, but refused to commit to anyone while she was at university. One thing led to another and Jake and Claire had ended up in her single bed together in her cramped campus room. It was the best sex Jake had ever experienced.

They saw each other a lot in the months that followed, but Jake's time at university was abruptly curtailed when Jake's father's company went into liquidation. Jake ran out of money fast without his father's financial support and ended up moving back home to get a job and support the family.

He and Claire stayed in touch, but the phone calls got shorter and shorter until they stopped all together and Jake had applied to join the police.

It was at his first meeting with the British Security Service after joining the Anti-Terrorist Branch that he saw Claire again. There she'd been, sitting at the end of the table.

They'd met for dinner afterwards, flirted, kissed a little. It was like the fifteen years in-between had never happened.

One day, Claire had said that he could call her and ask for information. She'd said it was useful to both camps and she'd be happy to help.

'I'm that good at sex? You're willing to break the rules for me?' Jake had joked.

The car was parked at the rear of Leeds train station. Jake opened the passenger door for Claire.

He drove without asking any questions, turning left and right onto side roads and checking several times that they were not being followed.

Finding a quiet street that he felt comfortable in, he parked up. They sat in the shade of an ancient horse chestnut tree that split the paving flags with its roots.

'What is it?' he asked abruptly, turning to face her.

Claire's hazel eyes shifted in colour from brown to green as she stared back at him. Her expression gave nothing away. Jake stopped himself from reaching out to touch her face with his fingertips. He could sense she was in work mode.

'You know back in May, when Abu al-Iraqi was arrested by the Americans in Pakistan?' she began.

'Yeah – the CIA has him? He's in Guantanamo Bay? So what's the problem? Why are you here?'

'They arrested him in a pre-planned operation. They'd been watching him and his network in Pakistan. They say he's head of al-Qaeda's European operations.'

'So?'

'That means what happened in London eleven days ago, Jake. Those sorts of operations. That's what he's involved in. Do you understand what I mean?' asked Claire.

Jake nodded.

Claire continued, 'After al-Iraqi was arrested, we picked up some chatter, some conversation.'

'OK. Who's been identified from the chatter? Anyone up here?' asked Jake, referring to the Leeds investigation.

'It's more than that. There were some odd phone messages left via al-Iraqi's contacts after he was arrested. Coded stuff...' Claire paused.

Jake glimpsed a look of pain in Claire's eyes and something he had not seen before – fear. For a brief moment she looked scared, lost and incredibly young again. It reminded him of when they'd first met at University. Her eyes today, they were the same innocent ones that he had known back then – the ones that looked at things not knowing how they worked. This was not the confident and in-control, career Claire.

'There are links to one of Wasim's contacts. We think Wasim was one of the recipients of the coded messages. He was at a training camp in Pakistan with several key people. Everyone in this particular group was taught how to make a new type of explosive at the camp. It's like nothing we've seen before. The trainers at the camps – they've learned from the Crevice operation that we can track orders of precursor materials like fertiliser. So their tactics and bomb ingredients – they've evolved…' She went silent for a brief moment. 'There are others involved. Something is going on. I'm worried… It's moving way too slowly on our side.'

Claire trailed off and looked away. Eye contact with him had ceased for the time being. He guessed that this signified the end of the information feed.

'Why are you telling me this now, Claire? You think I haven't been saying this exact same stuff since Operation Crevice?'

Jake felt a mixture of arrogance and bewilderment. He had been pushing this with senior management for the last few months. They just would not listen. He was constantly being told that 'the Service should lead' and 'if they say the job is dead, it's dead'. Clearly he had been on the right track. But management was still telling him he hadn't got enough for a criminal investigation.

Jake's eyes narrowed as something else dawned on him. 'But al-Iraqi was arrested in May? Two months ago! You've known about these coded communications for two months?'

'No!' Claire shot back. 'I found this out yesterday! I'm telling you today! Look. You need to take a look at this.'

Claire glanced around quickly to check there was no one in the street before surreptitiously palming him a piece of paper. 'Let me know if the police know anything about this number and address, will you? Please? As a personal favour to me?' She sounded desperate, pleading.

It was the first time Claire had *ever* asked him directly for information. The moment wasn't lost on him. The Security

Service already had access to police-intelligence databases and the HOLMES system, but she was explicitly asking what he knew.

'I need to get back,' said Claire.

'What? You're going back now?' Jake laughed, thinking she was joking.

'Yes, I have work to do,' she said, as she looked squarely into his eyes. There was no smile. She was serious.

'That's it? You came all that way just to tell me that? And you're not even staying for some breakfast?' he joked back to hide his annoyance.

She was silent and turned to stare dead ahead out of the windscreen.

Jake realised it was pointless to argue.

At that precise moment, he knew he didn't have the words to change her mind.

Jake pushed the BMW's gear stick into the drive position and the pair retraced the short distance in silence. At the station, Claire looked at him earnestly before leaning forward and kissing him on the lips. Without a word she got out and walked away to hunt for a return train to London.

Jake sat in his car at the taxi rank with the engine running. He could hear the honking horns from the taxi drivers, telling him to move off their patch, but he ignored them.

Her voice echoed in his head. 'There are others involved.'

She'd travelled all that way just to tell him that? Ask him that? Give him that piece of paper? It made no sense. Why?

Was it *that* sensitive that she didn't want to transmit the information any other way? Jake knew that was how the bad guys worked. Messages and letters were passed down from al-Qaeda command; a network of contacts ensured the messages were delivered to the right people. Who was Claire scared of? Who did she think might have listened in to that conversation if they'd had it on the phone instead of her travelling three hours to Leeds and three hours back to London on a train?

Jake looked at the note. Hastily written in blue pen was a London address: '*Sullivan House, New Southgate, north London*', together with a phone number. There was no name. Maybe they didn't know who was using the phone?

Claire was aware that Jake sometimes broke into addresses without getting authorisation from the head of Intelligence or a court. Was that what she wanted? Why didn't she get her own guys to do it?

The morning sun was starting to get hot. It blinded Jake as it shone straight in through the front window of the BMW. He lowered the sun visor.

He needed breakfast. Then he needed to get to work on what she'd given him. He would have to go to London later in the week and find out what the hell this address was all about.

24

Tuesdays were meeting days; the day when Jake's satellite arm of the investigation spoke face to face with the London team via a video link.

'Now, CCTV. Who's here from CCTV today?'

Malcolm Denswood, the senior investigating officer on the operation, took centre stage on the pictures being beamed up from London.

A black-suited arm appeared toward the back of the table. 'I am, sir. DS Chris Barnby.'

'You have some news for us I hear, Chris?'

'Yes, sir. It's more an oddity than anything else. As you know, we've been looking at the CCTV from Woodall Services on the M1, just south of Sheffield. That's where the bombers stopped to fuel up the Micra at around 0505 hours as they drove down to London. Asif Rahman, the bus bomber, who pays for the petrol, is wearing white tracksuit bottoms. In every other CCTV clip we have of him after that point, he's wearing dark blue or black tracksuit bottoms. We checked the inventory of all the items that were found in the Micra at Luton. The white tracksuit bottoms are not there, sir. It's odd.'

'That is odd. I'm not sure it takes us anywhere as far as the investigation is concerned, though. Anyone have any suggestions on this?'

There was silence.

'Sir?' Maria, one of the MIR receivers down in London put her hand up and fidgeted in her seat excitedly. Jake had met her a few times. She was sweet, but a bit dim. Everyone knew it.

'Sir, if the tracksuit bottoms weren't in the Micra, Asif must have taken them with him and blown them up. *Or* lobbed them out of the window, sir,' said Maria.

The comment was met by silence from Denswood and the rest of the room.

There was giggling from the team up in Bradford. Maria had stated the obvious. There were no other alternatives. One of those two things had to have happened. Jake was sure Denswood didn't need Maria to tell him that. The question was why the tracksuit bottoms were missing, not how.

People often stated the obvious in these meetings, but with the belief that they had stumbled upon the meaning of life. It always made Jake smile.

Jake suddenly had a vision of Maria sat proudly in front of Denswood in a tartan Sherlock Holmes deerstalker hat, thinking that she had solved the case. He started to giggle along with the Leeds MIR team. The giggle was louder than he had wanted it to be – Denswood heard it down in London over the video link. He turned toward the camera.

'DI Flannagan, do you have some input on this?' Denswood looked directly into the camera as he spoke, straight at Jake.

'Errrr… Yes, I do, sir… I'd imagine that trip was a fairly scary thing for one to be doing that morning. I'm thinking the most likely explanation is that Asif shit himself on the way to blow himself up and soiled his pristine, white tracksuit bottoms, sir?' Jake kept a straight face as laughter erupted from both the Leeds office and the London side.

Denswood waited for the laughter to stop.

'Thank you, Jake.' Denswood coughed. He was trying hard not to smile.

Denswood concluded the meeting by reminding everyone that there was a job to do. 'We've a lot to get through here, but if we all pull our weight and put enough meat in the top of the machine, I'm determined that we'll get some sausages out of the bottom.'

The video link was severed and Jake returned to his desk in the Dudley Hill office.

Jake had a lot of time for his big boss; he really put his heart into the job. Yet Jake feared Denswood was not always very effective on his own – especially in such an overwhelming investigation with so many pieces of information to muddy the waters. This single bomb factory at Victoria Park looked way too convenient. Jake didn't like it. Not one bit.

25

From the inventory list that had been made of every single item found in the Victoria Park flat, the team of receivers down at the Major Incident Room in London were beginning to send up action after action to Jake's team of detectives in Bradford.

Jake's team were supposed to investigate the object and let the MIR know what they'd found out by sending them back a message. The MIR looked at the message, indexed it and linked it to other information on the HOLMES computer.

HOLMES stood for Home Office Large Major Enquiry System and was a blatant backronym designed to crowbar in a reference Arthur Conan Doyle's famous sleuth.

The HOLMES system had been dreamt up years ago in the wake of mistakes made during the Yorkshire Ripper investigation. Peter Sutcliffe had come up several times during different lines of enquiry, but the investigation team at the time had not connected the different pieces together, which had led to Sutcliffe killing more. HOLMES was supposed to connect the dots, attempting to avoid such mistakes in the future.

Jake was beginning to hate the requests coming out of London to investigate items found at the Victoria Park premises. Each night in his dreams, Wasim was sending him on wild goose chases and mocking him when he came up empty-handed.

He called Helen on his mobile.

'Boss, it's Jake.'

'Hey, Jake – how's things? I hear it's going well up there?'

'Helen, HOLMES is creating its own problems by swamping the investigation team with infinite actions. It means that the intricacies of literally everything have to be investigated in minute detail.'

'Well then, there's plenty for you lot to be getting on with?' his boss replied, unfazed.

'Way too much evidence to suggest that, Helen!' said Jake in annoyance.

'What do you mean?'

Jake hesitated for a moment, then dived in. 'This all seems a bit, well... convenient. They wanted us to find this bomb factory. We were handed it on a plate. Does that not ring alarm bells with you? Have you seen the living room area? You can't move for evidence, you can't even walk across it. There's everything here that's been used to conduct this bombing operation. I don't buy it. We're missing something. Something they wanted to hide by giving us this place. I'm sure of it,' he said, with total conviction.

Helen laughed. 'Well you scoot off and find it, Jake. In the meantime we'll concentrate on the actual hard evidence we've got.'

'Yeah, I'll do exactly that, Helen,' he replied dryly.

Jake was sick of it. He couldn't take much more of these stupid actions.

'Helen, there's only so much we can do to investigate the hell out of a tube of toothpaste. Why do I have to make a member of my team drive to Peterborough to visit a company that supplied the packaging for that toothpaste more than a year ago? What does that have to do with a terrorist bombing down in London? It doesn't solve anything.'

'Put enough meat in the top and we'll get sausages out the bottom – you know how it is, Jake,' said Helen, repeating Denswood's familiar mantra.

'But why aren't we looking at the motives behind it? What if the evidence we're looking at doesn't give us the motive? If it doesn't tell us why?'

'What do you mean? We know their motives. They were extremists and they're dead anyway. The whys and wherefores don't even matter in this.'

'We found empty plastic packaging for ice at the Victoria Park flat, Helen. They bought ready-made ice. It matched up via HOLMES with a receipt that was found close to the seat of the blast where Wasim martyred himself. Using the details on the receipt we went back to the store and looked at the CCTV. Sure enough, Wasim went to Asda in Pudsey at 0520 hours with one of the other bombers on 6 July. They bought fifteen bags of ice that day…'

'Good result. That shows that the system is working then? We're slowly finding out stuff like this and HOLMES is doing its job?'

'Fantastic. Yes. *But…* this stuff is only us telling about *how*. Not *why*. Not *who orchestrated this…*'

'We just keep doing the right things, Jake. Follow the evidence.'

'And isn't it just lovely we have so much to follow?'

'I don't see your point, Jake.'

'Why did they plan the bombings that day? In all the planning materials we've removed from the scenes and the bomb factory, there was no mention of the G8 summit in Scotland, nor the Olympics announcement.'

'So what?'

'It doesn't make sense.'

'Jake, we've not found a single indication anywhere that they planned around any significant event. It was probably just coincidence that the G8 summit was on and the Olympic host city was announced the same week the bombings happened…'

'But maybe they knew that the G8 summit meant that London would be short on security personnel with everyone up in Scotland? Did they even know that the Olympics announcement would be made that week?'

'Well, if they did, none of them documented it,' replied Helen.

'Yeah, but don't you think that's really strange, when they'd planned everything else to the nth degree? Why no mention of it in anything we've found? That's my whole point. There is nothing. There is nothing to follow but packets of ice and tubes of toothpaste.'

'I don't know, Jake, but I do know that you need to get on with the actions coming out of the MIR – that's what's important right now. Don't get distracted,' said Helen as she hung up.

Jake couldn't fathom any of it. He was starting to believe that no one really knew what was going on.

26

Jake found the address that Claire had given him using his police issue *Geographia Atlas of London*. Battered and bruised just like him, it was one of the few things that had survived the accident two weeks ago in Leeds. Its days were numbered though. Satnav was now being fitted in the faster, marked London police cars. Jake liked his old blue hardback book. He'd liberated it from a marked police car in the rear yard of Brixton station one afternoon several years ago.

The drive down to London from Leeds that morning had been slower than he had anticipated. There had been a fair few lorries on the two-lane A1, but the lack of traffic police compared to the featureless M1 meant he could get a wriggle on without worrying too much about being pulled over.

On the journey, he'd reflected on the news Claire had shared with him up in Leeds about the coded messages left following al-Iraqi's arrest. She'd said she thought one was to Wasim. He guessed that another must have been to the place he was going to look at today. Despite running the phone number and address through all the intelligence databases he could think of, nothing of interest had come back.

The address Claire had given him corresponded to a sixties-built block of flats on a nondescript, north-London housing estate. The tower block bore over him like a giant as he got out of his car and made his way to the main door. He spotted a bin store directly adjacent to the path. There was no mistaking its horrendous stink;

he could make out a strong odour of rotten vegetables. But there was something else – an unexpected chemical smell.

Inside the brick-built bin store were seven large communal containers. He peered into a couple. Cabbage leaves, carrot peelings and scores of empty bottles of hair dye. Someone obviously had a lot of hairdressing work on.

The communal entrance door to the flats was ajar. Broken. The sign next to the lift indicated that flat fifty-eight was on the eighth floor. As he walked up the stairs, he remembered that Mrs Rahman had said the front of her son's hair had turned lighter. The box hedges at Victoria Park – they'd changed colour too. Hydrogen peroxide was a bleaching agent but it could also be used as rocket fuel. It was highly flammable – explosively so if you got rid of the liquid it came in.

Could someone here be using hair dye to make a bomb? Just like Asif had for 7/7?

Jesus. These guys had bombs too?

Jake arrived at the eighth floor and found number fifty-eight. He put his ear to the door and listened. No sound emanated from within. He knocked, intending to use a cover story about looking for a friend, but there was no reply. Jake gently pressured the door. He could tell that just the Yale lock at the top had been applied. He pushed hard against it. The door swung open straight into the living room.

The place smelled familiar; peppery, spicy, with synthetic undertones.

He followed his nose to the back wall of the lounge. The stench was at its strongest by a sixties-looking wooden sideboard. It was the sort that had once held a turntable and a decanter of whisky on top, but not now.

Jake looked underneath it for wires but found none. He gently pulled the sideboard out from the wall before fetching a knife from the kitchen, which he used to prise off the back panel. Inside, he found five large, clear plastic food tubs containing a strong, spicy-smelling yellow goo.

The stench was blistering now. The sticky yellow mixture looked similar in texture to the substance they'd found on the plates at Victoria Park. This must be where all that highly explosive hair dye had gone. He had to think fast.

Water. Add water. Make it less concentrated and less flammable, he heard a voice in his head say.

He went to the kitchen. Under the limescale-covered tap, in a stained washing-up bowl, he spotted a selection of glasses which he filled with water and carried back through to the lounge.

He repeated this until he'd added four glasses of water to each tub. The mixture seemed to suck up the water like a sponge. Was it safe? There was no way of knowing. He had to get out of there. He had to call this in.

He replaced the back panel of the sideboard, carefully pushed it back against the wall and returned the glasses to the sink. He left the flat, closing the door behind him. It was like he'd never been there.

Now to tell Claire.

27

'Claire, it's Jake.'

Jake was crouched in a garage forecourt area adjacent to the block of flats he had just left.

'Jake – you OK?' Claire could hear the unease in his voice.

'No. That address you gave me. I think I just saw explosives in there.'

'You went inside? Are you nuts? I didn't give you that intelligence for you to go snooping around inside the fucking flat! I asked you what you knew! That information came from the Americans, from the NSA. If they find that out, I'll go to prison! You said you'd look at it. Not go into the flat!'

'But I've found something. I've tried to make it safe. I'm pretty sure it's some sort of peroxide-based explosives.'

'Jake, you've got to let this run. You can't claim the glory for this. Not unless you have some of your own, definitive evidence to lead you there!' she said angrily before hanging up.

Jake stood there looking at the blank screen of his phone. It was the second time in two weeks he'd been in this predicament. Did she really think that he was going to do nothing after what had happened on the seventh? Which one of them was nuts?

Jake considered his options. He'd illegally entered a premises using intelligence that he shouldn't have had. If that substance in the sideboard had been explosive, he hoped it wasn't any longer thanks to the water he'd added. Jake didn't even have enough information to go and apply for a search warrant at court. He couldn't go and speak to the bosses. He was in enough trouble as it was and he'd have to tell them he'd broken in. That was a non-starter.

Jake called Claire again.

'I can't fucking believe you went there,' Claire shouted down the phone as soon as she picked it up. 'That's the last time, Jake! You know anything that I give you is for intelligence use only! You don't tell anyone I've told you. You don't use it or act upon it in isolation. If you do, the trail leads back to me – I go to prison!'

'Claire – I'm sorry. You can't blame me. Somehow you've got to get that place on the radar tonight.'

'It is on the radar. Just low down. You sure it was explosives? Positive?'

'The smell, it's distinctive. I recognised it from Victoria Park. The substance is gooey just like what we saw there. You said the other day they were learning how to make new substances in Pakistan, Claire. We've got to make this official.'

'I can't just bloody tell them that my friend, DI Flannagan, broke in and illegally searched the place after I breached the Official Secrets Act by passing him the intelligence. Plus, it's the Yanks' intelligence. They'd extradite me for less! Look, I'll do my best. It won't happen fast – twenty-four hours if we're lucky. I need to pull in a couple of favours to elevate it without arousing suspicion,' Claire said, clearly still upset.

'I'm sorry, Claire,' replied Jake, as the line went dead again.

28

Wednesday
20 July 2005
1740 hours
New Scotland Yard, Westminster, London

Jake drove south to Scotland Yard. He parked underneath the high-rise police headquarters and called his boss. Helen's answerphone clicked in straight away. He decided against leaving a message.

He made his way up to the fourteenth floor. Sitting at a computer terminal in the corner of the large office, he spent several hours scouring the police intelligence systems. He was hunting for something that he could legally use to mount an investigation into Sullivan House and the gooey, sticky, peppery substance he'd just discovered.

There was nothing. The Security Service had not alerted the police. God only knew how long they'd been aware of the people there, he thought.

His only hope was that Claire would punch something through in the next twenty-four hours. He couldn't tell a soul. He'd already been in trouble for the extra-curricular work he'd done up in Leeds. Here he was two weeks later, exactly the same. The only difference being that Jake hoped he had messed with their explosive mixture just enough. Perhaps they'd realise it was now inert and abort their plans? It might just give the Security Service enough time to sort themselves out.

Jake would call Claire tomorrow afternoon. Give her the twenty-four hours she said she needed. Tension was still high at the Yard. Suspicious-package calls had gone through the roof. Everyone was tired, including Jake. He needed sleep.

He'd not been home in two weeks. He'd run out of clean clothes. Now was a good time to collect supplies.

It was a gorgeous evening, yet London was deserted. Normally there would be hundreds of people wandering around the city in weather like this, he thought. The windows of his car were wound down, yet there was an eerie silence across the capital, broken only by the sirens of police cars as they hurtled from place to place.

On arrival back at the sari shop in Whitechapel, Jake unlocked his door and walked into his stiflingly hot and rancid-smelling flat.

The mouldy washing-up looked like it was about to grow legs and run off. Nice. He opened the windows, got undressed, pushed the pile of clothes from his bed onto the floor and lay down.

He looked at the ceiling. This was no life. Fighting everyone. Fighting simply to do the right thing. How could it be that the NSA, CIA and Security Service knew this stuff? Knew that people had died. Knew that there were others, yet didn't inform the police when they were the only agency that could actually make arrests?

Sleep found him suddenly, unexpectedly.

29

The sun woke Jake, its strong rays breaking through the dusty Venetian blinds in his bedroom. He'd overslept; he was supposed to be back in Leeds.

He got up, showered and began making the trek across London. On the way he received a call from one of the team, asking him to pick up a copy of an exhibit. The exhibits office was close to the Oval cricket ground. It wasn't too far out of his way so Jake agreed.

The place was busy when he arrived. Jake decided to eat breakfast in the canteen whilst he waited for them to retrieve and photocopy a book that had been found at Victoria Park.

By 1230 hours he was still waiting, so he made his way down the stairs from the canteen to hurry them up. As he entered the office, he hit a wall of commotion. People were frantically grabbing masks and forensic kits and running out of the door.

'What's going on?' Jake asked one of the exhibits team.

'Another attack! Chemical substance at Oval Tube station,' replied the exhibits officer, grabbing his stuff.

Jake followed him as they ran to the car park. They jumped into a waiting unmarked car, which pulled away sharply, Jake in the back seat. Only seconds later, they were getting out again at Oval Tube station. The place was in chaos. People fanned out from the station's entrance in all directions – some screaming, some crying.

93

Jake and a couple of the officers from exhibits leapt the barriers. The escalators had stopped. They ran down as people continued to stream up. At the bottom – on the northern-bound platform – sat a Tube train only partially in the station, its doors open.

Jake charged onto the Northern Line train and along several carriages. He began to check for dead or injured before it even occurred to him that he might need some personal protective equipment.

A smell of acrid smoke hung in the air. One of the exhibits team shouted for everyone to be careful.

Up ahead, located toward the middle of the third carriage, Jake could see a black nylon rucksack with its contents strewn across the carriage. Spilling from a large, clear plastic container was a yellow cake batter which foamed as it hit the floor of the Kennington-bound Tube train.

Jake recognised it immediately. It was the hydrogen peroxide mixture spewing from one of the food tubs he'd sabotaged at Sullivan House just a day before.

'Stop! We need protective clothing and masks!' shouted one of the exhibits team.

Jake's reply came instinctively, 'We don't. It's inert. I know…' He stopped himself mid-sentence as he realised what he was saying.

'Move back! You can't tell from here! It might go off!' shouted back the senior exhibits officer.

Jake turned and retreated as cautioned.

Thank God he'd been to Sullivan House the previous day; there appeared to be no fatalities or seriously wounded.

They evacuated the station and stopped new people from trying to enter, but it was hard going in all the uproar and confusion – he was in plain clothes. It was always more difficult to convince the public to listen to you when you weren't in uniform and wore no helmet. He hoped the lids got there soon to organise the crowd control.

Outside the station there was utter panic. Lunchtime on a Thursday and Clapham Road was heaving.

Their next most pressing task was to cordon the place off. Jake's priority was to preserve the crime scene and sort out who among the throngs of people there needed to be interviewed.

It was going to be a long day.

30

Thursday
21 July 2005
1245 hours
Oval Tube station, Kennington, London

Jake stood on the corner of Clapham Road. This busy cross-roads in the shadow of the Oval cricket ground was completely blocked by emergency response vehicles. The noise was incredible. Sirens wailed from every direction; police cars, fire engines, ambulances – all anxious and wanting to do their bit to help. The suspect or suspects were long gone. Jake had no idea what they looked like or which way they'd taken off. There was no point tearing down a street without knowing who you were looking for in this mayhem. Whoever it was would be caught on CCTV – or so he sincerely hoped.

Jake gathered himself, 'Crime scene,' he said aloud, kicking into action. 'Sort the scene out!'

Catching bad guys meant having evidence to put them in prison. The evidence came from what you could prove they'd done at the scene of the crime. Placing them there meant fingerprints, DNA, physical exhibits they'd left behind, fibres from their clothing, explosive residue. He needed to preserve them. There was nothing worse than having the fire and ambulance services trample all over the scene unnecessarily.

He grabbed two uniformed police officers getting out of a small car and identified himself. They looked young. Both kids. One ginger and tubby, the other skinny and dark.

Fatty and Skinny had new uniforms, new hats. Their eyes were wide and scared – like rabbits caught in headlights. They were probationers. They'd never forget this day as long as they lived. Jake had no other option – he needed help right now.

'There's been an attempted attack. There's a substance on the Tube down there. I need you two to stay up here at the entrance. Make sure you stop any firefighters or paramedics going down onto the platform. There's no fire and no wounded down there. They can do what they like up here. This is a major crime scene and I don't want a million boots walking all over it. Tell your control room that information, OK?'

'Control Room are saying it's a possible chemical attack, sir – are we OK here?' asked Fatty, looking even more nervous.

'You'll be fine – trust me. Go on. Get on with it!' said Jake, gently nudging Fatty in the direction of the Tube entrance.

A small crowd of people had gathered by the railings that separated the road from the pavement. There were six of them – four men and two women. An older woman wearing a lacy cardigan was crying on the shoulder of a younger bloke in a beige suit. The rest were talking on their mobile phones. Jake went over to the group and raised his warrant card in identification.

'I'm a police officer – any injuries or walking wounded?' Jake asked the shell-shocked group.

A stocky guy in a green T-shirt, whom Jake immediately thought looked like a builder, spoke for the group.

'We were in the same carriage. We saw what happened. He tried to blow his rucksack up. He was chanting something and fiddling with something. I dunno what – it looked like a wire. Then there was a loud pop, a bang, and then this stuff flew out of his rucksack. It went all over him and onto the floor. It was burning his back. He was screaming. I grabbed him but he got away. Ran off.'

Jake said nothing at first. He just looked at them. Each one of them. For a moment everything around him stopped. Time stood still. There was a silence. Peace. All these people. Six people. All with a story and a life. All six might be dead had Jake not been to that flat yesterday. What was Claire playing at? What was the Security Service playing at?

Jake was jolted back into the real world again as the other woman from the group spoke up.

'What do we need to do?' she asked.

A blonde in her early thirties with long straight hair, she was wearing a floaty floral dress and cream patent-leather shoes. She was what Jake would term an absolute stunner.

'Well. I'm going to need statements from you all. And I need you to take your clothes off...' Jake raised one eyebrow in her direction and smiled at her. 'Your clothing is evidence. There will be fibres and residue on them that we'll need. I'll organise for you to be taken to a local police station. We'll get you all some new clothes so we can take those ones.'

There was a general look of bewilderment on the group's faces.

The blonde piped up again slightly annoyed, 'But I'm going to a wedding. I've got to be there. What clothes are you going to give me? You can't take my new dress!'

'Don't worry. I'll make sure you get to the wedding looking just as fine as you do now.'

Jake turned and walked back over to Fatty and Skinny. Fatty was arguing with a red-faced firefighter who was claiming he needed to go down to the Tube.

Jake spoke to Skinny, 'I need a van. Those six people over there—' Jake pointed to the group '—they all saw what happened and were on the carriage with the suspect. At least one of them has touched the suspect. All are significant witnesses. Get a van and get them to Brixton. Don't let any of them go anywhere. I'm going to organise a team to take their statements and clothing.'

After trading mobile numbers with Skinny who approached the group and explained what was going to happen, Jake called the Reserve Room at the Yard.

'Roley? I'm down at the Oval...'

Roley interrupted, 'Oooh be careful down there, son. Chemical attack they've said. Nasty, nasty!'

'It's fine. Don't think it's anything to worry about. Look, I've got a group of significant witnesses here. I need five people to do statements and clothing at Brixton. Can you organise that for me?'

'Of course I can, son. Call ya back or someone will shortly.' Roley hung up.

By the time Jake arrived at Brixton police station, a total of fifteen witnesses had been rounded up. There was no chance he was going back to Leeds for a while. He knew that much.

31

Thursday
21 July 2005
1400 hours
Oval Tube station, Kennington, London

The blonde stunner was called Alice. She was single. Jake en-sured that he took her statement first. She flirted outrageously with him and he tried desperately to stay in professional work mode, but ended up giving as good as he got. He had to ask for her dress and shoe size before popping out to a local branch of Principles and purchasing a strappy aquamarine dress and gold kitten heels for her. He even shocked himself by making sure to choose a dress that was shorter and more revealing than the one she'd originally had on.

Back at the station, Jake got on with the other interviews. Alice had disappeared with her assigned WPC, who swabbed her for explosives, took all her clothing and bagged it all up.

Later, when she returned, she was beaming. She was very happy with Jake's choices. As he watched her twirling around in the interview room, showing off her new outfit, Jake thought that she looked incredible. Even better than before.

On the Tube, Alice had been in the seat closest to the sus-pect when he'd tried to detonate his device. It should have been her in the black body bag – not just her pretty wedding clothes. She would have died had it not been for Jake going to Sullivan House yesterday. Instead, she was standing there in a stylish new outfit in front of an admiring detective.

Jake smiled at her. 'You look fantastic.'

'Well thank you, my gorgeous personal shopper. But it still doesn't help solve my dilemma. I've got to be in

Hertfordshire at my cousin's wedding reception this evening!'

That was a tough one, thought Jake. The Tube was shut and London was gridlocked. There wasn't much chance of her making it out to the sticks in time.

'We can't have you dressed like that and not getting to this wedding now, can we? If I get you to Euston station, can you catch a train from there in time?'

'Yes, but how are you going to do that? It's going to take me hours!' wailed Alice.

'Don't panic,' said Jake, 'I have a plan.'

He got up from his chair and grabbed Alice by the hand. She didn't resist. She squeezed his palm back as he led her through the police station's corridors. There were bomb survivors pointing and laughing at the clothes they'd been bought by the other officers. Two were fighting over who claimed a short-sleeved shirt, and another was asking if they could swap the red Marks and Spencer's jumper for a blue one.

Jake led Alice through the station and out toward the back yard. Every warm-blooded male that they passed turned and glanced admiringly at her.

Jake helped settle her in the front passenger seat of the BMW, closing her door gently. Checking that she was strapped in correctly, he proceeded to put his foot to the floor and drive with blue lights and two tones all the way across London.

Travelling directly north from Brixton to Euston station took just over ten minutes. Alice's smile lit up the inside of the car the whole way.

Jake stopped in a service area adjacent to the train station.

'Thank you, Detective Inspector Jake Flannagan,' she said as she leaned over and kissed him on the cheek.

'You're most welcome,' he replied.

'Perhaps I'll be in touch, when this all quietens down?' she said. 'Take care.'

Alice got out of the car and walked to the station.

It had been an extraordinary few days. Alice and many others could have been dead – but instead, here she was in a new dress, new shoes; she'd had a whirlwind ride in a police car with flashing lights and sirens, driven by an admiring detective *and* had an amazing story to tell to the other wedding guests about why she was late.

He couldn't ever envisage things quietening down. There was never enough time to see his kids or his girlfriend as it was. There were people to catch. No time for anything. Jake envied Alice as she waved a final farewell at the top of the steps and moved closer toward her point of exit from London.

'Enjoy the wedding, Alice – thank me in the next life,' he said to himself as he pulled the car back into the road and sped off back to Brixton.

The drive back was more relaxed. Thousands of people were walking the streets in the late afternoon sun; there were no Tubes. The pavements were busier than Jake had ever seen them, teeming with people trying to get home from work. The main roads were jammed with traffic.

Sat at a set of red traffic lights at the top of Great Portland Street with his window wound down, Jake watched two men with briefcases saunter past his car. Engrossed in their conversation, there were smiles and laughter as they chatted and walked. Jake wondered if they'd have had that conversation on a crowded and noisy train.

Two weeks ago Wasim and his gang had maimed and killed fifty-two of these people. Today someone had tried again, but they'd failed.

Londoners were a hardy bunch. They just got on with it. They had to. There was no choice. Bomb or no bombs – life had to go on. Jake imagined that this was how London behaved during the Blitz. People pulled together. They looked after each other. Through all this doom and gloom they still found time to laugh.

Even Jake had forgotten the earlier chaos for a moment or two as he enjoyed his time with Alice. Two people thrown together in a terrible situation could still find that spark, that attraction. A moment of fun.

32

Back at Brixton, Jake continued taking statements. More witnesses had been directed to the station. All wanted to help catch the people responsible and all sat there patiently waiting for their turn to be seen.

It was 2300 hours the next time Jake grabbed a chance to look at his watch. Time for a cup of tea and a bite to eat, he thought, making a move for the canteen.

The serving hatch was closed, metal shutters locked in place over the counter. Two vending machines lit up the corner, touting their wares at him like a couple of brothel windows in Amsterdam. Chocolate-bar dinner it was to be, then. Jake fished around in his pocket for some change and dragged out forty-four pence. There wasn't even enough for any chocolate – just enough for a cup of mouth-blistering tea, in a small beige plastic cup, two-thirds full.

He sat down at a table in the deserted canteen and pulled out his mobile to dial Claire's number. It rang several times before clicking through to answerphone.

He hung up without leaving a message and sipped the braised brown liquid, scalding his tongue in the process.

His phone rang.

'Hi,' Jake answered, hoping it was Claire.

'Jake, it's Helen. Can you meet Ian from exhibits at Golders Green underground station at 0030 hours please?'

'What for?'

'They need to drive the train from the Oval to Golders Green, separate the carriage the suspect was in, lift it off the tracks there and put the carriage on the back of a lorry so that exhibits can take it away to deal with forensics. Ian is going to travel on the carriage for continuity of the exhibit. You need to meet him at the other end, make sure he's happy and that everything goes smoothly when they lift it off. Oh, and most importantly, give him a lift back into town.'

'OK,' replied Jake wearily.

'We've block-booked a load of rooms at the Cumberland Hotel at the top of Park Lane. Get your head down there when you've finished that – I need to talk to you in the morning at the Yard.'

'What time?'

'0900 hours.'

Jake finally got his head down at 0430 hours. Going home to check on Ted wasn't an option.

33

Friday
22 July 2005
0915 hours
New Scotland Yard, Westminster, London

Jake stood outside Helen's office. He'd been waiting for fifteen minutes. Two DIs before him had walked out without saying a word. There was pressure to get results. Everyone was too busy for chit-chat.

Helen's office was just wide enough for a desk and a couple of chairs. It was cosy, yet there was no handshake and no eye contact. It was unlike her.

'You OK, Helen?' Jake attempted pleasantries to normalise the situation, when really all he wanted was for his boss to get to the point.

'We're splitting the team in half. Half on the 7/7 bombings – Operation Theseus – and half on the 21/7 bombings – Operation Vivace. Vivace is our priority – we have live suspects who have tried to detonate devices. Forget 7/7.'

Helen was in full 'telling mode' – there was no negotiating.

'But, Helen – they're the same job. Same group of people,' interrupted Jake.

'Where's the evidence of that? It's just copycat stuff – that's what the Security Service have told us…'

'They did? They said there was no connection?' Jake couldn't believe what he was hearing.

'You heard me, Jake! That's what they said! They've given us a few names. People that they suspect. There are surveillance teams looking for them now.'

Helen looked him directly in the eyes. It was time for Jake to listen and not speak.

'I want you to go to Harrow. One of the names we have – possibly one of those involved yesterday – well, I want the next-door neighbour interviewed. He's a white Muslim convert who was seen dancing around in the garden in the early hours of the morning after the suspect left. You will *not* make arrests without permission. You will *not* go rogue.'

Helen passed Jake a sheet of paper with the name and address of the person she wanted interviewed. 'You come back when it's done – I need you on Vivace. These guys are alive and running around somewhere.'

Jake got up and left the room. He said nothing to Helen as he left. He walked to the end of the corridor and started to climb the stairs to the sixteenth floor. He could hear footsteps above him and looked up to see Detective Chief Superintendent Richard Smith on his way down. Normally a jovial chap who said hello, today he didn't even make eye contact.

'You OK, guv'nor?' asked Jake, trying to catch his attention.

DCS Smith looked at him. His eyes were red. He looked exhausted and upset. 'Not really. We just shot someone dead at London Bridge.'

'Jesus!' exclaimed Jake, genuinely surprised.

'It was a mess. I think we shot the wrong bloke.' DCS Smith looked down at the ground and continued his walk down the stairs.

Jake just stood there, rooted to the spot. Two terrorist attacks on London and now police were shooting people dead? The wrong people dead? This wasn't London any more. This was a place he didn't recognise.

He'd lived in the capital his whole life; thought he understood how it worked, what made it tick, what excited it. He knew the good and the bad and still loved it. But this? This wasn't London. He thought about his daughters. Was this the place he wanted them growing up?

34

Jake stood in the stairwell of the fifteenth floor and called Claire.

He didn't wait for her to say anything. The moment he heard it connect, he started shouting.

'What the fuck? Tell me! Just what the fuckin' hell are you lot doing? Wednesday fucking night I told you there were explosives in that place. Wednesday fucking night! They would have killed loads more on Thursday had it not been for me!'

'Jake, Jake... calm down,' Claire tried to talk over him.

'And now, this morning, you lot have got the world's biggest fucking surveillance fucking operation on in London. You knew all the names all along! You knew, for fuck's sake!'

'Jake. Stop it!'

'Stop it? It's a good job I did. You didn't try to stop it did you?' Jake's temper had got the better of him.

Claire came back at him. 'Really? So how the fuck did you find your way to that flat, DI Flannagan? How? Who gave you the leg-up?'

'You wanted me to check it out, not actually go in there – you so said yourself. We've shot someone by mistake just now – needlessly. It could have been avoided had we nicked that lot on Wednesday!'

'Yes, I wanted you to show an interest in that flat. Snoop around. You did. By hook, by crook, by being clever or by sheer luck, Jake – you should be thanking me that you went there, not fucking screaming at me… And as for shooting the wrong bloke – maybe they shouldn't give guns to stupid half-wits like you police officers!'

The line went dead. Claire had hung up on him again.

'Halfwits?' Jake mumbled to himself as he walked down the concrete stairs.

On his way out of the building, Jake's mobile rang.

It was Helen. She sounded flustered. Bad news travelled fast amongst police officers. Jake knew instantly what it was about.

'Jake – cancel going to Harrow. There's been a fuck up… we've shot someone. We don't know who it is yet,' Helen continued. 'This is getting out of hand. We can't cope. The Met can't cope. We need to catch these maniacs. Fast. There's a bomb factory in north London this lot used, just been found…'

Jake had to bite his tongue from shouting the words 'Sullivan House' down the phone.

'Jake, you need to organise the guys over there to make house-to-house enquiries. Do what you do best. Find these people.'

'Message understood, boss,' he said as he left the building.

Jake didn't ask the address before he hung up. He sorely hoped that Helen hadn't noticed.

35

Jake pulled up at the sixties tower block in north London for the second time that week. This time around, though, there were several ATB officers by the communal front door, drinking coffee from takeaway cups. It reminded Jake of a picket line.

'What *are* you lot *doing*?' he snapped.

'Just grabbing a cup of coffee, guv,' said one of the more senior DCs.

'What enquiries have you done? What have you found out?'

There was silence.

'Throw that fucking coffee away. Get your fucking arses moving and start banging on doors. I want answers. Who lived here? Who were their friends? What car did they drive? Where do they work? There are terrorists on the loose and a man's been shot dead; you're standing there drinking coffee. Move it. Now!'

They threw their coffee into a bin and walked off. Sometimes you needed to crack the whip to get people moving. Even in situations like this, thought Jake.

He got back into his car and called Claire.

'Jake – I'm sorry. Thank you. I flagged the address up as best I could. It was given to a team to look at. Not fast enough. Thank the Lord you got there and messed up their explosives,' she blurted out.

'I don't get how you can have all that intelligence and not see the wood for the trees. It was obvious,' replied Jake.

'I'll call you back,' said Claire. 'I have some things I need to sort out.'

It was too muggy to sit in the vehicle. He got out and leant against the side, wondering when Claire would call him back with an update. Bruise-coloured clouds shrouded the sun and darkened everything, including Jake's mood.

Jake was annoyed with Claire, but he was also annoyed at himself for being annoyed with her, which made it even worse. They'd been seeing each other again on and off for a while now. When they were together it was intense – just like it had been when they were at university. Yet he'd been fighting with himself not to become too involved, because she'd given him no indication that she felt the same as he did.

They had good times, laughter, great sex and interesting conversations. Jake liked her. Maybe he liked her too much? But recently he'd seen little of her. She didn't seem to want to commit to anything more. Her behaviour was unsettling. It meant that he had begun to enjoy any attention he could get from other females. A bit like the rah-rah-skirted woman in the club – before the guilt set in.

Jake hated himself for becoming emotionally involved with anyone, but he desperately needed to be needed. He didn't really understand why. Perhaps there was an emotional deficit there as a result of his father not being at home when he was little.

Jake mostly satisfied his needs with work. There was always someone that needed him at work. And when there wasn't and Claire wasn't around? His flirty nature reared its ugly head to stave off the loneliness. But that led to him getting more annoyed at himself that the desire for praise and attention crossed over into his private life. He'd failed. Mustn't let that happen.

'Do some work, Jake. Don't think about it!' he told himself.

An elderly lady walking her poodle headed toward him along a pavement made half of wonky, grey paving slabs and half of well-levelled tarmac. The dog had chosen the smooth side and had given the old lady the rough. As the fluffy white canine reached Jake's car, it cocked his leg and urinated over his rear tyre. Jake laughed; the woman smiled back at him.

'It's funny how dogs have to do that, isn't it?' he said with a chuckle.

'Yes. He never fails, this one. If there's a car, he has to do his business on the tyre!'

The old girl, with hair as snowy as that of her dog, must have been in her eighties. To Jake's ears she sounded like a local. The clear north-London twang gave it away. There was no hint of any Kent or Essex rural country burr – as was more evident with Londoners based in areas to the south and east.

'I can tell you've lived here your entire life,' said Jake with a big smile.

'How can you tell that?' She was genuinely interested. The fluffy white dog was now sniffing round Jake's shoes. He began to worry it might cock his leg again.

'I'm a detective,' winked Jake. 'It's my job to know these things.'

The old lady gave out a tinkly little laugh. 'Are you here about them lot on the top floor? Those Mussulman bombers?' she asked.

Jake was startled. He looked at her straight on, but she seemed neither jokey nor senile. Her body was old and frail, but her mind was clearly as sharp as anything.

'I am,' he fired back. 'Do you know them?'

'Pain in the arse, they are! Making noise. Coming and going at all hours of the day. Not like us. Have you checked on their friend in Gilbert House?' The woman motioned toward an almost identical 1960s tower block, a few streets away.

'No. How do you know they have a friend in there?' asked Jake, curious now.

'Edna. My sister Edna lives in that block; lived there for thirty years. I've lived here for over twenty. We've never had any trouble here. Them Mussulmans move in and now look, police everywhere. Been moved out of my home 'for my own safety'. I've seen them going in and out of an address by Edna's. Not sure of the number. Ask the caretaker. Number four he lives at. He knows them.'

The woman had barely finished speaking before Jake was on his toes, thanking her as he sprinted in the direction of Gilbert House.

Jake arrived at flat four, Gilbert House. For once he didn't actually know what he was going to ask. He was out of breath. He banged on the door. A man in a jumper that Val Doonican would have been proud of answered.

'I'm DI Jake Flannagan. Can I come in and talk to you please?' Jake held up his leather-bound warrant card. The man nodded and allowed him into the small flat. The swirly carpet was almost identical to the jumper – green, brown and orange.

'I'm investigating the attempted bombings yesterday. We're working in Sullivan House, top floor,' said Jake. He needed to know that the man understood the gravity of the situation before he continued.

'I know they've sealed it off. I suppose you want to know about their friend's place over here?' asked the caretaker.

Jake wondered if he was the only person in the entire area that didn't know what was actually going on.

'Yes. What number is it?'

'Forty-three. The flat was empty, then I saw one of the Sullivan House guys go in there this morning. The big one – really tall fella, he is. Came out wearing the full gear like those Muslim ladies wear. I don't know what it's called, that outfit. But top to toe. Black robe thing. You know.'

'How long ago?' asked Jake.

'About twenty minutes ago.'

'Which way did he go?'

'Walked up toward the shops on the main road.'

Jake raced as fast as his feet would carry him, up toward the main road in the direction that the 'big woman' in the burka had headed. Twenty minutes was quite a head start, but how fast could a very tall man in a burka move, without drawing too much attention to himself?

36

As he ran, Jake called the Reserve Room for assistance. There was no one nearby to help, but a request was lodged for local uniform to be on the lookout.

He reached the end of the estate and hit the main road.

'Left or right, Jake? Take your pick?' he said.

On the opposite corner was a sweet shop with a shabby red awning advertising soft drinks. The place looked tired and dilapidated. Window stickers from the previous November still proclaimed 'Fireworks sold here', but the door was open and they looked like they were still trading. Jake scoured the outside of the building and spotted a small CCTV camera looking back at him. He dashed across the road and in through the open door. An elderly Indian woman with a tie-dyed sari draped over her right shoulder sat on a high stool behind the raised counter. There was no time for pleasantries or introductions.

'Police. Your CCTV, does it work?' Jake pointed at the camera.

'Yes,' she said.

'Does it record?' Jake asked. There were many systems that didn't record because they weren't set up right. It always amazed Jake. What was the point of CCTV that's not watched or recorded?

'Kumar! Kumar! Kumar?' called the woman up a set of stairs to her left.

A twenty-something lad with a goatee beard and ripped jeans appeared. The woman spoke frenetically to him in Gujarati before he turned to Jake.

'Yes, mate what can I do for you?' asked Kumar, with a thick Cockney accent.

'Your CCTV, does it work and record?'

'Yeah, course it does, mate.'

'I need to see if it's caught someone walking in the road opposite. Can you show me it?'

'Sure – come with me.'

He led Jake into a storeroom at the back of the shop, filled almost to the brim with boxes. In one corner sat a precarious-looking shelf holding a computer and a monitor.

Kumar sat on a large box of Walkers crisps. He'd logged on before Jake could even blink. He navigated through the windows, menus and submenus of the computer to access the footage. Jake was pleased that he'd met Kumar.

'How far do you need to look back, mate?'

Kumar pulled up four cameras. The screen split into quarters to show each of the different views.

'Twenty minutes, half hour? I'm looking for a big woman in a burka. Try that camera there, the one that catches the street.' Jake tapped the top left of the monitor's screen.

Within minutes, Kumar had footage of a very tall, fully burka-clad silhouette walking toward the shop. The figure was carrying a white handbag. The time on the footage showed 1732 hours. Jake checked his watch; it was 1758 hours. The figure approached the junction and turned to its right. Jake had exactly what he was after, the direction of travel.

'Kumar, you're a star! Well done. That's just what I needed!' Jake shook his hand warmly and bolted out of the shop.

37

Jake began to sweat as he sprinted along the pavement in the heat of the late afternoon. He slowed down as he reached some playing fields at the end of the road. There was a small car park which sloped down to bushes and a wooded area.

It was a wide open space. There was nowhere else for the guy to have gone; he had to have walked to the bottom of the playing fields.

When Jake got to the bottom, there was a steep verge down onto the North Circular Road. Two lanes sat side by side with stop-start traffic crammed into every available piece of space. A sea of different coloured cars and vehicles panned out before him. A smog of traffic fumes hung in the air.

Jake ran down the verge to the main road.

Had the guy in the burka met someone here? Got into a car? There was a bridge and a bus stop on the other side. Jake looked up and down the road as he tried to catch his breath. There was no sign of the burka man on any pavement. There was no CCTV to help this time either.

Jake stood there. What now? Where was he going?

Jake walked back up the verge, which gave him an elevated view of the road across the stationary traffic.

There were four kids watching him from the playing field – he'd run past them on his way down to the road. They'd been playing football. One was the goalkeeper in front of a makeshift goal created out of BMX bikes.

Jake jogged toward the boys.

They looked about twelve years of age at the most. Two were white with freckled faces. One was Asian looking and the other black with braided hair. The black boy, who was closest to the ball, instinctively picked it up as Jake got nearer. It made Jake wonder how many times they had had their football taken away by a man in a suit.

'Boys, I'm a policeman,' he said as he took out his warrant card and showed them. 'Did you see a really big woman in a black dress with her face and head covered? She came past here a bit ago?'

The group of boys stood in a semicircle. They looked back at him blankly.

'Nah,' said the black boy, holding the football protectively to his chest.

Jake exhaled loudly. They were clearly more interested in their game.

'OK. Thanks,' said Jake, as he turned away from the boys.

As he started back up the incline toward the sweet shop, the black kid shouted after him in his north London twang.

'You meant a burka didn't ya, mate? Not a dress! A burka with the veil and that?'

Jake was pleasantly surprised that the kid knew the right terminology. He stopped and turned.

'Yes. I did. Did you see a big, tall woman on the road over there in a burka?'

'Nah,' shouted back the kid as he practised his keepie-uppies.

Jake gave up, waved his hand to thank them and carried on walking. The trail had gone cold.

The smallest white kid with freckles shouted after him. 'I tell you what though, mate – we did see a massive big fella wearing one about ten minutes ago!'

Jake spun back round. 'What? Where?'

'Down there at that bus stop – got on the bus. It's number A232 – that's the only bus that stops there. Every fifteen minutes,' said the black kid, pointing at the bus stop on the other side of the road, beyond the bridge.

'We was laughing at him. There's no way that was a woman. Way too big. And he was walking like a man. It was a man! You sure you ain't looking for a man in a burka?'

'I was. I *am*! Thanks, lads!'

38

Jake turned and legged it back down the verge. He sprinted up the ramp and onto the bridge. Above the sea of traffic again, he could see a bus coming toward the stop. It was the next A232. It had to be. The kid said it was the only bus that stopped there.

Jake ran down the ramp leading to the opposite side of the road. The bus had slowed and was caught in heavy traffic, not moving. Jake picked his way between the cars and down the middle of the stationary traffic, making a beeline for the driver's side of the bus. The driver, a fat white guy with a ruddy complexion wearing a maroon tank top and a white short-sleeved shirt, pushed open his window.

It suddenly struck Jake that the burka man might be carrying a bomb in his white handbag, or potentially wearing a suicide vest.

'Police. The bus in front of you, the A232 on this route – do you know who's driving it?' Jake asked.

'That'll be Arthur Clack. He's a good bloke. Is he OK?' asked the driver from his window.

'I need you to pull over and get him on your radio. Can you do that? Now. Right now!'

The driver shook his head. 'The control room will have to do it. I can't contact him directly from my radio.'

'I need it done straight away. I'm from the Anti-Terrorist Branch.' Jake flashed his badge. 'There's a terrorist suspect on his bus. A man wearing a burka, disguised as a woman.'

'OK, OK! I'm pulling in,' said the driver as he indicated, pulled the bus onto the pavement and began talking into the radio mike in his cab.

Jake waited anxiously. The seconds seemed like hours.

'The control room wants to know who you are. They want to speak to you before they contact Arthur and stop his bus.'

'Get them to call me on my mobile now.' Jake recited his number to the driver who relayed it via his radio.

Jake's handset flashed and buzzed in his hand.

'DI Jake Flannagan. Who am I talking to?'

'Scott Rodman. Duty Manager, Mainline Passenger Transport.'

'Scott, there's no time to waste here. There's a suspected terrorist on Arthur Clack's bus. A tall man dressed in a burka. He may be armed and he may have a bomb. I need you to get hold of Arthur right now, keep him calm, and find out if the burka man is still on the bus. Do it now, Scott. Call me back.' Jake waited for a response.

'OK. I'm doing it.'

The line went dead.

39

Friday
22 July 2005
1455 hours
A406 North Circular Road, north London

Jake's nerves were getting the better of him. He kept his eyes glued up ahead, expecting to hear an explosion and see a plume of smoke.

The traffic was moving again. He couldn't wait any longer. Seconds and minutes were important. Lives were at risk. He couldn't have another busload of passengers blown to pieces.

'Everybody off the bus, now!' shouted Jake at the top of his voice down the aisle of the single-decker vehicle. 'Now! Get off the bus. Police!'

The fifteen or so passengers alighted from the vehicle, followed by the driver. Jake grabbed him and led him back onto the bus.

'Mate, you're gonna have to drive. As fast as you can after the A232 up ahead,' said Jake, as he nudged the chubby guy toward the driver's cabin.

'But...'

'If you don't drive it, I will. And that will just be more painful for you to watch than it will be for me to do. Now move!'

The driver closed the pneumatic doors and quickly put the bus into gear. He pulled off the pavement with a huge crunch and careered into the inside lane. Jake clung to the side of his cab.

The traffic had thinned slightly and the driver was clearly in his element, flashing his lights and sounding the horn. 'Get out of the fucking way, you stupid old biddy!' he shouted, gesticulating through the window at an old lady in the outside lane, blocking their path.

As they hit a clear piece of road, the speedometer neared 65 mph and a half grin appeared on the chubby driver's face.

Jake's phone rang.

'HELLO?' Jake shouted. He could barely hear above the clatter of the diesel engine that was being worked harder than it had ever been before.

'Detective Flannagan? It's Scott Rodman. I've spoken with Arthur. The big burka guy is off the bus.'

40

Friday
22 July 2005
1505 hours
A406 North Circular Road, north London

Jake waved at the chubby driver to slow down as he shouted into his mobile at the bus company's control room. 'Where? Where did he get off?'

'Golders Green Road,' came the reply from Scott in the control room. 'Shall I hold the bus where it is? I've told the driver to hang on. It's two stops along from you.'

Jake suddenly saw Golders Green Road on his left as they flew past it. 'STOP! STOP!' he shouted.

The bus driver slammed on the breaks. Jake lost his grip on the driver's cab and careered forward into the windscreen. He smashed into it as the vehicle came to a halt against the kerb. Jake touched his forehead. Blood.

'Sorry, mate. So sorry. You OK?' The driver got out of his seat and held out his hand to help Jake up. 'You're not a professional tumbler, are you?' he joked.

'What?' Jake was confused and slightly dizzy.

'We get them all the time. They say we've braked dangerously when we haven't, then they claim for some made-up injury. You look like you might have an actual claim though,' winced the driver as he looked at Jake's head.

'It's fine. I'm fine. Thanks for your help.'

Jake got off the bus. He knew he must only be a couple of minutes, if that, behind the burka man now.

He could taste the blood running down his face as it dripped into his mouth. People in cars and on the street were turning to look at him as he pounded down the road, some asking if he needed help. He ignored them. He knew head wounds always bled badly and appeared worse than they actually were. He had to keep going.

Jake got to the end of Golders Green Road; a one-way system with lots of traffic lights, an underground stop and a coach station. There was no sign of the burka-clad man.

'Fuck!'

He couldn't do this on his own any longer. He called the Reserve Room at the Yard and explained to Roley what had happened – that he hoped the suspect was close but he didn't know where.

'OK, son. Uniform know you're there. They're on their way. Stay where you are. I'm despatching two cars from the Yard to help. Sit tight. You're no good to us dead or missing, son.'

Jake looked down at his white shirt. It was slicked with blood and almost completely crimson; a deep carmine-coloured shroud.

Roley was right. Stand still. Wait.

Jake tried to catch his breath. He sat down on the kerb and watched as blood dripped from his chin into the road. It dried quickly on the hot, dusty tarmac, turning dark brown. The constant dripping slowly began to form a congealing mound of bloodied mess.

Where was this guy? What was his next move? Was he running to hide or was he still in attack mode?

Jake heard sirens approaching. Then all at once there were several police cars in the centre of the one-way system. He could tell from the fluorescent yellow dot on the back windows that these were armed response vehicles.

Jake ran over. He had to keep control of the situation – they'd shot one too many innocent people today already.

An officer jumped out of the ARV and immediately went to the boot, pulling out a Heckler & Koch MP5 machine gun to inspect before loading.

'I'm DI Flannagan. I put in the call,' Jake said, making a beeline for the armed officer.

'Jesus. You OK, sir?' replied the policeman, staring at the blood pouring from Jake's head wound.

'I'm fine.' Jake waved away his concern. 'We're looking for a guy in a full burka.'

A total of six uniformed officers had gathered around him now, but none of them showed any glimmer of understanding in response to this instruction.

'You know what I'm talking about, yes?' asked Jake. He glanced desperately from face to face for some sign of understanding.

'Sorry, sir, we've not had that new diversity training yet,' replied the officer holding the Heckler & Koch.

Jake shook his head. The kids he'd spoken to earlier had known what a burka was. How was it possible these armed police officers didn't know this stuff?

He took a deep breath.

'The suspect is wearing a robe from head to toe and has his face veiled. The garment is black or dark in colour, and he was last seen carrying a white handbag. He's over six feet tall. We are looking for a *man*, not a woman!'

'Do we know if he's armed? Could he have a bomb?' asked the officer who had been first on the scene.

'I don't know. But let's ask ourselves that fucking question before shooting anyone else dead today, shall we? No assumptions! I want you speaking to people, in the station at the bus stops. Someone will have seen him, seen where he went. Talk to them. Ask questions. Find him. Go!'

The officers scattered in different directions.

Jake stood covered in blood, in the middle of the junction littered with police vehicles. The shoulders of his suit were now completely black.

Jake's legs felt heavy, his head woozy. He suddenly had a vision that he was wearing a suit of armour covered in blood, the phone in his hand transformed into a shield bearing the George Cross; the scene the centre of a battle with marauding foreign warriors trying to take his crown. He stood atop a hill, his men sent to fight rampaging foreign thugs in all directions.

A National Express coach pulled out of the station and managed to weave its way onto Jake's imaginary battlefield, pulling him back to reality. Then it was gone in a flash of white.

Jake stood there and replayed the coach pulling away in slow motion in his head, transfixed.

'Burka,' he heard himself say.

He'd seen it.

A slit in the dark material with just a pair of eyes looking back, staring at a badly bleeding man and wondering what had happened.

'THE COACH! HE'S ON THE COACH!' Jake screamed at two newly arrived police officers nearby. They spun round as Jake ran toward their marked police car.

Jake jumped into the driver's seat. The keys were thankfully still in the ignition. The two officers followed him, one in the front and one in the back. The one in the front started screaming into the radio mike that was pinned to his chest. Jake didn't hear what he said. Everything was going into slow motion. He was concentrating only on the back of the coach, which was now disappearing over the brow of a hill ahead of him. The junction was blocked. Only the pavement was free of traffic. Jake slammed the Vauxhall Astra into gear and sounded the horn as he mounted the pavement and drove down the pathway. People scattered in all directions to get out of the way.

'Two tones. Put the two tones and lights on!' Jake shouted at the officer sat next to him.

The officer hit a huge red button on the dashboard's centre console and the car's siren started wailing.

Jake left the pavement at 40 mph and hit the road just as they reached the brow of the hill. There was a squeal of tyres as Jake pushed the accelerator to the floor and sped over the top.

The coach was in sight.

Driving on the wrong side of the road, they gained on it quickly.

As they got closer, Jake could see the coach driver looking in his wing mirror. The coach's brake lights went on. It slowed and stopped. Jake drove around it and blocked its path, preventing it from moving further. The three of them jumped out of the car.

Jake ran to the door, which was already opening with a pneumatic hiss, and stepped up and into the coach. There were terrified faces everywhere he looked, except one. One face up the aisle and to his left wasn't looking at him. The head was turned away. When it came to face him, just the eyes were visible – the eyes through the slit in the burka. Jake noticed a white handbag sat in the luggage rack above the tall figure's head.

There was no time to think. No time to be scared. Only time to do.

Jake pushed his way up the aisle and lurched toward the suspect, grasping a handful of the black material at the neck. Adrenalin filled every space in his body as he hauled the burka-clad figure from its seat and down the coach. Despite the weight and height of the suspect, there was no resistance as Jake dragged the figure down the stairs. Outside the coach, he pulled the suspect to the pavement, kneeled on their chest and partially pulled off the face veil.

It was a man.

Jake had got his man.

'You are under arrest for terrorism. You tried to blow people up on a train. You do not have to say anything but it may harm your defence if you do not mention, when questioned, something which you later rely on in court!'

41

Friday
22 July 2005
1822 hours
High-security custody suite,
Paddington Green police station, central London

Jake gazed at the grey tiled floor as he slumped against one of the two sinks in the Gents, grateful that it bore his weight.

He looked up into the old mirror. A tired and bloodied man, whom he barely recognised, looked back at him. He needed to clean up, to go and buy a new shirt and suit. He stripped to his waist and began to wash the blood off.

Injuries hurt, but the pain went away. Wounds always healed and Jake was no stranger to them; he was a risk taker. The only fear he had was the fear of losing or coming second. These were options he tried not to entertain.

There were reasons for Jake's bullishness. Growing up, he'd wanted to climb trees, ride bikes fast, run with the other kids; all things his mother didn't like. So he had rebelled. He would do things that the other kids were too scared to do: skip from garage roof to garage roof, climb the wrought-iron drainpipe up the side of the flats; jump his BMX bike across the ravine at the woods.

When Jake did get hurt, he was surprised to find that the pain wasn't that bad. He believed that his mother's fear of danger was sorely misplaced.

Yet there were reasons for her fears.

Jake's mother had lost two daughters in childbirth.

She'd never gotten over it. Jake often thought that if it hadn't happened, he might not have existed. Things happen for a

127

reason, he always reminded himself. If he could make his mark on the world, change the course of lives, then his existence on this planet was warranted. He was needed.

But at the back of his mind he'd lived with a nagging doubt. She'd always wanted daughters. Was he his mother's wooden spoon? He had an urge to prove himself, to be the best in his mum's eyes; to show her that he was made of tougher stuff.

The fearful think things are impossible.

The stupid don't care or understand what you think.

The brave do things and worry later.

His head wound – a large cut to the left of his forehead – needed stitches, but it had finally stopped bleeding. The cut meant that his eyebrow drooped across his eye. It looked awful but he wasn't aware of the pain. The stitches could wait until later. He might even meet a nice nurse who would flirt with him and give him some attention in the process. Going to the hospital was never bad in his book.

Jake dressed himself and made his way toward the custody suite.

Paddington Green police station was a strange, white sixties creation consisting of a central tower block surrounded by a triple-storey, five-sided building. It reminded Jake of a single birthday candle on a cupcake.

The first and second floors of the tower were restricted access. Beneath the tower, on a raised ground floor, was the custody suite used solely by the Anti-Terrorist Branch for their prisoners. They called it 'the most secure police station in the country' – a police station within a police station.

The place had been designed to hold IRA terror suspects in the 1980s. Blast doors, anti-ram barriers, CCTV and several full-time security guards kept the place secure – and kept the IRA out – should one of their own be held in the clink.

Jake went downstairs and buzzed to get into the secure holding area.

On his arrest at Golders Green, Samir had been given a sterile white forensic suit to wear over his burka. He'd then been transported in a car with its interior thoroughly covered in fresh plastic sheeting. The inside of the vehicle had looked to Jake like a scene from *ET*.

At the station, Samir had been placed directly in a cell with its floor and walls covered in fresh brown paper. Everything had been done to ensure that any potential evidence, such as explosives residue, was preserved on Samir's body and his clothes. Nothing must be picked up along the way, or left behind.

Samir was taken out of his suit, then stripped, swabbed for explosives residue and redressed. His clothes were seized and replaced with a fresh forensics suit.

Then he was booked in, asked a series of questions by a custody sergeant and given information about his rights.

It took two hours until an urgent interview could be arranged – and that was before they'd even taken fingerprints.

During the lengthy booking-in process, Jake had learned that the man in the burka was called Samir Shafiq. He was twenty-one years old, originally from Somalia and he spoke English fluently.

Most of all, Jake had learned that Samir wanted to talk – that he didn't want a solicitor present during the interview. That's why the stitches, new shirt, new suit and nurses were going to wait. If your man wanted to talk, you got on with it, there and then. You sat there and let him talk to you.

Samir was brought out of his cell and handed over to Jake, who stood by the custody desk.

'Samir, we've asked you repeatedly if you wish to have a lawyer present and you have said no each and every time. I'm now going to take you to the interview room and we can talk in there.'

Samir said nothing. He nodded. His eyes were wide. Jake started to sense fear in them. 'It's just you and me having a chat,' said Jake.

42

Friday
22 July 2005
1845 hours
High-security custody suite,
Paddington Green police station, central London

Jake led Samir to a small and windowless interview room with just one desk and four chairs in it. On one side was a series of shelves on which sat a DVD video recorder and a separate audio recorder.

Each device would record two true-to-life copies of everything, so everyone could be doubly sure nothing had been missed. There were two cassette tapes that went into the audio recorder and two DVDs that went into the DVD recorder.

Jake began the spiel that he knew off by heart, ignoring the laminated prompt cards lying on the table in front of him.

'This interview is being recorded and may be given in evidence if your case is brought to trial. The recordings are audio – sound – and visual – TV pictures.

'We are in an interview room at Paddington Green police station in London and I am Detective Inspector Jake Flannagan of the Anti-Terrorist Branch. I am interviewing – please state your full name.' Jake paused and indicated to Samir that he should speak.

'Samir Shafiq.'

'At the conclusion of the interview I will give you a notice explaining what will happen with the recordings of this interview and how you may get access to them.

'I must remind you that you have the right to free and independent legal advice at any time – day or night. This interview can be delayed for you to obtain legal advice. You can ask for a solicitor to come and sit in this interview with you – but you have said that you do not want a solicitor. Why is that, Samir?'

'I don't know. I don't need one, I don't think.'

Jake was surprised. Samir was looking down the barrel of a minimum of thirty years in prison for this. As with most crimes, you had to prove guilt, prove intent, prove that the suspect had a guilty mind. A cornerstone of the English justice system: '*Actus reus non facit reum nisi mens sit rea.*'

It was the only Latin that Jake remembered. The only Latin he'd ever bothered to learn. It was written in the front of the first criminal-law book Jake ever read at university. There was no translation; he'd had to look it up. It always surprised Jake that the police never taught this stuff fully to students at Hendon. The Latin translated to: 'An act is not necessarily a guilty act unless the accused has the necessary state of mind required for it.'

That's why police interviews were so important. You had to prove the accused's guilty mind. The fact that he had done something wrong wasn't enough. The courts demanded evidence of a 'guilty mind'. The interview is where that proof most often came from.

'It's your choice. You've chosen not to have a solicitor – fine. You are under caution. You do not have to say anything unless you wish to do so, however it may harm your defence if you do not mention when questioned something which you later rely on in court. Anything you do say may be given in evidence.'

Once they'd got past the formalities, Samir seemed more relaxed.

'OK, Samir. We can talk as long as you want, but I need to ask you something urgently. It's urgent because we are concerned lots of people are going to get hurt or die. I need to know – are there any more bombs anywhere?'

'Not that I know of.'

'What does that mean?'

'It means what I said. Bombs are bombs. They kill people. Do the people of Iraq, Afghanistan and Palestine know when the next bombs are going to be dropped?'

131

'Maybe not. But we are talking about London – not any of those places. And the bombs in those places are dropped by trained professional military personnel on military targets – not on Tube trains and buses by people wearing backpacks.'

'I am a soldier of Allah.'

'Are you? You didn't act like a soldier when you dressed as a woman and tried to escape on a bus. I've never seen any soldier ever do that. *Ever.* If you're a soldier, where is the rest of your army now? The other members of your unit that you normally fight with? Have they fled dressed as women too?'

Samir said nothing.

Jake needed to keep up the tempo of the interview. He didn't want Samir to have too much time to deliberate and start to make up his answers. Keep asking questions quickly, thought Jake. He needed the first thing that came into Samir's head. That way there was less time for suspects to think up a strategy; less time to evade the questions being asked of them.

'You're from Somalia?'

'Yes.'

'When did you come here to the UK?'

'When I was nine. I came here with my aunt and uncle. They were given political asylum here.'

'You grew up here in the UK after that?'

'Yes.'

'That was good of us – the UK, I mean. We gave you somewhere to live. Educated you. Did you go to college?'

'Yes.'

'You're twenty-one now, right? Are you working?'

'No – I study Islam.'

'So, when did you train to be a soldier... of Allah, I mean?' Jake wondered if Samir could tell he was being sarcastic.

'Every day I read Quran. This trains me. We don't always do jihad by going abroad and firing guns and using bombs. Before we do that we must have jihad within ourselves,' answered Samir calmly.

Most people would have been annoyed at Jake's dig, yet Samir remained impassive. Maybe Samir was stupid?

'You live on your own?' asked Jake.

'Yes.'

'At Sullivan House?'

'Yes.'

'So what's your trouble then?'

'What do you mean?

'You fled a war-torn country. Asylum means your family must have been persecuted in your own country. You come here. My country allows you in. Feeds you. Gives you somewhere to live. Educates you. Then it sends you to college. Then, even when you're not working, we give you your own flat, free of charge, for you to read religious books and go down the mosque every day... I don't get it – what's your trouble?'

'This world is like a toilet. Who wants to spend all their life in the toilet, when something better is waiting for them? My people are being bombed every day. Women and children raped and murdered in Afghanistan and Iraq by butchers.'

'Whose words are they?'

'What?'

'You said "raped and murdered by butchers"... You've seen this happening or did someone tell you about it?'

'I have been told by people who have been there.'

'You believe everything you're told?'

'These people speak the truth. I trust them.'

'What if they were telling lies? Just to make you do what they wanted you to do?'

'I've seen videos and photos of these things.'

'Given to you by the same people that told you that these things were real?'

Samir was silent again.

'Samir. How do you think I found you?'

'I don't know.'

'These people that you trust... The people that tell you the "truth". Do you think maybe that they might be messing you about? Telling you lies that you are their friend, when in fact you are not? Telling you that they will protect you, when in fact they are telling us where you are?'

133

Samir was silent. He stared at Jake.

Jake could see it. In the corner of Samir's eyes. It was work-ing. A seed of doubt had taken root.

43

Friday
22 July 2005
1910 hours
High-security custody suite,
Paddington Green police station, central London

Jake allowed the silence to go on much longer than he would in a normal conversation.

'Let him fester and think,' Jake's inner voice said.

Silence was awful in this environment for a suspect who was now beginning to self-question and reprocess everything that they'd once believed in. They couldn't run. They couldn't hide. They couldn't block out what you were saying. It was even rumoured that some of the walls of the building had been specially designed with white tiles to make the view perfectly symmetrical. This was to help prevent suspects from focussing on an image in their heads that might block out interrogation.

After what seemed like an age, Jake spoke again. 'We can come back to that later, Samir. Let's move on. Tell me *why* you did it, Samir. Let's talk about that.'

Jake had consciously shied away from asking 'Did you do it?'

It may have passed Samir by, that Jake had deliberately skipped this, the million-dollar question. Yet, by moving on, Jake inferred he already knew the answer. This was his subtle way of playing mind games.

Samir responded, 'You will not listen to our words. Only when we show you our blood will you listen to our words.'

Probably the most profound thing he's said all day, thought Jake. But yet again they sounded like someone else's words, not Samir's.

'So by blowing yourselves up on Tube trains and buses you make us listen to your words?' Jake asked.

'We need to make you and your government listen. If that's what it takes, then that's what we will do.'

Jake needed more. It wasn't enough to prove intent. It was close but not perfect.

'So when you went onto the Tube on 21 July, 2005, you wanted people to listen by seeing your blood?'

'Yes.'

'By blowing yourself and others up, you would have made people listen?'

Jake had gone in for the kill quickly. The opening was there.

Samir couldn't see it, but his next answer would change the course of his life from here on in. If he answered, he was saying he was guilty and had a guilty mind. It was like playing tennis. Jake had served for the match. Would Samir notice that Jake's next shot had topspin lob on it before he hit it back? Or would he lose everything?

'Yes – that's right.'

Samir was stupid. He was fucked. He'd admitted his act, and admitted that he had a guilty mind. Jake could let his guard down a little.

Jake sat back in his chair and took a moment to really look at the human being in front of him. He suddenly saw a boy sitting before him, not a man. The interview had been a walk-over. Jake wasn't even trying. He was like Roger Federer, playing tennis with a kid who didn't know the rules of the game; a child opponent versus a three-time Wimbledon winner who did this for a living.

He felt a slight pang of remorse. Samir was more immature than he'd realised.

'Samir – tell me about your life. Tell me about you.'

'The aunt and uncle I came with left me. I lived with foster parents more or less as soon as I arrived here in Britain. I missed my own parents. They didn't have enough money to come. They sent me, paid for me to come. Said my life would be better here.'

'The foster parents – were they Muslim?'

'No. They were white. English. Christians. They were nice. But I was different. I didn't fit in. I drank alcohol and took drugs to escape. Chewed khat. I was nobody. When I left school I met some other boys from my part of the world. East Africa – Ethiopia, Eritrea, Somalia. They were like me; had no identity, were going nowhere, taking drugs and getting drunk. We started going to a special Thursday-night club at the mosque.'

'And what happened there?'

'They made me feel like I was family, part of something; one of them. They kept me in a room, made me stop the drugs and alcohol. It was hard but they didn't give up on me. To take my mind off the pain they showed me videos of what was happening abroad – all the killings. Then, when I got better, they took me and my friends on trips to the countryside, to the forest. It was cool. We were all brothers together. The feeling I had missed since I left Somalia. They made me feel special – wanted.'

For the first time, Jake felt a twinge of empathy for him. He understood Samir's desire to feel wanted and needed, to feel part of something. Jake had that desire too. His own neediness and loneliness also drove him into the arms of strangers; women that would boost his self-esteem just like Samir's friends had done. But Samir's friends had played on these feelings, had manipulated him and led him to do terrible things.

'What did they do on the trips?'

'At first it was just walking. Then we ran. They made us train. Then they taught us to build hideouts. We played war games. I liked it.'

'War games?'

'Yes. They made us pretend that we were being hunted; that people were trying to kill us. Then they would leave us in the forest. One night at first. Then two. Then a whole week. No food.'

'And why did they do that?'

'They said it was training for when the UK and US began wiping out all Muslims. That if we wanted to stay together as a family we'd have to learn how to hide together.'

137

'The photos and videos you mentioned earlier – the ones of women and children being raped and killed…'

Samir interrupted him, 'They said that it had started – Muslims were being slaughtered. That we had to help before it went too far. That you were not listening to us. That we had to give our blood to make you listen and to stop the killing. The videos, I watched them over and over when they kept me safe. They said watching them would help me to stop the drugs.'

Jake had seen it before – a chance for attention, to feel wanted… He knew those feelings himself.

Samir didn't like to be alone; he was guileless in many ways. Had that innocent look when you first saw him. He just yearned to be part of something that he'd lacked in childhood. But now here he was, clearly in too deep, not knowing know how to swim. He'd never considered the outcome of being caught, he'd been so focussed on just trying to fit in and be part of the crew. He had no strategy for this eventuality.

Samir had been manipulated and used. He was happy to kill for these people; happy to kill himself. He hadn't expected to still be alive, sat in a police station, powerless and helpless.

The men who had brought Samir to this point, they were the ones Jake wanted to get hold of. They were the ones who needed to be stopped. Going after Samir was like going after a helpless drug addict, the user. If you wanted to make an impact you needed to get the dealer, thought Jake.

'Samir – would you have been happy killing those people on the Tube and happy killing yourself on 21 July?'

'That's what I wanted. I would have been in Paradise with seventy-two virgins now. Instead I am sitting here with you. This is all wrong. Everything has gone wrong.'

Jake knew that Samir had expected to die, yet here he was in an interrogation room, suddenly having to think about his future, realising he'd failed in his quest.

Jake was positive that at this precise moment, given the chance again, Samir would have taken the option to have been shot by police at the coach station.

'Who has been telling you this nonsense?' asked Jake.

Samir looked as though the fight had gone out of him. There was a hollowness there. Jake was used to hardened criminals beginning to negotiate with him by this stage of the interview. Yet Samir was vacant. He was broken. There was no attempt to do a deal.

Jake was reaching a dead end. He could sense that there was no spark left to play off. When you shook up a normal criminal in an interview, they'd react like a carbonated soft drink. But Samir was like an empty bottle. There was no vigour, no animation, no fizz. Nothing remained.

Jake stood up. He looked Samir in the eyes.

'Can you not see you've been used, Samir? You are a dangerous individual. But you're a small fish in a huge sea. You're deluded and you can't or won't see that.'

There was no point in continuing the interview. Samir had nothing else to give. It was a job for another day and possibly another team member.

Jake concluded the interview and turned off the tapes.

Jake was certain that they'd find no evidence at Sullivan House about *who* had brainwashed Samir or *why* he'd been brainwashed.

44

Jake watched the news as he ate his dinner, if he could call it a dinner that was. A meal of two bacon sandwiches.

The headlines were dominated by the arrest of two more of the 21/7 bombers in Operation Vivace.

Jake wondered if the newsreaders seemed to like this new diversion into home-grown terrorism. It gave them plenty to talk about. 'At around 11 a.m. today, armed police surrounded two houses on a rundown estate in the White City area of London. They fired tear gas and stun grenades into the premises where two of the four suspects were arrested.'

The bacon tasted good after the stint at work he'd just done; meetings for the past twelve hours solid. It seemed that everyone in the world was now a terrorist. The Branch wasn't going to be able to cope if this was the new reality, thought Jake. He couldn't believe their current funding and manpower would stretch. The Security Service was growing in number too. It seemed that everyone had been caught on the hop by the global threat that Islamic terrorism now posed.

Jake burped as he finished his last crust. He looked down to see that the ketchup from his sandwich had dripped onto his shirt.

'For God's sake!' he sighed heavily to himself.

He was going to have to change it before he went out with Claire. They'd decided to meet at Tiger Tiger in Haymarket for a drink that evening.

As he stripped off, the phone rang.

'Jake, it's Claire – I can't make tonight.'

'What? You can't? Are you sure? Can't you get out of it? What's going on?' Jake knew he sounded needy as soon as the words left his mouth.

'It's work – been called in last minute. You must have heard about the arrests today?'

Jake sighed. 'How come they need you on that now? The Met has split the job in two: 7/7 is Operation Theseus and 21/7 is Operation Vivace. We've been told to treat them as totally separate and unrelated. What's the real story? Tell me what's going on.'

'I can't, Jake… You know what it's like here… I can't share it with you at the moment. Just…'

'OK, another time.' He hung up the phone without allowing her to say anything more; his way of protesting.

He walked to the fridge in his small flat and opened the door. Beer and the leftovers from yesterday's meat-feast pizza were the remaining delights that it had on offer.

The news was still on. He shoved a slice of pizza into his mouth as he turned over to the football. 'Fuck you and your terrorists. Fuck the lot of you!' he shouted with his mouth full.

He cracked open his first can of lager. His palate watered as the scent hit him; the ritual of the habitual drinker.

Ted the cat was scratching at the cork wallpaper, begging to be let out.

He hated it when she massaged the wall with her claws, like a cheese grater. It was like she was throwing out a challenge to him. 'What are you going to do, Jake? Lock me out? Not feed me?'

Jake couldn't be bothered to move, and growled like a dog at her.

In response, Ted promptly jumped down from the window ledge and coolly wandered over to Jake's yucca plant, which was sat in the corner of the lounge. She leapt up into the plant pot and relieved herself in disgust. The soil would have to do as her litter tray for now.

That made at least two females in his life that he wasn't on perfect terms with right now, thought Jake.

45

Back in the office, after a weekend without Claire and a flying visit to see the kids, he realised grimly that it was almost a month since the first bombings. And where were they now? No further on, it seemed.

Jake sighed and went to find a quiet room with a TV and DVD player. He had been tasked by Denswood to undertake a special job. He'd been given some film footage to watch. Jake had not been told *how* it had been obtained, but he knew it had come from MI6 and that the method by which it had been acquired was top secret.

It was of Wasim and had been filmed in Pakistan at some point during the winter of 2004. Wasim was sat in the corner of a room, in front of a fabric backdrop patterned with red and cream stripes. Jake had researched the material. It was readily available in Pakistan, but you couldn't purchase it in the UK.

On his head, Wasim wore a red and white chequered scarf. A traditional keffiyeh, it was tied tightly around his forehead with the loose ends left flowing down behind him.

Jake watched him carefully as he spoke.

'We are at war and I am a soldier. Now you too will taste the reality of this situation,' said Wasim chillingly, yet with a familiar Yorkshire brogue.

He had travelled to Pakistan in November 2004, seemingly in good health, but on the TV screen Wasim looked extremely thin. He'd lost a lot of weight compared to the family pho-

142

tos Jake had seen. Maybe it was the stress of saying farewell to his wife and daughter? That couldn't have been easy. Or maybe he'd picked up a stomach bug like on his previous trip to Pakistan in 2001, when he'd had to return home through ill health?

Jake thought back to February 2004 and the conversation he'd overheard Wasim having with the Crawley lot on that windy and rainy night in Sussex. He'd sounded like he never intended on coming back from the trip to Pakistan. He'd even resigned from his position at the school where he worked. It looked to all intents and purposes that he had planned to become a martyr abroad – on foreign soil.

But then he'd come back. Why had he returned home in February 2005? The intention to return to the UK from Pakistan had surely been made over there. It looked like someone, somewhere, had convinced Wasim to return, in order to undertake a suicide mission on home soil. That, or he had sought permission to do it – and it had been granted.

Al-Qaeda logos were plastered all over the footage, together with claims that it had been produced by the al-Sahab video production house. It seemed to Jake that there were lots of messages in this video. Hidden messages. He just couldn't decipher them at the moment.

The clock kept showing 8.50 on the cartoon start of the video, the time that the bombs went off. Had this been agreed in advance? Why was that relevant? What were they trying to say?

Wasim continued his sermonising. '…Raise me amongst those whom I love like the prophets… I and thousands like me are forsaking everything for what we believe… Our driving motivation doesn't come from tangible commodities that this world has to offer… Accept the work from me and my brothers and enter us into the gardens of paradise.'

Over and over again, Jake watched the video of Wasim explaining why he would soon martyr himself. He watched it two hundred times, possibly more, until eventually he could no longer stand it.

He needed a break.

All he could see in his head was Wasim talking to him. He was tired.

He got up, made himself a coffee, then logged on to the internet and trawled through the news reports covering the 2001 Twin Towers attacks in New York – the attacks that made bin Laden and his al-Qaeda network known to every household in the world.

Jake looked at the time that the first plane had hit the World Trade Centre.

0850 hours.

The time on the clock in the video.

The time of the attacks in London.

If al-Qaeda were claiming this attack, saying they had also attacked London, why not release Wasim's martyr video immediately?

If they'd filmed it and had it in their possession, why wasn't it released on 7 July – as soon as the bombings were perpetrated? That would have got them maximum media exposure, surely?

Why had this footage taken so long to come to light if they were responsible?

Had someone been holding it back until the last of the 21/7 lot were arrested? If so, then the 7/7 and 21/7 attacks must surely have been connected?

If someone had had since the winter to edit the footage and put all the al-Qaeda graphics on top, thought Jake, then why wasn't it ready to go by 6 July?

After all, that was the original date that the attacks had been planned for – before Wasim's wife had been rushed to hospital with pregnancy complications and everything had been delayed.

46

Jake was drunk; his team had all gone back to their hotels.

He called Claire.

'Jake, what is it?' Claire sounded like she'd just woken up.

'Hey, you OK? I miss you! What are you doing?' Jake slurred down the phone.

'Well, I was sleeping, Jake. And by the sounds of it, you should be too.'

'I just wanted a friendly ear to talk to. Everyone hates me. Those that don't hate me have gone home. I'm on my own. I want you to talk to me.' Jake had to shout above the late-night revellers packing the crowded cobbles.

'Jake, get some sleep. Call me in the morning.'

'When are you coming to see me?' he pleaded.

There was no response.

Jake stared forlornly at the call-ended sign. Claire had hung up on him.

'I *need* love! I'm going to find someone to love me tonight...' he shouted to no one in particular, before tagging onto the back of what looked like a fun, lively crowd. He followed them into a club playing loud music. The door staff took some money off him. He had no idea how much. He didn't really care. It was noisy; there were people dancing and drinking. They were the type he needed right now. Not the sleeping type. Not the grumpy type. Not the fundamentalist bomber type... but the happy type; the drunken type.

145

When Jake awoke the following morning, he wasn't alone in bed.

47

Tuesday morning meant that it was time, once again, for another update meeting between the Leeds team and the Major Incident Room down in London. Jake felt as though these video conferences were starting to eat away at his soul. He could see that they were all working in separate silos which should have been joined up, but weren't. There were now around three thousand people on the job. They had created a monster.

Back in London, the Major Incident Room would decide what actions would be undertaken for the rest of the week. Jake wondered whether the slower some people could perform an action, the more money they hoped to pocket in overtime.

That morning was the usual. The analysts seemed to be no further forward with the phone data from the bombers' phones and the MIR manager had talked a lot about systems administration management, how many new staff had been brought in and how much overtime was being undertaken.

Jake had had a month's worth of this. They'd not come up with anything. He was starting to feel that things weren't looking too rosy.

He murmured under his breath, 'Jesus H Christ. We've got three thousand people working on this and we still haven't made any progress?'

Jake's head hurt; he seemed to be drinking more and more in the evenings. It didn't matter which day of the week it was. He drank to blot out the boredom of filling in pointless reports twenty hours a day. He drank to alleviate the loneliness of nights in his hotel room. He drank to blur the thoughts of Wasim's world.

When he slept sober, Wasim was with him there too.

Jake's drunken world was the only place Wasim didn't inhabit. Jake found himself going there more and more often.

The only drop of pleasure he could wring from the situation was the thought of what he was doing with the money he was being paid to investigate Wasim. He derived great amusement from the fact that he could deliberately spend it on alcohol, clubbing and – when Claire snubbed him – potentially meeting women for no-strings-attached encounters. He wanted to use his salary for everything the extremists were opposed to. All the Western extravagances that the fundamentalists were against.

Swallowing four paracetamol, he opened the first file of the day. Yet another MIR action created via the HOLMES system. It read: Investigate rice packet DB/14 found at Victoria Park.

He cursed aloud to Lenny who was sat opposite.

'Fuck me, Lenny! We've done pitta bread, pasta, now rice. We've investigated 265 items in the past three weeks. I'm fed up of finding out where food was made and looking at fucking sell-by and use-by dates. All this stuff! We're knee-deep in it. There's *too much* of it for one flat. How did they move around in there? They wanted us to look at this stuff. They even left the receipts so we could go and visit the shop they bought it in and investigate the bastard CCTV to see them actually buying it. Why? They're trained terrorists. Why would they leave this trail behind for us? This isn't right. We're missing something else.'

'Yeah,' nodded Lenny over his computer monitor. 'No one we're interviewing seems to know anything. None of their stories add up. It's all shit.'

'Well…' replied Jake, 'there's going to be an end to this shit…'

He stood up and dropped the note about rice packet DB/14 in the bin. This wasn't the first time he'd done this and it wouldn't be the last where MIR actions were concerned.

'I can't bear it, Len. I just feel like we're getting nowhere.'

'I know, boss. No one has a handle on this case. We need to do something different.'

'So what else do we have, Lenny? What do you suggest?'

'I dunno, guv. Witness statements? You could look at those?'

'I like your style, Lenny – try a new approach. At the moment, nobody can see across the board.'

Jake went to the store cupboard and grabbed a couple of unopened boxes of computer paper. He needed a fresh start. He filled the printer trays of every printer in the borrowed office to the brim with blank sheets of paper.

This would be a new beginning, he thought.

Jake settled down to begin the mammoth task of printing out every single witness statement obtained in the entire investigation to date. All 1,392 of them.

'Cup of tea please, Lenny. Two sugars.'

48

There was little that Jake didn't know about the 7/7 witness statements by the end of trawling through almost 1,400 of them. But it had thrown up absolutely nothing new.

So he'd gone through the exhibit records. There were already thousands. He'd looked at every description and every photo of the items that had been found in the Victoria Park flat to date.

Still nothing.

He was back to square one.

He called Claire, sober for once.

'The investigation is going round in circles,' he said. 'We're all working in silos.'

'Well, what about the friends and relatives up in Leeds? Have you got anything out of them?' she asked.

'I don't believe any of the witnesses up here. Half of them don't know anything and I worry that the rest of them are not credible or are covering their tracks. No one wants to speak to us properly. And we're inundated with exhibits. That's all we do. We just spend every day investigating a new object from the flat.'

'Then speak to London. Get them to send you more help?'

'No one in London is taking this by the scruff of the neck. No one has got an overview on this. No one is telling us what's really going on. We need to look at something else. We need to know what you lot know, Claire. Who's behind this?'

'We have no idea either, Jake! What else have you got?' she asked.

At this stage, Jake didn't know.

Later that evening, Jake lay in the bath in his hotel bathroom. The water was going cold.

'What else have you got?' he repeated Claire's question before submerging his entire body under the water.

He sat back up. The water ran out of his ears and nose. He could almost recite by heart the thousands of inanimate objects his team had been given to investigate by the MIR. They were overwhelmed by the stuff – inundated by actions – as if they had packets of food coming out of their ears like bath water.

He got out the bath and pulled on a hotel robe before calling Lenny.

'Len, do you think it's all been put there, dumped in one place for a reason?'

'Evening, guv. Good weekend? Do I think what has been planted where?'

Jake dispensed with the niceties and continued, 'All that stuff in the Victoria Park bomb flat. It's telling us nothing, but it's keeping us busy. Keeping us from finding out other stuff. I wonder whether they were very happy for us to find this treasure trove of evidence. One that's taking ages to investigate. We have a hideously slow chain of request and command. The whole thing is painful and useless.'

'Yeah – but how do you take control away from the MIR? We have to do their bidding. That's what we're here for, right?'

'No. We have to stop doing their work and come up with some leads of our own.'

'What about re-interviewing the witnesses, guv?'

'Len, you've said it yourself that we can't rely on witnesses. This stuff is time critical. CCTV disappears. Witnesses forget things. People wash their cars and dispose of clothes. The faster you can get to these things, the better. Already we're a month down the road! We need something that can't lie to us.

Something permanent, but something that tells a story. How about we look at the… phone records?'

'But the analysts down in London are working on investigating the bombers' operational phones, boss.'

'Yeah, but who is tasking them? What are they looking at? We're not getting any breakthrough information from them. That team is deathly quiet. They're not detectives. What the hell are they actually doing?'

'I really don't know. There are loads of dirty phones. The bombers had tonnes of pre-paid, unregistered handsets, and they changed them regularly to avoid detection. There might be all sorts on those.'

'Yeah. Exactly, Len. Phone records. They can't lie to us or forget stuff like witnesses can. They're not being washed to remove clues. We should be able to use them to look back in time six months or maybe even further? That data is impossible to fudge or tamper with.'

'So what are you going to do with that data, boss? Why is it so important to you?'

'Well, we can pinpoint where each handset was when it made a call or sent a text, because the network exchanges signals with it from the nearest mast. Once the phone sends a signal back, that mast or cell-site location is recorded by the service provider.'

'So we can track them according to their cell-site locations?'

'Yeah, from the list of phone communications that a network provider holds, we can work out exactly where our suspects were calling from and therefore where they've been, over a period of time. They'll light up like a beacon. We need that phone data, Lenny. It'll create a framework over which we can overlay the rest of our evidence.'

49

Monday
8 August 2005
0800 hours
Dudley Hill police station, Bradford, West Yorkshire

There was an urgent call from Helen. She sounded distinctly unhappy.

'Jake, the MIR manager has been on the phone to me. He's moaning that you've got 150 actions outstanding. He's threatening to report you to Denswood.'

Jake skirted round the subject.

'I don't think we're making headway fast enough here, Helen. The route we're taking is a scenic one – or worse, it might not even be the right way.'

'The actions from Victoria Park have got to be done, Jake. There could be something in there; we've got to work through each item properly.'

'Helen, this is pointless. It will take eighteen months to complete all these billions of actions and this crazy system will still never solve the job. If we put crap in, we'll get crap out.'

'But, Jake, there's a system in place and it's there for all of us. We all have to do what we have to do.'

'I understand that, but what if the systems are not being used in the right way and by people who aren't detectives. A lot of the guys in the MIR have a background in traffic or community policing. Where is their detective nous? They're not investigators. I want to know who helped the bombers commit these crimes, Helen, and why. None of the instructions sent up from the MIR are helping us to do that. There's no crossover between any of the teams. I'm getting a different story from every other person I speak to. You know yourself what a rabbit warren HOLMES is. It's a self-propagating system. It's not really solving the job.'

'Jake, just have more faith. We will solve the job in time, if we follow a logical route and use the proper system.'

'But we don't have time. We need to get moving from point A to point B. I need leads now. I need stuff cross-referenced with our other counter-terror cases. I need to know who we've seen before. No one's got a handle on it! What if whoever masterminded this whole thing has no connection whatsoever to the bomb factory? What if he's someone that they only made one phone call to?'

'Stick with it, Jake. The analysts will throw up all the phone numbers to the MIR. We'll get there…'

'I've been looking into the phone stuff, Helen. Since May, the four bombers have been using four different operational handsets each. One of them used three. We're approaching twenty phones already, and that's not even including their personal ones. Then there's the seven-page request form that needs to be filled in and signed off by the right people every time we ask for data from a phone network. The analysts have made nearly 4,500 requests to phone companies for information in the last fortnight alone! They are requesting everything. It's the same with the MIR. We're creating our own haystack and burying the needle ourselves. This won't work. Both the MIR and the analysts are banking on the system throwing up the important stuff. They're doing their best, but we simply do not have the manpower to use the system in this way and the analysts are not detectives. They don't see what we see…'

'But, Jake, that's what the MIR is there for.'

'Helen, the analysts are saying that they are focussing on two hundred priority numbers. Then there's two hundred and fifty to three hundred calls and texts for *every single one* of those numbers. That's around sixty thousand communications to look at in the entire investigation. Which one of those calls is the important one? It's there, I'm sure of it – but I don't think an analyst is the person that's going to find it for us.

That's where all of our leads are. We need a magnet to retrieve the needle from the haystack, Helen. No one has got the helicopter view on this. A witness statement or a phone call or a piece of evidence has no meaning in isolation. You have to give it meaning. You have to link it into other things in order to understand the context. On its own, it's worth nothing. No one is doing that. It's like giving too many chefs a single, stand-alone ingredient to cook with. It doesn't work until you put all the ingredients together. *Then* you can bake the cake. But the starting point needs to be the phone data. It's pure. It's the primary constituent in this recipe. I need that phone data.'

Helen sighed. She could see his point.

'I'll get the MIR to send you the data. Get those bloody actions done too, Jake.'

50

Jake had told his team to be in for 0830 hours. He'd made tea for each crew member, but began the meeting with two unclaimed cups slowly going cold. They were sat on pieces of paper adjacent to empty chairs. He'd written on the paper: 'I must not be late for meetings.'

The entire team were slipping into laziness. They didn't understand what the MIR was trying to get at. They took statement after statement that had little or no evidence in it. It was just background noise as a result. There had been some sloppy work over the past few weeks as they'd all plodded through the pointless MIR actions. Putting your brain into 'neutral' wasn't what good detectives did. They worked better at identifying problems – why they were not moving forward – and then did something about it. Major investigation or not, you worked the same way.

Jake couldn't stand it any longer – he intended on making sure the team turned up on time and worked hard.

'Right. We'll make a start without Martin and Alex – and on that point: we work hard. We play hard, *but* we fucking turn up for work on time with our brains engaged on the job. Anyone who does not do this from now on will go back to London. There are plenty of spaces on the disclosure team going. Is that understood?'

The seven of Jake's team present nodded. No right-minded detective ever wanted to work on the disclosure team in a big case like this. It basically meant life as a librarian, indexing the items that they'd already investigated so that evidence could be accessed quickly and more efficiently. To Jake's team this spelled never leaving their computer screens, never leaving the office, never interviewing a real witness and never seeing sunlight for years. If they thought they were hard done to in West Yorkshire, this was far more tedious work. People didn't want to be stuck in the office, alone. The disclosure team was where bad detectives went to die.

Jake continued, having got their attention, 'I will be issuing you new actions as of today. You will refer the MIR back to me should they call you direct. You will not tell them what you are doing, under any circumstances. You will report everything to me.

'I've read all the statements and looked at every exhibit. I'm certain that we do not have the full picture. This is because we cannot necessarily trust anything we are being told by those we are interviewing. Whether or not they had some suspicion that something was going to happen, there may well be those who want to protect their friends, colleagues, neighbours or loved ones. Treat everything in those statements as very suspicious. The exhibits we are looking at have been left for us to find. It's the picture that they and others want us to see. I'm not happy with that. I want the whole picture. The true picture.

'I have the phone data. This includes data from the bombers' personal handsets. That is what we'll be working on – that's where we'll find our leads. I am convinced that we are looking for at least one more bomb factory. I think Victoria Park is staged. Yes they manufactured something there, but they wanted us to find it, and all the things in it. Our primary objective at this stage is to find other premises that may have been used for storage or manufacture of explosives. I'm convinced that we already have the information but haven't realised its significance. They'll have contacted the supplier of those premises at some stage by phone. We talk to everyone they spoke to. We assess every single person with the same question in mind: 'What was the reason this person was in contact with the bombers?'

Jake dismissed the meeting.

51

He'd sorted out his team, but it still wasn't enough. He needed to build a magnet strong enough to find the needle in the haystack. Jake needed his own analyst. One he could work alongside. One who knew their stuff inside and out. One who had an investigative police background.

Big Simon.

Big Simon had joined the Police Cadet corps back in January 1980, aged just seventeen. He'd said it was like being paid a full-time wage just to play football down the park. Jake had met him in the Organised Crime Group when Simon worked on the Intel unit and graded the intelligence reports before they were put on the system.

Big Simon loved data. He was addicted to data and addicted to food. Jake knew that he could be kept fully focussed as long as he was provided with a double helping of Olympic breakfast at the local Happy Eater every morning and kept entertained with some puzzles to solve.

Jake loved Big Simon because he was the one person guaranteed to laugh at all his jokes.

Big Simon had been what was known as a lid once, a bobby on the beat. He'd pounded the streets of London years before Jake. Then he'd become an analyst in the days before they'd 'civilianised the jobs' as Jake termed it. Back in the old days, only ex-coppers became analysts, not fresh-faced university graduates. Simon had been so good and so sought after on major cases that he'd been working all hours, but he'd got fed up of the constant pace. Now twenty-two stone, he was getting on and he missed his family. He wanted stability, so he'd taken a job as a lecturer in the police training school at Hendon – until he'd been dragged into the ever-expanding clutches of Operation Theseus.

Jake and Big Simon shared a love of malt whisky and had formed an unlikely drinking alliance when they'd worked together on organised crime. Jake knew who he needed on his team. He needed Simon to help him to sift the data, like panning for gold.

Currently, however, Simon wasn't even being used for his analytical skills. He was working on the witness-statement team, not with Jake's lot, who were mainly involved in analysing the inventory items coming out of the bomb factory.

Jake wanted to motivate Simon.

He needed to dangle the carrot in front of him – the puzzle that was yet to be solved.

52

Jake and Simon headed to Dot's Café and Sandwich Bar, handily located opposite their building. Jake's promise of a latte and mention of something top secret had been just enough to entice Simon across the road.

Dot was a sprightly West Yorkshire lass with a dirty trucker's laugh. She was in her sixties, but still looked pretty good for her age. She wore a striped blue pinny over her jeans and jumper, was an outrageous flirt and Jake liked her a lot. The café was tiny – room for just four tables – but the food was excellent.

It was time to fill Simon full of frothy coffee and let him know what needed to be done.

The blue gingham tablecloths and Dot's cheery face, lifted their spirits as they sat down for a conspiratorial chat.

Lattes to hand, Jake took the plunge. 'So I've got an idea, but I need to get someone to help me, because I don't know whether it's actually possible with the software we have.'

Jake was feeding Simon the bait. Simon's eyes lit up.

'What exactly do you want to do?' asked Big Simon curiously.

'I've got to be honest. What's been going on in London is laughable. The analysts are not detectives. I've become frustrated with what's going on. I want control of the phone data. That's the only clean data we have. It's not tainted by time or by perceptions. It's real. It's the only thing we have that says where those bombers were and what they were doing in the run-up to the attacks.'

'Why do you need me?'

'Basically there are sixty thousand lines and there might be ten pieces of information on each line. I need to analyse six hundred thousand pieces of data and give some meaning to it. I want to make that data useable to the investigation to drive things forward. We've now got at least five telephone numbers for each bomber because they each had numerous personal and operational handsets. I don't believe that the analysts down in London know where to start. They're overwhelmed with it. They're not being tasked properly and don't have a clue about how to solve it themselves.'

'That's a lot of data, Jake. I can't think of any job I've ever worked on that's been even a quarter of that size! What software are they using to look at it?' Simon sounded excited.

'They're using Excel.'

'Excel? You are joking! Nothing else?' Simon's excitement had turned to abject horror.

'Exactly,' nodded Jake in agreement. 'It's not working, Si. They're swamped. We need something to mine the data, to match it up with other parts of the investigation quickly; to get rid of the rubbish and shine a light on the important parts...' Jake was hoping to see a spark in Simon's eyes.

If it *was* even possible, Big Simon was the man to do it. A big challenge like this was a seductive premise to an IT geek like him.

'It's certainly a challenge. The biggest I've ever seen. Don't get me wrong, I'm very up for it *and* you know I love working with you, Jake, but...' Simon trailed off.

'What?' Jake's mind was searching for what Simon could possibly say.

'You realise, it's highly embarrassing for me, from a personal point of view?' said Simon, cleaning his glasses with a serviette.

'Why?' asked Jake.

'Because I trained the analyst team leader in London,' he sighed. 'He was shit then, and he's still a bit shit now.'

'Then think of this as a chance to right some wrongs,' smiled Jake, 'both yours and mine. I need to know what software is available to do the job properly.'

Simon's ears pricked up. He was looking enthusiastic at the prospect of a puzzle coming his way. 'To get a handle on the data, we'll need i2.'

Jake was aware of i2. The Met used it as a mapping tool to connect up who was in contact with whom. It was mainly used as a graphics program by them but had originally been designed for BT and was capable of manipulating massive amounts of data so that it made more sense.

'I've never actually used it to do telephones,' continued Simon, 'but technically it is possible to throw a load of phone data in there and see who has been talking to whom.'

They drank their lattes and returned over the road to the police station.

Big Simon grabbed his laptop and Jake transferred some of the phone data onto a memory stick he'd bought especially.

He gave it to Simon to upload, but Simon looked wholly unimpressed when he opened the files.

'It's all in Excel, on one spreadsheet, but it needs sorting. The raw data needs converting into some sort of format that the i2 system will accept.'

Jake was none the wiser. 'So what does that mean in layman's terms, Si?'

'Hmmmm… I'm going to need two days to tart up all the formats and kick it into shape.'

'Will it be difficult?' asked Jake.

'You're talking to one of the police's leading i2 experts. I eat, speak and shit i2. And I teach this stuff for a living.' He smirked. 'If you buy me another coffee and a muffin… and a packet of crisps, it shouldn't be a problem.'

53

Thursday
11 August 2005
1731 hours
Dudley Hill police station, Bradford, West Yorkshire

Jake walked into the office, juggling a couple of tea-stained mugs full of steaming brew. 'Any joy yet?' he asked.

Big Simon was sat in front of his laptop with a particularly frustrated look on his face.

'I've sorted out the data and uploaded it to i2, but the fucking software has crashed again on my laptop! I've not got the right cables with me today, but we can retry it tomorrow on the office computers. They process HOLMES so they're quite beefy. They should give us more power.'

Friday
12 August 2005
1511 hours
Dudley Hill police station, Bradford, West Yorkshire

'Any luck, Si?'

Jake had watched Big Simon upload the i2 software onto the West Yorkshire Police computer system from a special dongle that very morning. He'd been pacing the office ever since, wearing a hole in the carpet. Every time he'd walked past and spied the screen, the bloody egg timer had been permanently stuck on show.

Jake didn't like the signals he was getting. It was just like being back down in London at the Met with their diabolical computer problems. Their hardware and software would often crash and be out of use for weeks, awaiting repair. West Yorkshire had middle-of-the-road but ageing hardware. The stuff worked, in the main, but took up huge areas of the office. Cumbersome CPU towers hogged every available piece of work space and fat, unwieldy CRT monitors crowded the desks.

The traditional police theory was that you had to choose between nice cars or good computers. It seemed to Jake that most forces went for the decent motors.

At least West Yorkshire didn't have a closed IT system, he thought. He'd once wasted a whole afternoon driving round Doncaster trying to print off a witness statement, only to discover that South Yorkshire Police didn't possess a single USB port or allow external uploads. A friendly manager at the local Tesco Supermarket had come to the rescue, letting him share their systems. He'd almost pulled his hair out that day. Now he was getting déjà vu.

'Oh no! Not AGAIN!' shouted Big Simon as he banged the desk with his fist. 'It just *keeps* freezing!'

'What's wrong with it?' asked Jake.

'The sheer amount of data in there keeps crashing the whole system. I've cut it down to the bare minimum but it still won't work.'

'Is there any way of getting round that?'

'We could do it in chunks, analyse some data at a time, but you'll miss the linkages between people if we do it that way.'

'So what do we do?'

'Let me call up the software company.'

Big Simon disappeared into a meeting room for some time.

Jake sat for a while at his desk, staring into his cup of cooling tea, wondering dejectedly to himself if this whole idea was just a hopeless case.

On his return, Simon looked brighter. 'They say we need more processing power.'

'And how do we get that?' demanded Jake.

'They reckon we need a new, specialist mainframe PC…'

'OK.'

'…with as much processing power as NASA!'

Jake took in a big gasp of breath. 'Jesus! Really?' he asked, shocked.

54

Simon giggled. 'Nah... I'm pulling your leg, Jake. But, look, it's not going to be straightforward. It appears that the tinpot machines we have here are just not up to the job. I've spoken to several people and they all say pretty much the same thing. We have a single purpose and that's sorting and mining a hell of a lot of data, therefore we need a machine that is superfast and efficient...'

Jake started to yawn and look blankly at Big Simon. He couldn't really get to grips with this techy stuff.

Simon realised that he was losing Jake here. He changed his approach. 'Let me rephrase it for you, Jake. What do you do if you want to make a road car go fast?'

Computers were really not Jake's bag, but cars and bikes – they were his babies. He brightened at this analogy. 'To make a road car fast – you cut down on its weight, strip out all the fat, get rid of the lardy luxuries.'

'Yes! That's right. You get rid of the radio, the back seat, the passenger seat, the spare wheel, the electric windows, the central locking.'

'We have to do all that?' asked Jake.

'We have to do all that,' replied Big Simon. 'It all has to go. What we need is a leaner machine. I reckon it can be done but we need a customised one – top spec, mind. But we'll end up with a machine that is built to race.'

'No good for taking the missus down the shops then,' chuckled Jake. 'Where do we start?'

'Well, we could get one done by Amersham computers. They're based down the road from the Bradford offices. I'll get onto them.'

Big Simon spent some time making several calls. Jake couldn't catch all of the information. He reasoned that he wouldn't have understood any of it anyway, but he was sure it was all technologically brilliant stuff. He trusted Big Simon.

'What's the damage then?' asked Jake, as he passed Simon's desk.

'Well, we'll need to strip out all of the things we don't need off their top-of-the-range computer. We need the fastest, biggest processor and we'll have to pay for them to put in the top graphics card money can buy. It will need to be designed just to process our stuff and to have nothing else running on it. No other police software *at all*. And I've asked them to put a fingerprint recognition system on it for security purposes too.'

'Do we really need that last bit, or is that just because you're a computer geek?' asked Jake.

Simon blushed. 'We'll need a shedload of cash for the supercomputer, a new screen, new mouse and various other bits and bobs – and it'll take a couple of weeks to build. Do you have a lottery win up your sleeve?'

'Fuck it,' said Jake. 'We'll put it down as a purchase of covert camera equipment. It can come out of the surveillance budget.'

55

Monday
15 August 2005
0730 hours
Longthorne Oak Hotel, central Leeds, West Yorkshire

As Jake sat down for breakfast in the hotel dining room, another hangover was trying to smash its way out of his skull. Smartly dressed businessmen and women wearing grey or navy were dotted around the room, alongside heavy laptop bags and small wheelie cases. Few people stayed more than one or two nights at the hotel.

Many of the white tablecloths looked like individual Tracey Emin masterpieces. Jake could see ketchup strewn across one, another encrusted with muesli, and a table in the far corner littered with a pile of chipped and dirty coffee cups.

Breakfast was a self-service buffet with a central table full of large silver-domed platters. The domes slid back to reveal that morning's delights, most of which Jake wasn't particularly impressed with. He didn't reckon much to the chef; he was pretty sure he could have done a better job himself.

Jake had learned the hard way that the scrambled eggs were to be avoided at all costs. Always full of huge pieces of shell. Jake wondered if the chef even bothered to break the eggs. Perhaps he just lobbed the whole lot into the pan and mashed them up as he cooked?

'Good morning, Jake,' said Lenny as he sat down opposite the boss.

'What's good about it, Lenny? Why did you leave me in that bar last night on my own?'

'It looked like you were having a good time with the blonde bit of stuff and her friend. You didn't want me cramping your style.'

'They took me back to their hotel. I could have been murdered, Lenny. We're supposed to look after each other!'

'Hahaha. *They* took you back, did they?' Lenny winked at Jake.

'Don't ask me what happened. I can't remember. I'm sure it involved nothing more than talking though.'

Lenny chuckled. Monday nights in Leeds appeared to be the new Fridays. 'Who were they, Jake?'

'No idea. Can't remember their names. Jane? Janet? Jan? And her mate with the great arse. They worked for BT. I was tapping them up for information on cell-site activity. All good background for the case.' Jake closed his eyes for a second and rubbed his temples. He couldn't remember much of it – just that female attention was the only thing that cheered him up at the moment. He tried to shrug off any aimless feelings of guilt; he hadn't actually been up to anything, he reasoned.

'You seen the papers this morning, guv?' Lenny slid a newspaper across the table toward his boss. 'Police Tracking Device found on 7/7 Wife's Car,' screamed the headline.

There was a photo of Salma Khan, Wasim's wife, standing next to her Honda Civic holding up the telelogger tracking device that Jake's team had placed on the car a month ago.

'How the fuck? Just how the fuck have they found that? How did she know?' Jake asked as he looked up at Lenny from the paper, astonished.

'She didn't know. How could she? It's been working fine. Her movements have been fairly consistent up until the last time we checked a couple of days ago.'

'Tea or coffee, sir?' asked the Polish waitress.

Jake and Len broke off their conversation. Jake covered the newspaper with his arm.

'Tea, please.'

The waitress filled Jake's cup and left them alone again.

'I just don't get it. They also ran that story last week about some of the forensic finds at the Victoria Park flat. The bosses are going to be well pissed off,' Jake said as he poured milk from the small white jug on the table into his tea. It looked like oxtail soup, it was so strong. He didn't care. He needed the fluid. He dropped four sugars into it and sipped. Maybe he'd avoid the breakfast this morning.

'You'd better call London and let them know, Jake.'

'I will do when I get to the office. You ready? I'm skipping breakfast here this morning.'

56

The office was fairly quiet when Jake arrived. A lot of the staff had come in early and gone straight back out on duty. Jake had taken to claiming one particular table in the corner of the room, on which he'd started leaving as much office paraphernalia as he could find – files, folders, notepads. He was just after a desk organiser now to complete the set, to fully deter any West Yorkshire staff from sitting in his favourite spot.

Jake called the SIO on the office line.

'Malcolm Denswood.'

'Morning, guv'nor – it's Jake Flannagan.'

'Morning, Jake – how are you?'

'Not too shabby personally, thanks, sir – but we've got a small problem... Have you seen the headlines this morning?'

Jake heard the SIO inhale. 'No, Jake. What is it now?' His tone changed.

'The lump we placed on the wife's car last month. The press have somehow found out about it and are running a story.'

'We kept that very tight, Jake. Very few people knew. How could they have found it?'

'I don't know. I did the applications. They went straight to you. DS Sandringham and I did the surveillance security cover on the fitting. I think a maximum of six people knew about it.'

'It's very disappointing, Jake. The team up there is tiny and we still can't keep things secret? Down here I could understand it; we've got hundreds of officers, most of whom are attachments from other forces. You put something in the HOLMES system and the world and his wife can read it, but this was highly classified. How do we stop this happening again? What's your suggestion?'

Jake was struggling for answers. 'Short of investigating the journalist and finding out their source, which is a major distraction from the day job, I don't know what to suggest.'

'Where would you start with that?'

'Maybe get a list of mobile phone numbers of everyone working on Theseus and Vivace. Get the journalist's mobile phone records. Cross-check the two. Might throw up a hit. Might not. It's a lot of work and it's kind of bolting the stable door after the horse has gone. It might help to stop potential future leaks though?'

'You're assuming that the journalist is using a human intelligence source, Jake. What if he's nobbled one of the staff to bug the office or something, and is listening remotely?'

'There is that, but he'd still have contact with the member of staff, wouldn't he?'

'You're thinking he's got a cleaner or someone to put a device there? I can't see that working. It might, but it's easily rumbled. I think he's probably a bit smarter than that.'

'There's always the "rough him up in a dark alley and make him talk" method, guv?'

'Ha! You came into policing in the wrong era, Jake. In the sixties and seventies that was their *only* method,' Malcolm laughed. 'Have a think about it, Jake. I'm going to come up in the morning for a meeting. There's another matter I want to discuss with you that I can't put in HOLMES right now; not with all this going on. I should be there first thing at Dudley Hill.'

'OK, sir. Will you be staying over or going straight back?'

'I'm coming back the same day. Back-to-back meetings all week. We're struggling to run both Theseus and Vivace as it is.'

'I'll get the kettle on for 0800 hours sharp tomorrow, guv.'

'Thanks, Jake.'

Jake hung up. He looked up at Lenny on the other side of the room.

'Do not let me get pissed tonight, Len!'

57

He was late. The very thing he chastised his own staff for.

The traffic was solid.

Lenny had woken Jake by banging on his hotel-room door at 0730 hours after he'd not shown up for breakfast as agreed.

He'd showered and dressed while Lenny got the car from underneath the hotel. Lenny was doing his best to cut through the traffic but they were now late. Jake had another hangover from hell. He shut his eyes and held his head in his hands. It throbbed.

Jake dialled Denswood's mobile number.

'Good morning, Jake. Where are you? We're waiting for you...' Denswood sounded annoyed.

'Sorry, guv, we're caught in heavy traffic; been a nasty accident I think,' Jake ad-libbed. He was sorely tempted to cheat and whack the blue lights and two tones on.

'How long, Jake?' Denswood sighed.

'I don't know. Depends if we can get round the accident. Maybe thirty minutes?'

'I'll make a cup of tea then, Jake. Soon as you can. OK?'

Denswood ended the call without saying goodbye.

Jake pressed the button on his handset to ensure it was disconnected his end.

'Is he all right?' Lenny looked across sheepishly at Jake from the driver's seat.

'He sounds fucked off. I would be. I told you not to let me drink! Why did you?'

'Jake – have you seen yourself when you get going? I'm going to video it one night and play it back to you. You cannot be stopped. You're like a runaway train! Always the same route, non-stop. You're going to the end of the line where you have a huge crash. I'm not your conductor, nor your father.'

'No. But you're my DS and if I give you an order, you should follow it.' Jake winked at him.

'So what happened last night?' asked Lenny cautiously.

'Well, it was the same old, same old; spent all evening going through the files. Then Thai green curry on room service and forty-day-old porn on the TV. I had to go and have a vodka and Red Bull at the bar just to get out of my bloody room. Then… well there was that cheeky hen party in from Hull.'

'And?'

'It was rude not to join in… Things got a bit messy after that.'

They got to Bradford at 0840 hours. Denswood looked less than impressed when Lenny and Jake finally arrived at the office. The second-floor meeting room was tiny. The pale, imitation pine table was supposed to host twelve people but the room was tiny, which meant that the table had been shoved up against the wall. It strangled the office chairs on one side – their headrests bowed solemnly at the two people sitting around the opposite edge.

The early-morning sun shone fiercely through the single window opposite the door. Jake had to squint as he walked in, just to try and make out who was sat at the table.

SIO Denswood was sat with DCI Helen Brookes.

'Morning, Jake. Morning, Lenny – sit down. Glad you could make it,' Denswood said with a note of sarcasm in his voice.

Jake managed a half smile as he pulled out the chair nearest the door. The sun was in his eyes. With a spotlight stuck in his face and only blurry silhouettes in the background to mark the other figures present, he almost felt as though he were about to be interrogated. Lenny sat on the other side of the room, over toward the window – leaving Jake to take the heat.

'Sorry we're a bit late,' said Jake as he started to wonder why this meeting was so cosy and if it might mean bad news.

Denswood peered over the top of his glasses, a sombre expression in his eyes.

Jake suddenly felt very sober – the headache gone.

'Let's crack on, shall we?' Denswood said in a humourless mood. Jake nodded in agreement.

'First of all, let's talk about this leak, Jake. How was the lump found? I've read the newspaper article. It's very clear they've discovered it and know that they've got a tracking device on their hands. How, Jake? How have they found it? Any ideas?'

Jake took a deep breath. 'Well, sir, it was hidden behind a plastic guard in the wheel arch. It was out of sight. Up until two days before that article was published, the device was working perfectly. We could dial in and out of it, download the data from it. I've looked at her pattern of movements and all the locations visited. They were consistent. She's not been anywhere new or out of the ordinary. It's very odd. One of two things has happened in my opinion. The lump either fell off because the magnet failed – and was rattling around behind the wheel-arch cover and they found it that way. *Or* someone told her it was there.'

'I'm hoping it was the former, Jake.'

'I was rather hoping that too. I checked with technical support to ask how many magnet failures they'd had like that.

'And?'

'None. They've only had two lumps found in the last five years – and neither of the magnets failed in those cases either. They said it's possible the magnet *could* fail – but of the two that have been compromised, both were found through someone alerting the target of a lump being on their vehicle.'

'So it was more than likely compromise? A leak?'

'That's the suggestion. It's not certain.'

'OK. Who would leak that to her and why, Jake?'

'The lump was put on there in the first few days of the job. There were only six people that knew it was there, four of whom are in this room now. The West Yorks technical support guys were the other two; they helped fit it.'

'Maybe it's one of them? What do we know about them?' asked Helen.

'They've been in West Yorks PTSU for some years. Both vetted and trusted. The only odd thing is that the walker, John, who fitted it, said he left me two voicemails the other week about changing the battery on the lump. I didn't get either of the voicemails he claims to have left. He was adamant that he left messages for me.'

'Has he dialled the wrong number and left the voicemail for someone else? That's how it's got out?'

'It's his work mobile. I asked to see his itemised bill to check, and he was right. It was definitely my number that he called. We need to talk to the mobile-phone company and look at where those messages went to, because I certainly didn't receive them.'

'Good. I take it we've disabled the lump that Salma Khan has now got at home and there's no way of her tracing that it was definitely us, Jake?'

'It's not marked. Neither she nor the newspaper can say for definite it was us, sir.'

'OK.' Denswood was satisfied for the moment and moved on. 'Next item on the agenda this morning. The compromised lump wasn't the main thing I was here to talk to you about, despite it being a conundrum that takes some beating. No, the actual problem I'm here about involves bomb victims. This is highly sensitive information. One of the seriously injured is weeping a green substance from the site of their amputation. The hospital has no idea why. I'm concerned that there was some sort of chemical or biological agent in the devices. If there was, we are in deep trouble. I don't know if that's the case so I'm choosing not to reveal that to anyone. I don't want this getting out and causing panic at this stage, Jake. I need you to look into it for me.'

'Yes, sir. No problem. Is it just one of the amputees at the moment?'

'Yes. The hospital has said it's very unusual. They've not seen it before. Helen will give you the details of the person concerned.

I don't want you talking to them – there's a dedicated team in London that's doing the victim contact and support. I want you to look at the bigger picture. Speak to FEL and assess if they or we have missed something.'

'Yes sir.' said Jake.

FEL was the forensic explosive laboratory based at Fort Halstead near Sevenoaks in Kent. Sevenoaks was one of Jake's old stomping grounds that he didn't mind visiting.

'We'll get on it.' He nodded back at the SIO.

'Thanks, Jake. Thanks, Lenny.'

'I'm going to make a tea, if anyone wants one?' Lenny asked as he got up.

'Thanks, Lenny, but Helen and I have an urgent meeting at 1000 hours. We're off to West Yorks HQ in Wakefield to discuss the lump compromise. They want to assess community tensions now the press are all over the fact that someone has been tracking the vehicles of the alleged bombers' families. It doesn't look good.'

Jake wondered what all the media fuss was about. Who cared about what the community thought as long as they got a result in the case?

Denswood must have seen the bemused look on Jake's face and he continued, 'It's important. We have to work with West Yorkshire and the community and it's their patch, Jake – so we'll go along and make all the right noises. It was good to hear what you've said this morning. Find out what happened to that voicemail. We can't have more of this stuff getting out,' he said, shaking his head grimly.

He and Helen got up and left the room as Lenny continued chatting to them on his way to make a brew. Their voices faded as they walked down the corridor and away from Jake who remained sitting in the meeting room. His head was spinning. It was a bad day. The hangover was back, now accompanied by a compromised tracking device *and* a possible biological weapon.

58

Jake and Lenny were sat outside the sari shop in the car. They'd driven down from Yorkshire together the night before. Lenny had dropped Jake home in Whitechapel before driving on to Surrey to enjoy a rare night at home with the wife.

Jake, on the other hand, had not even had Ted to keep him company. He had called her from the back window, but she was nowhere to be seen. She'd deserted him after he'd deserted her for Leeds. In the end, he'd stopped calling her name and closed the window. When Claire then didn't answer her phone, he'd given up on both the women in his life and decided to get a good night's sleep instead.

Lenny looked quietly contented. 'Are we off to the British Medical Association then, Jake?' he asked, as he pulled away from the kerb and into the busy rush-hour traffic.

The amputee suffering from the 'green gunge' complications had been a victim of the bus bombing. Fortuitously, whilst trawling through the HOLMES system, Jake and Lenny had happened upon a highly appropriate expert to help them solve their medical mystery. Her name was Professor Sandy Groom-Bates and she had actually been caught up in the carnage of 7/7 herself.

An Australian who'd been living in London since 2001, she'd given an interview with a Sydney newspaper saying how she had immediately come running out of her office to help victims of the Tavistock Square bombing. She'd been working for a journal based in the British Medical Association building, next to the spot where the Number 30 bus had been blown to pieces on 7 July.

She'd been hailed a hero in her native Oz for assisting with the victims and their injuries and had since been interviewed dozens of times by media outlets Down Under.

Her police statement said that she was a professor of wound microbiology and Lenny had subsequently dug up her profile to discover that she'd been a medical doctor for fifteen years prior to that.

'Just the person we need to see,' said Jake, when Lenny had presented all the details to him.

Jake had called the BMA to speak with Professor Groom-Bates the previous afternoon. He'd been passed from person to person before eventually being told she was off sick from work. Finally he'd been put through to her manager, Dr Herbert Watson, who'd seemed strangely evasive on the phone and had agreed to meet Jake the following morning.

Lenny parked in a taxi rank in Endsleigh Place at the north end of Tavistock Square. They walked in silence across the busy road toward the red-brick BMA building. What a difference forty days had made. The place looked back to normal. There was no indication that anything had happened there at all, thought Jake.

The BMA receptionist smiled at them as they approached the front desk.

'We're here to see Dr Herbert Watson,' said Jake.

The receptionist punched in a number on her console and handed them both passes.

After a few minutes, a greying man in tweed trousers and a bright pink jumper appeared from down the hallway. His out-fit made him look like an elderly hare-brained inventor from a children's TV show.

'Detective Flannagan, I presume?' said the man in a public-school accent.

Jake proffered his hand. 'Jake Flannagan. Good to meet you.'

'I'm Dr Herbert Watson. Follow me, please.'

The doctor led them down a hallway toward the back of the building and up two flights of stone stairs to a stately looking office with a dark green, deep-pile carpet. Dark wood panelling covered two walls and a packed bookshelf framed another. Opposite the door, a gigantic Georgian window overlooked a central courtyard.

The doctor sat at his desk with the window behind him. Jake and Lenny sat in studded leather chairs on the other side.

'You're here to speak to Sandy Groom-Bates, I understand?' The doctor wasted no time getting to the point.

Lenny pulled out a notebook and pen.

'That's right,' Jake replied. 'Professor Sandy Groom-Bates.'

'No, not professor,' said the doctor. 'Correction. She wasn't a professor at all.'

'A GP?' asked Jake.

'No, not a GP. She wasn't a doctor either.'

'But that's what she said in her police statement. What did she do here exactly?'

'She was an editor on a medical publication.'

'Don't you need medical knowledge to do that?'

'You need a certain amount of medical knowledge but you don't have to be a GP or have a PhD, as such.'

'She told both us and the newspapers that she was a doctor and a professor in wound microbiology.'

There was a long pause.

Watson gave a sharp intake of breath. 'Um, no... she wasn't. She had very little medical experience and... well... it now appears that she lied about a lot of things. After the bombings, she sent various emails to an Australian newspaper that purported to have come from a friend of hers. The emails praised her work in helping victims. An Aussie journalist did some digging on her qualifications and found them all to be false. The newspaper gave us a heads-up about two weeks ago that she wasn't even a doctor. She'd done a year's training in a Sydney hospital as a laser therapist, and some sort of diploma qualification in health management. The rest appears to have been completely made up.'

'So how did you not know any of this – you're her manager, aren't you?'

'Well… I *was* her manager…'

'Was?' Jake interrupted. 'Have you taken disciplinary action already?'

'You've not heard? Oh. We instigated an enquiry just over a week ago. She tendered her resignation immediately but we were duty-bound to continue. Then, just this morning, I got a call from her father. She was found dead in the early hours at her flat in Shepherd's Bush. It's all very tragic. She was only in her mid-thirties.'

Christ, thought Jake. Green gunge and now another dead body so soon after the bomb blasts. Maybe they did have some sort of lethal outbreak on their hands?

59

'Do you have her address please?' asked Jake.

Watson scribbled out an address on a piece of paper and handed it to him.

Jake passed the piece of paper to Lenny. 'Can you get hold of the nick that's dealing with it, Len? I think it'll be Hammersmith and Fulham who'd cover that one. Tell them not to touch anything. I want to have a look first.'

Lenny got up and left the room.

The doctor continued, 'Since we started our internal investigations I've heard all sorts. I hear that she claimed to have given birth to twins who then died, had incurable cancer but made a full recovery, had hip-replacement surgery, went overseas to help with earthquake and hurricane victims, was stalked by various people in this building, and had relationships with people that have now been found not to exist. Her life appears to have been one big fantasy, I'm afraid to say. And now she's dead. What a desperate tragedy...'

Jake was curious about something. 'When my colleague, DS Sandringham, looked her up, he read that she was once involved in a study that looked into blood clots? Was that here with you?' he asked Dr Watson.

'I think that might have been during her time in Australia interning at a hospital. She did nothing here but edit a journal. I know that she used to carry a stethoscope in her bag at all times, but that really had nothing to do with us. That was her own personal one. Like I say, she was away with the fairies quite a lot. We always thought she lived in a bit of a fantasy world.'

'I understand. Look, what we really wanted to speak to her about was a rather delicate medical issue. One of the survivors of the bus bombing has experienced some unusual medical complications. There are signs of a green fluid leaking from the site of their amputation. None of the other victims from this bomb scene have these symptoms. It's very strange. Now Groom-Bates is dead, albeit that people are saying she didn't do much, is she the fifty-third death of 7/7 – not including the bombers? Was there some form of contaminant in the bus blast?'

The doctor thought for a moment before he replied, 'Well, when a limb is blown off, it's not clean. It's torn off; ripped away. The blast will have carried with it all sorts of nasty contaminants; debris from the bus, blood and other bodily fluids. We saw bone fragments from the bomber embedded in victims. They even found a set of intestines at the door of our building. If that sort of debris has got up inside the wound, it's very difficult to get out.'

'She treated some of the victims, is that right? Could she have had something to do with this?' asked Jake.

'She claimed to have treated the wounded. I'm not so sure she did. No one from the team saw her go onto the bus, but none of us really know.'

'If there was a toxin involved that caused this, could she have died from the same substance? Has anyone else here had side effects?'

'To my knowledge, there have been no reports of people from the BMA falling physically ill. However, I'm sure you'll understand when I say that many people are still missing from work. We're dealing with an enormous amount of post-traumatic stress. People are still coming to terms with some of the horrors they saw on the day that bus exploded. It was unspeakable, ghastly...' Dr Watson trailed off, shaking his head.

Jake knew only too well the grisly scenes from that day. He had had no counselling. His nightmare was one where there were no answers to the crime and where Wasim continued to taunt him from the grave.

Dr Watson composed himself and placed the tips of his fingers together. He spoke quietly but pointedly. 'Look, it might be that Sandy took her own life, Mr Flannagan. Her behaviour changed markedly when we instigated the initial enquiry into her qualifications. She knew that her fantasy world had been found out. Maybe she felt she had nothing left?'

Jake had heard enough and stood up. He shook Dr Watson's hand, thanked him and left his office.

Lenny was outside the door. 'They've preserved the sudden-death scene at the flat for us, guv,' he said.

60

It took them forty minutes to reach 'Professor' Groom-Bates's flat. Jake didn't need to look very hard to find it. There were two police cars, an ambulance and an unmarked black van all parked right outside the block she lived in.

Next to the black van were two men in black suits and black ties. The men in black worked for a secretive organisation and often encountered bugs and nasty-smelling things. Unlike the film with Tommy Lee Jones and Will Smith, though, they didn't hunt aliens. They worked for the undertakers. Jake always thought it was an awful job. They picked up the body regardless of what state it was in and how many pieces, placed it in a big bag, took it to their van and delivered it, in cases like these, to the local mortuary.

'Morning, gents. What floor are they on?' asked Jake.

'Fifth floor,' said one of the men in black.

Jake nodded at him in thanks and walked across the wide pavement toward the high-rise art deco building that was flanked by a lowly supermarket and an estate agent. 'The Pennines' was written in big, bold black letters on a white background above the doorway.

They took the lift to the fifth floor. The smell hit Jake as soon as he got out. Even fifteen minutes after death, bodies had an unmistakable smell. It was like nothing else. A hideous, sweet and musty stench with an excruciating cheesy undertone. It was a million times worse than a rotting carcass in a butcher's overwarmed storeroom.

There were three uniformed officers standing at the threshold to flat 544. The wooden door had been forced open from the outside. The stench in the hallway was almost unbearable.

Jake wasted no time. 'Morning all. I'm DI Flannagan. Who found the body?'

'I did, sir,' said a tall, nervous officer wearing a name badge. The name badge proclaimed him to be Brian Roberts.

'And what was the reason for your visit here today, Brian?' asked Jake.

'Father called us from Australia; hadn't heard from her for two days. Said it was really out of character as she called him every day. Always at the same time on the dot.'

'You forced open the door?'

'Yes, sir, I could smell it at the time. It's gone now the door's open.'

'It stinks up here, Brian! You've just got used to it and can't smell it now. What have you found out about the circumstances of her death?'

'Neighbours say she is a professor or doctor at some big hospital in central London. They don't know which one. Said she used to talk about herself a lot. Number 545 says that he saw her a few days ago and she ignored him – looked upset. She's in bed. Looks like she died in her sleep. Nothing suspicious. Shall I show you, sir?'

'Yes, please.' Jake nodded.

Brian led Jake into an airy studio apartment. Light from a large window bounced off the blindingly white walls and laminate floor. A dark blue sofa bed sat opposite a huge television hung on the wall. The screen was off.

On the sofa bed, a white duvet was pulled back to reveal a woman's naked body. She was lying supine, propped up only slightly by two pillows behind her head. Her dyed red hair looked lank and her skin had a yellowy hue to it. Large, well-fed bluebottles buzzed around the room. They'd clearly discovered the body before the police had.

Jake stood by the side of the bed and looked down at the body. She was skinny. Very skinny. Her breasts, despite being small, were sagging over her body. She was almost too thin. Drugs? Anorexia? Hyperactivity? Illness?

There was no blood. No fluid. No puncture wounds on her front. Her eyes were open and staring toward the TV. The white sheet that she lay upon was still white.

A small bedside table held a lamp, a phone and a glass of water. Jake checked around the bed. There was no sign of tablets or needles – or a remote control for the TV – anywhere in the vicinity.

She was thirty-six. How had she died?

61

'What did you do when you came in here, Brian?'

'What do you mean, sir?'

'Was the TV on or off when you came in, Brian?'

'It was on, sir, but…'

'But you turned it off and didn't think that was relevant?'

Brian sighed. 'I turned the TV off, sir. Yes.'

'Where's the TV remote control now, Brian?'

'I put it in the cabinet under the screen…'

'Where did you pick it up from?'

'Err, erm. Err, I, err, think I got it from the table there, but I can't remember.'

'How long have you been in the job, Brian?'

'A year, sir.'

'At how many sudden-death scenes have you been the first officer to attend, Brian?'

'Two, sir. This is my second.'

'Have you turned the body over, Brian? Looked at her back?'

Brian sighed again. Jake knew what was coming.

'Err. No, sir.'

'So you said you think she died in her sleep. But if the TV was on, she most probably had her eyes open because she was watching it? Not because someone suddenly woke her up in the dead of night and scared her to death?'

'I've fucked up again, haven't I, sir? Yes, you're right. Sorry. Won't make that mistake again. Fair point,' smirked Brian.

Jake wasn't amused. It was typical of uniformed supervisors to send inexperienced officers to sudden deaths. He couldn't bite his tongue any longer. Brian was acting like a schoolboy. His attitude to this was all wrong. Someone had died. It was their job to find out how; find out if foul play was involved. This wasn't a game or a maths lesson.

'Are you fucking stupid, Brian?' Jake's tone was sharper.

'In what way, sir?'

'What if she's got a knife in her back, Brian? What if this is a murder scene? What if the killer's fingerprints were on that TV remote before you rubbed them off and moved it, so it looks like it's not relevant to the investigation? What if she's died from a highly infectious and communicable disease and you've just picked it up off that remote that you hid?'

62

The colour drained from Brian's face. Jake was astonished that Brian could not see the obvious nor understand how a crime scene should be treated.

'Put your gloves on and turn the body over, Brian. Inspect it. It's your job to determine if she's been murdered. That's why you're here, you stupid idiot. This is a murder scene until you decide it's not. You do not move objects anywhere. You *do not* pick things up and turn things off! Got it?'

'Err. Yes, sir... Sir, I, err, I also turned her mobile off as well. It was ringing and getting on my nerves. So I turned it off. I've maybe rubbed the fingerprints off that too. I wasn't wearing any gloves. If you do check it for fingerprints, mine will be on it.'

Jake rolled his eyes. What did they teach at police training school these days? He couldn't remember being that stupid. Ever.

'Where are your surgical gloves, Brian?'

'In the car, sir.'

'Go and get them. You need them at a crime scene, Brian. They are no fucking good in the fucking car, are they?'

Brian said nothing. He turned on his heel and jogged toward the hall. Jake was alone with the body in the bedsit. He just stood there. Lenny and the other two officers remained on guard at the door.

He always needed time at a scene, to just stand there and look – to understand where he was and how people would use the space in normal circumstances. It was important to think about the way people normally moved around in it. That way he could identify things that were out of place.

The place looked clean, spotless in fact. Everything was dusted to within an inch of its life. Groom-Bates was obsessively clean. The washing up was done. Was this a suicide? Had she cleaned it knowing that people were going to look around? Suicides normally did it clothed in Jake's experience. He couldn't remember attending a suicide scene where they had been naked. They were always clothed because they knew people would come and look at them. They thought about it before they acted. They wanted clothes on to protect their modesty – as if to ameliorate death, our most immodest state.

Jake surveyed the scene calmly and quietly.

The glass of water by the bed was half full.

She was naked and in bed, watching TV.

Her phone was by the bed. It was off, as Brian had said.

Jake figured there would be no last text messages or phone calls to friends and family, just a couple of calls from her father.

There appeared to be nothing out of place.

He knew suicide was far more prevalent amongst men. Three times as many men committed suicide compared to women.

In Jake's mind this didn't look like a suicide. But what was it?

Was it something she'd caught off the bus at the blast scene that had killed her?

Had she even been at the blast scene?

Brian ran back into the room, panting and holding a box of surgical gloves. Jake took a pair out of the box and pulled them on.

Brian just stood there.

'Put a pair of gloves on, Brian. We're going to inspect the body together.'

Brian donned a pair of gloves and followed Jake to the bed.

'Right. We're going to lift her up and look at her back. Help me out.'

They pushed their hands under the unyielding body of Groom-Bates. She was rigid. They could feel her cold skin through their gloves. It was fragile, like paper. They turned her on one side. A small pool of maggots sat under her body, eating away at the dead flesh of her back in a recess of the mattress.

'So no knife, no bullet hole, Brian. You're a very lucky man.'

And crucially, thought Jake to himself, no sign of any green gunge.

They laid the body back down again.

'Right, Brian. We don't know how she died. The post-mortem will decide that. I'll talk to the coroner. I want you to seize all the prescription medicine in the flat and her mobile phone.'

'Yes, sir. I forgot to ask, sir. Why are you interested in this case? Aren't you Anti-Terrorist Branch?'

'Forty days ago she claimed that she was at or near the bus bomb site. I need to understand what killed her.'

'Yes, sir.' Brian looked as confused as ever. Jake decided it was pointless trying to explain or asking him to do anything else.

Jake walked to the entrance where Lenny was waiting.

'It's time for lunch, Lenny. Let's find a nice café while this little lot sort themselves out.'

63

They hunted for a café as they walked. The place was awash with traffic, mainly large goods vehicles. Westfield Shopping Centre was under construction behind the row of shops on the other side of the green.

'Jesus, it's still pandemonium around here! They've been building that place for more than two years. How long is it going to take?' shouted Jake above the noise of the lorries.

'God only knows. Maybe till 2008, they're saying. I dunno. Do they really need a shopping centre here, so close to London's West End?' Lenny was unimpressed.

Along the route, the eatery options that presented themselves were not particularly enticing. They had a choice of sharing a table with a fat, hairy trucker or dining next to a builder showing off his arse crack.

Jake turned and looked back at the Pennines apartment building where the men in black would be bagging up Groom-Bates by now.

'Change of plan. Let's to go the Regency, Lenny.'

The Regency was special.

Lenny smiled. They jumped in the car and drove to New Scotland Yard. The underground car park was full again. The security guard waved them away. Lenny parked on a double yellow line outside The Feathers pub on Broadway. They would get a ticket from the council traffic wardens but hopefully they'd get it written off.

They passed the three-sided, spinning New Scotland Yard sign, which cost the Met around £200 per year to power and rotate. Jake thought he recognised the face of a female reporter doing a to-camera piece for one of the television news channels. The Met were talking about buying the freehold for the Yard, which they currently rented. If the Yard ever moved, Jake wondered how many of the local businesses would survive the disappearance of all that ready cash flow. He couldn't ever imagine it happening though. He was sure the Met were all set to buy the place.

The Regency Café was loved by detectives and worth the extra walk. Opened in 1946, its lavish interior had featured in several films. Daniel Craig had filmed a particularly brutal scene there for *Layer Cake*. The film had been so well received that the bookies already had Craig as favourite to snap up the role of 007 in *Casino Royale*.

On the way, they passed a newsagent and Jake noted that one paper had gone with the headline, 'The Name's Bland, James Bland'. They were touting Clive Owen as the better man for the job.

The café was buzzing as usual. Cappuccino-coloured tiles went from floor to ceiling. Formica tables with four fixed plastic chairs around each one meant you had to slide across clumsily to take a seat. Red gingham half-curtains were pulled across the lower panes of the windows, shielding customers from the road.

Jake and Lenny queued up diligently, ordered and paid.

Cash only and everything was cooked to order. The servers were in full voice, shouting out the orders ready for collection at the top of their lungs. The husband-and-wife team had the loudest voices Jake had ever heard. In another setting they could have been opera singers, he thought.

Jake sat down opposite the serving counter with his mug of tea.

'What's your plan for the lady "professor" then, Jake?' Lenny asked, sliding into the seat opposite him.

'We need speak to the coroner's officer – let them know our concerns. I want to see what the post-mortem turns up.'

'Two sausage, two eggs, bacon, bubble and beans!' screeched the woman from behind the counter.

'Do you think we need to go to the post-mortem? Do we need to be present and get samples, Jake?'

'We'll have to let Denswood decide that. I wouldn't think so personally, not unless they can't establish cause of death straight away.'

'Two eggs, two sausage, two bacon, bubble, fried slice, beans and chips!' bellowed the man at the counter in a deep guttural growl.

'What're your thoughts on her and how she died?' Lenny asked.

Jake sipped his hot tea.

'It's a strange one. She was young. She was very skinny though. Maybe drug misuse? Difficult to say. The place looked clean and tidy. Whatever it was that took her, did it all of a sudden – I don't think it was a gradual thing. She was clearly well enough to keep the place tidy.'

'Suicide? Could she have done something to herself? Suddenly decided to do it?'

'What, in bed watching her last *Family Fortunes* show na-ked, Lenny!'

'You're probably right. The blast then? Something to do with that? Is she the fifty-third victim?'

'I don't know, Lenny. Got my doubts. Let's wait for the PM.'

'Two cheese on toast with beans and egg!' screamed the woman.

'House!' called out Jake, like he'd won the big bingo prize fund.

64

Jake pulled up alongside the double-storey white gates. A ten-feet-high wall ran around the perimeter, securing the mortuary building. Large red signs stated in bold white lettering: 'No Parking, 24-hour access required. Unauthorised vehicles will be towed.'

Death was indeed a twenty-four-hour business, thought Jake.

The mortuary was nestled amongst plush, high-rise apartments that had sprung up out of the old gasworks like invasive bamboo.

Security at mortuaries was always high. Not that the dead were going to escape. It was more that the dead had a story to tell – the story of how and why they had died – and there were sometimes people who didn't want that story to be heard. The bodies needed to be protected so that the integrity of that story was sound.

Grief also did strange things to people. Sometimes the bereaved felt the police and authorities were adopting the wrong course of action and wanted to take their loved ones home, or just didn't want them at the mortuary at all. Jake could commiserate with those feelings all too easily.

Lenny got out of the passenger seat and went to the silver box on the wall by the gate. Jake watched him state his credentials into the intercom and wave his warrant card for identification purposes before the gate swung open slowly on a tiny motor. Jake pulled into the small yard and parked as Lenny walked in behind and found the buzzer to get access to the building.

Inside, a light-grey, tiled floor was met with white tiled walls – yet the tiles did nothing to mask the smell of death, which hit you as soon as you walked in. They were greeted by a man in his late fifties wearing a white lab coat. His hair was unkempt and his face showed several days' worth of stubble.

'I'm Derek. I'm the lab technician who'll be assisting the pathologist today.'

Derek didn't proffer his hand to shake. Jake wondered how many dead bodies Derek had handled that morning already. Shaking hands wasn't a particularly attractive scenario in this environment.

'I'm DI Flannagan and this is DS Sandringham,' he replied.

'This way, please...' Derek wandered off in front of them, following the path of the highly polished, grey-tiled floor as it snaked its way down along the corridor.

They passed through a set of double swing doors and into a large room that was tiled floor to ceiling like the hall, but with harsh fluorescent lighting and gleaming stainless-steel furniture. Four examination tables sat side by side, each one designed to hold an adult cadaver on a raised section that looked like a sieve. The drain holes were there to allow any bodily fluids to drip down into a reservoir underneath and be channelled away unseen.

At the far end of the room was a slim, elegant, red-haired woman in her late forties. Jake had met Dr Angela Farthing some years earlier whilst working on a previous case. She didn't look like she'd aged a day.

Given the unusual circumstances of 'Professor' Groom-Bates's death, Jake had put in a special request for a registered Home Office forensic pathologist to undertake the post-mortem examination.

Dr Farthing donned surgical gloves and a white lab coat as she looked down at the lifeless, naked figure of the woman Jake had found in bed at the Pennines.

'Good morning, Inspector. Please tell me what you know about this lady and her death?' she asked him, primly.

'Good morning, ma'am. She was thirty-six years old. Lived on her own. Australian by birth. Worked as an editor of a medical journal at the British Medical Association building in Tavistock Square. Bit of a Walter Mitty character by all accounts and appears to have lied about her qualifications and background. She claimed in a newspaper article to have treated the injured on the bus that was blown up outside the BMA building on 7 July. She has no high-level medical qualifications. Her moment of glory in the media unwittingly undid and laid bare her lies to her employer and those around her. She was found dead at her bedsit. It's a very strange case.

'Crucially, and what I really want to know is, could it be possible that she picked up some contaminant in the process? Some toxin, bacteria or infection that's killed her?'

'Thank you, Inspector. Let's get started then.'

Dr Farthing began pawing at the skin around Groom-Bates's left shoulder. She moved down her left side to the foot, across to her right foot and then back up to the right shoulder.

'Her back please, Derek.'

Derek pulled the 'professor' onto her side so that the doctor could look at her back.

'I see the flies found her. Thank you, Derek,' she said, referring to the hole in the base of Groom-Bates's back.

Derek gently laid the cadaver down onto the examination table again, whilst Dr Farthing spoke into her Dictaphone in preparation for her report later.

'No signs of bruising. No puncture wounds. Slight decomposition of lower back with the presence of fly larvae and localised egg laying. Larvae are small. Are you looking for me to determine time of death, Inspector?'

'No, ma'am,' replied Jake.

'You don't want me to test a sample of the dead larvae, then?'

'No, thank you. Neighbour saw her alive twenty-four hours before we found her dead in bed. Time of death is not terribly important in this case.'

Dr Farthing raised her eyebrows, pursed her lips and continued.

'So, this "contaminant" that you mentioned… Have you any idea what type that might be, Inspector?'

'We don't know. One of the victims who was badly injured on the bus, an amputee, is showing signs of a green fluid weeping from the site of their amputation. Coupled with Professor Groom-Bates's death, there is a distinct possibility that there was a dirty bomb on that vehicle in Tavistock Square on 7/7.

'We know that there are countries out there experimenting with munitions containing biological agents. Maybe there's some involvement? Difficult to say at this stage.'

'OK. Understood… Derek, could you do the brain for me, please?'

Derek nodded. He picked up a scalpel in his right hand and flattened down Groom-Bates's lank hair with his left. On the very top of her head, he cut a cross in the skin. Then he peeled it back as one would peel an orange, folding her forehead over her face and two flaps over her ears, to reveal the white skull underneath. Jake had seen this done maybe ten times during his police career, but it still made him wince.

Derek then picked up a small, hand-held, electrical circular saw and turned it on. The whir of the motor reminded Jake of the dentist. Derek began cutting around the top of the skull with the saw. There was a smell of burning as the saw blade clattered around the bone. The cerebral fluid ran out and into the sink. Derek then lifted off the top of Groom-Bates's skull like the lid from a jam jar. With the top of his fingers he pulled out her brain, cut the cord attaching it to the spine and placed it onto a weighing scale behind him.

'One thousand, three hundred and forty-three grams – no sign of haemorrhaging,' said Derek as he picked up the buttery mass off the scales and passed it to Angela.

Angela made a visual examination before placing it on a stainless-steel table to her left and dissecting it.

'Brain appears to have been starved of oxygen – probably at or around time of death, I would say. Let's look inside her, please, Derek.'

Derek moved to Groom-Bates's torso. He dug hard at the sternum with the scalpel and ran it down over her chest and toward her pubis. He pulled open the slit he'd made, the yellow fat visible under the skin. From behind the lower part of the ribs, he lifted out a white, j-shaped sack. It was about the size of a grapefruit. Jake recognised it instantly. This was the stomach. Its contents shifted about waywardly as Derek lifted it – like food waste in a bin bag.

The smell was already bad, but Jake knew the worst was yet to come. Nothing could mask it or prepare you for it.

Derek placed the stomach in a stainless-steel bowl before cutting it open to let its contents spill out. The smell was unbearable. It hit Jake like a smack in the mouth. He wanted to throw up. Like distilled essence of rotten eggs mixed with concentrate of rotting cauliflower leaves, but in a heavy gas. It hovered; so dense you could almost see it, touch it.

He always wanted to throw up during post-mortems. Trying to detach himself from them was almost impossible. Standing there, watching them take place, it was an assault on every sense that you owned. Seeing a dead body in situ was easier, thought Jake. In the morgue with the body being cut open, cut up and things being said – every one of your senses was wide open and being abused in the most revolting of circumstances. Vision and sound were bad enough. Then there was the smell. It got the back of your throat. You could taste it, it was so strong. You could see the colour drain from onlookers' faces. You had to fight the urge to gag. Jake had seen plenty of people faint as the smell from the stomach contents hit them.

Angela sifted through the bowl of stomach lining and stomach contents with her gloved fingers. 'Undigested food; last meal appears to have been crisps and a bar or two of chocolate – perhaps just half an hour before death. Nothing out of the ordinary about the stomach or its contents.'

Jake started to lose his focus. He began to think about the body parts he'd seen in Tavistock Square. About the intestines found at the door of the BMA. He had to concentrate on something else, otherwise he was going to gag and be sick.

He shut his eyes and tried to name every Premiership football ground in the country to distract himself. It was no good... the smell wouldn't go.

He gagged. Acid reached his taste buds. It had been a few years since he'd done a post-mortem. Jake forced himself to swallow half a mouthful of sick back down.

Lenny smirked at him, highly amused to see the boss clearly displaying signs of discomfort. Jake knew he'd get a ribbing for this.

'I'll wait outside,' he said, as he walked out. He'd seen enough.

65

He'd been sat in the car for forty-five minutes. What sort of life was this? Watching dead people being cut up, to find out if they'd been killed by some other dead people, who'd blown themselves up?

An advert was playing on the radio: 'Tonight is the eightieth Euromillions draw. £25 million could be yours!'

'I *wish it was* mine,' replied Jake to the radio. 'I'd give up this poxy game for sure!'

Lenny appeared at the open car door, laughing at him. It wasn't cool to walk out of a PM in police culture. You had to be the 'roughty-tufty-nothing-phases-me' type. Showing emotions or weakness like that was frowned upon.

'They've finished,' said Lenny. 'Doctor wants to see you in the office.'

'First time that has ever happened to me, Lenny. Honest. I just couldn't stomach it,' said Jake as he got out of the car.

'A lightweight – that's what you are, Jake. You'll be asking for weekends off and a 9-to-5 office job next.' Lenny winked.

Jake traipsed across the car park, head bowed in mock embarrassment.

The smell still lingered in the tiled corridor. The door to the office was ajar and Dr Farthing sat at a white, brightly lit, laminated desk, making notes. A large window in front of her overlooked the autopsy theatre. The lab coat was gone. She was wearing a smart black skirt suit with a grey pinstripe in it, and an expensive-looking, cream silk blouse. She looked more like a city lawyer than a pathologist.

'Inspector – how are you feeling?' She placed her royal-blue, Mont Blanc pen down carefully on her writing pad. Jake detected a hint of sarcasm in her voice.

'I'm feeling a lot better now that you're no longer digging around in a dead body and have taken your lab coat off. Nice suit.' Jake looked her up and down appreciatively.

'Flattery won't get you far with me, Inspector. Sit down,' she requested in a schoolmistress tone of voice.

Jake sighed and sat down. She smiled at him as if he were an incorrigible pupil.

'Your woman, Miss Groom-Bates, she's a very odd one. I'd suggest that deep-vein thrombosis started in the legs, and a piece of the blood clot broke off into the bloodstream, which then blocked one of the blood vessels in the lungs. Oxygenated blood was almost totally restricted, which caused sudden death via a massive pulmonary embolism. Natural causes. No signs of any biological blast contamination or foul play. I say very odd only because she isn't among any of the high-risk groups for DVT. She certainly wasn't overweight or obese, for example.'

'Do you know of any contaminants in a blast that could cause a blood clot like that?' queried Jake.

'If it were a dirty bomb – I'm talking radioactive – there could possibly have been contaminants in there which might have triggered it. I've also read of cases in which suicide bombers have deliberately infected themselves with things such as hepatitis prior to a blast, to inflict maximum damage. But if this was a dirty bomb or a serious epidemic you'd have lots of people affected by something like that. I've taken tissue samples, blood samples for toxicology and I've taken vitreous humour as well – that will tell us more.'

There was a slight upturn at the corners of her mouth as she stared at him. She'd done it on purpose. She knew he didn't have a clue what vitreous humour was.

Jake played along. 'Vitreous humour? I'm assuming it's nothing to do with comedy?'

Angela smiled. 'No, Inspector. Vitreous humour is the fluid within the globe of the eye, between the retina and the lens. It's ninety-nine percent water. It's isolated from the rest of the body and is a great post-mortem sample for toxicology analysis. Was your woman using drugs?'

'Not that I know of.'

'Well don't judge prematurely. The toxicology samples will tell us for sure,' Dr Farthing replied.

Jake nodded in agreement. 'Well – it's certainly a puzzle. But if anyone will find any anomalies, it's you, doctor. Don't suppose you fancy a chat about it over a drink tonight?'

There was a pause. '…I'm busy tonight. Maybe some other time.'

Angela stood and shook his hand far more formally than he would have liked, as if to usher him out and away.

Jake got back in the car.

'Everything all right?' asked Lenny.

Jake slumped back in his seat, arms curled over his head, slightly dazed. 'It was really surreal…'

'What happened?' asked Lenny, shocked. 'What did the doc say?'

66

'Well…' began Jake, confused, 'she turned me down!'

'What?' guffawed Lenny.

'I know!' said Jake in disbelief. 'My advances were rebuffed! Can you believe it?'

'I meant about Groom-Bates, man!'

'Oh, yeah, that…' Jake realised he was distracted and tried to pull himself together. 'She thinks it's natural causes. Blood clot in the lungs. Weird.'

Lenny tried to jolly him along. 'She was a fake professor. Weird in life and weird in death. She was having a tough time, about to lose her job. You can get blood clots through stress though, you know?'

'Can you? I'm surprised I've not keeled over and kicked the bucket before now then.'

Lenny laughed as he pulled out of the car park and past the high-rise penthouses. 'Where to now, boss?' he asked.

'You, you lucky man, are headed for a weekend off, Lenny!'

'Am I? Fuck me, I've forgotten what they are!' He beamed. 'Last day I had off was the weekend before the bombings, second and third of July!'

Lenny was acting like he'd won the Euromillions draw before it had even taken place, thought Jake. He felt a pang of envy when he remembered that spark of excitement. What it felt like to be given a spare weekend off to go home and see his family.

Heading toward central London on Cheyne Walk, the traffic slowed to a standstill in both directions. The houseboats to Jake's right, just before Battersea Bridge, were all sitting very low in the mud and not moving. The tide was out; they were waiting for the water to flow back underneath them at some point tonight. Jake realised he'd missed London.

Beyond the houseboats, he was mesmerized by Battersea Bridge for a moment, deep in thought.

'IRA,' he mumbled to himself.

'What?' asked Lenny.

'Hammersmith Bridge,' Jake replied.

'No! That's Battersea Bridge!' Lenny chuckled.

'I know. The IRA, they tried to bring down Hammersmith Bridge with explosives three times. In 1939, 1996 and 2000.'

'I didn't know they did it in 1939. Can I drop you home and take the car back to mine then, Jake?' Lenny asked. He was excited. He'd be home with his wife by 5 p.m. if all went to plan.

'Now 1996, that was a bad year for London. The IRA tried to blow up Hammersmith Bridge in April. They'd blown up South Quay in Docklands in February, just two months before, with a lorry bomb. I was one of the first on scene.'

Jake began to remember the complete devastation he had seen; the huge hole in the ground where the lorry had been. Every building for half a mile was completely wrecked. Debris and concrete everywhere. Some buildings had moved on their foundations, the blast had been that strong.

'Wow. I didn't know you went there,' Lenny said, wracking his brains to understand why Jake was talking about this stuff on a Friday afternoon.

'I was on the late shift. Bomb went off at 1900 hours. Heard it go off the other side of the river. Incredible noise. They'd given a coded warning. The area was evacuated. Two news-paper sellers refused to move. Stayed in the cordon. Both killed. There wasn't much we could do to be honest, not once it had gone off. I was fascinated with how the blast had travelled. You could see it. It had gone up to some buildings and totally destroyed them. With others it had gone through windows; not damaged the outside too much, but ripped the insides to shreds and dumped it out the other side. Incredible sight. That event, that was what made me want to be Anti-Terrorist Branch.'

There was silence in the car. The houseboats were gone. Battersea Bridge was behind them as they plodded along Chelsea Embankment, nose to tail with the rest of the traffic.

'It's a way of life for terrorists. It's what they do. They never stop. You have to catch them.'

'I know. You having the weekend off, Jake?' Lenny asked, trying to change the subject.

'I've got a weekend with Ted... I might do some work.' Jake sighed.

'What work?'

'The telephone stuff the analysts are doing down here. I've managed to get hold of a few more bits of it. I'm gonna take a look at it. I think there's stuff they're missing – important stuff.'

'Why don't you go and see the kids? We can do the phone stuff together on Monday?'

'The bombings happened forty-two days ago, Lenny. We still have no idea who helped them do it. Another two days until Monday. Another week for me to get my head round the mountain of telephone shit. Another month before we've got anything decent to work on. Another six months before we've got suspects to look at? It's taking too long. We might even have some sort of dirty bomb on our hands!'

'But you've got to have a rest from this stuff, Jake. It will eat you up otherwise. Maybe that's why you're drinking so much?'

'You think I'm drinking too much?'

'I think you're drinking every night to escape what we've got our face in every day. I think we all need some downtime to recharge – even you!'

'Maybe...' Jake sighed again.

They hadn't moved for several minutes. Traffic was at a standstill.

Jake pushed open the car door and got out. He shut it and leaned in through the open window.

'Spin round, Len. Get yourself off home. Have a good weekend. Pick me up at 8 a.m. Monday morning, my place.'

Jake turned and walked toward the pavement. As he reached the kerb he heard Lenny hoot the car horn. He turned and looked at him.

'Rest, Jake. Rest!' Lenny mouthed to him over the noise of the traffic. Jake nodded back and started to stroll along the pavement in the late-afternoon sun.

67

Jake crossed the road, zigzagging between the essentially station-ary cars. He stood against a wall and looked across the river at the Buddhist Peace Pagoda in Battersea Park. The sun bounced off the mudflats as a small motorboat made its way downstream in what little water was left available in the middle of the river. The golden Buddha surveyed the scene from the other bank, staring back at Jake from underneath its pagoda.

'Religion,' Jake snarled at it with contempt.

He pulled his Nokia from his pocket and dialled Claire. It rang, but there was no reply. Almost immediately he got a text back from her.

'Can't talk. What's up?'

They began texting each other. Jake couldn't understand why she could manage to text but couldn't talk. Was he a secret? What was she hiding?

He texted back.

'I'm off this weekend. Hoping we could see each other?'

'I can't come out tonight, I've got too much work on. Sorry.'

'What about the weekend?'

'No. Too busy. Sorry.'

Jake fought the emotions. Was she was trying to tell him to get lost? That she didn't care about him, didn't love him? He tried calling her again. Again she didn't pick up.

The phone buzzed in his hand. Another text from Claire.

'Call you later.'

He knew she wouldn't.

'I wish you'd just fucking tell me the truth, so I know where I stand,' Jake shouted back at the SMS.

Maybe he did need to drink. Jake turned on his heels and walked off toward the barracks.

'If you won't love me, someone else will,' he growled to himself, heading for the nearest pub.

Jake wandered down several side streets on his route away from the river, as he hunted for a pub. There wasn't a single one to be seen, just posh houses and apartments with expensive cars parked outside. He turned onto the main thoroughfare. Surely he'd get a decent pint on the King's Road?

The road had, up until 1820, been the King's private route to Kew. Only the King and a select few were authorised to use it. The riff-raff were banned. The route was said to have 'afforded the best overland access from Westminster' – quite important really, when you were passing through swamps that were plagued by robbers and bandits.

Jake looked left and right up the road. There was no sign of any king, nor any swamps or robbers today, just lots of traffic.

Several Routemaster buses lined the thoroughfare, chucking out smoke as they sat there. They looked like elegant, cougar mothers next to their low-floor-chassis daughters. All the grace of Joanna Lumley parked up next to the equivalent of Kat Slater from *Eastenders*, thought Jake – and soon to be phased out due to the upcoming Disability Discrimination Act.

He spotted Habitat and the Curzon cinema on his right and remembered that there was a pub, The Trafalgar, nearby. Perfect for being alone and drowning one's sorrows, thought Jake. The Spanish and French had lost most of their ships in the battle of Trafalgar and the British had won. Jake would celebrate Nelson's win. He sauntered off up past the cinema in the direction of the pub.

Once through the double doors and into the darkened pub interior, he relaxed. At the large bar in front of him, the old men dotted along its length appeared like guards looking over the parapet of a castle wall, protecting an alluring barmaid.

Jake stood at an unguarded part of the bar and made eye contact with her. Long dark hair, tight black trousers and a fitted waistcoat open just enough to reveal the crown of her breasts. She wandered toward him with a smile.

'What can I get you?'

Jake struggled not to look at the part of her cleavage that was on display.

'A pint of your finest lager, please.' He got the words out quickly, determined to avoid dropping his gaze.

Deftly, the barmaid reeled off a long list of lagers. The bar was noisy and she had a soft voice. Jake only heard Carlsberg and settled for that. He watched amid the other guards as her petite figure bobbed about, grabbing a glass and pulling his pint.

Jake paid for his beer and chose a sofa positioned with a good view of the street. He sipped the cold lager. People walked along the pavement outside carrying expensive-looking paper bags from designer shops.

He flinched as he heard a booming, barrow-boy voice bellow his name from the doorway:

'Jake Flannagan! As I live and breathe!

68

Jake looked up. A whippet of a man dressed in smart blue jeans and a beige Armani T-shirt was running his hands through a thick, black curtain of hair and grinning at him from the doorway.

It was Zarshad Ali.

He wandered over and plonked himself in the low sofa opposite. Jake suddenly remembered that Zarshad lived on the council estate over the back of the pub.

'You get that car you was after? The Civic? One of your Yorkshire mates came and collected it from me. Can't remember the geezer's name.'

'Yes, thanks – it was perfect, Zarshad.'

'Good, good. Can I get you a drink? Join you for couple, Jake?'

There were strict rules about meeting registered informants. You had to go through a controller to authorise it. Jake knew that he should decline the drink and move to another pub – that was the ethical, professional Jake thinking. But he wasn't here.

'Get me another Carlsberg, mate. Thanks.'

One drink wouldn't hurt. He'd let the controller know tomorrow. Jake downed the remainder of his pint in three gulps.

Zarshad returned and plonked a fresh pint down on a low table in front of him. 'She's a bit of fucking treacle, ain't she, the barmaid? She'd get it good and proper!'

Jake laughed.

'What are you doing down the King's Road, Jake? You weren't checking up on me, were ya? You know I'd come to you if I had something?'

'You know I'm always straight with you, Zarshad. We've had our arrangement for the best part of five years now. If I wanted your help, I'd call you, like I did about that Honda Civic.'

'Yeah, I know. You're a good bloke, Jake. You don't fuck people about. You still with the Organised Crime lot?'

The reason they controlled meetings with snouts was to ensure that the structure of the relationship remained sound; that the police were in control and not the snout. Zarshad was pumping Jake for information about what he was doing, and not the other way around.

'Yeah – still doing that.' Jake decided to play it safe. You had to keep control. Knowledge was power and the less Zarshad knew, the less control he had.

'Cool. What ya looking for down here then? I know all the bad boys round here. I could do with some extra money, if I can help with what you're up to.'

'You're interrogating me, Zarshad? Isn't it supposed to be the other way around? I ask you the questions. Why are you so interested in what I'm doing here? Don't take the fucking piss because you've bought me a pint.'

'Yeah, yeah, you're the boss,' said Zarshad. 'OK. You got me. I saw you through the window and wondered what you were up to, if you were working? I'm doing fuck all at the moment. Supplying the odd motor, nothing more.'

The smile broke again on Zarshad's face and his eyes followed. Jake could tell he spoke the truth. The skin between his eyebrows and his upper eyelid moved. He knew it was almost nigh on impossible to contract the muscle that ringed the eye, unless in a genuine smile.

Jake picked up the pint Zarshad had got him and took a swig. 'Cheers, mate.'

Jake didn't answer questions from snouts – that way led to disaster.

No, he was the one who did the questioning.

69

A used-car trader of Pakistani heritage, Zarshad had grown up on a Chelsea council estate living alongside extreme wealth. It stared him in the face and the draw was strong. He wanted what the rich had too.

So he took it.

Normally it was their cars parked in the street which he rung – a process of giving a stolen vehicle the identity of another vehicle so that it could be sold. Sometimes Zarshad would take the rich men's daughters. He was a good-looking lad in his early thirties with the gift of the gab. He dabbled a bit in drugs and a certain type of rich chick was attracted to him on a short-term basis.

When Jake had arrested him in possession of a stolen car, Zarshad had expressed an interest in helping out with the huge investigation he'd been running at the time, but only in exchange for Jake helping him get off the charge, of course. That's how those relationships started. You scratch my back and I'll scratch yours.

In the end, Zarshad had got a police caution instead of going to court. Jake liked him. He was an honest criminal; he didn't dress himself up as anything else.

'What you up to then, Zarsh? What's going on in your life?' asked Jake.

'Same old stuff, really, mate. I've not been setting the world alight with anything. I'm a bit down on my luck. Girlfriend fucked off to Marbella and didn't come back a few months ago. Met an ex of hers out there, I think. She says they have a "history" that can't be thrown away. Shame. I liked her. But look at me… I'm just a mug with fuck all who lives in a one-bedroomed flat, ain't I? Hardly marriage material?'

'What's the ex got that you haven't got then – two or three bedrooms more? A bigger cock?' chuckled Jake.

Zarshad smiled.

'I don't fucking know. Can't get any sense out of her over the phone. She says that the sex was the best she'd ever had with me! Said she loved me. Said she wanted to be with me. Then it all changes overnight. No reason why. She can say what she likes though, can't she? Just words. Actions speak louder than words, don't they, mate?'

Zarshad downed the remaining three quarters of his pint in one go.

'Fuck it, let's have another one. Fancy a shot as well, Jake?'

Jake looked at the dregs in the pint glass sat on the table. He really should leave, he thought. Shouldn't be here with a snout drinking. But where was he going to go? To another pub? Back home? Zarshad was what – the lesser of two evils? Better than being on his own.

'Why not? Go for it. I'll get the next one,' said Jake, picking up his pint and downing the remainder in solidarity with Zarshad.

They both had absent girlfriends who said one thing and did something else. Why not drown their sorrows together?

70

As the number of pint and shot glasses on the table grew, the pub got busier and noisier. Jake's head was beginning to feel a bit fuzzy. He looked down at his watch. They'd been drinking and talking about the problem they both had in common – women – for nearly two hours.

Zarshad set two fresh pints down on the table among the pile of empty glasses, before returning to the bar to collect two shot glasses of something strong, dark coloured and medicinal smelling. He passed one to Jake.

Jake held it aloft and said, 'To the absent and the dead. Gone but never forgotten. To family!'

'They certainly need me to drink to them!' toasted Zarshad in agreement. He threw back the glass, slamming the liquid to the back of his throat.

'I've never heard you talk about your parents, Zarshad. They alive?'

'My mum passed away when I was young. My dad's alive, I think – I haven't seen him in ten years.'

'Wow. Why's that?'

'My fucking father and bloody Tablighi Jamaat. He's very religious. He doesn't agree with my lifestyle – the drinking, the women, the drugs. But he's the reason I am the way I am. He spent his life ramming Islam down all of our throats. He made me learn the Quran, verse by verse, from a baby. Fucking years and years of it there was. I think the first words I said were

216

out the Holy Book. He wanted me to follow a particularly strict sect of Islam. Then when I was eighteen, he organised a marriage to my cousin... I wouldn't have minded too much but she was a fat ugly bitch!

'I caused a major family upset when I refused to follow him down the same religious path and marry her. It's all about money. Her brother was supposed to marry my sister. My father was getting a small fortune for her in dowry money and was paying fuck all for me marrying the ugly bitch. All this religion and it was just a frigging business agreement. The business just happened to be family.

'I told him and his religion to go fuck themselves. That's why I choose to live my hedonistic lifestyle, I suppose. I'm still rebelling.'

Zarshad picked up his pint and held it up for another toast. He looked across at Jake and nodded at him to do the same. Jake complied.

'And prepare against them whatever you are able, of power and of steeds of war, by which you may terrify the enemy,' Zarshad said.

Jake looked at him confused but swigged from his pint all the same.

Zarshad explained, 'Chapter 8:60, from the Quran, or part of it. I'm at war with my bloody father and this beer is my power over him who is the enemy.'

Jake suddenly had Wasim's video in his head. He could see the cartoon clock showing 8.50 a.m. The bombs had started to go off at 0850 hours.

'What does Chapter 8:50 say, Zarshad?'

Zarshad looked at the ceiling and scrunched up his face, willing himself to remember.

'And if you could but see when the angels take the souls of those who disbelieved... They are striking their faces and their backs and saying, "Taste the punishment of the Burning Fire"!'

Zarshad smiled triumphantly. He poured the fresh pint down his throat in reward.

'Jesus fucking Christ!' said Jake.

'What? Jesus? He's in the Quran too?'

'It was 8.50 a.m. *That* time. The time of the attacks was symbolic,' said Jake.

71

'What?' asked Zarshad.

Jake wasn't listening. His mind was racing at a million miles an hour.

People often saw investigations like building a jigsaw puzzle – collecting all the pieces and then assembling them in the right way by copying the picture on the box. It was a method even a child could do. You could probably even teach a chimpanzee to do it, thought Jake.

Find all four corners, then find all the straight edges. Build the outside of the puzzle, getting an idea of how big it was. Fill in the centre using the image on the box with all the pieces that you have left.

The puzzle *had* to fit together. You *knew* it would.

There were a number of problems with the puzzle method. Firstly it assumed that you already had all the pieces needed to complete it. Then it assumed you had a good idea what the picture was supposed to look like when it was finished.

It worked reasonably well with simple crimes like a man knifing his partner to death in their kitchen in a row over the dinner. This was the type of crime where you already knew who your victim was, where the crime took place, could prove what the murder weapon was and you had a prime suspect. Easy. You had all the pieces. An idiot could prosecute that offender. You just had to put the pieces together in the right way, using the set method, and prove a guilty mind.

What if you had no idea what the picture was? Had no idea how many pieces of the puzzle there were? What if some of the pieces were missing? Or someone was deliberately giving you the wrong puzzle and the wrong picture?

Jake didn't use the puzzle method. Instead he stored pieces of information like pennies. Each penny lived in the arcade of his brain. He would place each coin into a specific slot machine in his head, the type you'd play on the seafront pier as a child with your mum and dad. Some called them 'sliders' or 'penny pushers'. They were also known as 'shovers' or 'coin cascades'. But Jake knew them as penny-falls machines.

They were the ones you dropped the pennies into, one after the other. They built up the coins in mounds and piles. Some pennies would fall on top of each other, just sit there and be useless, but some would back up and form a little chain. When Jake had enough pennies in the right places, eventually a quantity would fall out in an avalanche. They'd fill the holder by his feet and make him a winner.

In Jake's eureka moments, the penny would drop into the right slot and all of a sudden the coins would fall into place. Lots of things that never made sense or he'd thought meant nothing all came together and screamed the same message at him in that one instant. And the solution to the case came crashing out.

Wasim had made his video in Pakistan, months before the attacks, explaining the reasons he would blow himself up and the reasons for martyring himself. That was a penny-falls machine in Jake's head. One that had never paid out. It had lots of pennies in it all piled up, waiting to be unlocked.

One of the pennies in the machine was something that Wasim had said on the video.

Jake played the footage back in his head. Wasim was sitting there in front of the red and cream fabric backdrop saying, 'We are at war and I am a soldier. Now you too will *taste* the reality of this situation!'

Another penny in that machine was the animated clock showing the time of the explosions, a big clock showing 0850 hours. The same time that the first plane hit the World Trade Centre on 9/11.

Eight fifty. Chapter 8:50.

Jake dropped another penny in that machine; the penny that Zarshad had just given him about what Chapter 8:50 of the Quran said: '*Taste* the punishment of the burning fire.'

'What are you on about? Time of what attacks?' Zarshad interrupted Jake's chain of thought.

'I'm working on the London bombings. I'm on the Anti-Terrorist Branch now.' Jake suddenly realised that he was getting into drunken-confession territory with a snout. The alcohol was getting to him like a truth serum; he was starting to say what was in his head without thinking.

'Wow – Charlie Big Potatoes you are now, Jake! Fuckers the people that did that!' Zarshad burped at the end of the sentence and smiled.

At least I'm not the only inebriated customer, thought Jake to himself.

'They blew themselves up at 8.50 a.m.' Jake picked up his pint and swigged a mouthful of the dregs. He held the glass against his lips, staring dead ahead. Straight through Zarshad. There was something nagging at the back of his mind, but the alcohol was now seriously inhibiting his powers of concentration.

The timings of the attacks had been planned seven or eight months before they were carried out. Others must have known the meaning of the timings, surely? That's why there was a huge animated clock in the video making a big point of the 8.50 a.m. time. The attacks had been planned with other people. This wasn't just four loners. Someone was saying, 'This has meaning. We know the significance of it.'

The bomb factory. It had been staged to make it look like it was just the four of them involved, but Jake had felt in his gut all along that this was wrong. There were others involved; maybe lots of them. The guys who tried to do the same on 21 July. It was a sign. It had a symbolic meaning. He needed to speak to Claire. There were more than just a few kids up in Yorkshire involved in this.

Jake was still holding his glass up to his lips, staring into space.

'Jake, what's wrong with you? Are you as drunk *as I am*? Snap out of it, it's your round. Go get the drinks.' Zarshad held up his empty glass.

'OK.' Jake downed the rest of his lager and stood up. He walked toward the bar, deep in thought. The same petite barmaid was still there, offering service with a smile. Jake didn't bother trying to conceal his interest in her breasts this time. He looked straight down at them. There was a crucifix on a chain around her neck; it nestled in her cleavage.

Jake ordered two pints and then walked back to where Zarshad was sat.

'The crucifix. A cross. The cross as the symbol of Christ,' Jake said as he plonked the beers down onto the table and stared out of the window again.

There was a sign on the wall opposite the pub. It read 'King's Road'.

'King's Cross – they separated at King's Cross. They went north, south, east and west. In the shape of a cross from fucking King's Cross! It's all symbolic!' Jake stood up suddenly and walked toward the door.

'For fuck's sake, Jake, where are you going? Stop being weird. You sound like my father. He'd tell ya there are no Christians left in England; all atheists – no one goes to church any more. That's why he'd say it doesn't count if this country is attacked. We're all fair game. He'd say it's not against his holy book to attack atheists...'

Jake wasn't listening. Zarshad's voice faded as he walked out of the door, his mind a mess. Fuzzy with drink, pennies, arcade machines and Wasim laughing at him. He stumbled into the street and waved at Zarshad as he walked past the window. He needed to be alone. He had thinking to do. The beer was no good for thinking. It was no good for anything except forgetting.

72

Jake awoke with a start. The room was light. The flimsy floral curtains did nothing to keep the sun out. His grandmother had been a poor sleeper her whole life, awake most of the time it seemed. He could turn up at any time of the day or night and she'd welcome him in. He wondered if she'd ever slept. Curtains that kept out the sun were not high on her agenda.

He wondered what had woken him. Then he heard it – there was a loud banging at his front door.

'Shit – what now?' he said to himself as he jumped out of bed.

He scoured the bedside table for his phone. It was nowhere to be seen. Where was it? What time was it? Had something happened? Another bomb?

The banging was getting louder. He walked down the hallway, opened the front door and was startled to see the twenty-year-old daughter of the sari-shop owner standing there looking at him. Jake was wearing just his boxer shorts and an embarrassed smile. She looked his semi-naked body up and down and smirked.

She was short, five feet two, with long dark hair and amazing eyes. Jake had seen her a few times but didn't know her name. She was wearing an orange sari draped partially over an exposed midriff.

'Err, hi. Wasn't expecting to see you,' he said awkwardly.

'Clearly.' She smiled broadly and her eyes sparkled.

'How can I help?' he asked, standing there self-consciously in his boxers and wanting to bring the conversation to an end quickly.

'It's your cat. She's been crying at your window for the past two hours. She knows you're in because she can hear you snoring. We can all hear you bloody snoring. It's like a foghorn downstairs in the shop. Maybe you should let her in and feed her?'

'Yep. Sorry.'

The young girl turned and walked down the stairs. She stopped on the half-landing below and paused, looking back up at Jake with a big smile.

'We all miss your grandmother. She was sweet, if a little old-fashioned. It's great to see you taking on the flat and not selling it. We know you're away a lot. We look after Edwina when you're not here, you know.'

Jake was comforted by her comments. 'Thank you. I miss my grandmother too. Very much. I really appreciate you looking after Ted. My job is a nightmare right now.'

The girl nodded and smiled at him as she continued her walk down the stairs and back to the shop.

Jake went to the kitchen. Ted was indeed yowling at the window to come in. He slid the sash window up and she jumped off the corrugated iron roof and onto the lino at his feet. She seemed really pleased to see him, rubbing herself all around his bare legs and purring loudly.

'Aww hello, Ted. Long time no see, babes. You look well. I can't say I'm surprised – I'd look well if the girl from downstairs was taking care of me regularly too.'

Jake stroked her soft black fur. She felt clean and silky. He reached into the cupboard and pulled out a tin of pilchard cat food, the only edible item in the entire kitchen.

He watched her scoff down the entire bowl. She was happy and well rested for once.

'Right, Ted, I should see the kids. It's been almost two months since we had a proper full day out together. Fucking job. It's all right for you – you've got the girl from the sari shop downstairs on your side. They've only got their mum. As amazing as she is, I think their dad needs to try and see them a bit more often too.'

Ted looked up from her food as he spoke, her green eyes locked on his as if she understood him. The sunlight made her coat gleam.

Jake's grandmother was not used to living alongside people of a different skin colour. Some might even have described her as a bit on the discriminatory side. Jake thought her whole generation were in many ways. By today's politically correct standards, she could have been termed a racist. Jake remembered her talking about the sari-shop owners downstairs. 'My neighbours are Indian, you know, but they are really very nice.'

Jake smirked at the backhanded compliment. She had been right in a way. About the daughter, at the very least – she really was very nice.

He walked to the bedroom to find his phone.

73

The girls were playing on the slide at the local park, a short walk from their home, though they hadn't walked. They had pulled on their roller skates to race down there like their lives depended upon it, the excitement unbearable. There had been a frenzy of activity to find their skates in the cupboard under the stairs, a frantic lacing up of their boots and then a bundle of bodies, arms and legs to get out of the front door, and see who could be first onto the driveway outside.

Tayte was the oldest at seven. She had Jake's eyes and similar colouring. The rest of her was her mother – tall, elegant, long hair, and both confident and sharp with her tongue. Megan was five. She was tiny in comparison. Nothing came easy to her but, like Jake, she was a fighter and determined to win at everything she did. She was more of a tomboy, liked her hair short and was comfiest in jeans and trainers. 'I don't want girls' clothes,' seemed to be her favourite saying. She was much more like Jake in her temperament too. She had her own way of doing things.

Jake sat at a battered, wooden picnic table next to some red, fixed play equipment. Bees buzzed among the dandelion clocks as the tallest conifer trees cast shadows. The shadows pointed at the playground in the middle of the park, like dark arrows on the lush grass showing where the fun was to be had. Days like this were what Jake remembered his life had been like before. Before the bombings. Before he'd joined the

226

Branch. Before his mother and grandmother had died. Before the split – and before he'd started drinking too much.

The girls had been really pleased to see their dad when he'd arrived at the house, the place that had been his own home too until he'd walked out. Stephanie had actually smiled at him when he'd arrived to pick them up. He had keys to the house but no longer used them. Jake wondered if the guilt he felt would ever leave.

Stephanie and Jake spoke very little – just like it was when they were married really. Friends, good friends, partners, but no longer lovers. They had been, once upon a time, before the kids. They'd had a good sex life but it had disappeared once the first baby had turned into two. Jake didn't really know why. He'd become consumed by his job, as Stephanie had with her own career and the children's increasingly busy lives. They'd just grown apart, as the cliché ran.

When the girls were around, or the family kept dropping in, there never seemed to be any time to talk. There was no chance to have grown-up nights out, nor a window to enjoy intimacy any longer. All he'd wanted was to be close to some-one. He didn't really understand why he'd not tried harder to work it through with her.

Maybe it was a failing within him, an inability to stick at it. He wondered if it was just his own psychological issues rather than a problem between them both. That's why he had walked out, he reasoned. He'd needed to work through in his own head what was going on.

After his mother and grandmother had died, he'd pushed all the emotions to the back of his mind and filed them in the 'I'll-deal-with-those-later' box.

He'd immersed himself in his work. He wasn't hiding from the box of emotions, or so he kept telling himself – there just wasn't time right now… He'd deal with it later.

The box was left abandoned, still unopened.

'Daddy, Daddy, Daddy – watch this!' Megan shouted as she slid face-first down the slide, launching herself off the end, like Superman freeze-framed in the air for a nanosecond, before landing with her chest on the tarmac at the bottom. She laughed and got up.

'You, you, you! Your go now!' She pointed to Tayte at the top of the slide.

Tayte looked down at her nice new blouse and favourite checked skirt, and shook her head.

'Chicken!' Megan stomped off and headed back toward the stairs for the slide.

The girls were growing up fast.

What had that space given him? Space to miss them growing up? Not to be a proper dad? Space to drink more? More time to work? His head was no clearer. He missed the girls. He missed Stephanie in many ways. Yes at first he'd had lots of sex – mainly with strangers whom he never saw again. Yes the sex was sometimes good, dirty sex. But the cost? He'd traded all this for some cheap thrills and now a girlfriend he never saw? Was that it? Is that what he'd done? Maybe if he opened the box and dealt with the grief of losing his mother and grandmother, maybe that was the key to it all? There was no time now. It would have to wait.

'Come on, girls. Skates on. Time to go home!' said Jake, standing up from the table.

74

Jake and Lenny were heading east with the windows down on the car. The majority of the early-morning traffic was trundling into the city in the opposite direction. Clear blue skies and no wind; today was going to be a scorcher. The pavements were busy with people dressed for the occasion.

'You didn't get drunk over the weekend then, Jake? I'm assuming that's why you wanted to drive today, unlike most days…' Lenny smirked across at him in the driver's seat of the BMW.

'I spent all weekend going through the phone data. I didn't sleep much. That data is an absolute gold mine. I did have a few jars on Friday night though.'

'After the post-mortem? You managed to keep it down without being sick, I'm amazed! So you hooked up with your bit of skirt on Friday, did you?' asked Lenny.

'Nah, bumped into someone in the pub, an old mate. We got chatting about religion. He knows his way around the Quran. Interesting bloke.'

'A devout Muslim in the pub, Jake? Pull over, you're fucking drunk and high on drugs, mate!'

Jake laughed.

'He's non-practising. Father was very strict, force-fed him Islam as a kid – so much so that he can recite it verse by verse. Likes a beer now though. More my type of bloke. He's all right.'

'Who is this guy? I've never heard you talk about him before.'

'Just an old pal. I've known him for years. Alex, his name is.'

You never called a snout by their real name to anyone. Only the handler and controller knew their true name and address and the snout would be assigned a pseudonym. Jake preferred unisex names that did not immediately reveal the informant's gender to outsiders.

He took informant handling seriously. He had to protect identities. It was a dangerous role for all parties, including Jake. You didn't blab about your informants to anyone, not even your best mates.

Being a police snout could be a lucrative business, as long as you got results. For information that led to a conviction, a police snout might get a lump sum of £2,000.

The Security Service operated an entirely different system. They used suitcases full of money to cultivate an informant, before the snout had even provided any information. These people were then paid a monthly retainer – sometimes as much as £2,000 per month, just to sit on the books.

Mobile phones and cars were also provided to sweeten the deal and ensure that the snouts were able to do whatever the Security Services wanted them to do.

Having been used to the results-driven system within the police, Jake found the methods used by the Security Services very odd. He felt that these snouts were just being paid on a monthly basis to remain in terrorism without delivering the goods. They lived off the money like a salary, became bored, and spent more time getting involved in illicit or extremist activity. Jake saw it breed within communities. Friends and relatives also wanted money for doing virtually nothing – or worse, actually used the money to become involved in dodgy activities when previously they wouldn't have bothered or have had the time or means to do so.

Jake much preferred the results-based system that the police used. The snout only got paid if they behaved responsibly and provided a measurable outcome to the police.

Running snouts was a very messy business, even when both you and your informant played by the rules.

That's why Zarshad was now just a friend called 'Alex'; an old friend that Jake had bumped into at the pub over the weekend.

Jake glanced over at Lenny in the passenger seat. 'I was talking to Alex about the timing of the attacks, about Wasim's video that's been showing on the news. The time of the attacks is a big thing. It has a meaning. Something we've all missed. Other people knew the significance. I don't think it's just the four of them.'

'We've been saying that for weeks, Jake. The MIR is all over the place. What does your lady friend at the Security Service say?' asked Lenny.

'The official line is that, on the ground, it's just the four lads up in Yorkshire involved in 7/7. I think Claire might have some more information, but she or the Security Service is trying to throw us off the scent.'

'Maybe the Security Service are just a shit organisation, Jake? I think we give them far too much credit. Some play with computers, some go out and play at being James Bond. But, actually, they're just a bunch of kids who know nothing about the world. Left hand doesn't know what the right hand is doing.'

'Why the lies about what they do or don't know then?'

'Because they can?' Lenny shrugged.

'What do you mean?'

'They can say what they like. They know we can't look at the intelligence they hold – no one can. Not even the politicians. They're their own keepers, answerable to no one. That's the way us police used to be in the seventies. No one could touch us. We did what we liked. If we made a mistake, we covered it up. We didn't have to put up with the shit from the courts that we do now.

'They lie because they can, Jake. Because they can get away with it. Of course they know more. Of course they've fucked up, but they're never going to admit it and we're never going to be able to prove that, are we?'

They were headed into the Blackwall tunnel. The sunshine was suddenly gone, replaced with neon light that flooded from the ceiling. An acrid smell of traffic fumes filled the car. They both wound up their windows.

The tunnel came to an abrupt end and they were dazzled by the daylight. They'd be at Fort Halstead soon.

The drive from the Blackwall tunnel to Sevenoaks took about an hour. They spoke little about work again until they started to climb the hill toward the Fort Halstead facility.

'What do you reckon they're going to tell us about the dirty bomb, Jake? D'you think it's caused an epidemic?'

'I don't know. I dread to think. To be honest, Len – I really hope they've found nothing at all.'

75

They drove slowly toward the barriers blocking the entrance to the facility. A security guard in a black jumper and black trousers stepped out of the small building next to the barriers, with a clipboard.

'If your name's not on the list, you ain't coming in,' quipped Lenny as they slowed down.

Jake stopped the car next to the guard.

'Who are you here to see, gents?'

'Professor Bowman. We should be on the list. DI Flannagan and DS Sandringham,' said Jake through the car's open window.

The guard scrolled down the clipboard, 'Yes. You know where you're going?'

'Yep, no problem,' said Jake.

The guard turned and waved back toward the building to give the OK. The metal barrier in front of them slid slowly skyward, leaving an open road. Jake drove carefully into the vast facility.

Situated on a hill overlooking the commuter haven of Sevenoaks, Fort Halstead had all the appearances of an army base without the army. Low-rise, red-brick buildings, neat streets and cut grass.

The place prided itself on being one of the world's oldest laboratories and the team in white coats continued to regularly test new types of explosives. However a large proportion of their work was the examination of debris or exhibits in criminal investigations, such as the 1988 Lockerbie bombing and the mainland IRA campaign during the nineties.

Jake drove along a deserted road to a building at the back of the facility. They were met in the car park by Professor Bowman, a wiry man with grey hair and small round glasses.

Jake and Lenny got out of the car. Bowman shook Jake's hand. It was a firm handshake. Bowman worked away from the public gaze. He met few people outside his team, but was a man of strong character. Jake often wondered what his background was. He reminded Jake of Q from the James Bond films, even in the way he dressed.

'Good to see you again, Detective Inspector,' said Bowman.

He led them into one of the buildings. The corridor had offices either side. Busy people in white lab coats were wandering up and down.

They settled in an office that had framed certificates on the wall. There were lots of them in an assortment of frame styles and sizes, both landscape and portrait. The room held a desk, but Bowman plumped for a green sofa instead.

'Sit,' Bowman instructed and indicated to two high-backed chairs opposite him.

Jake and Lenny sat down. Lenny took out a notebook.

'Thanks for taking the time to see us today. It's really appreciated,' said Jake.

'No problem at all. It's an interesting piece of work. More than happy to have got involved. Malcolm Denswood at the MIR in London sent me the hospital reports and photos of the amputee last week. I've been through all the information in some depth.'

'And? Anything?' asked Jake, leaning forward in his chair.

Bowman opened a large brown file and peered into it. 'Hmm, it's odd. Did the bombers spend any time in Iraq do you know?' he asked, looking between Jake and Lenny.

'I don't know. It's possible. We know Wasim Khan, the ringleader, made a video which specifically mentions the war in Iraq as being one of the reasons for blowing himself up in London, and we know that he travelled a fair bit in the last five years. He spent some time in Afghanistan, Pakistan, Saudi Arabia, Israel and Palestine, according to the Security Service reports. They've made no specific mention of Iraq. Not that that means anything to be honest. They don't mention a lot of stuff they know to us. What do you think this has to do with Iraq?'

'Clostridium perfringens,' Bowman announced with a smile, as if it should mean something to Jake.

'What? What the hell is that?'

'I've been in touch with my colleagues at Porton Down, the biological-weapons facility. Clostridium perfringens is a biological agent that can be used with explosive munitions. It's a very common bacterium. It can be found in decaying vegetation, the intestinal tract of humans, other vertebrates, insects and soil. It's also the third most common cause of food poisoning in the UK and the US, thanks to the fact that it has the shortest reported generation time of any organism at just 6.3 minutes. You find it has an absolute ball reproducing at all-day buffets. It loves reheated gravies, lukewarm soups and cooled-down casseroles. If ingested, you may well get diarrhoea, vomiting and fever within the next ten to twelve hours. It doesn't hang around.

'However, having said all that, when used with explosive munitions it doesn't just cause food poisoning. It causes something far more serious, something known as "gas gangrene".'

Jake's palms started to sweat. He felt slightly sick.

76

'What does that mean? What does it do?' Jake struggled to get his words out.

Bowman glanced down at his notes. 'Gas gangrene. British naval surgeons described it back in the 1700s. You've not heard of it? Well, the first recorded death rate was as high as 46% when tracked back in 1871. It became a common problem with bomb injuries during the American Civil War and World War I. Hundreds of thousands, perhaps millions, died from it in the trenches. A soldier would get a blast injury, they'd amputate, but the soldier would have become infected from the Clostridium perfringens bacterium that was present in the trenches. If there was faecal matter from the soldiers relieving themselves in the trenches, so much the worse. The symptoms are a build-up of gas and fluid leaking from joints and limbs. It's dangerous. The typical incubation period is frequently short, but incubation periods of up to six weeks have been reported. Antibiotics tackle it effectively – but there was little of that back in 1915.'

'OK. So I get all that. But what's the connection with Iraq?' asked Jake.

'Well, we do know that in 1986 and 1988 the US Government shipped a quantity of Clostridium perfringens to Iraq, along with anthrax, and some other nasty biological things for weapons. Some reports cited they had up to 5,000 litres of Clostridium perfringens for use with explosive munitions during the nineties.

That's why I wanted to know if the bomber had been to Iraq. But you say he hasn't?'

'As far as I know,' shrugged Jake.

'Well, I still think this person is showing all the signs of gas gangrene. It's the sort of thing that we would have expected to see two hundred years ago. I mean, even by the time of the Falklands War in 1982, we'd stopped hearing about it. There wasn't a single case reported throughout that whole conflict. That's how far things had come,' Bowman said with a frown. 'But if he's not been to Iraq, and they've not shipped any over, then I can only assume that this case must have been caused by some sort of accidental contamination, rather than a designated biological weapon. Clostridium perfringens can be prevalent in black pepper, and we know that was a key ingredient in these bombs.'

Jake was reminded of the spicy, pungent fragrance.

'We've tested the remaining bomb ingredients that were left in the flat,' said Bowman, 'and nothing was flagged up. But it is possible that they used an entirely different batch and disposed of the packaging somewhere else.'

Jake looked quizzically at Bowman. 'Hang on. So you said this gas gangrene could be treated by antibiotics? If it can be treated by antibiotics, why has this amputee got it? I'm pretty sure that when they amputate, the patient is pumped full of broad-spectrum drugs by the hospital. Why did this patient get this condition?'

'It's a good question, one that I have struggled with myself. The usual antibiotic treatment for Clostridium perfringens is penicillin. Penicillin normally knocks it on the head. But sometimes antibiotics alone are not effective because they may not penetrate infected tissues sufficiently. If this amputee was potentially allergic to penicillin, they'll have most certainly been treated with an alternative, probably clindamycin. However, it's becoming increasingly clear that clindamycin alone is not always successful in treating this bacterium. The experts at Porton Down tell me they're currently seeing new strains of Clostridium perfringens that have become resistant to certain antibiotics.

'I've looked at the blast pattern and I've looked at where this patient was located on the seating plan in relation to the bomber. I'm wondering – if the bus bomber had recently been abroad, could he have picked up this germ and been carrying it in his body?'

Jake thought back to what he knew about the four bombers and nodded in agreement. 'Yes, I can see that being plausible, Professor. I researched why a couple of the bombers lost so much weight. Turns out that they'd had stomach bugs, which they'd picked up from training camps when travelling abroad. Wasim, for example. We know he became so ill back in 2001 on a visit to Pakistan that he had to return home to the UK. And Asif, he lost a load of weight between November 2004 and February of this year. His normal clothes didn't fit him. His mum said she didn't recognise him when he got back from his trip. He somehow picked up something really nasty out there. Friends and relatives said he was constantly complaining of feeling ill.'

The Professor raised his eyebrows. 'So my thinking is that this bug could possibly have been expelled from the bus bomber's body, as a result of the explosion, and contaminated the bomb victims' wounds,' he reasoned.

Lenny looked nonplussed. 'Well, we found the bus bomber, Asif Rahman, in a number of pieces, but I know for a fact that his bowels and intestines were intact. His torso was on the roof of the BMA's building.'

'How on earth did you know that his body was up there?' asked Professor Bowman incredulously.

'The team said they were being plagued by an enormous flock of seagulls in the square. The birds were very interested in something on the roof. When we got some of the guys up on a cherry picker to have a look, they spotted a torso and we DNA'd the remains,' grimaced Lenny.

'Then perhaps the device on the bus was in contact with faecal matter infected with Clostridium perfringens? Did the bombers defecate onto the bombs or into their rucksacks, for instance?'

Jake looked at the floor intently. There was something at the back of his mind gnawing away at him. It suddenly came to him. 'The trousers, Lenny!'

Lenny turned to him with a puzzled look on his face. 'What d'you mean?'

Jake was getting animated now. 'The petrol station CCTV at Woodall Services on the M1! You remember, Lenny. When they were travelling down to London early on the morning of 7/7 in the Nissan Micra? The CCTV showed Asif wearing white tracksuit bottoms as he got out to pay the cashier for the fuel. Then when we saw him again on the CCTV at Luton train station, three hours later, he had dark tracksuit bottoms on. We never found those white tracksuit bottoms. Like I said in that meeting, he must have had a little accident on the way!'

'You're right!' said Lenny. 'The mysterious case of the missing white tracksuit bottoms! He's obviously shat himself and got changed. Must have been covered in it.'

'And then he put his filthy trousers in his rucksack with the device,' said Jake.

'So you believe that the bus bomber was suffering from a severe stomach upset, defecated in his tracksuit bottoms and after changing into a clean pair, he stowed the soiled garment in the rucksack with the bomb?' asked the Professor.

'That's exactly what I think could have happened,' said Jake, 'and when the bomb exploded, the faecal matter on the trousers could have contaminated the entire scene with the bacterium. There's us thinking that they were terrorist masterminds. Thinking they'd created a bomb containing a biological agent, hell bent on spreading an epidemic. When actually that bacterium was there totally by chance. All because Asif had a dodgy tummy. They didn't hatch a deliberate dirty-bomb plot at all!'

There was a moment of silence as the three of them took this information in.

The Professor broke the lull. 'Well, it's certainly an interesting theory, but just a theory nonetheless. You're right to say that it doesn't seem like a deliberate dirty bomb, but I wouldn't like to place my bets on exactly what caused the gas gangrene – it's a highly unusual set of circumstances.'

A split second later and Jake's brain was whirring again. 'So what's the prognosis, Prof.? How do we help to get rid of the gas gangrene?'

'I'll speak with the biological weapons people at Porton Down and get them to liaise with the hospital medical staff directly. They'd be the right experts to speak to in terms of creating the ideal treatment programme. They have all the latest research on the newer resistant strains of Clostridium perfringens. Hyperbaric oxygen therapy has had good results in tandem with special cocktails of the newer antibiotics.'

Lenny and Jake thanked the Professor and left, still reeling slightly from what they'd discovered.

77

The West Yorkshire team had convened to converse via video link with the meeting room back at Scotland Yard. Their Tuesday-morning meeting was once again dominated by the bomb factory at Victoria Park.

'We've removed roughly half of the items out of Victoria Park in the past six weeks. It's a very slow process. We're taking photos of each exhibit. The photos are being sent to the MIR for actioning and, as you'll see in front of you, we're continually forwarding copies up to the Leeds team,' Ian Thetford, the exhibits officer, said into the camera.

'Thanks, Ian,' replied Jake. 'I have a few questions about the bomb factory, having seen it first-hand. There's a lot of stuff in that flat. It's knee-deep in junk. You can't even move room to room in some places because there's no clear walkway. How did they use it as a factory with that much stuff in there? It would have been impossible to get anything done! Most of it looks like it's just been lobbed in there as an afterthought. It's as if there might have been another location, but this was all that they wanted us to find.'

'I can see your point, Jake, but the place is teeming with evidence for us to get to grips with. The forensic explosives lab has confirmed our belief that the hydrogen peroxide was smelted in there. The bedroom area has been subjected to extreme heat, so much so that the paintwork on the door frame has bubbled up. The windows had to be kept open at all times because of the fumes. They used masking tape to secure the net curtains to the window frame to stop people looking in. It was definitively and without question the location in which they manufactured the hydrogen-peroxide-based explosives.'

'But…' Jake was about to ask Ian another question when he was interrupted by the voice of Denswood, who was chairing the meeting as usual from the London end.

'Thank you, Ian. Thank you, Jake. So this week's actions will be sent out by the MIR. Same time again next week please, folks,' he concluded. The screen in Bradford went black. The meeting was over. They'd cut the link in London.

78

Jake sipped his posh latte under an expanse of glass that was framed by gilded mosaics and wrought iron. The upmarket boutiques and restaurants in the ornate, restored arcade made Jake feel a bit like he was back in London. The Crystal Palace of the north, he thought.

Comfy seats and rich strong coffee were all very well but it was actually the gorgeous, blue-eyed Latvian waitress that kept him coming back here.

Len plonked himself down opposite Jake.

'Back here again, are we, Jake?' smirked Len, as Jake watched the waitress saunter past, clad in a tight black dress.

'I could masturbate about the coffee alone here, never mind the waitress,' Jake winked back, as he polished off his first latte of the afternoon.

'I've been looking at the Victoria Park stuff,' said Lenny, changing the subject, his voice more hushed now.

'Oh yeah?' asked Jake.

'There's a couple of things that bother me...' Len watched as the waitress returned. 'Two lattes, please, my love. One for me, and one for your stalker here,' Len said, cocking his head in Jake's direction as he spoke. The waitress giggled as she shimmied off to fetch their order.

Len continued, 'The day we first found the Victoria Park flat, Karim Rahman showed us those phones and that piece of paper he'd found on top of Asif's wardrobe. D'you remember?'

243

'Yes, I remember.'

'I checked with the MIR. They've not done anything on those two telephone numbers yet. That information has been totally overlooked.'

'Jesus!' said Jake in disbelief.

'Karim called all the numbers in those phones' contact lists. He was desperately hunting for his missing brother. Some of the people he got through to said they knew Asif. But the two guys who gave Karim the biggest runaround were the ones whose phone numbers were written on that note he found. Their names are Shahid and Shaggy.'

Jake smiled at the waitress as she placed the lattes on the table.

'Karim first tried the bloke called Shaggy, who said he was from Sheffield. He said he didn't know Asif, and apparently acted quite bizarrely on the phone. But they had definitely spoken several times before the bombings if you look at the phone records. They certainly did know each other,' said Lenny, with cream from the latte he'd started to drink on the end of his nose.

He continued, 'I did a subscriber check on Shaggy's number. It came back as a pay as you go phone and no subscriber was listed. I've traced a *possible* address in Sheffield for a Shaggy. We could go and check him out? We have the handset's IMEI details. It might turn something up?'

'Lunch in Sheffield it is tomorrow then, Len. Good work. But wipe that fucking cream off your nose. If it doesn't work out with Claire, you're embarrassing me in front of the future Mrs Flannagan, you knob!' Jake looked sideways at Len and then up at the Latvian waitress standing in the doorway.

Len laughed and dabbed at the end of his nose with his serviette.

79

The weather had been glorious for months. Jake wondered if 2005 would be remembered for just three things: its sunshine, London winning an Olympic bid and mass murder on home soil.

His head hurt again, but that was normal these days. He was spending close to £700 a week getting drunk in Leeds city centre during evening hours.

Lenny was driving. It was a good job. Jake imagined that his own blood-alcohol level was probably still well over the drink-drive limit. Lenny was well known in the force for his habit of not concentrating and he frequently went the wrong way, but the M1 to Sheffield was an easy journey, even for him.

They wound their way south down the motorway in the BMW.

'So what do we know about this bloke, Len?' asked Jake.

'Nothing much. He's called Shaggy. It's a long shot but you never know,' Lenny continued, looking ahead as he drove.

'Fuck me, Lenny, it's a bit on the light side, isn't it? He has the same name? That's it, is it?'

'You make your own luck, Jake. You've got to be in it to win it, like you always say. This is the only way we'll find out if it's the right bloke or not, isn't it?'

Jake was in no mood to argue. 'Yeah, yeah, yeah. You're right, Len. You can do the talking when we get there. My head's banging. You be the good cop, as normal. I'll be the bad one.'

He relaxed back into the headrest and closed his eyes. The motion of the car quickly lulled him into sleep.

'Jake! Wake up! We're here,' shouted Lenny as he pulled on the handbrake sharply.

They'd parked up on what looked to Jake like a council housing estate with low-rise, pebble-dashed homes. Flat, black tarmac ledges served as pavements and spindly little trees sprung up at regular intervals along both sides of the road.

'Number eleven. Over there.' Lenny pointed toward a blue door a few spindly trees down from them.

Jake did his usual external property recce. He glanced at the cupboard that housed the gas meter. There was just one white door. He checked the number of wheelie bins in the front garden – again just one.

The number of meter cupboards and bins were always helpful in signposting how many separate dwellings might be in any one building. Jake could tell this was a single dwelling. Good, he thought. The less people he had to deal with the better.

The black picket fence in the front garden was rotten. Several of its wooden posts had broken, and the gate lay on an overgrown lawn like it was drunk.

Lenny walked up the paved part of the garden and into a small recess that housed a blue front door.

There was no bell. Lenny rapped hard on the top glass panel. After a few seconds there was movement in the hallway. Blurred patches behind the translucent glass changed shape.

'Who is it?' A male with a Pakistani accent shouted.

'It's the police, sir. Could you open the door please?' Lenny said in his most authoritarian tone.

'No! Fuck off!' said the figure as he moved away and back to where he'd come from.

Lenny looked at Jake and shook his head. They couldn't leave now. They had to speak to this man.

Jake moved into the recess. Lenny stepped out. Jake banged on the door with fist: 'Open up please, sir. We need to speak to you urgently!'

The Pakistani voice replied again, 'And I'm telling you now to be fucking off!'

Jake and Lenny looked at each other and raised their eyebrows. This man's reaction was unsettling. It was unusual. There was no telling why he'd acted that way – but Jake wasn't about to leave it at that.

'Open the fucking door!' Jake shouted. The glass shook as he hammered on it again three times.

The figure moved back toward the door.

'What do you want?' asked the man.

'I want you to open the door,' Jake lowered his voice as he spoke.

'I'm not opening my door!'

'OK. This is very simple! You open the door or I kick it in! Your choice, pal,' said Jake. He waited for a response. None was forthcoming.

'You've got ten seconds to open the door!'

Jake waited for what seemed, to him, like most of the morning. There was silence. He walked back out of the recess and glanced up and down the street, looking for anyone obviously watching them. There was no one. The curtains all seemed still, the street was empty, the front gardens abandoned.

He turned back toward the door and quickly sprinted a distance of ten feet or so toward it. Three feet short, he hopped onto his left foot and then extended his right toward the lock. He felt like Roy Keane going in for a tackle, studs up.

His foot slammed with a bang, right beside the handle, as the door took his full weight. There was the sound of splintering wood and a crack as the reinforced window split. The door swung open and wood from the frame flew into the hallway toward a lone figure.

Jake and Lenny could now see the man who'd been swearing at them.

80

They didn't flash their credentials.

Badges and IDs were for when you were doing things legally. The official line would be: 'You don't have to reveal your name in terrorism cases and that's why I didn't show him my badge, Your Honour.'

The man was in his seventies. His white hair and unkempt white beard contrasted with a dark blue dressing gown and matching slippers. His mouth was hanging open in shock. He looked utterly bewildered as to why these two Cockney coppers were trying to get into his South Yorkshire home. He said nothing.

'Where's Shaggy?' asked Jake

The man's confusion got visibly worse as he stared back at Jake.

'Me?' said the man.

'You got a mobile phone, Shaggy? Don't move. Stay where you are, just tell us where it is,' said Jake.

Jake could hear Lenny attempt to pull the door to behind him and then fiddle with the broken lock.

'Please do not be hurting me. Phone is on table in living room.' The man began to look more scared now than confused. Jake walked past him and picked up the battered handset that was lying on the coffee table.

Jake had brought with him both the mobile phone number and IMEI number of the handset that they'd identified from the reverse billings.

He dialled *#06# on Shaggy's mobile and brought up its IMEI number; he checked it against his notebook. Wrong one. This wasn't the phone that had exchanged calls with Asif or Karim.

Jake looked around the room. Orange carpet. Velour furniture. A mantelpiece full of photos of children slowly growing up, going to college and graduating from university.

This was all wrong.

He felt it in his gut. This was the wrong place. This was the wrong bloke. It was too late to undo this mess. This sometimes happened. A bit of crappy information added to a bit of the wrong attitude, multiplied by a hangover, equalled a fucking shambles.

'Always press ahead when you end up in this situation,' Jake heard the voice in his head say. The bad guys or even the good guys with the wrong attitude don't actually know you've got it wrong.

'Come in and sit down, Shaggy, please,' said Jake in his best calming voice.

'What is it about?' Shaggy asked, the stress on his face clearly visible.

'We are looking for a man called Shaggy that made some phone calls. We thought that might be you. Do you know anyone in Leeds?' said Jake.

'No. I am not going out much these days, isn't it? My wife, she is dead and my children work down there in the London banking. I don't go out much. I don't see many people,' Shaggy said, his face crumbling.

Jake decided that they needed to beat a hasty retreat. He fished out the remaining cash he had left in his pocket from the previous night out on the tiles… £200.

'Thanks, Shaggy. Get your door repaired, mate. Take care,' Jake said, as he handed over the big wad of notes to the bemused old man.

Lenny said nothing. Jake walked out of the door and Len followed his lead, waving the remote-control key fob at the car to unlock it from behind his boss. Jake got in the passenger side. Lenny climbed into the driver's seat.

'Drive, you useless tosser!' shouted Jake, laughing and wincing all at the same time – appalled by their morning's antics.

Lenny started the car and pulled away in a hurry.

81

After lunch in Sheffield, Lenny and Jake returned to the office in Bradford. They'd both agreed not to mention to anyone that they'd even been to South Yorkshire; it had never happened.

Amersham Computers had called whilst Jake had been kicking an innocent old man's door down. The supercomputer was ready. Big Simon had brought their haul of techno goodies back to the office and set it all up. It had taken him hours to get all the software and data loaded onto it.

Jake walked into the office to hear a 'Fucking hell!' from Big Simon, followed by a long, slow whistle through his teeth.

'Jake! It's not crashed! It's actually fucking working!'

Jake flew over to look at the new supercomputer's screen. On it, the full phone data was listed in glorious working order.

'Christ, and this is just the start?' Big Simon asked. 'How do we even know what they were thinking? What their state of mind was when they made these communications?'

'Si, we need to treat this investigation like any other organised crime. Forget the scale of it. Forget the fact it was terrorism. These are the issues that everyone's been getting bogged down by. We need to look at it like they were planning a bank robbery. We need to take all emotion out of it. That way we can find out how they did it and who helped them,' said Jake.

'I know, I know. We need to get back to basics. What did old Roger from CID used to say back in the good old days? I

251

don't want the people the suspect speaks to most. I want the people he speaks to the least. The things they do the least are the things that are the most interesting.'

'Yeah, yeah, forget the girlfriend he's texting goodnight to every night,' laughed Jake, 'although those are by far and away the best texts…'

Simon smirked. 'No! We need the one number the criminal speaks to over the course of a series of months, then goes silent on. D'you remember?' Simon was scrolling through the data now. 'Roger used to say look for the one final, rogue message in the run-up to the robbery. That proves they've finalised something, broken off communications, and then gone back to double-check the plan. That's what we're looking for.'

Jake and Simon had spent most of the day playing with their supercomputer, getting to grips with the system, uploading more data and creating pivot tables. Jake was cheered by their progress.

Now the office was almost dead. There was no talking or banter; just the whirr of computer fans and the tappety-tap-tap of computer keys as the MIR staff input information into the HOLMES system. The rest of the troops were out chasing where loaves were made and when they'd been shipped to here, there, Timbuktu or the bomb factory. Hours wasted digging up information that wasn't going to solve anything, thought Jake. Then again, kicking in some innocent bloke's door hadn't solved much either, and besides, Jake didn't think he could afford to do that every day.

Jake looked at his computer screen. He had to find some focus. He pulled up Karim Rahman's statement again:

On top of my brother's wardrobe, I found a piece of paper and a mobile phone. The paper had two mobile phone numbers on it, one against the name Shaggy and one against the name Shahid. When I looked in the handset's call log, both the Shaggy and Shahid numbers had previously been called from the phone.

I called the Shahid number. A man answered. He had a West Yorkshire accent. He said that he knew my brother from the mosque, but I'd never heard of the mosque he talked about. Then the man terminated the call...'

Jake went over to Simon. He gave him Shahid's number. 'Can you give that one a run through the new system please, Simon? HOLMES tells me that we've done fuck all with it so far.'

'Leave it with me, Jake.'

Nothing had been done on it at all. Jake was shocked. He'd been forced to spend weeks investigating rice packets when things like this number hadn't even been properly scrutinised.

Jake watched Simon use the fancy fingerprint scanner to log on to the new supercomputer and access the 600,000 individual pieces of data. The big man smiled as his screen lit up. He was in his element.

Simon typed the last six digits of Shahid's phone number into the find field and hit the return key. i2 displayed things in a different way to Excel. It was more of a visual tool. The supercomputer took a few moments then came up with a hit. Jake looked at the time and date of the call. It was the phone call Karim had made looking for his missing brother. The one he'd talked about in his statement. Jake sighed.

Big Simon manipulated some windows and looked in more detail at the results that the computer had found.

'There are actually seven matches for this number...' Simon beamed.

'Seven?' Jake said loudly. On the other side of the office, two MIR staff had stopped tapping their keys and were looking directly at him, waiting to hear what was coming next.

'That's an interesting number. When was the first call?' he asked, much more quietly this time.

Jake watched as Simon manipulated the data. It was like he was manipulating time. Whizzing downwards, backwards from 26 August 2005, Jake was being allowed to look back before the fifty-two victims and four bombers has died. The computer stopped. It had completed its task. Jake looked at the date of the call that had been highlighted.

08/04/2005.

'Nearly three months before the bombings, Jake. Call-pattern spread is very narrow. They certainly ain't best mates,' Simon said as he continued to play with the computer. 'The call was made to Shahid. From Wasim. From Wasim's personal handset.'

'What the fuck? That can't be right? Made from Wasim to Shahid? Not Asif?'

Simon tapped away excitedly on the keyboard. 'That's correct. First two contacts are Wasim. Then the next five are Asif.'

'OK. Let's give those calls some context – what was going on around that time?' asked Jake.

Jake checked Wasim's travel dates. Wasim had arrived back from Pakistan on Tuesday, 8 February 2005. Jake knew that Wasim had been in contact with an unidentified clandestine contact in Pakistan on Sunday, 10 April. The person in Pakistan had been using phone kiosks to call Wasim. The calls stopped at 0900 hours on Thursday, 7 July 2005. The day of the bombings. The caller clearly knew what was going to happen and had stopped trying to make contact.

Lenny walked into the office with two cups of tea. He sat down next to Jake and pushed a chipped white mug toward him.

'Lenny, when did Wasim first purchase any hydrogen peroxide? What date?' asked Jake.

Lenny fished out a notebook from his pocket and fumbled around with it for a few moments before finding the information he needed.

'Thursday, 31 March 2005 was the first purchase, boss. Wasim purchased five litres that day,' replied Lenny.

'That's all a bit coincidental,' Jake murmured as he looked upwards at the ceiling, mulling it all over.

'What's coincidental?' asked Lenny.

'You know the other number we were looking at? The other one that was with the Shaggy one?'

'The Shahid one?'

'Yeah. Well, we just searched for it in the supercomputer on the off chance. Turns out it's been in contact several times, not just with Asif – but with Wasim too,' said Jake.

'That's interesting. How come that's not been identified already?' asked Lenny, surprised.

'See, this is exactly what I've been saying all along with this shit, Lenny! None of these personal phone billings have been entered into HOLMES properly. The analysts have been concentrating solely on the operational handsets, but there's been bleed over from the bombers' activities onto their personal phones. No one's had the full picture of what they've been up to. Nothing important seems to have been actioned unless it's related to a fucking rice packet! Who knows what's actually been done and what hasn't?

'Anyway, it's important because of the timings of the calls. Wasim called Shahid on 8 April. That's a week after he made that first hydrogen peroxide purchase. Moreover, that's just two days before those Pakistan phone-kiosk calls start. Wasim is in full operational attack mode. Everything Wasim is doing at that point is working toward the end goal. To my mind, Shahid is possibly involved.' Jake looked Lenny straight in the eye to gauge his response.

'I'm with you, Jake. I never argue with your theories, I like them,' winked Lenny.

'Take Shahid's phone number, Len. Run it through West Yorkshire's intelligence and crime-information systems for me. Find out what they know about him. I'm going to speak to the guys at the Security Service,' said Jake.

82

Jake was alone in the office.

The walls were made of sound-deadening blue cloth, which gave the place a sleepy sort of silence. Everyone had gone home or back to their hotels; it wasn't unusual for him to be here on his own. Jake liked the peace at this time; he had time to think.

He was just getting ready to leave Dudley Hill when he saw Claire's number flash up on the small screen of his Nokia. He'd left a message earlier for her to call him back. Security Service employees were not allowed to take their mobile phones into their actual office suites at Thames House. They had to be turned off before entering and placed in metal cabinets outside. They were advised to turn them off even before they got near their building, but not everyone did. The mobile phone mast on the roof meant that foreign security services could potentially track and target those handsets which 'pinged' on the mast on a daily basis, because it was very likely that the people who owned them worked in the building directly below.

'Hey, gorgeous – how are you?' he asked Claire as he picked up her call. He worried for a split second that he sounded far too enthusiastic to hear from her.

'Not too bad. Things are pretty grim this end. We're under a lot of pressure to deliver stuff that we either don't know or had forgotten that we knew. What about you?'

256

'Working hard. Thinking hard. Drinking hard. There's not a lot else to me at the moment. The pub is the only place I can escape this shit.'

'I wish we had the drinking time down here, Jake, honestly I do. Think yourself lucky.' Claire sounded tired.

'Well, you could always pop up here and I could show you the best that Leeds has to offer.'

'Ha. I know you're the best Leeds has to offer, Jake. And trust me, soon as I can get away, you can show me. Is that what you've called me for?'

'I feel bad now. No, that wasn't why I left a message. I need a favour,' he said.

'I'm all out of favours, Jake. I've only just got out of the last mess you put me in. The audit trail highlighted that I'd looked at the phone records for Sullivan House. I had to come up with a hell of a story to sort that out for you. If this is Leeds stuff you're going to have to put it through your normal channel. Speak to your official contact. I can't help you.'

'You know that takes ages and I'm never confident that I'm being told the truth. You lot know loads that *you're not* telling us.'

'It's arse covering basically, Jake. Be persuasive. Use your charm. Ask them why they think Wasim moved address five times in 2004. I can't keep doing this stuff for you. Sorry. Look, I've got some holiday booked; maybe we can grab some time away together? Do you fancy a trip down to Cornwall, to the old house?'

Jake had been to Travannon House twice before. It was a beautiful old place overlooking a sheltered cove near St Austell. He was envious of the incredible scenery and much of Claire's life growing up there. He jumped at the chance. 'That would be great. When are you off?' he asked.

'I'll text the dates to you later. I've gotta go. Miss you,' she said as she put the phone down.

The office returned to silence. Dusk was beginning to fall outside. The staplers and pen pots were casting shapes on the tabletops as the sun made its retreat.

Jake put his elbows on the desk and let his head fall forward onto his hands. He closed his eyes. He imagined himself lying sprawled on a blanket on a Cornish beach, the breeze buffing his cheeks, as he breathed in hazy lungfuls of sea air flavoured with a mixture of clay and gorse bush.

He didn't want what he had right now. This life – he wanted to spend time away with Claire, or see his girls. Wasim was with him every moment, especially in the small hours. He was drinking too much. He knew that. It was almost as if he couldn't function without it. The night before last, his kids hadn't wanted to talk to him on the phone when he'd called to say goodnight. Then he'd burst into tears brushing his teeth this morning. He didn't really know why.

Just a couple of drinks tonight. No food. Early night.

A break would do him good.

83

Jake had awoken that morning to a white expanse of hotel-room ceiling, with what looked like a new light fitting in
the middle of it. He'd lain in bed for ages, wondering why his
light had been changed during the night.

As he'd looked down, he realised that 'just a couple' of
drinks must have turned into many more. He vaguely remembered talking to a group of girls at a bar who'd then dragged
him to a club. He couldn't even remember which club it was.
The attractive, twenty-something brunette with whom he was
in bed must have been one of them, surely?

An hour later, he'd said his goodbyes and made his way back
to his own room, wearing the previous night's clothes.

'This has got to stop, Jake. We can't carry on like this. You're
going to kill yourself, or catch something nasty,' he said to
himself as he looked at his reflection in the lift mirror.

Time for a shower, fresh clothes and then a dash to get to work.

Jake's team worked at Dudley Hill from the Monday of one
week through to the Friday of the following week, without a
break. That made a shift of twelve days on the trot. They had
two days off with their family, or whatever or whomever they
had in their lives, then they had to be back at Dudley Hill at
0900 hours the following Monday.

That meant just sixty-five hours' break every two weeks.
Jake couldn't comprehend how anyone had enough time to
conduct anything vaguely approaching a normal lifestyle or

relationship. To him it seemed an impossible task, given the distance they were away from home.

Lenny was sat at his desk in the office as Jake walked in.

'Morning boss. Good night last night?' asked Lenny with a wry smile. He was in a good mood. Jake envied him in many ways. He was happily married. He only ever spoke positively about Mrs Lenny. They still did things together; shared good times despite twenty years of marriage. It was a feat Jake had failed miserably at.

Lenny was happy and that made Jake happy. Lenny was going home for his sixty-five hours with his wife today.

'Lenny, I really need breakfast. You can brief me on what you've found out about that Shahid bloke over a cup of tea and a bacon sandwich.'

Lenny and Jake made their way over to Dot's café across the road. Dot had confided in Jake that she was making a killing out of the Met officers being there. Over the past seven weeks she'd purchased a new coffee machine, some new tables, had painted inside and out and taken on two of her granddaughters as waitresses.

Jake sipped his mug of tea.

'What do we know about Shahid then, Lenny?' asked Jake, before squirting ketchup onto his roll.

'I've run him through the West Yorkshire CIS system. It says he's of Pakistani heritage, Muslim, thirty-two-years old, successful businessman – owns a number of supermarkets with his older brother who is very well connected. Oh, and he once had his car broken into. I also did some checks through Intel down at the Yard. He comes up as a victim of an assault. Was bashed up by some guy in London a year ago. I've not been able to look at the London crime report for the assault yet, but that might give us something. What did the Security Service say about him, guv?'

'They've not said anything. My contact has the arse with me. I've got to use the official channels, she says.'

Jake bit into the bacon roll. Ketchup oozed out of every side as he sank his teeth into the front of it. It dripped onto his plate. He chewed lazily; chewing time was thinking time.

'OK, I want to keep moving on this one. Find out if they took photos of him and his injuries after that assault and I want to know what that fracas was about. Can you sort that this morning, Lenny?' asked Jake.

Lenny pulled back his shirtsleeve to reveal his wristwatch.

'It's already four minutes past noon, Jake. I won't do it this morning, but I'll do it straight away,' said Lenny cheerfully, as he got up and walked out of the café door.

84

The office was dead apart from Jake and Lenny. The satellite staff had taken their actions for the day. Jake knew they'd be banking on getting them done early so that they could speed their way back to London and miss the Friday traffic.

Lenny was still on the phone to the intelligence unit in London, trying to locate the crime report for Shahid. It baffled Jake why, with the exception of HOLMES and the Police National Computer, none of the UK's forty-three police forces had compatible software packages that could communicate with each other. Fax and phone were still the go-to tools.

Jake picked up the phone to call his 'official' Security Service contact, Joe West, at Thames House.

Skinny, with unkempt blonde hair, he reminded Jake of a weather-beaten, malnourished surfer. Jake sat with the phone to his ear, listening to the rings, as he waited for Joe to pick up.

'Joe West speaking.'

'Hey, Joe. How are you?'

'I'm OK, Jake, how's it going?'

'Busy. We're working on something up here that may be interesting. I need you to run a name and phone number through your systems and let me know if you have anything.'

'I'm off today and this weekend, Jake. Is it urgent? Can it wait until Monday?'

'I want to move on this today, Joe. Things are taking too long to progress at this end.'

'I'll call the office for you and ask them to contact you about it. I don't know who's in or what they've got on though, Jake. So I can't guarantee it'll be soon, sorry,' he replied.

'Fine. Thanks. Have a good weekend, Joe,' said Jake as he ended the call.

'Every fucking Saturday and Sunday off, those bastards!' Jake mumbled under his breath as he scrolled through the phone records again.

There was something rhythmic about the seven calls between Shahid and the bombers. The calls came in four blocks. April, May, June, July... Why?

Lenny sat down opposite Jake with a notepad. 'I've managed to get some details from the crime report relating to Shahid Bassam, guv. That London assault back in 2003; Shahid was attending a mosque down in East London.'

'What was he doing down there, then?' asked Jake.

'Well, there appear to have been some undesirable types protesting outside about something. A big group of skinheads were demonstrating. One of them got into an argument with Shahid and punched him in the face. Got charged with ABH then pleaded guilty at court. He got one hundred hours community service; no compensation awarded.'

'Any witnesses? What was it about?'

'I don't know exactly what it was about. Crime report is very basic. But they took some photos of Shahid for the court case. I've got a copy on the email. He's a big old lump.'

'We should talk to him,' said Jake.

'Do it Monday?' Lenny asked pointedly; Lenny wanted to go home.

'Let's get it out of the way, Len. I'll call him and have a chat on the phone. Sounds like it's a wild goose chase. He was probably just one of the bombers' mates or something...'

Even as the words came out of his mouth, Jake's gut told him that this wasn't a wild goose chase at all.

85

Friday
26 August 2005
1600 hours
Dudley Hill police station, Bradford, West Yorkshire

Lenny was pacing up and down the corridor. Jake could see him through the narrow pane of glass. Mrs Sandringham would not be happy. Her sixty-five hours with her husband were counting down.

'I know, Sue... Not my fault... I'm sorry... Oh, I forgot... Sorry... It's important...'

Jake glanced at the supercomputer's flatscreen monitor. He had dates and numbers swimming before his eyes. There were patterns of contact that looked interesting then turned into irregular patterns... then floated upwards.

It had been a long week, made even bleaker by the fact that he had nothing in the diary to look forward to this weekend.

Jake spoke to himself as Lenny continued to try to placate Mrs Sandringham on the phone outside the office door.

'So four blokes did a job. I can't rely on anything except what can't be disputed. Anything any person has said *can* be disputed. But machines and systems don't lie. Phone calls don't lie... I know the dates that they travelled to and from Pakistan. I know the date they blew themselves up. Forget everything else. Why would you stop calling the bombers once the bombings have taken place? Who kills contact then and why?' Jake mumbled to himself.

Lenny came back into view through the pane of glass on the office door.

'OK, I won't, I'm always careful, love you too,' Lenny said into his phone, as he ended the call with one hand and pushed the door open with another.

'Jake, we have got to catch these fuckers soon. My marriage is going to end in divorce otherwise!'

Jake smirked.

'I love that about you, Lenny – you'll divorce your wife rather than leave me to catch these bastards alone.'

Lenny sat down opposite Jake at the desk.

'You see, you've just proved my theory, Lenny. Friends and family keep calling. They keep in touch. If you didn't turn up at home tonight, Sue would call, wouldn't she? If she didn't know what had happened to you, she'd keep calling until she did, wouldn't she?' Jake was half talking to Lenny and half talking to himself now.

'If I don't turn up tonight she's going to come looking – and it'll be for you, Jake! She knows this is you making me stay!'

'I need tea to help me think, Lenny, tea!'

Lenny walked toward the door.

'I can't believe that I'm sacrificing time with my wife to make you fucking tea, you wanker!' Lenny kicked open the office door with his foot and headed for the kitchenette up the corridor.

Jake looked back at his screen.

Those rhythmic calls between Shahid and the group, he couldn't get them out of his head. They had to mean something.

Lenny walked back into the office holding two mugs of tea, with a digestive hanging out of his mouth. He looked at the phone numbers crowding the supercomputer's screen whilst he munched on his biscuit and glanced at his tired, drawn-looking boss.

'I don't know why you didn't just leave all that data back with the analysts down in London. Why bother making more work for yourself, guv?'

'Lenny, a piece of intelligence is useless unless you give it meaning. If we let analysts run wild in the MIR, all this phone data will just be left and we'll get nowhere. Analysts are not supposed to solve things for you. They're just there to give you the data.'

'But they're the experts, boss. Why not leave it to them to sort out?'

'Lenny! It's all very well an analyst telling us that telephone A has been in contact with telephone B, but they won't be able to tell you who was on the end of the phone having that conversation. Now a detective worth his or her salt should be able to work out why those two numbers might have been in contact with each other. And if they really know their stuff, then he or she might also be able to find out who may or may not have been at the end of that number, *and* what they've been up to.

'Lenny, those analysts might have been on some fancy-sounding courses but that doesn't make them into a detective in a couple of weeks or months. Ten years it took us, with all our policing experience. There's something funny about this Shahid, I can just feel it in my gut and the supercomputer is agreeing with me.'

'What is it, boss? What did you find out?'

'Well, from the phone records on screen here, we can see that this Shahid has been in contact with at least two of the phones belonging to the bombers *and* the landline of the parents of a bomber. Hence he's lied about knowing people whom he clearly does know. There's a rhythm to the calls, monthly almost. Then they stop. I'm going to give him a ring.'

Jake picked up the phone on his desk, ignoring Lenny's pleas for Friday-night clemency and punched in Shahid's mobile number. A number he now knew off by heart.

'Yes,' a man with a Leeds accent answered the call.

'Is that Shahid Bassam?' asked Jake.

'Yeah. Who is this?'

'I'm Detective Inspector Flannagan from the Metropolitan Police. I need to talk to you about Wasim Khan.'

'Why? I didn't know him,' replied Shahid.

Bingo, thought Jake. Shahid had just handed him a huge gift without realising it. He had referred to Wasim in the past tense.

He knew Wasim was dead. He knew who Jake was talking about instantly. He was lying.

'It's just a formality thing, sir. We're just tying up some loose ends. Where are you now?'

'Well, I'm in my supermarket, aren't I?'

'Which supermarket is that? I'm nearby. I'll come and see you straight away. Won't take long,' replied Jake

'Al Siddiq. 442 Harehills Road,' said Shahid.

'See you in thirty minutes.' Jake hung up the phone without giving him an opportunity to say anything further.

Lenny's mouth fell open and the digestive biscuit dropped onto the dark green carpet. It smashed into several pieces at his feet.

'But... now? It's Friday? Sue is gonna kill me! We're doing this right now? Interview tonight? No, Jake... please.'

'Lenny, he's a liar and I want to interview him. I'm not waiting till Monday. I can't leave him to disappear over the weekend now I've spoken to him on the phone. We need to see him face to face, today!'

Jake grabbed the car keys off the table in front of him and pulled his jacket off the back of his chair.

Lenny plonked the two mugs he was carrying down onto the desk. Hot tea splashed up onto his shirt cuff and over the desktops.

'Oh fucking great, I've created my own little storm in a teacup!' muttered Lenny. 'For fuck's sake, boss. We only get sixty-five hours a fortnight off, sixty-five fucking hours! And we're doing this now?'

He trampled across the broken digestive on the floor and toward the office door, which was already swinging shut behind his boss.

86

The traffic was heavy. The revellers were already out in force. Stag and hen parties turned the streets into one great big fancy-dress do at weekends. A man dressed as a giant banana was talking to a group of girls wearing white T-shirts, candyfloss wigs and pink fluffy scarves. A man dressed as an onion was shouting at his friend, another banana, to hurry up.

Leeds was so small in comparison to London that Jake noticed the contrasts more easily here. Things were in closer proximity to one another. Side by side, they were more visibly in his face. As Jake looked at banana man and onion man, who were clearly drunk, he thought about how close they were to the place that had spawned suicide bombers; those who claimed they hated alcohol, music, women, money and capitalism. Jake wondered what Wasim would have said when he passed a scene like this just a few months ago on a Friday, the Muslim holy day. What would he have said on the day of prayer after a week of making explosives – explosives to blow exactly these sorts of people up?

Jake suddenly felt an affinity with banana man and onion man. They stood for the things he did. Life was for living, having fun.

'We going the right way, Lenny?' asked Jake. Lenny had the map book open on his lap.

'Yeah, up here. Keep going straight. Up toward the brewery.'

They spotted the bright green and red signage of the Al Siddiq supermarket and parked in a road opposite.

The place was enormous and surprised Jake. Fresh fruit and veg were displayed in huge pallets outside on the pavement, watched over by Pakistani men who wore sandals with no socks. Loose, un-lidded bins overflowed with commercial waste and the street was strewn with rubbish. Inside were rows and rows of tinned produce with men stacking shelves down every other aisle. The lack of chilled cabinets, dearth of female staff and complete absence of an alcohol section all felt strange and unfamiliar to Jake.

Jake spotted Shahid before he'd even got through the door. He'd made sure to memorise his photo off the report Lenny had found. He was difficult to miss, a big, muscular bloke like that. There was something different about this fella, thought Jake. He noted straight away that he was wearing a lime-green Pakistani cricket top with a Pepsi logo emblazoned across the width of his chest.

'Yes, sir. What can I do for you?'

'DI Jake Flannagan, police. We spoke on the phone. We need to talk in private,' said Jake, intentionally not checking his name first. He wanted Shahid to realise that they already knew what he looked like to put him on the back foot straight away.

Jake noted how, all of a sudden, the bulk of the sockless shelf stackers disappeared. He wondered if some of them were wary of their immigration status now that the police had turned up.

Shahid ushered them into a small, windowless office at the back. It was clad in pine that someone had applied some sort of dark stain to. There was a desk with chairs, and two large, pale-grey filing cabinets stood in the corner.

Shahid motioned for Lenny and Jake to sit. Lenny knew better than to sit. He knew the drill. He stayed by the door so there could be no swift exit or entrances for anyone.

'Can I get you a drink? Perhaps some mint tea?' Shahid asked

'No, we're fine. Thanks.'

'So how can I help you?' Shahid said as he sat behind the desk.

'We're investigating the London 7/7 bombings; I want to know how you knew Wasim Khan.'

'Oh, yes, terrible thing that's happened there.' Shahid sounded calm and respectful. 'But I don't know him.'

'You sure about that?' asked Jake.

'Yes,' replied Shahid.

'That's an interesting response...' Jake realised that this might be a long night. And no one knew that he and Lenny were there. They hadn't asked for any approval or sign off for this and they hadn't left details of where they'd gone. They were there on a whim, without backup. Then again, if he was going to have it out with this fella, the office was as good a place as any. He needed the seclusion from prying eyes just as much as Shahid did.

87

Jake sat opposite Shahid. Shahid leaned back in the large, leather-backed office chair to put his hands behind his head and his feet up on the desk in front of him.

There was a long pause.

'Do you have children, Shahid?' Jake glanced back at Lenny; he wanted Lenny to know something was coming.

'Yes, I have two boys, why do you ask?'

'When one of your boys has done something wrong, would you know what that thing was, totally, before you bothered to go and speak to them about it?'

'Yes,' replied Shahid nonchalantly.

'So when he lied to your face, while looking you in the eye, you could challenge him?' Jake put on a deliberate, fake smile. He hoped Shahid could see just how false it was.

Shahid said nothing.

'So that when the little fucker lied to you, you'd be ready to reprimand him? Ready to smack him?' Jake had never smacked his kids but he knew plenty of people that did.

'I probably would, yes.'

'What makes you think I would come here without knowing things before I talk to you, Shahid? What makes you think you can look me in the eye and lie to me?'

Shahid crossed his legs on the desk. They were on his turf. He was showing them that this was his domain and he could do what he liked. That he thought he was still in charge.

'If you have questions to ask me then ask me,' he replied.

There was an arrogance about this man. He was arrogant in a way that Jake had previously seen whilst working with suspects on the Organised Crime Group. Arrogant like, 'I'm better than you and you can't touch me.'

But on this job, interviewing friends and family of the bombers, Jake hadn't yet seen anyone quite like this. This man was a very different sort of Muslim.

Jake was used to the interviewees being helpful, humble, meek.

Then it clicked: it was bravado. His tone, his manner – bravado to cover his lies.

Victims often act one way. Witnesses act another way.

And suspects trying to cover their tracks acted like Shahid.

'I've asked you two questions already, Shahid. And neither of your two answers I'm satisfied with. The first question I know you're lying about, and the second one all you've done is ignore.'

'Now hang on.' Shahid took his feet off the desk and leaned forward.

'No, Shahid, you fucking hang on.' Jake stood up abruptly. His chair caught the back of his legs and fell backwards onto the floor with a crash. Jake's voice was a half shout.

It caught Shahid off guard.

Because of this guy, they'd missed the early Friday-night getaway. Every time Shahid insisted to them that he didn't know Wasim, some more of Lenny's sixty-five hours with his wife would be eaten into.

Jake was getting pissed off. Still standing, both arms resting on the desk now, he leaned over and stared Shahid directly in the eyes. 'I'm going to give you one last chance, Shahid. Answer me like you think I'm some sort of fucking idiot again and you will be *really* fucking sorry.' Jake's words were resolute and purposeful. He asked very slowly and deliberately this time. 'I want… to know… how you… knew… Wasim?'

'I didn't.'

Jake had had enough. Shahid wasn't going to tell the truth unless he put him under real pressure. He had to bluff it. But he was also banking on the fact that no one who was actually guilty had ever called him on a bluff.

He had nothing concrete except the phone records, and a complete and utter feeling of being given the runaround by someone who was clearly lying to them. But he couldn't reveal what he knew. You hold back your kings and your aces. You play your fours. Just like in poker, he reminded himself.

He needed Shahid to think that they knew everything, without him finding out that they only had some phone links.

Jake glanced at the door. Lenny was acting like a bouncer. Shahid was cornered.

Neither he nor Lenny would now get home at a reasonable hour that evening, which made him angry but, equally, his aim was to use that anger to full effect in playing a part. It was all he had left in his armoury.

He stood up straight, to his full height, all the while looking Shahid in the eye. Then he picked up his notepad and, with huge force, slammed it down on the desk, bellowing in the loudest voice he had. 'For fuck's sake! Right, Len, I've had enough of this wanker! I've given him his chance. Ring London! Get the custody suite ready. We can keep him down south for a month! He can decide down there what lies to tell!'

Shahid looked alarmed. He obviously wasn't used to the sight of a Metropolitan Police copper with a Cockney swagger getting loud and unpleasant in his office on a Friday evening. He was clearly very unsettled by it. His demeanour changed instantly.

'But I can't go down to London. I'm giving Dawah. Me and my brother in Bristol this weekend!' he said anxiously. 'My voluntary work. It's all planned. There's ten of us going. I can't be in London. We're staying at the mosque over there. It's all arranged. We're doing our neighbourhood visits.'

Jake knew he had no authority to arrest him. He was making his own luck here, but it seemed to be working. He grabbed his handcuffs and swiftly moved around behind the desk as if to arrest Shahid, but just before Jake made contact with him, Shahid threw his arms up in the air.

'Stop, look I didn't know him. He just used to visit someone that I rent a room to!'

Fuck me, that worked, thought Jake.

Jake and Lenny exchanged glances. If there was really nothing fishy here, why would he have covered that up?

'Right,' said Jake. 'Get up. Follow my good detective sergeant to our car. Take us to this friend.'

'Err, well, he's done a runner. I can't take you to him,' replied Shahid, shifting uncomfortably in his seat.

'Where's the place you used to rent out to him?'

'I've got a sandwich shop. There's a flat above there.'

'Right, Len, you're driving,' shouted Jake as he chucked the car keys at Lenny.

They marched Shahid out of the office and through the supermarket to the car parked across the road.

'You're in the back with me, mate, *with* the handcuffs on,' said Jake.

Shahid might have lost some of his front, but Jake had no intention of dropping his.

88

Shahid was quiet. He spoke only to give a rough indication of where the flat was located. Jake was glad he'd put the handcuffs on him. It was still a game of cat and mouse and Jake had to show that he was in control. Shahid could still be dangerous, even if he was looking fairly worried.

And look worried he did. Jake watched as a bead of sweat danced its way down his face and onto his lip. As they got into the back seat of the vehicle, Jake moved toward Shahid, pushing him right across the vehicle and against the car door, behind the passenger seat on the other side. The child locks were on in the back; they couldn't be opened from the inside. Shahid was trapped.

You always sat prisoners behind the front passenger seat, not behind the driver. Jake had learned that the hard way when still in his probationary period as a uniformed constable. He'd arrested a shoplifter; she'd been playing the buy-one-get-one-free game at Asda. On the way to the station, Jake had sat the shoplifter behind Stan, the officer driving the patrol car. The shoplifter hadn't been handcuffed and had been chatting away happily the whole time. Halfway there, the woman had suddenly gone crazy and grabbed Stan round the throat from behind. Jake had been too slow to stop her; their vehicle had left the road and hit a lamp post. Luckily it was just the car and the lamp post that had been hurt, but Stan blamed Jake for the mistake and refused to work with him ever again.

Jake had six months in the job versus Stan's twenty-two years, but he still got the blame. She'd been his prisoner and he had been sitting next to her.

All three of them could have died that day. He never forgot that lesson from the panda car.

Looking across at Shahid, Jake couldn't help but wonder what this bloke had done. Finding out what that thing was – that was going to be hard work.

Shahid directed them to a pay-and-display, council-owned car park.

'The room is in there, above the sandwich shop,' Shahid said, pointing with both handcuffed hands to a large, external staircase that ran from the car park up to some first-floor flats above the retail units.

They got out of the car, climbed the wrought-iron stairs and passed through a shabby wooden door that was unlocked. The place smelled of cooking fat. The beige carpet underfoot was filthy, black and sticky in places.

'That door there, Wasim knew the guy who used to live there,' Shahid said, indicating a blue door with the letter 'C' on it.

Jake knocked on the door and a short black guy with a goatee beard answered. The stench of cannabis almost knocked Jake out.

'Yeah? Whadda ya want?' asked the black guy.

'I need you to step out of the room and go and wait downstairs for me, mate,' said Jake, flashing his badge. 'Police business. Nothing to do with you – it's the room I'm interested in.'

Lenny took hold of the black guy and led him down the corridor. Jake and Shahid were alone in the room. He told Shahid to sit on the bed.

Jake glanced around, taking it all in. It was just one large room containing a double bed, two wardrobes, a chest of drawers and, in the corner, a weightlifting bench. The carpet was light grey with a deep pile.

'Where's the bathroom?' Jake asked.

'Shared bathroom down the hall,' replied Shahid.

Jake stood in the middle of the almost bare room, his arms crossed, his back to Shahid. Lenny had returned and guarded the door.

Opposite Jake were three massive double windows that looked out over the road at the front of the property.

Across the road he could see children in a playground, avoiding the calls from their parents to come in for their consecutive teas.

The sun was getting lower in the sky. It generously shared its last warm rays across the patchwork of hand-shaped leaves belonging to the horse chestnut trees that towered over the park.

Jake knew that Wasim had frequented this area of Leeds often, according to the cell-site data they held on his mobile calls, but so what? What did that prove? That Wasim came here for the pleasant view? Surely not, thought Jake.

He desperately needed some evidence, yet despite it being a large room, it was pretty much empty. There was nothing to go on.

What the fuck have I got myself into now? thought Jake as he stood silently bereft in the middle of the room. Was this just another dead end? Like the trip to see Shaggy had been? The confused look on the old man's face after they'd kicked his door down in Sheffield jumped into his head.

The room was bare and stark, a far cry from all that junk piled high in Victoria Park. He remembered Geoff, the EXPO's words, 'Rather them than me in that small place with a load of explosives equipment... What if it all went up in one go? What sort of idiot assembles all three parts of a bomb in one tiny flat?'

Jake looked over at Shahid, who was still sweating.

Why was Shahid so worried?

Jake felt that he had few options here. Either he had to nick him or, well, there was no plan B.

Staring out of those large windows, it occurred to him that the curtains looked brand new, whereas the rest of the room looked tired and worn.

New drapes? Jake went over and touched the heavy, blue-velvet curtains. They didn't look like they had been used at all. There were no net curtains.

He wondered if parkgoers got a nice view in from across the road when the lights were on inside the flat.

And then he saw it.

89

There, on one of the white, UPVC window frames. One small piece of roughly torn, off-white masking tape.

It was stuck to the right-hand edge of one of the frames.

In all the places Jake had ever seen, in all the places he'd ever searched during his entire career, he'd only ever seen masking tape stuck to one other window frame.

'I want you out! I'm seizing control of this room! Gimme the keys. I want every set of keys there are!' he shouted.

Lenny looked at Jake, totally bemused.

'What's up, guv'nor?'

'I'll tell you later. You won't believe me. Take our friend down and put him back in the car. I need to make some calls.'

Lenny pulled Shahid to his feet and led him out of the door.

Jake pulled out his mobile and called Denswood to explain about the masking tape he'd found.

'And that's the basis for you saying it's a bomb factory?' Malcolm Denswood laughed down the phone.

Jake took a deep breath. 'Sir, it's got a theory behind it. Look, when Wasim and his team had been cooking up explosives in the Victoria Park flat, we know they'd had to keep the windows open because of the fumes. The chemicals were so strong that all the paint had blistered on the window frames and the hedges outside had died. To stop passers-by peering in, they'd taped the net curtains to the window frames. They

279

used masking tape to do that! We saw the masking tape at Victoria Park in the same place. This room is no different! And the bloke's a liar. I don't know why, but he's worried sick about something.'

'You want me to send a forensics team on a hunch?'

Denswood wasn't backing down, but nor was Jake. 'I'll take whatever resources you can give me, sir,' he replied.

'Look, I'll send you one bloke. That's all you're getting. And Jake – think yourself lucky. It may have escaped your notice, but it's a Friday night, for Christ's sake!'

90

Jake's one forensics guy had arrived. Rick Benson wasn't particularly happy about being sent up from London on a weekend's wild goose chase to Leeds. Jake made him swab the room several times.

At the third time, Rick sighed loudly. 'What are you hoping to achieve from this?'

'I want it all swabbed. Again. Thoroughly. I want to know if there are fingerprints and explosives in here. If we find any other fingerprints in this room, they might be other potential bombers.'

'But it's too big to swab properly and it's too bare. There's nothing in here that's of any use to us. You can want all you like, but you won't always get it. It's almost two months after the event. Some other bloke's been living here since then.'

'What about the carpet?' asked Jake. 'What about taking all the carpet up?'

'What is that going to prove? How does that move this investigation on?'

Jake rolled his eyes at Rick's lack of enthusiasm for the job in hand. 'Look, we've found one bomb factory but a bomb consists of different parts: the main charge, the initiator, a power source and a trigger. If you're properly trained, you'd never manufacture or store each of the parts in the same place because it's just too dangerous. You'd construct the different

281

parts in different places and keep all the parts separate as long as possible. It's common sense. They've been up to something in here. Shahid is a liar. I want to find out what's in that carpet.'

Rick wasn't convinced. 'Mate, the carpet won't fit in my van. I've been told this is a low-key search. You're out on limb here. It's a load of old bollocks. No one is giving this any significance.'

'I want to know what's in the carpet,' repeated Jake.

He remembered that he'd once spilled emulsion paint on a brand new carpet back home. He knew at the time that Stephanie would go through the roof; it had only just been laid. So he'd wet down the carpet, then put a damp flannel on the back of the hoover instead of attaching the bag. When he'd vacuumed, he'd caught everything in it and most of the paint had come up, thank God!

'We need a hoover,' said Jake, 'here's some cash. Go and get me a hoover. Let's see what's been in here.'

When Rick returned from his shopping trip, they vacuumed one square metre of the carpet together, and Rick took a Pandora's box of dust back down to London with him.

91

Jake gripped his coffee mug tightly between his hands in an attempt to bury his frustration. He sat in a small office on the second floor, looking at the TV screen, his notepad and pen beside him. His mug held just water, which he sipped at regular intervals, trying to fight off the dehydration from another hangover. It wasn't working.

The meeting room in London appeared to be bursting at the seams. There were people stood on all sides of the table and not enough chairs to go around.

'We're currently looking at all the slack space for anything of use, sir,' continued one of the forensic computing geeks in London.

Lenny began to giggle.

'Slack space – you've seen plenty of that, hey, Jake?' whispered Lenny as he nudged Jake with his elbow.

'Forgive me for sounding stupid, but what exactly is slack space?' asked Denswood.

'Well, lots of people in the police who know nothing about computers and how they work mistakenly believe that once a file is deleted on a drive, it can't be recovered. In fact, all that happens is that you delete the filename and the ability of your computer to find it again. Any information in the file remains there, on the hard drive as before. That means that the space is open; it's slack. Sometimes even when the space is overwritten with something else, another file, we can still see fragments of what was there originally. Does that make sense now for the novices?'

The computer geek sounded a little too smug to Jake's ears.

'And how long do I need to allow you to look into this slack space before you can tell me if there's anything decent in there?' asked Denswood, sounding slightly annoyed. He didn't like the tone of the condescending PC nerd either, thought Jake.

'We currently have seventeen drives, sir. That's an awful lot of slack space to be looking at...'

'Do you need more manpower?' asked Denswood.

'Each file, each space needs to be looked at and assessed individually. Of course, more people would us help, sir.'

'How many do you need? Ten, twenty? Just tell me. We need to move on with this stuff.'

'I need to look at how much capacity we have currently and come back to you later today, sir. Is that OK?'

They were no further forward and Jake had gleaned little else from the others who spoke throughout the rest of the meeting. It seemed as though everyone was literally looking into slack space. Things were limping along listlessly. The MIR was churning out actions; various small teams were going through them and sending them back to the MIR, only to generate yet more actions back from them.

'Have you got anything to add, Jake? Have your team found anything of note?' Denswood barked over the video link, startling Jake.

'Yes, sir. I have a question. I'd like to know if the stuff we hoovered from the flat above the sandwich shop has been submitted for analysis yet by exhibits?'

'Yes, Jake. It's been sent off. We're awaiting the results,' replied Ian, the exhibits officer.

'You're still convinced this was a bomb factory, Jake?' asked Denswood. 'Have you made any progress with owner of the place yet?'

Jake took a sip from his mug of water. His throat was dry.

'Yes, sir. I am still convinced. The more I talk to Shahid Bassam, the more I dislike him and the more holes I find in his account. What he's trying to cover up with those lies is a different question.'

'Like what? Give me an example of the lies,' asked Denswood.

'I'm still looking at what he's said and pulling it apart. He claims that he first met Wasim by chance outside a mosque one day. That's a lie. The phone records show that they were in contact for quite some time prior to the date when he claims they initially became acquainted. There are other inconsistencies but I'm working on how to prove them at the moment. It sounds minor, I know, but, well, I don't like him.'

'I need more than a hunch, Jake. Let's wait and see what comes up on the forensics. Thank you, all. Same time again next week please.'

92

It was video link time with London again. Jake turned on the monitor and camera. Someone at the other end accepted the video call and the TV screen filled with a blurred image. The cameras took a while to warm up and the picture remained fuzzy for some time after the screen came on. He could see hordes of officers beginning to traipse into the meeting room at Scotland Yard.

Someone had left yesterday's newspaper on the table. Jake thumbed through it. The front page was dominated by a photo of a devastated New Orleans. Hurricane Katrina had caused a storm surge. At least 80% of the city was flooded, and thousands were believed to be dead. It was being reported that law and order had completely broken down and people had to fend for themselves. There were complaints that the US government was doing very little. Michael Jackson had indicated that he was going to launch a charity single to help.

On an inside spread, Jake spotted a photo of Wasim Khan. There was an article about his suicide video, which had been broadcast by Al Jazeera TV.

The meeting started as Jake was still reading.

'Good morning all,' announced Denswood. 'Let's get straight into this, I've got a lot on today. I'm assuming you've all seen the video of Wasim Khan on the news? If you haven't, the MIR has a copy. There are no surprises contained within it, to be quite honest. He talks about the reasons he decided to martyr himself. Iraq, Afghanistan and Palestine are all mentioned. It's the sort of thing we've seen before, created by other suicide bombers on the internet. We've had people looking at it for clues as to where it was made. Initial assessments are that it was filmed in Pakistan at some point between November 2004 and February 2005.

'The video has been released by al-Qaeda's media arm and uses their graphics. Take from that what you will. What strikes us as odd is the length of time that they've left before releasing the video. It could be that they were just waiting for the dust to settle on the blast sites... Next item: DI Flannagan. I believe that Ian from exhibits has some news for you. Ian?' Denswood paused.

Jake closed his newspaper.

Ian cleared his throat and took the stage. 'Yes. The hoover contents from the flat above the sandwich shop. The results have come back. We were looking to see whether the sample tested positive for any form of explosives. In particular *some* trace of hexamethylene triperoxide diamine, otherwise known as HMTD. HMTD is highly explosive. It's mainly used for initiators as it responds well to shock, friction and electrostatic charges. It would be very easy to set off a bomb via an HMTD initiator using a nine-volt battery like the one Asif Rahman purchased in Boots before he blew himself up on the bus. The hydrogen-peroxide-based explosives we found at the Victoria Park flat would have needed an initiator. HMTD would have been highly suited to this purpose...'

Jake realised he was holding his breath.

The exhibits officer continued, 'We normally find HMTD traces in quantities measured in micrograms, but in this case, we didn't...'

Jake's heart sank.

'No. This time we found something very different. In this case we've found it in milligrams. To explain, that's a thousand times more HMTD explosive than we would normally expect to find. To put it another way, there was enough explosives residue from that one, single square metre of carpet to blow up the whole street. Frankly I'm amazed the hoover alone didn't set off an explosion!'

There was a collective gasp from all those listening on the video link.

Jake felt a mixture of excitement and elation.

'Well done. Now how are we getting on with the owner of this property?' asked Denswood in a flat, emotionless, tone. He seemed wholly unimpressed by this news.

'Thank you, sir. Well, I've spoken with him a couple of times. He's constantly changing his story about what happened. He's going to admit he's lied, I think, and possibly that he's disposed of evidence. I think we should arrest him, sir.'

'Do you think he's directly involved in the plot, Jake?'

Jake paused. He ran through all the possible pieces of evidence he knew about the flat. The text messages between the bombers that he'd read; the phone data that he'd pawed over. It all said Shahid wasn't the mastermind behind the bombings. But the look Jake had seen in Shahid's eyes, the feeling in his gut when the man spoke to him, Jake knew there was something more to this whole thing.

'I don't think so, but he's hiding something. Whatever he's hiding is important…'

'What makes you think that he's going to say any more to you while under arrest and in interview, Jake? If we arrest him and take him to Paddington Green, what incentive is there for him to tell the truth then?'

'It's not so much about him telling the truth; he isn't doing that even now. It's more about getting under this bloke's skin. Finding out what he has to hide, what he keeps in his house, the books he reads, what's on his computer, if he keeps porn mags under his mattress. We need to know what makes him tick; we need to make our own luck. Arresting him gives us those options, the opportunity of turning something up.'

Jake had finished making his plea. There was a lull.

Denswood didn't speak immediately. He was thinking.

'Hmm… I'll talk to the Security Service, see what they know about him, get their views on it, but I'm of the opinion he's more useful as a witness than a suspect, unless you can convince me otherwise, Jake?'

Jake hated this about the Anti-Terrorist Branch. In any other area of policing, they would have had Shahid banged up in a cell, sweating, while Jake rifled through everything he could get his hands on from his home, his place of work, his car. No one was that good; they all left little clues behind about what they were really doing. They could swear blind to your face, but they normally slipped up somewhere along the line. Jake could always find something of interest if he looked hard enough. But this wasn't any other place...

'Yes, sir,' he sighed.

Denswood moved on.

93

Jake and Lenny parked on what looked like a recently relayed, block-paving drive. A white Transit van faced the large bay window of the 1930s semi. Two stickers were visible on its rear doors; one a St George's flag and, next to it, one proclaiming 'English by birth, a Gooner by the grace of God.'

Jake knocked at the pillar-box-red front door. A broad, bald-headed man answered, wearing a black sweatshirt, stone-washed blue jeans and white trainers.

Kenny Savage was thirty-five-years old. Jake had done his research before contacting him. Kenny had a criminal record that included two assaults, one transgression for pitch invasion at Arsenal and a penchant for protesting outside of mosques. He was said to have links to the British National Party.

'Good morning, you must be Mr Flannagan?' Kenny extended his hand toward Jake to greet him. Jake was surprised at how well spoken Kenny was. He didn't sound at all like the fascist, right-wing, football hooligan that Jake had been expecting.

The two men shook hands. Kenny stood to one side of the door and ushered Jake and Lenny inside. In the hallway was an expensive-looking mahogany side table below a crystal-framed mirror. The carpet was a rich, dark burgundy with a luxurious feel. The place was plush, thought Jake, as Kenny showed them into the living room.

Kenny gestured for them to sit on a large, white, leather settee.

'Can I get you a tea or a coffee, gents?' asked Kenny.

'Coffee, white, three sugars for me please,' said Lenny.

'Haha, a man after my own heart, sir,' came the reply.

Jake didn't normally accept drinks from people who'd had run-ins with the Old Bill through fear that they might spit in it, or worse. But Kenny seemed quite civilised and pleasant. Why not?

'I'll have a tea, please. White, one sugar,' replied Jake.

'Give me two seconds,' said Kenny as he made his way to the kitchen.

Jake looked around at the meticulously arranged living room. Cream walls, a huge blush marble fireplace with large orange crystals in the grate. Photos of an attractive blonde woman in her thirties and two young girls sat on the mantelpiece above. The place smelled of upmarket, lavender air freshener.

A few minutes later, Kenny returned holding a tray with three mugs and a selection of foil-wrapped chocolate biscuits in a variety of different flavours.

'Blimey, we don't get treated this well by anyone,' quipped Lenny.

'Happy to help you gentleman as best I can. Even if it's just with a few biscuits,' said Kenny as he passed out the cups and sat down in a white leather armchair opposite them.

'So you said on the phone that you wanted to talk about Shahid Bassam?'

'Yes, you were listed on the files as a witness to the incident in which Shahid Bassam was assaulted. The crime report is a little bland. It simply says that you were demonstrating near a mosque in the East End about the spread of Islam, which you disagreed with. Shahid Bassam was nearby and, after a short altercation, your friend punched him in the face. But there was nothing further on the report. Can you tell us anything else about the incident?' asked Jake.

Kenny cradled his mug in both hands and leaned his huge frame forward toward the two officers. 'Well, there is a bit more to it. I'm sure the report said that I'm a member of the BNP. I am, but don't share all of their views. I'm part of a group that's splintering off from the BNP. We are against the Islamification of the UK. We're based around firms within football supporters' clubs. We're patriots who think Islam is wrong.

'That demonstration was about them building a huge, great big, mega-mosque on that East End site. Seventy thousand Muslims they'll have worshipping up there. The boys at the Inter City Firm of West Ham are up in arms about it. How can you build a mosque that size? That's bigger than St Paul's Cathedral for fuck's sake. That's bigger than Old Trafford! We can't have that!

'I've grown up here. I've got two beautiful girls, a wife and a family. I don't want my kids growing up in a society where they might be forced to wear a burka.

'Great big mosques mean more Muslims moving into the area. The place becomes a ghetto, hundreds of them living in the same house. Illegal immigrants from Pakistan and places like that, people who work like slaves for no money at all, in Muslim-only companies. That forces people like me out, forces down the wages in the local economy, the place slowly becomes a slum and the houses end up being worth nothing. The richer Muslims become the landlords. They buy up all the cheap housing stock and bring in more illegal immigrants to work as virtual slaves. It all starts with the mosque. We can't have it.'

Jake was silent for a moment. He thought about Shahid's supermarket up in Leeds and the men with no socks; the men wearing sandals who'd all scattered when he'd arrived.

'OK. I'm not sure I buy into your apocalyptic view. Tell me why you and your friend had an altercation with Shahid?' Jake asked.

'Look at me. I'm twenty stone. I'm big. I stand out from the crowd. Bassam turned up in his flash Range Rover. I was told by the Inter City crew that he was a bigwig from up north. They'd seen him before. I wouldn't let him past in the road. Stood in front of his car, wouldn't move. He gets out, the flash cunt, all fucking bling, but wearing the traditional Muslim clobber. Comes over to me and says, 'You will never win this fight.' My friend thought he was going to hit me so he just punched him first, straight in the fucking face. Bassam got back in his car and drove into the mosque area – it's just a load of Portakabins at the moment, but it's a huge site. Next thing I know, the Old Bill turn up and they nick my mate.

'They reckoned we called him a Paki. We didn't! I don't give a fuck about him being a Paki. I'd happily live near him, but I won't have him and his type turning huge parts of the country into ghettos. I won't have a mega-mosque that takes over London and dwarfs St Paul's Cathedral. This is a Christian country. If Pakistan is so fantastic, why do they all come here to live? Why not stay over there? They come over here, take our jobs, turn the places they live into cesspools just like where they came from. Why? You tell me, Mr Flannagan, why would they do that? Why should we sit by and watch that happen?'

'You'd happily live next door to a "Paki"? By that you mean Pakistani, Mr Savage, yes?' Jake asked him.

'It's a colloquialism, isn't it? Paki? You know what I mean, don't ya?'

'I tend to call people by their actual name, myself, Mr Savage. Rather than a term which may be deemed offensive.'

'Offensive? What?'

'Well, the term "Paki" could be construed as a racist slur,' said Jake carefully.

'What do you want with me? I'm trying to be helpful! My mate should never have been nicked. That Paki was going to assault me and now you're calling me a racist while eating my chocolate biscuits, which, I might add, are brown like some people's faces. Not my face though, thank God. Imagine that? Fuck no, the thieving, dirty, darkie Paki cunts!' Kenny let out a big belly laugh as he finished his sentence.

Kenny's mask had well and truly slipped. The pleasant, well-spoken man that had greeted them at the door was gone, replaced by a racist, swearing thug.

Jake glanced at his mug of tea. It tasted odd. He placed the half-eaten chocolate biscuit down on the glass coffee table, along with his half-empty cup of tea.

'Listen…' said Kenny '…I'm just winding you up. I know all you coppers think the same as me underneath. You're just not allowed to show it. So I won't say any more about it, OK? You didn't tell me why you were interested in Bassam anyway? What's he done?'

'We just wanted some background on him. Wondered how he had come to get involved in a fracas with "nice" men from Strood, like yourself, up in London, outside a mosque.' Jake hoped he had accentuated the word nice enough for Kenny to see he was being sarcastic.

'Look, I own my own air-conditioning company. I own my own home. I pay my way, pay my taxes, play by the rules. I have a proper family with proper Christian values. My girls are treated with respect in their community. They can go out and work. They can be equal to men. All they have to do is make sure his dinner's on the table at six.

'The Pakis, they come here as a minority, screaming at the top of their fucking stupid voices, and it's us that should fucking fit around them, us that should give way to their demands. Fuck 'em! They can fuck off back home.

'Look what happened in London – 7/7. Fucking shitters, that's what we've got for decades of pandering to these cunts and trying to appease them. I saw this coming a mile off. They start moving into an area and it's like a plague. All the white people's businesses are undercut; they go bust. The Muslim businesses move in. They don't let the money out of their own little circle. All cash, no paperwork, nothing done properly, no taxes and people working like slaves for a pittance…You have kids, Mr Flannagan?'

Jake looked up at the happy, smiling girls in the photo on the mantelpiece and was reminded of his own.

'Yes,' he replied.

'Then I need say no more to you, sir. Your own head will tell you that what you hear from me is right. Would you want a fucking great big mosque on your doorstep? They have hundreds of mosques in the area already. Why do they need a new one this big?'

Jake had heard enough.

'Thanks for your time, Mr Savage.' Jake stood up and walked toward the front door of the house, without offering the man his hand.

As they left and made their way toward the car, Kenny continued chuntering from his front door.

'Shahid Bassam is not what he seems, Mr Flannagan. Look past that polished facade and the nice car!' he shouted.

94

They left the sleepy Medway town behind, as Lenny drove toward the motorway. They were silent. Both thinking about the man they had just met.

'What do you reckon then, boss?' asked Lenny. 'He seemed a nice sort of chap. Successful businessman, runs his own company.'

'Jesus, Lenny, he was like Jekyll and Hyde! Charming and awful all at the same time! The thinking man's thug. He could live next door to you and you might never even know his views.'

'Yeah, but do you think he really called Shahid a Paki during the demonstration scuffles? I could understand why there might be a fight, but what did Shahid mean? "You will never win this fight." What did that mean?'

'I don't know, Lenny. It could mean anything.'

Jake had come away with a nasty taste in his mouth. Was it the tea or the bile spewing from Kenny? This man who had seemed so normal and sensible on first meeting. He made Jake question his own views.

The nice house with the white leather sofa. It could have been Shahid's living room, thought Jake. Shahid Bassam and Kenny Savage were two peas from the same pod in many respects. Neither were what they first seemed.

'I wonder, boss, if Kenny and Shahid aren't so different after all? Two ends of the same horseshoe, perhaps? They both want to keep their wealth and profits within their own communities. And what's wrong with that? Is that racist?'

Jake shook his head. 'I just can't figure him out. Maybe he just has a deep-seated, illogical hatred of anyone new? Anyone who looks different? It felt like an aggressive hate aimed at deliberately stirring up trouble, like rioting football hooligans.'

'Nah,' disagreed Lenny, 'I think it's more about protectionism.'

'You didn't say much in there, Lenny.' Jake looked across the car at his colleague.

'No.'

'Why?'

'Some of what he says I agree with. He's right about some stuff. He's racist, yes, but no more racist than most people. He just says what he thinks. Does that make him bad? I know it's not politically correct and work would sack me for agreeing with him in public but I don't want any more Muslims here either.'

'Don't be stupid. How can more mosques mean more Muslims? And so what if we have more Muslims anyway?'

'I think that's his point, It doesn't necessarily mean more. It just becomes a magnet and the whole area becomes more Muslim. It becomes a concentrated mass in one place. Segregation takes place. It's that segregation that then breeds pockets of extremism. Us and them. I don't want them on my doorstep either, mate...' Lenny tailed off.

They sat in silence. Jake closed his eyes. He slept.

95

The sun had started to disappear below the headland as Jake had passed Launceston on the A30. He had driven the last forty minutes in the dark whilst listening to a crackly phone-in show on a regional radio station. As he drove westwards in the warm car, local voices were thrashing out the case for Land's End to be the first UK stop on the Olympic torch relay.

The drive down from Leeds had taken him more than seven hours; he was tired. It had been almost three months since he'd had any real time off work. There was still so much going on with the investigation, but he desperately needed to see Claire, spend some time with her and, truth be told, he needed some space away from the investigation.

It was having a strange effect on him; he couldn't explain it. The more he found out and the more he did, the less he trusted anyone else to do a thorough and proper job on things. It was like they didn't care, like the result didn't matter. As long as they travelled a course, their destination was unimportant. What was the point in that? He'd even begun to question Lenny's commitment to getting the result that mattered. He needed some space.

He'd been trying to call Claire all day but she wasn't picking up. She'd be there by the time he got there, he reasoned. The phone signal was so patchy in places. It faded in and out like the crackly local radio station.

Grade II-listed Travannon House had been built during the 1700s. Stucco rendered and painted white, the building was surrounded by camellias, azaleas and rhododendrons, and could still be seen some way back down the road, even at night.

The property had been owned by Claire's father's family for five generations, but for the past couple of years the eight-bedroom house had been occupied solely by Claire's mother and a housekeeper.

Claire's father hadn't visited the house for more than ten years because of the divorce; a divorce in which alcohol had played a large part. An addiction to spirits had dragged Claire's mother off to an early grave aged sixty-three. The housekeeper had found her in bed on Boxing Day back in 2004, empty bottles strewn across the bedroom floor.

The place was now a £5,000-per-week holiday let. Anne, the housekeeper, lived in an annexe to the rear of the main building and kept the place running smoothly.

Jake pulled onto the gravel drive to the side of the house; the housekeeper's Mondeo estate was the only car there. As he extracted himself from the work BMW, Anne came out to greet him wearing a big smile.

'Good to see you again, Jake! Claire not with you? She driving herself down?' Anne held out the keys to the house in front of her.

'She's not here yet?' Jake asked as he took the keys.

'I spoke to her yesterday. She said you were both coming. I assumed you'd be arriving together,' replied Anne.

'I drove down from Leeds – up there working. Claire was in London. The traffic was really bad. Lots of sheds on wheels. Maybe she's just caught in traffic? She told me she was leaving first thing in the morning, but maybe she left it a bit late?'

'Probably. The heating isn't on in the main house because it's been really sunny and warm. There's plenty of wood if you get a bit chilly. Firelighters and kindling are next to the grate in a basket. There's milk, cheese and bread and the usual stuff in the fridge.'

'Great, thanks, Anne,' said Jake as he walked toward the main door.

The house had been lovingly looked after by Anne for years. She'd tried to look after Claire's mother too, but in the end, the house was the only one that had benefitted from the care and attention.

After stowing his bags upstairs and getting a fire going, Jake settled in front of the TV to watch the 9 p.m. news. George Best was in hospital, a group of police cadets had been washed out to sea by a typhoon in China, and the US had killed thirty terrorists in Afghanistan.

Jake tried calling Claire again. This time he got a message saying that her phone was switched off.

The fire was warming the room up. Jake took off his shoes and put his feet up on the sofa as the newsreader explained that George Best had a kidney infection and was in intensive care.

Jake thought about his own drinking. Did he crave it? Did he need it? Not like Best obviously needed it and couldn't stop, not like Claire's mother. Why did he keep drinking? Maybe Bestie was lying in hospital right now asking himself that very same question?

Jake put his head back on the sofa. He'd never met Claire's mother. He'd seen photos of her. She'd been a beautiful lady back in her day. Claire didn't speak about Patricia much. He'd been told that the drinking had become a real problem in the early eighties, after the birth of Claire's younger brother. The toddler had somehow found his way out of their townhouse in London and into the rear garden on his own. He'd drowned in the family's fish pond. Claire had been playing in her room when it had happened. She'd been ten at the time.

When Patricia's drinking became too much, Claire's father had tried to get her help, but he couldn't cope on his own with Claire too.

Claire had moved in with her uncle and his family. Her father had totally immersed himself in his job, and it was agreed that Patricia would go to Travannon House. The place would be closed to lettings and Anne would try to help her quit the booze.

Patricia's isolation only served to make matters worse. Things spiralled out of control. She attempted suicide on more than one occasion. Claire's parents divorced and Claire ended up at boarding school.

300

Claire adored Travannon House. She missed her mother, despite her being a drunk. She hated her father for taking the easy option, rather than trying to look after her and her mother. It was a disease after all. She just needed help. Splitting them all up was never going to do any good.

Jake knew that Claire's move to live with her uncle's family had apparently been a disaster, and Claire had been eager to escape to boarding school.

Jake wondered if Patricia was waiting, like he was, for Claire to arrive. There was a photo of her on the side table by the fireplace. She was stood there smiling with her arm around a very young Claire in a field somewhere; maybe even a field near here, pondered Jake.

He looked around the room. There were photographs of Claire everywhere, yet not a single photo of her younger brother – not one. Jake realised he didn't even know the boy's name. He was never mentioned. Like a dark secret that should never be spoken of. Claire didn't ever mention him. He'd ask her when she arrived.

96

It was getting light when Jake awoke. He'd fallen asleep on the sofa. The embers in the fire still glowed. Breakfast TV was just starting, but the set had been on all night. He looked at his phone. No missed calls. No text messages. No Claire?

Jake got up and walked to the large side door that looked out onto the driveway. Just the Mondeo and the BMW were visible to the side of the house; Claire hadn't made it down? He walked out onto the gravel drive just to be sure she hadn't parked on the grass at the front for some reason. In the early-morning light, a mist hovered on the sand dunes that overlooked the beach. There was no other car.

He went back into the kitchen and tried calling her mobile again. Answerphone. Maybe something had come up at work for her? Surely she'd call and let him know?

He needed a shower and some breakfast. He'd walk down to the beach maybe, while he waited.

Jake arrived back at Travannon House just after 1300 hours. He'd spent most of the morning in St Austell getting some fresh air, and seeing if he could pick up a more reliable mobile-phone reception than that on the beach. He hated being on his own. He'd drunk tea and eaten scones with clotted cream overlooking the harbour.

He was now starting to get worried about Claire. It was unusual. She'd not said anything about being late and had

302

not returned any of his calls. Her mobile was still going to answerphone. He'd managed to get hold of her office whilst he'd been in St Austell. They'd refused to give any information about her at all and wouldn't even confirm if she worked there. Although that was to be expected insofar as Jake's dealings with the Security Service were concerned.

At 1900 hours, Jake collected up his toiletries and repacked his belongings into his bag. Something was wrong. He'd decided to drive to London to make sure she was OK. As Jake walked down the hall, he noticed a photo on the wall. A small boy stood on his own in a garden, in front of a yellowy, London-stock-brick wall. He looked sad. The frame was different to the others. Newer. Maybe that was the younger brother who'd died?

Jake placed his bags in the boot of the BMW. He knocked on the annexe and explained that he felt something was wrong, giving Anne instructions to call him if Claire arrived or was in touch.

He set off at speed. It was nearly three hundred miles to London. He'd try to do it in four hours if he could.

97

Jake walked up the stairs to Claire's apartment. She'd chosen it because she said she could walk to Thames House in fifteen minutes and it was handy for Victoria Station. The block was a newbuild on the corner of Gillingham Street and Wilton Road, lots of curved steel and glass. Jake had put on a suit and tie especially and buzzed all the buzzers for long enough until someone had gotten fed up and let him in without asking. As he reached the third floor, one of the neighbours appeared out of their front door.

'Good morning', said Jake politely to a thirty-something blonde in a tight, powder-blue skirt suit.

Jake had met only one of Claire's neighbours in the past, and this wasn't that one. He was pleased because it meant it wouldn't blow his cover story. He needed to get inside Claire's flat without the usual problems that might be associated with an overzealous boyfriend looking for a girlfriend that had not been returning his calls. These things could quickly be misunderstood.

He'd still not heard anything from Claire. There had been no answer when he'd finally arrived from Cornwall at midnight. The lights on the third floor had been off. Her car was parked in the residents-only bay by the front doors of the block. He'd gone home, waited another night... and still he'd heard nothing.

Jake was carrying a black folder under his arm. The blonde neighbour eyed it warily.

'Can I help you? You're not a resident here?' she asked.

All surveillance and intelligence operatives used cover stories that had to be decent enough to withstand a bit of questioning. This was why, in the folder, Jake carried a false photo-ID card proclaiming to be from Johnson, Brady & Bobb Surveyors. It was old, he'd used it a lot in the past and it had become a bit dog-eared and battered. All the more believable though; these things got better with age.

He opened the folder, which also had pens, paper and a tape measure inside, and made sure that the woman got a good view of these as he searched for his ID. He pulled out the laminated card and held this up fleetingly – just long enough for her to see his photo but not inspect it much further.

'I'm a subcontractor from the builders who put in the balustrades on the stairs when the apartment block went up. Just checking for structural integrity,' Jake said as he replaced his ID and zipped up the folder.

'OK,' she said as she turned and walked toward the lift. Jake watched as her trim figure, hugged by the pencil skirt, disappeared behind the sliding doors.

He waited as the lift numbers counted downwards, then watched from the window until he saw the blue pencil skirt leave the building.

The back section of his folder was secured by another zip, inside which he had a pick gun. A lock-picking set was hidden underneath the papers. He pressured the door to see which locks were on. If the door gave a few millimetres when he pushed it, he would know that not all of the locks had been applied. But there was no give and it felt solid. Claire had obviously not just popped down to the shops when she last left the flat. Both the deadlock and Yale were definitely on.

Jake took out the lock-picking set and pushed two different levers into the mortice on the lower part of the door. He felt the tumblers move. A cheap Italian lock in a building like this? Jake tutted to himself. The lock opened within a few seconds. He placed the pick gun in the Yale lock and pulled its trigger several times, vibrating the lock into the same state as Claire's key would. A second lever opened the door. It had taken less than thirty seconds to get inside Claire's half-a-million-pound flat.

Jake pushed her door closed. The Security Service employed some bright people – but despite all their computer skills, he despaired that they still didn't understand how to make their own homes secure.

He pulled out two sets of latex gloves. As he struggled with putting the second set on over the first, he wondered why the hell they weren't both sitting by the sea together eating fish and chips. Where was she?

Jake made his way down the hallway leading to Claire's living room. Dark solid-wood floors were coupled with panelled doors and fancy ceiling coving. Jake knew that Claire's salary as an intelligence analyst at the British Security Service would struggle to cover just the service charge and the utility bills at this place. He'd always assumed that Claire's father, a banker in the City, was where the money came from. She saw her dad infrequently and he seemed to just throw money at her. Guilt money maybe? Jake had often wondered.

He walked down the hallway and looked into each room. He checked the bathroom; it was dry. No water on the floor, sinks, bath or shower screen. No one had used it this morning. No damp towels, no wet toothbrush in its normal holder.

In the bedroom, the bed was made, with a suitcase next to it. He turned the small case on its back and unzipped it. Claire's clothes for her holiday stared back at him, all packed and ready to go. He zipped the case back up as best he could wearing his two pairs of surgical gloves, and put it back in its original position.

He had a quick glance in the wardrobe and spotted a man's designer suit hanging amongst Claire's clothes. It wasn't one of his. The brand was Armani, nice. Two grand's worth at least. A spasm of doubt gripped him, like a sharp sinus pain between the eyes. Whose was it?

He moved to the spare bedroom where Claire often worked late at night on her computer. She often said that most of what the Security Service knew could be found on the internet, and a lot more. You just had to know what you were looking for and where to look.

Sunlight bounced off a glass-topped desk, highlighting a thin layer of dust over everything. Jake noticed that there were breaks in the dust layer. The new iMac, which Claire had received as a birthday present from her father, was missing.

98

Jake entered the living room, which overlooked a central communal garden. Claire's car keys were on the coffee table alongside her purse and mobile phone.

His heart was thumping heavily.

'Think, Jake, think…' he said aloud to himself.

He remembered a conversation he had had with Claire, some months before the bombings. They'd been drinking cocktails in a bar; they were both slightly drunk. She'd grabbed him, kissed him on the cheek and had said in his ear, 'If something happens to me, just look in the box by the bed.'

He'd laughed it off at the time. Asked her if the computers she worked with at Thames House were likely to blow up. She'd said nothing in response, just smiled.

Jake went back to the main bedroom. There was a white bedside table with a single door; he pulled it open. Inside he found three tatty paperback books, some frayed hairbands, a vibrator with no batteries in it and a porcelain Dusty Bin figure from the 1980s television game show *3-2-1*. But there was no box.

Jake picked up the Dusty Bin figure. It had a slot in his head.

'A box by the bed…? She meant this? A money box?' Jake looked at the four-inch-high figurine in his hand.

He shook it. It was empty. He pulled out the rubber bung from the bottom and looked inside. Nothing. Still holding the

308

figurine, he walked back out into the dark hallway. He checked through the spyhole in the door. The communal stairway was clear; it was time to leave the flat. He pulled the door shut behind him and didn't lock the mortice. He might need to go back.

Claire's apartment block stood on a corner. Immediately opposite the main entrance was a newspaper shop. Jake crossed the road. Within five minutes he was leaving the shop with all of the previous week's CCTV on a DVD.

99

He sat down at his own computer, pushed the DVD tray into the computer tower and selected the CCTV-viewing-software icon.

Within a few seconds, he was watching footage from the previous day. The Asian shopkeeper was selling cigarettes to some kids at 1534 hours. Jake played around with the settings until he found the camera that looked toward the door of Claire's block.

He made himself a coffee. CCTV wasn't always a quick job, especially when you weren't sure what you were looking for. Each frame of film had to be watched, sometimes several times. Claire had been missing for three days. This was going to take some time.

He rewound the digital recording and went back in time to 1900 hours on Sunday night. He'd spoken to Claire on the phone at 1930 hours; she'd said she was just arriving home after finishing up at the office. It was a good point from which to start looking.

At 1900 hours, Jake could see that the parking space, which now held her car, stood empty. At 1918 hours, Claire's silver Volkswagen Golf pulled into the space. Claire got out of the car and went into the main entrance of the block. Excellent. This was a start, thought Jake.

He played the CCTV footage forward at five times its normal speed, slowing it down when he saw movement at the

310

main doors of the block. Each twenty-four hours would take him about five hours to watch. He settled down to begin.

He'd been looking at the CCTV for around sixteen hours. It didn't make sense. He'd seen Claire go in, but she hadn't come out. Jake had even seen himself arrive and leave on the same CCTV, but Claire still hadn't come out. He needed sleep. He threw the pile of washing that sat atop his bed onto the floor and climbed in, fully clothed.

He closed his eyes. The darkness of sleep crept over him. Suddenly he was chasing Wasim's car down the motorway, sounding his horn and desperately trying to make it pull over. Reflected back in the car ahead's mirrors, he could see Wasim looking drunk or drugged as he drove. Jake had no voice. In the dream, he was shouting but no sound came out.

He awoke suddenly. He was standing up in his bedroom holding a jumper in one hand. His bedside table had been knocked over and his lamp was in pieces on the floor. He sat down on the bed, head in hands.

The nightmares were getting worse. More recently they'd started to become physical night terrors. He would often wake to find himself standing, fighting imaginary things in the room he was in or, worse, breaking things. Deliberate drunkenness was sometimes the only way to stop himself waking up.

He began to cry. He wanted it to stop. Where was Claire? What was going on? He lay back down, sobbing to himself, and fell back to sleep.

When he awoke, he was sweating; the clothes he'd fallen asleep in were damp. He thought he had heard Ted at the window, but there was silence. No black cat appeared.

Jake took off his wet clothes and threw them into a heap on the floor. He showered quickly and then sat back at his computer with a black coffee.

He'd been fixated on the idea of spotting Claire coming out of the building, but she certainly was not visible on exit. He'd watched all the footage now.

He'd missed something. Part of the answer was here. It had to be.

If she were dead inside the apartment, he would have smelled her, wouldn't he? It didn't make sense. He'd definitely missed something. He thought back.

What else had stood out?

Jake rewound the CCTV to watch the sections where more than one person had entered or exited the building at the same time. He noticed two men leaving in a white Ford Transit van.

Jake rewound to the section where the two men had arrived at the building. They'd arrived separately. Not together. Very odd. Maybe that's why he hadn't bothered with them on the footage yesterday?

The first man, short, stocky and dressed like a delivery driver, arrived at the building at 0650 hours. Jake watched him use the intercom, whereupon, after a brief discussion, he entered the building. Someone had let him in. Then, less than two minutes later, Jake saw the white Transit van pull up outside and a second man get out of it, before it moved off and parked in a loading bay.

The two men, both dressed in overalls, left the building together on Monday at 0721 hours, the same day Claire was supposed to have left for Travannon House.

He watched the same section of CCTV over and over again.

Presumably, the first man had let the second inside, and a third, the driver, had been waiting in the van. Half an hour later, as the two men exited the building together, they were carrying a red holdall. Jake had not previously noticed it, but the bag looked heavy. Each man held a handle and had a strap over his shoulder. Each time Jake rewound and rewatched the footage, frame by frame, he became more convinced by the obvious weight of the bag. Why did a large, red sports holdall require two men to carry it together?

Claire was only slight; maybe they'd drugged her and somehow fitted her into the bag?

As the two men walked out of the doors, one of them appeared to flick his head. It was an obvious movement as the man left the foyer. Jake rewound and reviewed it again and again. It was more deliberate each time he saw it. The man was clearly indicating something to someone as he came out, with a nod downwards and a jerk of his head to the right. Within a few seconds of the head movement, the white Transit van returned and moved across Jake's field of vision from right to left. It was so fast that you couldn't even see the registration with the naked eye.

Jake needed to get the registration of the white Transit van, but these images were too grainy and the cameras weren't facing in exactly the right direction. He needed more footage from a different angle so he could see the number plates. He grabbed his stuff and left his flat.

Twenty minutes later and Jake was standing back at the entrance to Claire's apartment block.

On foot, Jake began to trace the route that the white Transit van had taken. He walked out past her Golf, still parked in the same spot it had been since Sunday night, wishing he could see her belted safely in the driver's seat. She would be laughing as she always did when, in a mock-stern voice, he graded her useless attempts at reverse parallel parking. But the car sat parked. Abandoned. Idle without her.

He headed up the street toward Victoria. The main road outside was filled with residential houses and high-rises with no cameras. Ahead he saw a bank. As he neared the entrance, he spotted a CCTV camera at the door. The angle looked ideal to catch cars moving up and down the road.

He headed inside, up to the teller sitting behind the glass screen, and asked to speak with the manager. After several minutes, a pale, rotund, forty-something woman in a badly fitting, taupe suit appeared. Her name badge proclaimed her as Sandra.

'Can I help you?'

'I hope so. You're the manager here?' he asked, pointing at her badge and producing his police warrant card with the other hand.

'Yes, what can I do for you?'

'I need to view some of your CCTV footage. The camera out the front.'

'You'll have to request that through our head office. I can give you the form to fill out...' she replied.

'It's a matter of national security, I need to look at it now. I can't wait. I need your help,' Jake interrupted, trying to play upon the gravity of the situation.

He knew the protocols, but the forms, that all took time. He didn't feel that he had the luxury of time right now.

'Follow me,' she said. Jake breathed a silent sigh of relief. Sandra was clearly excited at the prospect of doing something to aid national security.

100

'What is it you're looking for?' asked Sandra, obviously hoping to glean as much information as she could to embroider the story when recounting it back to her mates in the pub.

'Three days ago, Monday morning, 3 October. I need the camera from the corner of your building,' Jake said. 'We are looking for a van...'

The 'we' was deliberate. His way of trying to make it look like it was more than just him.

'...that we think may be involved in some form of surveillance for a terrorist group.'

There was a short gasp from Sandra.

'OK,' she said, as her eyes widened and she became engrossed at looking at the screen.

'It's a white Ford Transit van,' said Jake as Sandra rewound the recording. 'We should be looking at footage from 7 a.m.'

Jake stood over the desk, eyes glued to the screen, as Sandra found the right part of the recording.

Jake knew that the van had travelled from the newsagent toward the bank at 0721 hours. He checked the current time on his phone against both the newsagent and the bank CCTV. They were five minutes apart.

CCTV clock times were as varied as people's watches but, on top of that, British Summer Time and Greenwich Mean Time made things even more confusing when some places didn't alter their clocks. It could be 0613 hours on the bank

315

CCTV and 0721 hours on the newsagent's CCTV and they'd actually both be showing footage taken at exactly the same moment in time.

Sandra wound through the footage to 0700 hours on Monday morning. She played it forward at three times the normal speed. Jake watched as several cars drove up the road; the camera angle was nigh on perfect.

'There!' Jake made Sandra jump as he shouted in excitement on seeing the white Transit van fill the screen. The clock time was 0716 hours. Three men sat in the front of the van, all wearing what appeared to be overalls.

Sandra rewound the images, frame by frame, using a special dial on her controller. Moving images were good except when you needed to read registration numbers, which often blurred as you froze the frame.

'May I?' asked Jake, indicating the chair where Sandra was sitting.

Sandra got up and allowed Jake to sit in the padded, high-backed chair. It was warm from her well-rounded bottom.

Jake moved the dial left and right to toggle backward and forward. You could read some of the registration on one or two frames and then the rest on the third.

'Yes... We've got it, Sandra,' Jake said through gritted teeth.

There was a pen and paper in front of him. He grabbed it and wrote down the registration number. Jake stood up and shook Sandra's hand vigorously.

As he left, Sandra shouted after him, 'Sorry, err... Where did you say you wanted a copy of the CCTV sent for evidence purposes? We keep it for thirty days.'

Jake turned reluctantly, remembering his role. 'Oh, yes... thank you. I'll be in touch about getting a copy. I'll let you know.'

'Glad I could help you,' said Sandra, beaming.

Stood on the pavement outside the bank, he called the Reserve Room. He asked the operator to run a PNC check on the registration of the white Transit van.

Jake never took the Police National Computer as gospel. Sometimes it could be a liability. The force's IT systems were limited. They took the DVLA database and added it onto the PNC. But the DVLA database changed by the second. It was a live database, whereas the PNC was only updated every few days. It was always playing catchup. Jake knew, unlike some, that even at its very best, the PNC was only moderately useful in an investigation.

'Sir, no reports, not lost or stolen, on a white Transit van registered to ABC Van Hire at 44 Mount View, Ilford, Essex. Anything else you need, sir?' asked the operator.

'No, that's great, thanks,' replied Jake.

Jake got in the car and looked up the address in his map book. He could be there fairly quickly on blue lights from central London. This was an emergency, he reasoned.

As he wove through the heavy traffic with the magnetic blue light on the car roof and the two-tone sirens blaring, Jake played out the different scenarios that might greet him at the car-hire place in Ilford.

Always be prepared, he thought.

101

The journey had taken longer than he had expected. There had been no room to get through the traffic. It was edging toward dusk when Jake arrived at Mount View and the vehicle-rental place was closed.

ABC Van Hire was in a small industrial unit; an office with a large enclosed storage area to its right. He pulled up outside the address. The lights were off inside. He'd thought that might be the case. There was only one way to get the owner to an address after hours. He couldn't wait until the morning.

Jake looked up and down the street. There was no CCTV anywhere to be seen and he could see no one inside the premises.

He took out his baton and broke the window in the door with one quick and purposeful swing. The burglar alarm went off immediately.

Jake walked back to his car and called the Yard again. The same operator he'd spoken to earlier answered his call.

'Yes, sir, how can I help?' The alarm was ringing loudly in Jake's ears. The operator could hear it in the background. 'Are you OK?'

'Fine. I'm at that hire place. Just arrived here. It's an insecure premises. Must have had a break-in. Can you create a CAD and send it to the local station? Just explain that I've attended and found the window broken,' Jake continued. 'I need the keyholder here immediately please,' he told the operator.

He waited in his car for about an hour until a grey Mercedes pulled up behind him and a very dark-skinned, Sri Lankan-looking man in a suit got out. The door to Jake's car was open and his magnetic blue light was still on top of the car. The man came straight over to him.

'Hello, I'm Rajid Patel. ABC Hire is my business. Did you find it like this?' asked the man, gesturing to the shattered glass in the door.

'Yes. Actually, I'd come here on an unrelated enquiry and found the window on the door broken. I think my lights and sirens must have scared the burglars off. It's your lucky day, mate,' replied Jake.

'Thank you, it's very kind of you,' replied Mr Patel.

'I'm Detective Inspector Jake Flannagan. I'm from the Anti-Terrorist Branch.' Jake offered his hand to the man. 'I'm looking into a missing-persons case. Needed to look at your files on one of your hire vans.'

Jake felt a slight pang of guilt about what he'd done. Mr Patel seemed like a decent, hard-working guy. He needed this information though, and certain ways and means served a purpose.

Rajid Patel unlocked the door to reception and silenced his alarm with the code. The reception area was small, but there was a large garage attached to the side.

'I should probably go and have a look around to make sure there's no one here, Mr Patel.'

Jake wanted to have a poke around for the white Transit van. He would've needed a warrant from a court to do that normally, but not for an insecure premises or when 'lawfully' accompanied by the owner, however.

'Good idea,' replied Mr Patel, waving Jake toward the garage area.

Jake glanced up and down the rows of vehicles and located the van by its registration. This was good news. He looked through the back windows of the vehicle. No red bag. No obvious signs of blood. He walked back through to the reception area where Mr Patel was waiting.

'No one out the back there – everything looks fine. The van I'm interested in is parked in the garage. I'm going to need to seize it from you, Mr Patel, and take it away for forensic testing.'

It was a statement; he was telling him, not asking.

'I also need to see the paperwork for the person who last hired the van, please.' Jake was feeling reassured that he had made the right decision to break the window. This would have taken another twenty-four hours had he waited until the morning.

He gave the registration of the van to Mr Patel who went looking for the paperwork in a back office. Things were going to be tricky with the Reserve Room from here on in. Jake knew he hadn't followed the right procedures; he'd need to wing it. He called them up to request that the van be taken away for testing and was immediately asked for reference numbers that related to the missing-persons report – a report which did not exist. Fortunately the operator accepted the line that Jake didn't have the documents to hand and complied with the request to simply use his name instead.

The van held a mountain of potential forensic evidence and clues as to what had taken place. Testing it might show up who the men were eventually. Their DNA and fingerprints would hopefully be all over the vehicle. Perhaps a stray hair from the driver's seat, cigarette butts in the ashtray, fingerprints on the mirrors. None of the men had appeared to be wearing gloves in the CCTV footage.

Most importantly, Jake wanted to know if there were traces of Claire in the back of the van. Was she dead or bleeding when they put her in the bag? Had she been struck and injured or even killed in the flat? Or was she still alive?

The forensics would take time though, a few days, a week, some of it maybe months – it certainly wouldn't be quick.

It was the hire record that Jake wanted access to tonight. That's why he had wanted the keyholder, Mr Patel, here, and why he couldn't wait until the morning.

Mr Patel returned with the file.

'Thank you, Mr Patel,' said Jake. 'Please put the file down. Don't touch the paper inside.'

Mr Patel placed the file slowly down onto the desk and looked at it like it might be contaminated with Ricin.

'It's OK, Mr Patel. The documents inside will most likely have fingerprints on them. I just don't want your fingerprints over the top of theirs.'

Jake put on the customary two pairs of surgical gloves as always, then picked up the file and thumbed through it.

The van had been hired under the name of Abdul Mahmood, a 22-year-old male from Ilford. There was a photocopy of a UK driving licence and a phone number at the base of the form. Jake copied the address and phone number onto a spare sheet of paper.

He placed the original paperwork into an exhibit bag and sealed it, just as two uniformed police officers arrived from the local station to escort the van to the forensic examination centre. He thanked Mr Patel and left. He had work to do. He had another lead; a name and an address.

Jake worried very little about the consequences of not doing things the right way, but he knew he was on very shaky ground here. He was supposed to be in Cornwall with Claire on leave. Instead, here he was in London, single-handedly investigating her disappearance and not a soul knew what he was really up to. Yet if he went through the normal procedures, he'd lose days, a week even. Time neither Claire nor he had to spare.

The bosses would pull Jake off the job straight away because of his personal involvement with the subject of the investigation. 'Not professional,' they'd say, and Claire would be dead by the time they'd finished writing the missing-persons report. Yes he was out on a limb, like he always was. But once he'd found her, they'd understand and pat him on the back.

102

The drive to the address on the hire record took less than ten minutes. Normally Jake would have done some research before turning up somewhere, got an idea about the people who lived at the address, had some sort of lead on what he might expect there. Usually he'd run the names through the intelligence databases first, through the PNC and past the Security Service. There was no time for that today.

Warrington Road, the street listed on the van-hire paperwork, was typical of the area: Victorian, terraced and turn-of-the-century. The beautiful period windows had all been ripped out to be replaced with white plastic UPVC and porches. But most importantly to Jake, the small front gardens were poorly concreted over in order to house lots of privately imported Japanese cars. In Jake's world, this was a hugely important nugget of intelligence. A large expat-Pakistani community in Japan made their living buying second-hand cars over there, exporting them via family networks to Dubai and then, in the main, onto extended UK family and friends as grey imports.

Jake parked outside number forty-two and walked up to the UPVC porch. He could see a shoe rack just inside the door that held one pair of men's shoes and several pairs of unused slippers, belonging to owners who were not present.

Jake might not have done any prior research, but there were some things he didn't need profiling databases to tell him. The neighbourhood was predominantly Islamic.

The porch was not locked. Jake stepped inside and banged on the inner wooden door. It was answered by a Pakistani man in his mid-sixties, who wore a white shirt and black synthetic-looking cardigan.

Jake produced his warrant card. 'I'm Detective Inspector Jake Flannagan, Metropolitan Police. I want to talk about Abdul Mahmood...' he began.

The man showed no flicker of expression, but immediately attempted to close the door. Jake was wise to this trick. He'd had it done to him countless times before. He'd already slyly wedged his foot in-between the door and the frame without the resident noticing. The door hit his foot. The man pulled it open and slammed it back again, more aggressively this time. 'Get out!' he shouted at Jake.

Jake pushed the door hard with his hand, knocking the man backwards. He stepped into the hallway, his shoes still on. 'I'm looking for Abdul Mahmood. Where is he?'

There was no response; the man looked confused.

'Your son is Abdul Mahmood? Yes?'

'He was... my son. He is dead...'

'When?'

'Last year, in Pakistan.'

'How?'

'Abdul died in an explosion. Him and his friend – December 2004. I've told the Security Service. I told them we are not interested in their money. Then they threaten us with the police...'

'The Security Service have been here? Why?'

'They tried to recruit his brothers as informants plenty of times. She said they would send the police if we didn't do as they wanted. You don't scare me...'

'December 2004...' Jake stopped mid-sentence; he suddenly realised that the date was significant. Wasim was in Pakistan at that time too.

The old man continued, 'Those are Muslim lands he was trying to protect. I am proud he is dead. His brothers, hounded by the Security Service, are now doing jihad too.'

Jake was frozen. He needed time to think. What was going on here? Who hired the van if it wasn't Abdul Mahmood? Someone using his licence?

'Arrest me or get out of my house!' the old man shouted, scrambling to his feet.

Jake turned around and walked out without saying anything else. The old man slammed the door behind him.

Jake got into the car. He sat there, his brain buzzing. The boy was dead. And so, it seemed, was that line of enquiry; Abdul Mahmood's driving licence was being used by someone else. Another extremist? It was common practice when one went off to fight with the view of not returning that others would use the identity and documents for fraud and scams. It was exactly what Wasim had discussed in Crawley with the Crevice crew. The question now was who'd used it?

Jake closed his eyes, replaying what had just happened with the old man over and over in his head. He looked at his notes. The mobile number for the person who'd hired the van was given on the sheet.

He changed the setting on his mobile to private so that it didn't reveal who he was, and dialled the number shown on the hire form. A generic voicemail message played out.

Pre-pay or pay-as-you-go mobile customers were very difficult to trace. All paid up in advance, there would normally be no details of the subscriber held anywhere.

Jake pulled away from the house. He needed to visit someone who could help, someone who wouldn't blow his cover.

103

Government Communications Headquarters or GCHQ was known by Jake and his colleagues as the Cheltenham listening service because it was their job to monitor radio and micro-wave signals. Mobile phones to them were nothing more than radios at a basic level.

The five thousand staff there specialised in different disci-plines of listening. These days a lot of it was actually visual, which meant they would monitor internet traffic too.

The journey to Cheltenham was slow going. Jake had decid-ed against using his blue lights on the motorway. It was now getting to the point where he didn't want to draw any more attention to himself than absolutely necessary.

Jake remembered driving at top speed with lights and sirens on for two hours solid during his training course, giving a running commentary to the instructor in the passenger seat of what he was doing, why he was doing it, what he'd seen and why he was reacting in a certain way.

For Jake, the commentary became a habit. He found it upped his concentration level when driving fast. He still did it in his head automatically. Sometimes he did it aloud to wake himself up. Especially if driver fatigue was taking hold, like now.

'Approaching hazard. Junction. Mirror. Breaking. Hard. Too fast, Jake. Too fast. Got control of lane one at junction. Traffic stopped. That's a nice arse on the left in the green on the pavement. Good spot, Jake. Control of lane two. Out into lane two. Mirror. Accelerate away from nice arse. Sadly…'

Two hours of driving lay ahead of him before he reached Cheltenham. He needed all the entertainment he could get.

GCHQ was housed in a swish, new circular building. Jake had been there once before. He had been amused to find out its nickname. Brilliant, he'd he thought, the Americans have the Pentagon and us Brits get the Doughnut.

The Doughnut had been open a year. It was the largest building project to house an intelligence agency anywhere in the world outside of the United States, but even then the place wasn't big enough to hold all its staff.

Packed with computer servers holding information and data that had been collected day-in, day-out, each server – and there were dozens of them – could hold a petabyte of data. Just one petabyte was equivalent to eight times the entire word count of the British Library. The electricity needed to run GCHQ's servers alone could power an entire city.

He had met Claire's cousin, Kate Collins, a couple of times. He knew she did something fancy at GCHQ related to picking up signals from hidden ships and anti-aircraft stations. It was maths-based; he didn't really understand it. He remembered chatting to her in the pub once, when she'd been staying at Claire's. As soon as Jake had heard the word maths he'd switched off. She'd gone on about how special she was, about how she'd done this and done that. She was full of herself. Good-looking with a thick mane of very long and very dark brown hair, she spent a lot of time at the gym and on her appearance. She was fit and attractive, but Jake found her terribly dull and boring.

Kate had a confidence problem. Jake had seen it. She was desperate to be loved by a man. Other men saw it too. This meant she had a bit of reputation, according to Claire. Jake had seen her eyes looking him up and down. He'd never mentioned it to Claire.

Kate lived near her father, a retired Royal Navy admiral, on the outskirts of Cheltenham. He'd wanted sons and had made no bones about the fact that he was disappointed in fathering only girls. He'd never spent much time with them as they were growing up. Jake wondered how much that had impacted on Kate's confidence issues and her decision to track down hidden ships with her obviously gifted, maths mind.

It was almost 2300 hours when Jake pulled into the cul-de-sac where Kate lived. The estate had been built in the eighties. Yellow bricks, white UPVC windows and a parking bay in front of the house, with her Ford Fiesta sat in it. Neat and efficient; a bit like Kate herself.

As she answered the doorbell, Jake deduced that she must have just been to the gym from the cropped sports top and three-quarter-length, Lycra leggings she was clad in.

'Jake?' Kate looked shocked to see him.

'Hi, Kate, can I come in? Need to talk to you.'

Kate stood to one side, confused. 'Yes, sure. It's late, what's going on?'

Jake walked past her into the spotlessly clean living room and sat down.

'What's happened, Jake? It's Claire, isn't it? What's happened to her?' Kate's face was ashen.

Jake got straight to the point. 'Claire is missing. I think she's been kidnapped.'

104

'What the fuck?' was all Kate could say.

'She was supposed to meet me in Cornwall. She didn't turn up. I drove back, couldn't find her. To cut a long story short, the last few days I've been retracing her steps. Done my own investigation. I think she was taken from her apartment building by someone in a van.'

Jake decided to leave out the part about the small bag.

'Oh my God!' Kate was visibly shocked.

'I need your help, Kate.'

'Yes, whatever you need. What can I do?' Kate sat down in an armchair across from him in her neat living room and leaned forward with her palms upwards. Jake sensed from her body language that she was genuinely concerned. He needed to know that she really and truly wanted to help before he could move on.

'This is all confidential. I know I can trust you. I don't know who's done this, but it seems that there might be some connection to her work, possibly terrorist extremists. I don't know how they located her address, but they have. It's also possible that someone at her work is involved. We need this whole thing to be kept quiet. Don't let her work know that I know.' Jake omitted the part indicating that no one at his work knew about this either.

'Wow. You think the Security Service has been infiltrated?' asked Kate.

'The van that was used to take Claire was hired using the driving licence of a guy who died in an explosion in Pakistan in December of last year. Someone at the Security Service has been talking to the family; his father told me that. And now Claire's missing. I don't know who I can trust or who or what the problem is. That's why I've come here. It's why, as family, I was going to ask you to help rather than use the official channels at this stage.'

Kate looked down at her bare feet, clearly in thought. She said nothing.

Jake continued. 'I want to know more about who this guy was that died in an explosion in Pakistan. I need you to run the phone number used to hire the van through your systems for me, and tell me what you have on it.'

'It's a big ask, Jake.'

'I know. I don't have many other ideas. I could go back to London, make everything official and hope that someone picks up the pieces quickly?'

'What do you mean official? Have you not properly report-ed her as missing yet?'

Jake sighed. 'No – they'll take me off the case because of our relationship. I can't have that happen. Not when I have leads to follow!'

'Have you checked her mobile phone location with the cell-site data?'

'Her mobile phone, purse and car keys are in her flat. She's not just gone off with someone else… that's not what this is. She's been taken properly, Kate. Kidnapped. They've taken her and her computer.'

'Why her computer?'

'I don't know, maybe she had something on it linked to why they took her?'

'OK. I'll do it.'

'Great. When?'

'Tomorrow morning, when I go in. First thing,' said Kate.

'Can I wait here, maybe stay the night, and you can give me the response personally rather than use phones or email?' Jake didn't want anyone listening in, but he was also tired after the drive and he sorely need to crash.

'Of course. It's a one-bedroom though.' Kate looked him in the eye a little too long as she finished the sentence. It was a mannerism she shared with her cousin. A look he'd seen from Claire many times.

'The sofa is fine, Kate. I snore, so you wouldn't want me to top and tail with you.' Jake decided to make a joke of it to avoid any awkwardness.

Kate laughed. 'Let me grab a shower and some bedding for you. I'm still in my gym kit, for goodness sake!'

Jake watched as the lithe, Lycra-clad figure bounded off upstairs. He heard the water running and smelled expensive bathroom products wafting down in clouds of steam.

Kate returned carrying pillows.

'I have some wine in the fridge. Night cap?' she asked Jake, who was still slumped on the sofa.

She was wearing an indecently short robe and her hair was wet. Jake couldn't take his eyes off her long brown legs.

She leaned over and placed the pillows behind him. He could smell her conditioner.

Jake moved away, twitchy at being so close to her under the current circumstances.

He brought the subject back to Claire to hide his blatant attraction. 'Have you any idea how or why she would get mixed up in something where she'd get kidnapped, Kate? She's just an analyst. Works in the office. I don't get it.'

Kate stood back up with a frown on her face. Jake wasn't sure if it was because he'd moved away or because of the mystery surrounding Claire.

'Analyst? That's... that's not what Claire does,' she said with her hands on her hips, looking at Jake like he was stupid.

105

'But that's what she told me she did for the Security Service...' Jake was confused.

'Look, Claire and I haven't been that close since we were teenagers, never forgave her for that business with my Dad. We don't speak that much really, family get-togethers and things and we've never really talked in-depth about what we do... But you can be sure Claire isn't someone who sits in the office all day. She's field based, doing what I don't know, but she's not an office-based analyst, Jake.'

'What? Really? I was operating under a totally different impression,' Jake said, taken aback. 'So what happened with your dad?'

'She can tell you that when you find her, but she's no angel, Jake.'

'Why would she lie to me about what she does?'

'Claire can be a bit of a stranger to the truth sometimes.'

'The suit in the cupboard?' murmured Jake to himself.

'What?' asked Kate, perking up at the thought of some salacious gossip about her cousin.

'When I went to her apartment, I checked her bedroom. I spotted a man's suit in her wardrobe. Designer. Expensive.'

'And it wasn't yours?' asked Kate, eyes widening.

'It wasn't mine,' said Jake ruefully.

'No way! The dirty slut!' shouted Kate, jumping up and throwing her arms out. 'See! I told you she couldn't be trusted!'

She seemed very excited; bouncy, bubbly, talkative. Maybe it was the endorphins? Had they rubbished that suggestion yet? Was she excited because of the exercise she'd just being doing at the gym or was she just excited that *he* was here?

She was blushing now. Maybe she really likes me, thought Jake. Why hadn't he considered it before? Because he'd thought she was dowdy and boring and now she looked sexy and was showering him with attention? Or because he was having doubts about Claire? About the man's suit in her wardrobe? About why she had actually gone missing?

His eyes were drawn to Kate's body. He made himself look away.

He loved Claire, didn't he? He was sure he did. That's why he was here trying to find her, wasn't it? Or was he simply trying to find her because her disappearance might be connected in some way to the bombings?

The suit in the wardrobe. The stuff about what had gone on with Kate's dad. He couldn't shift it from his mind. It was there, eating away at him. There could be an innocent explanation? He was trained not to jump to conclusions. But Claire had been distant with him recently too. Very stand-offish.

He could handle her having sex with someone else. Mistakes happened. Alcohol played a part. He understood that. He knew all too easily how that could happen.

But the suit in the wardrobe? That was premeditated; malice aforethought, mindful. Not just a physical thing that had happened on the spur of the moment?

'Have you eaten?' Kate asked him, changing the subject with a slight smile.

'Not a great deal, not lately.' Jake wondered if they were talking about food. He hadn't expected this. He was here because of Claire, but he was feeling less and less certain about her.

'You're worrying about her, aren't you, Jake?' she asked. 'Don't. Claire's a grown woman. She can look after herself. She's certainly not the innocent little girl she makes herself out to be.'

Kate's mood had changed. He could see that she had gone from excited to seductive. She moved closer to him, stood in front of him as he sat on the sofa.

'You want something?' Her chin lowered toward her cleavage, and she looked at him through her eyelashes, her gaze lingering too long. It was almost daring him. Where did girls learn how to do that look? There was no mistaking it.

Or was she just trying to distract him from missing Claire?

Her cheeks were rosy from the gym and the hot shower. Her wet hair dripped onto his shirt. The fluffy white robe she had on was held shut precariously with just a cinched-in towelling belt.

He was fighting against himself now. His girlfriend was missing and now he couldn't take his eyes off her half-naked cousin.

It was wrong. He knew it. *But that made it all the more sexy.* Was it revenge he wanted? Would fucking her cousin give him revenge for all the times she'd cancelled dates recently? All the times she'd put the phone down on him? For that suit in the wardrobe?

He shifted uncomfortably in the chair as he felt his erection growing.

'STOP IT, JAKE!' a voice in his head screamed at him.

'What have you got? Anything tasty to tempt me with?' Jake couldn't believe what was coming out of his mouth. If she was baiting him, he was baiting her back. Bad Jake. This was going to end in tears. Eventually.

Kate chuckled and sashayed off into the small kitchen. This was happening. They hadn't been discussing food, had they? Jake was confused.

'Come and have a look and see if I've got anything you fancy!' she called.

Jake lay in Kate's bed, looking at the ceiling. The kitchen floor had become slippery, like their bodies. They'd moved to the sofa, then her bedroom.

He'd ejaculated; all of it inside her.

For a split second, as the oxytocin hormone had coursed through him, Jake had felt invincible. A moment later he had hated himself again. Now, as he lay in bed next to her naked sleeping body, he despised himself more than ever before.

Jake looked at the bedside cabinet. The neon digits on Kate's alarm clock said 0300 hours.

What the hell had he done? He didn't even have the excuse that he'd been drunk. He couldn't remember the last time he'd had sex sober. This had been different. Yet all Jake could think about was Claire.

106

Jake awoke to find Kate had gone. He'd slept through. No nightmares.

The sex? Had that stopped them?

Jake was sticky. He went and showered. As he thought of Claire, his heart sank. He wondered how long Kate would be. Would she get the information he needed?

He flicked on the TV. He would just have to wait.

On Sky News more deaths were being announced in both Iraq and Afghanistan and a UN weapons inspector was comparing Blair and Bush to the Nazis. There was also a report on the first meeting of the London organising committee for the 2012 Olympic Games.

Jake turned over. There was a chat show on.

'Do you really think David Cameron could be the next Tory Party leader?' asked the female host, whom Jake vaguely recognised.

'Michael Howard has bowed out of the leadership race today, recommending David Cameron as their next leader so yes, it's a possibility. And at just 38-years-old he would be a very young Prime Minister, if he were to win the next election, although that is five years away,' replied a rent-a-mouth columnist.

Jake turned the TV off. It was three months since the bombings. The media headlines seemed to have all but forgotten about what had taken place in July. They moved on so quickly, thought Jake. Yet who was he to judge? Here he was, struggling

335

to cope with his girlfriend's disappearance and then having sex with her cousin. Was he crazy? The guilt made him feel sick to his stomach. How had he ended up with Kate? Maybe he'd moved on quickly too?

The latest edition of the *Daily Telegraph* sat on the coffee table in front of him. Jake picked it up and tried to distract himself. There was a splash about raids on the IRA's criminal empire in Manchester. The IRA had denounced its armed struggle against the English ten days previously. The Asset Recovery Agency was pursuing a £30 million property empire alleged to have been built by the group. Was the denouncement because the ARA was trying to take the leader's money? Was the criminality the bigger brother to the armed struggle?

Jake dozed off on the sofa; it had been a short night.

He was awoken suddenly by an excited Kate crashing through the front door. She leapt onto his armchair and sat astride him, kissing him frantically.

'Whoa, tiger! Calm down!' Jake managed to rescue his tongue back from her.

'Hello! I've missed you!' Kate was like an over-exuberant child who'd come bounding in after her first day at school.

He palmed her away. She looked like she was going to cry.

'Before we do anything else, I need to know how you got on today with that phone number?' he said in a measured tone.

Kate smiled. 'I've got a few bits in my bag for you, but it's gonna cost you!'

She backed away, and wriggled her hips as she pulled up her tight, black office skirt, then sat down on the chair opposite the sofa, her legs splayed open wide. She wasn't wearing underwear.

107

They were naked and twisted among the covers and pillows on the sofa.

'At least your makeshift bed is some use,' she quipped as she kissed and caressed his neck.

Jake froze. It was no good. He was torturing himself. He realised he could no longer carry on with this charade. 'I can't do this again, Kate. I'm sorry.'

Jake knew he had to broach the subject of Claire.

'Look, Claire is my girlfriend. This is crazy. I love her. You're her cousin. What the hell are we doing?'

'You think Claire is some sort of saint? That she hasn't been playing around? Plenty of her conquests have hurt me!' said Kate petulantly.

'Is what's happened between us getting back at Claire, then?' Jake started to feel awkward. He stood up and began grabbing his clothes together in a pile. Had it been him that had been used here?

'I know what's happened between us shouldn't have happened. I'm worried about Claire as much as you are.' Kate untangled herself from a sheet and placed her hands on his arms.

'I've always liked you, Jake, and this was my one chance to be with you. I took it. I enjoyed it. Now it's done. I hope Claire is found safe and well. That's why I've put my job on the line to help.'

Kate smiled, but Jake could see the sadness behind her eyes.

'Thank you, Kate,' he said. He appreciated her help. He was just a bit overwhelmed at who this shy girl really was, and how she'd practically thrown herself at him. He felt guilt too at what had happened between them, when he should have been out looking for her cousin.

'What did you find out at work, Kate? I really need to know.'

Kate pulled some handwritten paperwork from her bag. It was just numbers written down. Jake looked at it; it made no sense to him.

Kate let out a deep sigh and shook her head as she watched Jake frown at her handwriting.

'I'm a cryptographer, Jake. It's what I do. Only I can understand what I've written down. If they stopped me with that paper as I left the building, no one would be able to make head nor tail of it,' Kate rattled away excitedly. 'First of all, your man, the one who accidentally blew himself up – Abdul Mahmood...'

'Accidentally blew himself up?' Jake interrupted.

'He and a friend had a little mishap whilst learning how to make peroxide-based explosives at a terrorist-training camp in December 2004 – blew themselves to pieces by accident.'

'Peroxide-based explosives? The same type used in the 7/7 bombings and the 21/7 attempt?'

'Yeah, looks like the Security Service knew what they were up to, well before they left the country for the training camp too... had them under surveillance as they left.'

'What?'

'It gets worse than that... Abdul Mahmood travelled to the terror training camp *with* Samir Shafiq, your failed 21/7 burka bomber. And it seems that someone else was at the same training camp at the same time.'

'Who?'

'Wasim Khan, of 7/7.'

'So both jobs are connected? You're saying 21/7 and 7/7 are linked?'

'Yes.' Kate was smiling broadly. She had clearly done a lot of work and was happy to be showing it off.

'So you're saying that the Security Service had the 21/7 burka bomber, Samir Shafiq, under surveillance *before* he left for a training camp?'

'Yes. They followed him to the airport in a car. There were at least three of them that went to the training camp. The Security Service even asked Special Branch to stop and question them at the airport... Samir Shafiq messed up his story. Said he was going to Pakistan for a wedding and then couldn't name the bride or groom. Idiot – hardly a terrorist mastermind, right?'

'And then two of them, this Abdul Mahmood and a friend of his, messed up during their explosives training and blew themselves up?'

'Yeah. Doesn't sound like their training regime was particularly safe. Or maybe they just couldn't follow instructions? I don't know.'

'What about the phone number, the one that was used to hire the van?'

'Vodafone pay as you go, not registered. SIM purchased in Ilford on 24 May 2005. Never used for outgoing calls. We don't know who owns the SIM or the handset, but I looked at the reverse billings, the incoming calls to that phone. Most of them came from a single mobile that is well known to the Security Service.'

'Who is it? Who was calling Abdul Mahmood's mobile?' asked Jake.

'Mohammed Biaj,' Kate replied.

'Who the fuck is he?'

Kate looked bemused. 'You've never heard of him?' she asked

'Should I have done? Who is he?'

'He's someone who's on the periphery of lots of jobs, has been for some time. He never actually gets his hands too dirty though. He puts people in contact with each other. You want to go to a terror training camp? Biaj puts you in contact with someone who can help with that. He's a facilitator.'

'And it was Biaj that helped Samir Shafiq and Abdul Mahmood get to a terror training camp?' asked Jake, although he could already guess the answer.

'Yes.'

'And the Security Service knows all of this? All this stuff that you've just told me?'

'Of course they do.'

'Wasim Khan, the leader of the 7/7 attack, did he know Biaj?'

'He may well have known him, but I didn't find any direct contact between them when I was looking through stuff today for you. I did notice some third-party connections though. Through the TJ mosque up in West Yorkshire.'

'TJ mosque? What's the TJ stand for?' asked Jake?

'Tablighi Jamaat.'

Jake had heard the name Tablighi Jamaat before but couldn't remember where.

'Why would Biaj be in contact with a mosque up in Yorkshire?'

'He's very active within TJ and Dewsbury is where their European headquarters is.'

'Who are Tablighi Jamaat?' he asked.

'I don't know loads about them. Some people call them the Jehovah's Witnesses of the Islamic world. They're classed in many countries as a sect. Their members travel a lot and go round spreading the word of Allah, or at least their version of it, to other mosques and Muslims.'

'I don't get it. How can Biaj be so well known and operate in plain sight of the Security Service?'

'Really? You can't see how that happens? Come on, Jake.'

'He's an informant.' Jake sighed as he said it. It was obvious.

'That's my best guess, yes.'

Jake began to wonder how Claire had gotten hold of the information she'd passed to him about the 21/7 bombs being made at Sullivan House. How had the Security Service known there was something going on at that place? Had Biaj told them? Told Claire?

After recording the details that Kate had given him in his notebook, Jake kissed her and they said their goodbyes. She looked tearful as he reversed onto the road. It would be a lonely journey back to London, he thought.

108

The Arabian coffee tasted bitter. Jake pulled faces as he sipped it. He added more sugar. It was strong, with a treacle-like consistency, just like it was served in a souk.

He checked the fingerprint and DNA dockets he'd had returned from the forensic examination centre. They'd had the Transit van in the dark and tested it with special lights. No bodily fluids had been found in the back. Fingerprints from various surfaces had been obtained and a cigarette butt from the ashtray submitted for DNA. All good news, but best of all was that they'd found no blood. He'd started to wonder if Claire had got into the bag voluntarily. How else could they have got her in there?

Jake was sat in a café on the corner of the market on Green Street. It was a few hundred yards from West Ham football stadium, a structure that dominated the skyline. At the end of the road, Bobby Moore was immortalised in bronze, held aloft by his teammates in a scene following England's 1966 World Cup victory. The statue had only been there a few years.

Queen's market was a seventies monstrosity; a covered area where local traders held a daily market selling meat, fish, leather goods and colourful head scarves. The council was threatening to close it down, but the locals were fighting against it.

The council said that no one paid their rent or rates there. They wanted redevelopment – luxury flats and a smaller market. The place was rife with poverty. There was already talk

341

of West Ham relocating to the Olympic Stadium after the London 2012 games.

The 1966 Bobby Moore from the end of the road wouldn't recognise this place. In his heyday it had been full of Jewish traders from the East End selling vegetables and clothes. Today all the locals emanated from the Indian subcontinent and parts of Africa.

The place was packed with people shouting, bartering and negotiating. Jake caught a few snatched words of Urdu.

He was eternally grateful to Kate for doing the work on the pay-as-you-go phone used to hire the van. He was finding it hard to get her out of his mind.

Jake had made a quiet visit to the Yard on his return to London to look up what intelligence the police held on Mohammed Biaj. There wasn't much; clearly the Security Service were not sharing what they had. Jake had been able to print out a photo of Biaj which he now sat looking at. He'd sellotaped it to the inside of the newspaper that he held in front of him at the table and pretended to be engrossed in reading it. The photo just looked like part of the paper at first glance, an old covert surveillance trick, but it made it much easier to compare the faces of passers-by to the face of the person you were hunting for.

Biaj was known to use the maze of the market for his clandestine meetings. There was no CCTV. The place was described as hostile for police-surveillance purposes. Jake could see why. It was almost impossible if you were white, like most police surveillance teams were, to blend in with the predominantly black and Asian locals. That was why Jake had decided upon using the café for some cover.

Arabic music spilled out across the stalls from the centre of the market. The smell of raw meat and fish filled his nose when the foul-tasting coffee wasn't near. Women wore black burkas or colourful saris, with the men in jeans of yellow, red and blue, or more traditional Islamic formal dress.

After about an hour, Jake spotted the swarthy Iraqi features of Biaj from the photo. It was the unusual nose – which was too small for his face – that gave him away. He was dressed in white shalwar kameez; loose trousers that were narrow at the ankle, with a long mandarin-collared tunic on his top half. He wore a crocheted skullcap and had a dense black beard, with a clear paunch underneath his shirt. Jake watched him as he walked past, deep in conversation with two much younger Asian men.

Jake got up and shadowed them as they left the market, but peeled off toward his car as the three men parted and went their separate ways to their own vehicles.

109

Biaj was three cars in front of Jake. The traffic was stop and start.

The Blackwall tunnel was ahead; three lanes of solid traffic. All around him the sun bounced off the cars' metal roofs and glared back from windscreens.

The afternoon's traffic fumes clogged Jake's nose. The month had been unseasonably dry and warm. He pressed the button on the door to close the window and keep the fumes out. A man in a Volkswagen next to him was bobbing up and down in his seat to the beat of Britney's 'Toxic'.

The song reminded Jake of his two girls. He remembered how they'd been glued to the live stage show on MTV. For this, the throbbing opening number, Britney had entered dressed in a black catsuit, atop a cartoonish-looking 'Toxic' bus. Jake shuddered at the sudden realisation of how close to home it all was.

Jake's mind wandered to Claire as he sat there in the traffic. Britney's lyrics stuck in his head. Was Claire toxic? Did she love him? Did he love her? Kate's caution about Claire being a stranger to the truth wouldn't leave him alone.

The traffic started to move in front of him. Biaj observed the rules of the road. He stayed in one lane and maintained a steady pace.

He was easy to follow; surprisingly easy in fact. Some people weren't. They would drive really slowly, stop and start or travel really, really fast and jump red lights. Those sorts of methods quickly shook off any car following them. Classic anti-surveillance tactics. Jake had expected Biaj to use exactly those methods; instead he drove normally. They entered the down ramp to the southbound tunnel ahead. Jake's ears felt the pressure change as they went under the Thames.

The southbound bore of the tunnel was straighter than the northbound and newer by some seventy years. Jake was always fascinated by the tunnel's history. The northbound tunnel had been in use by horses and carts during Queen Victoria's reign, which meant that it had to be curved, rather than straight, simply because the horses would bolt if they saw the light at the end of the tunnel.

The traffic was fighting and vying for any tiny piece of space on the road to get into the entrance of the tunnel, creating a real bottleneck of traffic. This bottle had a leak though, and the cars sprayed out the other end into the sunlight of south London. The Millennium Dome's huge white expanse to the left watched as more than a hundred thousand vehicles a day flowed past.

This part of London was legendary for all the wrong reasons. Behind the Dome was a place called Shooter's Hill. During the seventeenth and eighteenth centuries it had been one of the most notorious places in England for highway robbery. The infamous Dick Turpin robbed the rich atop of it.

What was Biaj doing over here, Jake wondered. His small black Toyota car was no Black Bess. He wasn't going to outrun anyone.

Jake was now four cars back, as the dual carriageway meandered its way up the hill. Biaj indicated and took the Blackheath slip road. A vast, open heath lay ahead at the top of Greenwich Park. It was a mile across, with no buildings, no trees, nothing. Just flat grass and a single bloody tea hut serving snacks and drinks.

Jake cursed. Blackheath Tea Hut was every surveillance officer's nightmare.

110

The tea hut had been there in one form or another since the reign of Charles II in the seventeenth century. A meeting point and watering hole for weary travellers before they braved going up and over the lawless Shooter's Hill, it was a last chance for fortification before the possibility of coming face to face with Dick Turpin.

At the little green wooden shack, drivers could park up, grab a cuppa and plot their next scheme. Bad guys loved the place because they could see for miles around and determine if they were being watched.

Unlike pretty much every other part of London, Blackheath had remained unchanged. Time had stood still for hundreds of years here. All the modern highwaymen knew it. The upper echelons of criminal empires staged meets near to the tea hut and had done ever since Jake had been in the police. People who didn't want to be seen together, didn't want to be knowingly associated with one another, they would just happen to be at the Blackheath Tea Hut at the same time. 'So what, Your Honour? Everyone knows the tea hut. It was just a coincidence they were there at the same time,' you'd often hear in the courtroom.

Surveillance teams couldn't stop close enough unnoticed to see who was doing what. The bad guys knew it and they'd have someone in a car as a lookout. If an unfamiliar vehicle stopped or if there was someone with binoculars looking at the tea hut, then the meet didn't take place; they were being watched.

Biaj was heading directly for it on the middle of the heath. He was slowing down. He was stopping at the tea hut. This was surreal. This wasn't right. Jake drove on. He couldn't pull up – he'd be clocked straightaway.

It was half a mile up the road before he could safely turn around. He drove back in the direction that he'd come. The heath was like a vast African plain, minus the elephants and giraffes. There were no trees. Nothing. Just open grasslands.

As he neared the little green wooden shack, he saw Biaj, who was out of his car by now and standing on a mound of mud. He was shouting at a man in an expensive-looking, designer suit who was getting out of a smart new Jaguar.

A red jaguar. Unusual colour for the new XF, thought Jake. It looked flash.

People who were going to buy an XF didn't usually want to be flash, because it wasn't that sort of car, thought Jake. It was a more understated, opulent type of vehicle. More popular in silver.

The colour was all wrong. This one was bright red, with twin exhausts and big fat wheels.

Too red.

It was in-your-face, look-at-me red. Like the devil. Like the blood that comes from an open wound.

Jake had seen one like it before. Where? Think, Jake!

The driver of the red Jaguar, the man in the designer suit, was now chatting away to Biaj. Jake slowed down to 30 mph. The man in the suit had his back to him. The way he stood, his hair, long on top and dark, but with expensive-looking highlights in it, his pale skin, the way he moved his arm, the suit. It all looked familiar. He was drinking tea; he had his back to the road.

'Turn, you bastard, turn!' cursed Jake. He slowed the car down further, just as much as he thought he could get away with without being spotted.

The man turned his head slightly to the right just as Jake passed. A split second. Jake had got lucky. He raced through the archives of his mind, trying to pinpoint where he'd seen that profile and vehicle together.

No. It couldn't be, could it?

The same face he'd seen that night they'd got drunk on cock-tails. The same face he'd seen dropping Claire off after work, the last time they'd actually made it to Tiger Tiger.

It was Claire's boss.

III

Jake almost drove the car into the bollards up ahead; his mind was reeling. What was going on here? Kate had suggested Biaj was a source for the intelligence agencies and here he was with a member of the Security Service, Claire's boss.

Lawrence Congerton-Jones.

Jake suddenly thought back to some of the things Claire had said and done. Kate had been adamant that Claire was not an analyst and that she did something out of the office. Was she really a field agent? Jake didn't think so. She wasn't surveillance aware and she wasn't practically minded. She wasn't even clued-up enough about security to have a decent lock on her front door. The one thing she was good at, was dealing with people.

Maybe she was an informant handler?

Claire had lied to him. Why? Whose side was she on?

When Jake had told her about the explosives at Sullivan House, she'd done nothing apart from rant and rave at him.

Shit! Claire knew everything he'd done! Was she even really missing? Was this some stupid game the Security Service was playing to find out what the police knew?

Jake stopped the car up the road, away from the heath. He was sweating. Nothing seemed real. He felt faint. He felt like he was looking down at himself. Sitting there in his little car; in a little tin box with wheels. He was a toy. This was a game.

Claire's voice kept playing on a loop in his head. That night at Tiger Tiger, she'd told him in a drunken confession that she was scared. 'If something happens to me, just look in the box by the bed,' she'd said.

But there was nothing in the box. He'd found the game out. He wasn't supposed to do that. She hadn't expected him to go to Kate and find out about Biaj and see him meeting Lawrence Congerton-Jones. He was one step ahead. Just. He needed to use this to his advantage. The Dusty Bin money box by the bed must be some sort of trap, a set-up. Had to be. Claire was one of the bad guys – bad girls.

Was Biaj one of her informants? Was everything they'd had together all a game to her? All a lie, their whole relationship? Was it all a trick to get him back for one of his drunken misdemeanours? Was he just an unwitting informant too, used to monitor exactly what the police knew and were up to? Maybe she was even involved in the bombings?

Jake drove to the nearest pub, The Princess of Wales, on the other side of the heath. He was shaking. He downed several whiskies while he collected his thoughts and decided what to do next.

112

Jake called Claire's boss, the man he'd seen on the heath with Biaj. Lawrence Congerton-Jones.

Anyone with a hyphenated name aroused Jake's suspicions for reasons unknown to him. Lawrence was no exception. Jake had never liked him.

He dialled the number for the Thames House switchboard and was surprised to be put through immediately to Lawrence's voicemail, where he left a message. Within minutes Jake's phone was ringing back, displaying 'withheld number'.

He answered: 'Jake Flannagan.'

'Jake, it's Lawrence Congerton-Jones here, returning your call,' he said, lengthening the 'O' in Jones considerably, in an exaggerated fashion.

Jake bit the bullet. 'I need to talk to you about Claire. She's missing.'

Jake waited for a response. The pause was too long. Lawrence was thinking.

Eventually there was a reply. 'I thought she was on holiday. Cornwall she said.' Lawrence's tone was even and without nuance. Jake now couldn't tell whether he knew anything at all.

'Yes, she was supposed to meet me there on Monday – she didn't turn up. I drove back up here to London to find her.'

'Have you reported her missing?'

Again Lawrence's response seemed odd. Unflustered, not at all anxious. Maybe Jake was overthinking it?

'Can we meet to discuss it please, Lawrence?'

There was another long pause.

'Of course. When?' came the reply.

'Now. In the coffee shop just up from Thames House on Horseferry Road. The place with the red sign.'

Jake didn't want Lawrence to have time to prepare for the meeting, or be able to plan anything.

'OK... yes... I'll... I'll be there in a minute.' Jake sensed a slight reluctance in Lawrence's voice.

'I'm sitting at the back,' said Jake, as he hung up.

Fifteen minutes later and Lawrence walked through the door, smartly dressed as always. He was accompanied by a large, heavyset man, whom Jake didn't recognise, but who was also sporting an expensive suit. Jake stood up and shook both their hands. Lawrence's accomplice stayed silent.

'A friend of mine,' said Lawrence, as they sat down. Neither asked for a drink. Unfortunate. Jake wouldn't be able to get the DNA off either of their coffee cups. He could have done with the saliva from the rims for comparison with anything found in the Transit van.

'Let's cut to the chase then, shall we?' said Jake. 'Where's Claire?'

'We have no idea.' Lawrence's response was curt.

'Look, I have reason to believe that Claire has been kidnapped. I want to know why.'

The two Security Service men exchanged a glance.

'How do you know that's what has taken place?' asked Lawrence.

'I know much more than you think.' Jake leaned forward and rested his elbows on the table.

'What do you mean?' asked Lawrence.

'Is that an Armani suit you have on, Lawrence?'

'What on earth makes you ask that?'

'It looks almost identical to the one I saw hanging in Claire's wardrobe. You must think I'm stupid, Lawrence. Expensive suits, flash car, meetings with informants on your own in Blackheath. That's not how the Security Service rolls, I know.'

Jake smirked at him, trying to pretend he knew much more than he did. Yet all he knew was that Lawrence had far too much money to burn and that something wasn't right. The suit in the wardrobe grated on him.

A shadow passed over Lawrence's face. Jake was beginning to push his buttons now. 'Look here. There's nothing to know, and even if there was, don't you think that I, as a Security Service agent, would know more than an oik in the police?'

Lawrence's brow furrowed like an unmade bed as he over-emphasised the 'O' in oik.

'Oik?' asked Jake, puzzled.

'Is this an official police investigation, Inspector Flannagan, or just some flight of fancy of your own? What police resources have you been using on this jolly of yours?'

'I'm doing my job. She didn't turn up for our holiday,' Jake said between clenched teeth.

'Oh really? Well one hopes you didn't have a police vehicle in Cornwall with you whilst on holiday? I've heard Claire talk about you using it for personal use, Inspector. I suspect your superiors would take a dim view of that?'

Jake was getting nowhere. This was pointless. He picked up his cup and resisted the urge to throw the dregs of his unfinished coffee into Lawrence's face. There were plenty of witnesses, not least Lawrence's colleague. There was no way he could say his arm had slipped and it had been an accident. The coffee was still hot and then he'd be had up for deliberately scalding the bloke.

No. It was not the right thing to do. He stood up to leave.

'I'm a detective inspector, Lawrence, not an oik; you'd do well to remember that.'

Jake walked away from the table and settled up his bill at the counter. Furious, he left the café without even looking over his shoulder. Once outside, he turned right and began to walk back up the street. He needed to calm down and think. He ducked into the entrance of a nearby office building and stood in a large air-conditioned lobby area with purple sofas and clashing green carpets, whilst he took a few breaths.

He glanced back at the street through the window and spotted Lawrence's heavy, presumably on his way back to the office. Lawrence was not with him.

Jake quickly retraced his steps and slipped back into the café. Claire's boss was no longer sat at the table; in fact, he was nowhere to be seen. Perhaps he'd gone to the toilet?

Jake made his way to the rear by the kitchens. Inside the Gents, Lawrence was relieving himself at the far end, staring off into the distance.

Jake stood at the next urinal along, hemming Lawrence in to the corner, and proceeded to pull down his own flies.

'Hello again, Lawrence,' he said.

Congerton-Jones visibly jumped as he realised who was stood beside him. Jake noted the surprised look on his face. The runny nose and telltale grains of white powder below his left nostril, gave away the fact that Lawrence had just been snorting cocaine.

'Tut, tut, Lawrence. Naughty boy,' said Jake, as he deliberately missed the urinal and turned, conveniently, to piss all over Lawrence's handmade, lace-up Louis Vuitton shoes.

'I'm surprised you didn't know I was going to do that, Lawrence. You, an agent of the Security Service. I thought you'd be one step ahead of an oik police officer like me?'

Lawrence stood open mouthed as Jake quickly washed his hands and walked out of the toilet.

113

Jake stood in the corridor outside DCI Helen Brookes' office. The door was closed. Helen had called him just twenty minutes previously and told him to get there. It had sounded like bad news. Jake guessed he was going to get a bollocking. He'd spent the weekend going over and over what he knew about Claire in his head, thinking about Lawrence. Thinking about his comment on the use of the car. That last one was really bugging him.

How had Lawrence known that he'd taken the car down to Cornwall? Claire was surely in on this whole thing? Was Claire trying to set him up? Maybe she had tried to make him take a tumble for the 21/7 stuff? Why? None of it made any sense.

The door to Helen's office opened. Jake stared into the small space and saw a man in a black suit whom he didn't recognise, sitting inside. Helen stood at the door.

'Come in, Jake,' she said.

Jake stepped into the tiny office and Helen closed the door behind him. Door-shut moments were very bad news. Jake's heart began to beat hard and fast.

'Sit down please, Jake.' Helen was being overly formal.

Jake sat down opposite the man in the suit. He didn't introduce himself or offer to shake Jake's hand.

Helen sat at her desk by the window but swung her chair around to face them both.

'What's this all about?' asked Jake.

'This is Detective Chief Superintendent Jim Powell. He's from the Directorate of Professional Standards,' said Helen, indicating the man aged fifty-plus sat opposite Jake.

The DPS dealt with complaints against police, internal investigations. Jake knew he was in trouble. The question was how much trouble?

'Jake, I'm here to inform you that you are being formally suspended from duty today. There have been several allegations made against you, some of which have concerned us enough to require you be suspended while we investigate them properly. You can have a Police Federation representative or a friend with you here whilst I go through the formalities with you and serve the relevant paperwork on you. Do you wish me to wait for a friend or representative to be present?' asked DCS Powell.

Jake felt sick.

'This is all bullshit. What are the allegations?' said Jake, trying to sound composed. His mouth had gone dry. His lips stuck to his teeth as he spoke.

Helen pushed a piece of paper toward Jake who picked it up and read: 'Form 163A: Formal Allegation of Complaints against Police Officers.'

DCS Powell began reciting from a duplicate version of the same form that he had in front of him: 'Point one – on or before 10 October 2005, you used a police vehicle for unauthorised private use. Point two – on or before 10 October 2005, you failed to properly instigate a formal missing-person's enquiry relating to the disappearance of Claire Richards. Point three – on or before 10 October 2005, you perverted the course of justice in relation to the collection and retention of evidence relating to the disappearance of Claire Richards. Point four – on 10 October 2005, you assaulted a Security Service officer by urinating on him.'

Jake sat there in silence. He was *really* in the shit if they could prove the allegations they were making. This was the problem with the DPS; they didn't need evidence to find you guilty and sack you. Internal discipline matters were found on the balance of probabilities. It was like a kangaroo court where they could present pretty much anything against you. They didn't have to follow the normal rules of evidence and procedure the same as a police investigation. The evidentiary standard required here was much, much lower than that required at court.

This was going to take a lot of sorting out.

'The serious nature of these allegations means that I must suspend you from duty. Your warrant card and the keys to the car that you've been driving, please.' DCS Powell held out his hand as he finished the sentence.

The journey home took him half an hour on the train. Completing the last part on foot, he turned off Commercial Road and walked up Caroline Street. As he neared his place above the sari shop, he saw immediately that the main entrance had been kicked open. The frame was split and had splintered. Inside, his flat had been ransacked. It was a tip. His computer was missing.

Jake stood there, looking at the mess. The furniture had been slashed open – white feathers spewed out of the cuts. The contents of the kitchen cupboards had been thrown on the floor. They'd been in a hurry. It didn't look like any job he'd been privy to in the police, too messy. The Security Service? The kidnappers? Lawrence?

114

The room was filled with a hazy red hue; he assumed it was dawn, but he had no idea *which* day it was. There was a strong taste of stale beer in his mouth. As he rolled over, he felt the deep ache of bruises all over his body. His left arm hurt badly. It was sore around the base of the bicep. Had he been fighting in his sleep again? He wouldn't even notice if he had broken anything in his flat because, right now, the whole of it wouldn't have looked out of place in a skip.

Jake dragged himself out of bed and opened the cupboards in his kitchen. He couldn't remember the last time he'd eaten anything. Was he even hungry? He didn't really know. There was nothing except for sugar and tea bags. Where had the beans gone? He was sure he'd seen four cans of baked beans the last time he'd looked, not that he could remember when that was.

He picked up his phone; the battery was flat. He found the charger and plugged it in. What day was it? Empty bottles lay strewn around the living room and kitchen. Jake didn't remember drinking their contents.

He flicked on the TV. BBC news was reporting on riots in Paris. The riots were slowly spreading to other towns and cities in France. Cars were being set alight everywhere following the deaths of two Muslim teenagers in a Paris suburb. The teenagers had somehow been accidentally electrocuted in an electricity substation, whilst being chased by the police. Heavy-handed tactics were being blamed. The news ticker running across the bottom of the screen announced that George Best was close to death.

'That happened quick! Bestie only went into hospital last week. What day is it?'

His phone screen lit up one corner of the room and caught his eye. He got up out of his chair to see if it had regained enough juice to switch on properly.

'Fuck me!'

He'd been suspended seventeen days ago. They'd taken his warrant card and told him that until the investigation was complete, he was not to use any of the powers of a police officer. Seventeen days ago.

'So where the hell have those beans gone?'

He wandered into his kitchen. The empty tins were sitting there in his bin. He didn't remember eating their contents; he couldn't remember anything of the last seventeen days. Jake made a cup of tea with eight sugars. Black. There was no milk. The tea revived him enough to survey the damage properly.

It was utter devastation. There were empty cans of beer on every surface, except the corner of the coffee table, which held a rolled-up ten-pound note. The tubular note was bloodied and crusted around one end, whilst the other was white and crystallised. It was sitting in a very thin layer of white dust. Jake winced and shook his head in disbelief. He felt a cold knot of fear well up in his stomach. He'd taken drugs as a teenager, then briefly when his father died.

Jake knew that most of London's cocaine was only about 15 to 20% pure. It was always cut and heavily watered down with other stuff – baking soda, flour, citric acid, cleaning chemicals, Italian baby laxatives. The nose often bled after repeated snorting. The extras were what wrecked people's noses.

His dad had died from the booze and George Best's liver was on its way out, yet Jake had never really felt over-burdened by his own alcohol abuse. Drugs, though, that was another matter. Jake still viewed drugs as the more evil and destructive twin.

'*Seventeen days!*' he chastised himself.

He was hungry, very hungry. He had to eat. He looked in his pocket for some cash but found none. He showered, dressed and began to walk to the café-cum-kebab shop nearby. On the way, he stopped at the cashpoint to withdraw £20. The machine said there were insufficient funds in his account. Jake pulled up a balance enquiry. Jesus Christ! He was £3,000 overdrawn and payday had only been eight days ago.

'What the fuck have you done, Jake?' he asked himself.

115

He placed a quick phone call to his bank, which revealed that he'd withdrawn £4,000 in cash in eleven days, £2,000 of which had been in lots of £500 in just over forty-eight hours. Jake had told them that he couldn't remember going to the cashpoint, but the bank pointed out that it was his card and PIN that had been used. Amounts had been taken out at 2359 hours and 0001 hours and the same cycle repeated less than forty-eight-hours later. The bank also refused to increase his overdraft facility, a request which had never previously been a problem.

Jake trudged back home and picked up the bloodied ten-pound note from the table. He needed to eat. He washed it in the bathroom sink. What was he going to do? This was all he had to live off for three weeks? Ten pounds?

He walked back to the café and ordered the biggest all-day breakfast they had. He'd be able to think straight once he'd eaten.

He sipped tea from a tannin-stained mug before scooping up some baked beans on his fork. His mouth and jaw ached.

It couldn't get any worse than this, surely?

'Hello, Jake,' said a thin, twenty-something girl, cradling a takeaway polystyrene cup as she sat down opposite him. In a short skirt, high heels and wearing ton of make-up, she looked like she'd been partying a little too hard. She must still be dressed up from the night before, thought Jake.

'Hello,' said Jake politely. 'Do I know you?' he asked.

The girl let out a laugh and smiled at him. 'Yes, you know me!'

Jake sat there looking at her. 'I've forgotten your name,' he said, buying thinking time.

'It's Joanne. We met a few weeks ago. You were very drunk. Wheler Street, you remember? You'd been out in Shoreditch drinking, I think you said. Took me back to your place.'

Jake knew Wheler Street. It was a bit of a walk. A cut through from Brick Lane onto Commercial Road. A railway arch, covered in graffiti and street art at one end, meant traffic couldn't drive down it. The arch made a vast section of the road dark even during the daytime. It was a place prostitutes hung out looking for clients; an area well known for streetwalkers since the days of Jack the Ripper.

On joining the force, Jake had been warned about the three Ps; paperwork, prisoners and prostitutes. He'd heard the many lines his colleagues had trotted out to them over the years, such as 'Sleep with me and I won't arrest you' and 'Let me take you away from all this'. He'd used neither in his life. He'd never had any urge to go near a prostitute before.

He looked at Joanne's teeth; they were poor for her age. That usually meant a heroin addiction. Her clothes were cheap. They looked worn and uncared for.

'Joanne, I really don't remember. I found you in Wheler Street though? You go there often?' Jake asked, in a way that made it sound as though English were his second language.

'Yeah. A bit. It's OK there.'

'Joanne, don't take this the wrong way. What did we do when we got back to my place?'

Joanne laughed again. 'We talked. Well, you talked. And then we took a lot of drugs.'

A vision flashed before Jake's eyes momentarily; the imprint of a pair of buttocks outlined in white powder on the glass coffee table, *his* glass coffee table.

She was smiling broadly at him. She looked a little like a badly kept Claire. Is that why she'd caught his eye? Is that how they'd got talking?

'Joanne, as lovely as you are, I'm sorry we've met like this. I won't be doing anything like this again. What drugs did we get and how much did I spend?'

'We got some brown. I told you I liked it and you insisted you wanted to try it. You *loved* it! Then you asked me to go and get you some more. The dealer wanted more money for the second lot though, so you might see a few different withdrawals on your card instead of just one,' Joanne was smiling again.

'I gave you my bank card and PIN number?' Jake's couldn't believe what he was hearing.

'Yeah. You got the card back though. The second lot of drugs was £1,000 instead of £200 from that dealer; so I took £1,000 out that day. Then I got some food and stuff for us.'

He looked at his bruised left arm. That's why it hurt so much. He'd injected heroin into it.

'Great to meet you, Joanne. I'm going to finish my food.' Jake didn't want to hear any more. He just wanted her gone.

She tried to milk her cash cow further. 'I was wondering if you wanted to do it again? I'd like to. You up for it?'

Jake looked at the scrawny prostitute that he'd invited into his home, taken drugs with and then entrusted with his bank card. How could he have been so stupid? Just doing any one of those things would have seemed beyond crazy a few weeks ago.

'I want you to leave me alone, Joanne, so that I can finish my breakfast in peace, please.' Jake looked her dead in the eye. He wanted her to get the message that she was no longer welcome.

'Aww, OK, Jake, I can pop over and see you later?' She winked at him and smiled, exposing her rotten teeth.

'No. I hope we won't meet again. Thanks.' Jake looked back down at his five-pound breakfast that was now getting cold.

'I saw the photos on your wall, you know, Jake.' There was a change in the tone of Joanne's voice; it had an edge to it now.

Jake looked up at her. 'What?' he snapped back. She was referring to his commendation-ceremony photos, which hung in his hallway.

'The police ones. Should I keep quiet about my latest client's activities, being an officer of the law 'n' all, Jake?' Joanne was half-smiling at him, but her eyes had narrowed. This was the prelude to blackmail.

'Your client? Did we have sex too?' asked Jake.

'Ha! So the drugs were fine, but now you're worried about the *sex*? I don't think you've even got it in you. All you did is whine on about your fucking missing girlfriend. Boo hoo! I think I'd go missing if I had a boyfriend as dull as you! I tried to have sex with you, just to shut you up. You boring prick.'

Jake got to his feet suddenly, scooping his plate up with his fingertips and depositing its contents all over Joanne. Before she'd had chance to realise what had happened, he'd grabbed her by the arm.

Jake whispered into her ear, his body blocking the view of the waitresses. 'That breakfast all over you now will be nothing compared to what I will do to you and any other fucking piece of shit that comes near me. I suggest you stay away and keep your mouth shut. Unless you have a punter in it, that is!

'You can finish my breakfast, Jo,' he called over his shoulder as he walked out.

116

Jake had to escape. He had to escape from himself. In just over two weeks he had gone from gifted detective on the Anti-Terrorist Branch to an officer suspended from duty, drinking heavily, using drugs and now bringing a street prostitute back to his own home. He couldn't believe that in his drug-addled stupor he'd been stupid enough to give her his cashpoint card and PIN, so that she could empty his bank account.

Walking back toward his flat, he felt a creeping despair. Was Claire still missing or was this all part of her master plan? He had just a couple quid left in his pocket and he was still hungry after emptying most of his breakfast over Joanne in the café. He'd had to hand back his police Amex at the suspension meeting, and because of his father's debt trouble, Jake had never trusted himself with anything more than a debit card. Just feeding himself now was going to be a major hurdle.

He slumped onto the torn sofa. It spat feathers from the slashes as it took his weight. What had they been looking for? What did he have that they wanted? He couldn't think. He leaned forward and picked among the sea of beer cans on the coffee table in search of some dregs; they were all empty. Instead, he found the porcelain Dusty Bin money box sitting in the middle of them. He picked it up, rolled it in his hands and looked it over again. He felt a loathing for himself like never before.

'You set me up! *You're a fucking bitch, Claire!*' he screamed as he hurled the empty china figurine at the wall opposite him.

The impact caused it to explode into different shards of white, green and red, which scattered across the floor.

By the skirting board, he saw something glint in the sunlight, something metallic and silver.

Jake walked over to the wall. Half of Dusty Bin's base was still intact, the bung now missing. Inside what remained he found a small key stuck with superglue. It would have been imperceptible from the outside and could only be detected now that he'd smashed the thing open. He picked it up and prised the ordinary-looking key from the broken base.

'OK, Claire. So this is what you wanted me to find, is it? This is what they were looking for when they trashed my place?'

He grabbed his mobile and called Anne at Travannon House. After a few rings, she answered.

'Anne? Hi, it's Jake.'

'Hello, Jake,' she said curtly.

'Has Claire called you?' he asked anxiously.

'No, Jake she hasn't… I've had the police from London here asking questions about you both, though. Asking if I knew where she was. Asking what happened the day you arrived. They told me you're in some sort of trouble, but didn't say what. They told me not to talk to you. When you didn't call me back that week, I assumed everything was fine, until I got the visit from them. That was three weeks ago, Jake! I've been worried sick. I've left you messages.'

Jake sighed.

'I'm sorry, Anne. There's been a lot going on. I've done nothing wrong. I was just trying to find her.'

'You could have called. Her father has been on the phone asking me the same thing. He's not heard anything either.'

'I don't know what's going on, Anne. It's very strange.'

Jake looked down at the small key in his hand.

'Anne, you've known Claire since she was a child, haven't you?'

'Yes, I have. Why?'

'Was she fond of that seventies and eighties game show, *3-2-1*? You know, the one with Dusty Bin in it?'

'Not that I'm aware of, she might have been. Her little brother's nickname was Dusty though. He was always climbing into small spaces and getting covered in it.'

Jake felt his heart jump.

'He was called Dusty?'

'You sound surprised?'

'I've found a key belonging to Claire. I think she's left it as some sort of clue.'

'There *is* a box of Dusty's stuff here. It's in the attic of the main house. Claire had the box down a few months ago. I know there's a padlock on it. I don't have the key though, never had it…'

That had to be it, thought Jake.

'I'm going to come and to see you, Anne. I'm not quite sure how I'm going to get to you yet, but I will be down.'

117

Jake walked up the path toward the familiar Victorian facade of
the house he had once shared with his wife and two girls before
the split. He had phoned Stephanie and asked for her help. She
was his one remaining lifeline. He had told her on the phone he
was in some trouble and that he needed to talk to her face to face.

As he pressed the doorbell, he was still wondering how
much he should tell her. How much did he need to tell her?
Stephanie opened the door wearing her favourite pair of faded
blue jeans.

'Come in,' she said, as she stepped to one side. 'You look
like shit.'

Jake crossed the threshold of his former home. It had
changed little since he'd left. The same furniture, same carpets,
same smell, same people. The only thing that was different was
the man that now stood in the hallway.

Jake. Jake was different.

Stephanie closed the door and wandered off into the kitch-
en at the back of the house. He heard her switch the kettle on.
He followed her and sat down at the large, round oak table by
the patio doors, which overlooked the small rear garden. He
said nothing. He was still searching for the right words, the
right tone – the right way to position it.

Stephanie sat down opposite him and passed him a cup of
tea. She'd remembered, without being prompted, that he took
two sugars.

'Go on then, tell me… You've lost your job, haven't you?' she asked, resigned.

'Not yet, but I'm close. I need to sort out the trouble I'm in…' Jake stopped himself talking. How had she known he was in trouble at work? Had the DPS been here like they had to Travannon House?

'What makes you say it's my job that's the problem?' he asked.

'Jake, I can see you're in a state. You look like something the cat dragged in. I know that job is the only thing you ever really cared about. You didn't shed a single tear when you walked out of this house to go and live on your own. All you've ever really cared about is your job. Being the best, getting the result. That drive to win, to solve everything – it consumes you, eats you up. You try to exclude everyone and everything – you disappear into a cave. You drink or seek solace somewhere for the night. The job makes a monster of you, Jake. It makes you do weird things. You're not the man I married. I don't know where he's gone…' Stephanie tailed off, fighting back tears.

Jake said nothing. She was right. She knew exactly who he was, what he'd become.

He felt ashamed. How had he arrived here? How had his journey brought him to this point? He suddenly felt a huge surge of emotion. Tears welled up in his eyes. He put his elbows on the table and his head in his hands, covering his eyes with his palms, as if that might stop him weeping, but it didn't. The tears flowed down his arms.

'I'm suspended. I'm under investigation for trying to do the right thing, but it doesn't look good. I'm a mess. I've been drinking a lot; I've been using drugs as well. I've fucked up… I need your help. I've got no cash. None at all. I need to borrow some money, and a car…'

Stephanie stared back at him for a few moments. She looked at him like she no longer recognised him and spoke through pursed lips.

'You walked out on me, walked out on our children, walked out on our marriage without even properly explaining to me…'

Stephanie stopped herself mid-sentence to take a sip of her tea. Jake could see that she was swallowing to silence the sobs. She composed herself momentarily. She wouldn't cry in front of him. She wouldn't let him see her pain.

Jake tried to find the words. 'I'm sorry. Deeply sorry. I've lost myself in the last few years. I've been an emotional coward. Instead of talking about stuff, about how I felt, I've hidden my feelings, hidden my emotions since Mum and Gran both died. Work was the one place where I could escape from things; it was the one place where none of those things were spoken about.'

'Like what? What things? What problems couldn't you discuss with me?' Stephanie looked angry, the tears gone.

'I was scared. Scared about being a dad, about getting old, about acting responsibly, about being a middle-aged bloke with two point four kids and living in the suburbs. I was scared about dying like Mum, and not having done all the things that I wanted to do before I did. I was scared of not having achieved something amazing to leave as a legacy for you and the kids. So I ran away from it all. I hid.'

'And since you've been gone, what have you actually achieved, Jake? More notches on the bedpost? Banged up a few more criminals? Cracked the most important case in the history of the Metropolitan Police? I bet you've not even achieved changing your bedclothes.'

'I've behaved badly. I've hurt you. I really am sorry. I can't change what's happened.' Jake wiped away the remaining tears from his face.

'You've created two amazing daughters, Jake. They're growing up without you, without you even realising. That's the real tragedy in all of this – not that you walked out on me, on us. You walked out on the two single most amazing achievements a man can ever have in life, his children. That's the legacy you should be thinking about, not whatever case you're working on… Why are you telling me all this now? What do you need from me?'

'Right now?'

'Yes, right now, why are you here?'

'I need £1,000 and a car.'

Stephanie thought for a moment, sighed to herself and replied, 'I can transfer money into your account, but I want it back. My brother has an old van sitting on his drive that he's trying to sell. He wants two or three hundred pounds for it. It's too small for what he needed it for. Use some of the money I'm lending you to buy that off Paul.'

Jake suddenly wondered if her question 'What do you need from me?' meant something different to how he had interpreted it. Had she been throwing him a relationship lifeline, a second chance at their marriage?

Was he still so focused on solving this case that he hadn't even seen that?

It was too late. Stephanie was already on her feet, walking toward the front door. She opened it and stood waiting for Jake to leave.

'I'll transfer the money into your account straightaway,' she said. She looked at the floor and waited for him to leave.

118

The 1990 Volkswagen Transporter van looked in terrible condition. Its blue paintwork was faded and lacklustre. Large patches of rust were eating away at it from inside and out, making the van look like it had brown spots all over it from a distance. It had no power steering, no air conditioning, no MOT and it had done 175,000 miles. But the radio worked and the diesel engine sounded as good as the day it rolled off the production line. Best of all it would be shown as 'no current keeper' on the Police National Computer. It had been sold at various times to different people who had failed to notify the DVLA that they were the owner. This suited Jake perfectly. If he had to walk away and leave it for any reason, no one could trace it back to him.

Paul, Stephanie's brother, was a landscape gardener and had needed a rough and ready vehicle to take garden waste, rubbish and logs to the local dump, but it had proved too small and no match for his newer LT van – the trips to the dump had become too frequent. The old VW Transporter had sat on his drive for several months and the MOT had lapsed. He was glad to be rid of it and let Jake have it for just £175, with a £25 discount on top if Jake wouldn't mind just ferrying the ancient two-stroke petrol mower inside it to the dump.

Jake accepted the discount gladly and didn't even bother to insure the van. Another paper trail to be avoided at all costs. The Transporter started first time. He drove it off Paul's driveway and straight to the tip to dispose of the mower, then began his journey south-west toward St Austell.

It was late evening by the time Jake pulled onto the gravel drive of Travannon House. Anne came out and ushered him into her annexe.

'How are you doing, Jake?' she asked as she touched his arm.

'I'm just keen to find out what's going on and where she is, Anne...'

'There's guests in the house, Jake. I've had to bring the trunk in here down from their loft; one of the lads helped me.' Anne pointed at a robust wooden chest sat on the tiled floor in her kitchen. It had metal handles at the sides that were painted black and a clasp at the front with a padlock. It looked like it might have been an old tea chest in a previous lifetime.

Jake fished the key out from his pocket – the one that he'd found stuck inside Dusty Bin – and pushed it into the brushed metal padlock. It slid in easily and Jake felt a surge of excitement. He turned it barely a quarter of a turn clockwise and the lock opened.

'Fuck me! This is it, Anne!' shouted Jake, his emotions getting the better of him, before he realised he'd sworn in front of the elderly lady.

He pulled off the lock and opened the lid. The underside had Chinese markings stamped into the wood. Jake had no idea what they said. A musty fragrance emanated from within; a mix of sawdust and dried leaves. Inside, the chest was filled to the brim with photos of all different sizes, some in frames, some not. Every single one held an image of the same small boy.

'What... what on earth are all these? Why?' Jake said disappointedly, as he rifled through the box. He bit his tongue to stop himself swearing again, this time in frustration. This was all she'd left behind? How was this going to help him?

Anne glanced through the pictures and shook her head in regret at each one she picked up. 'I know you don't know...' she began.

Jake looked at her. 'Know what?'

119

'Dusty's death marked a turning point in Claire's life, Jake,' announced Anne.

'What do you mean?'

'When you told me she was missing, I was worried about her. Worried she'd done something awful, something stupid. She's suffered terribly during her life – I could understand if the pain was too much for her to go on.'

Jake was confused. What was Anne trying to tell him? 'Go on,' he replied.

Anne's face crumpled in grief as she spoke. 'The death of her brother, Dusty, was a tragedy, but her misery continued for many years afterwards. Both she and her dad went to live with her uncle. He turned out to be an evil man, wicked beyond belief. He abused her repeatedly. Then, when her mother died too, she locked Dusty's stuff away and out of sight. I guess she felt that if Dusty didn't exist and was locked away, then the abuse never existed and all those dreadful memories could be locked away too.'

'Was nothing ever done? She never mentioned it to me, ever.'

'Kate, Claire's cousin, caught them one afternoon. Frank, her uncle, claimed it was a one-off and it was all consensual. Claire's father blamed her for encouraging Frank in some way. He was sure it was down to some sort of mixed signals she was giving, that it was a one-off thing. It was repeated rape though.

374

The family couldn't bear to face up to more trauma after Dusty's death. No one talked about it; it was just swept under the carpet. Claire was sent to boarding school. Her father and uncle fell out and they barely spoke again. She's moved on. She hates her father and despises her uncle. He was utterly obsessed with her.'

Jake wondered if Claire had left him this information because she couldn't bring herself to tell him in person. Maybe the pain of it all was too much to bear?

As Anne picked through the framed photos, Jake spotted a flash of vermillion card nestling down one side of the chest. He grabbed hold of a corner and pulled it out. It was a folder. It looked new and clearly didn't fit with the other battered items the old chest contained.

Inside he found several intelligence reports on MI5-headed notepaper and a poorly photocopied planning application.

Jake skimmed through the intelligence reports:

Drugs Importation

'...There is strong evidence to show that drugs in large quantities are being imported into the UK by certain members of the West Yorkshire Muslim community...'

'...Purchase of the drugs abroad is done via the transfer of goods or monies through UK charities set up directly for this purpose...'

'...Considerable funds, raised from the sale of these drugs in the UK, may be used for clandestine purposes but is beyond the scope of this investigation. The illegal drugs importation itself poses no direct threat to national security and is therefore not a matter for this agency.'

'...Agents are using the drugs importation as a method by which to recruit informants via blackmail...'

'...Information is not being passed to law-enforcement agencies on the drugs importation...'

'...Agents have become directly involved in the sale/use of illegal drugs...'

Jake thought back to the moment he'd spotted Lawrence in the Gents – the telltale white substance under his nose. Was he part of all this? Had Claire uncovered his moneymaking secret?

Money Laundering

'...Large sums of money, believed originally to be for terrorist purposes, have been found to be crime related...'

'...Money is being used to purchase property and businesses...'

'...A small group of individuals are exerting control over entire communities...'

'...The local populace are excluded from other communities and are used as workers and cash cows...'

Tablighi Jamaat

'...A rogue element has infiltrated this sect... unidentified individuals are believed to be attempting to exert control over businesses and populace...'

Jake turned his attention to the planning application. It was for a huge seventy-thousand-capacity mosque in East London. None of the names on the planning application meant anything to him.

On a separate piece of paper, he saw the name of Mohammed Biaj written next to the numbers two, zero, one and another two, followed by a question mark. Was it the code for a combination lock?

Jake saw himself standing in an amusement arcade. There was a penny-falls machine directly in front of him. He had a huge coin in his hand, but he didn't know how to fit it into the machine. It was too big. It made no sense.

'Can I make you a sandwich, Jake?' asked Anne, dragging him back into reality.

'That would be good, Anne. Thanks.'

'It doesn't help you much, does it, Jake?'

'Right at this moment, Anne, no. I have absolutely no idea how this all fits in...' Jake shrugged as he waved the documents and bits of paper in his hand at her.

'No, I suppose not. It doesn't help that Claire's handwriting was always awful at the best of times...'

Jake looked back down at the notes. Anne was right – it certainly was Claire's handwriting. Dashed off as quickly as possible. Had she written these notes just for him?

120

'So what's the latest on the job then, Len?'

They sat eating club sandwiches, warmed by the sunlight streaming in through the glass front of the café. Below them, colourful narrow boats bobbed gently as Regent's Canal shook hands with the Paddington arm of the Grand Union.

'What of the fifty-third victim? The pretend professor who was found dead at her flat? Anything on her?' asked Jake.

'Toxicology on "Professor" Groom-Bates came back negative. No traces of drink or drugs in her system. No radio-activity. No infection. Overall consensus is that she definitely died from a blood clot on the lungs. Only, it seems weird that the one thing she died from is the one thing it appears she actually had some knowledge of. When I dug into it, I found that she'd actually written a thesis on the cause of embolisms whilst studying for a basic certificate of health care. In any case, she was just as much a victim as the rest of those poor people. She got involved in the circumstances of that day and was affected by it. Just like all of us, I guess.'

'Poor girl. What else is new?'

Lenny wiped the mayonnaise from the side of his mouth. 'Well, boss, latest on the green gunge is that Professor Bowman at the forensic explosives lab was right. There was no chemi-cal attack. Looks now as though it *was* gas gangrene from the Clostridium perfringens. Everyone I've spoken to says it could well have come from his dodgy belly, what with him shitting

378

his trousers and chucking them into the rucksack. But the source hasn't conclusively been found.'

Jake nodded. 'So the dirty bomb could just have been, what? A dirty mistake?'

'Potentially. The hospital has changed the treatment plan for the patient who was allergic to the initial prescribed regime and they're recovering well. The new antibiotic combination they've put them on and the hyperbaric oxygen chamber have put them back on track, which is fantastic news.'

'What happened with the stuff about the lump on the car and the newspapers? Did we ever get to the bottom of it?'

'Have you not seen the memo?' asked Lenny, looking shocked.

'I'm suspended, Lenny. Anyway, you know I never read my bloody emails, even when I was in the office!'

Lenny looked serious now. 'Denswood sent round a note, hard copy, urgent. They reckon former and retired police officers have been paid by the press to hack into voicemails. Nothing's been proven at this stage. It's just a rumour, but we've been advised not to leave any more messages for anyone via phone.'

'Jesus, I had a load of voicemails go missing!'

'Well, that may well have been the reason. Could be that someone was paid to hack into them.'

'Blimey, Len. There was me thinking Wasim's wife was a top AQ operative and she'd used her years of counter-surveillance training to find the bloody lump!'

'Nope, may have been the journos all along. They wanted answers. They need to print something and there's been no developments in the case. Maybe they've had to try some unusual methods to fill column inches?' replied Lenny.

'Any update on Shahid?' asked Jake.

'The boss is still adamant that we're going to use him as a witness and we're not going to pursue any of the criminal allegations about wasting police time, perverting the course of justice or withholding information.'

Jake looked incredulously at Lenny. 'I just don't get it. What's all that about?'

'Denswood says that if we prosecute him, we can't use anything that he says as evidence in the case, and we need what he says as a narrative to prove the timeline of events.'

'But he's a liar! So we're presenting lies as evidence now?'

'They're convinced that if we put his case in front of the CPS, they won't run with it. I have my own misgivings about bloody Shahid. He's a big fish in a small pool up there – an important source of employment. His cousin is good friends with the local MP and a mate of his is on the local Police Consultative Group. We have to do what we're told by the boss,' said Lenny ruefully.

Jake finished up the last of his sandwich and moved his plate away. 'You wanna see something strange, Len?' he asked, tilting his head to one side.

Lenny's eyes lit up. To him, Jake's definition of 'strange' was always worth a look.

Jake pulled the set of plans out of his inside jacket pocket and laid them down on the table in front of Lenny's plate.

'What's this?' asked Lenny.

'It's a planning application.'

'For what?'

'For a mosque in East London. They're proposing a building that'll be large enough to house seventy-thousand worshippers. Plus accommodation, shops, businesses. A whole, self-contained enclave on a disused, inner-city, brownfield site.'

'And? What's this got to do with anything?' asked Lenny.

'I've done some work on it. You remember that demonstration where Kenny Savage witnessed that fracas with Shahid?'

'Yeah,' replied Lenny.

'Well, we never really looked at the significance of what they were protesting about, did we? The reason Kenny was there that day was because he was in opposition to the building of this mosque in East London. This place is going to be the biggest mosque in Europe. It's going to be the new headquarters for Tablighi Jamaat. Bigger than St Paul's cathedral!'

'Who the fuck are Tabliggi Jam-whatsits?'

'They're a bit like travelling preachers. Someone described them to me as the Jehovah's Witnesses of Islam. They're grassroots missionaries, but hard line, neo-fundamentalist. They go around spreading their version of the Quran to different mosques across the country. Some of them preach that Muslims shouldn't mix with non-Muslims. They're not about converting Christians or other religions to Islam. It's like they don't really recognise any other religions, they only preach to other Muslims to try and convert them to their very strict way of thinking. They say they're apolitical and non-violent, but very little is known about them. They don't seem to have any formal structure that's written down anywhere. It's all word of mouth and fairy tales. They want strict adherence to a very traditional, old-school form of Sharia law and believe in Sharia-controlled zones around mosques. They are well known for helping to get the kids off drugs…'

'The sort of thing that Wasim used to do?' interjected Lenny.

'Exactly that. They get hold of the addicts and make them go cold turkey to get them clean and off the drugs. The wider Islamic community believe they're doing good work. You remember in the nineties, when Wasim was doing it as part of a gang…'

'Yeah, the elders didn't know what to do about the kids that were addicted to drugs. It was a real problem.'

'That's right. So in agreement with their frantic relatives, Wasim's twenty-strong crew would sweep up the addicts and hold them in a flat until their drug cravings had disappeared. I reckon he was already part of Tablighi Jamaat way back then, Lenny.'

'Really? OK. So what's so special about that then?' asked Lenny. 'That sounds like good work to me.'

'Well… that is good work. But what if someone were to infiltrate that group and deliberately prey on those unfortunates who are involved in drugs and crime? What if someone used it as a cover for picking the most vulnerable kids and radicalising them? If they're holding them to make them go cold turkey, they could do anything they wanted with them. The brain does weird things when it's coming down off drugs. What if they're using that time period to indoctrinate them? They could use the drug-cleansing process to forcibly radicalise these kids, make them do whatever they wanted?'

'What, like, "I've found God and thank you for helping me off the drugs, Lord"?' asked Lenny.

'Yes, that sort of thing. But we're talking hard-line extremism here, Len.'

'So, I still don't see what the connection is here between this planning application and the bombers.'

'I don't know either yet, Lenny, but I wonder if it's all connected through this Tablighi Jamaat movement somehow. That mosque that Wasim used to visit up in West Yorkshire was their European HQ, you know.'

'And what do they think about it?' asked Lenny.

'Well they say it's nothing to do with them. Same as the international headquarters in India. No one seems to have sanctioned this new mosque in East London or know anything about it. But someone clearly wants to create an even larger base here in London. A hard line Islamic enclave which could become Britain's first Sharia-controlled zone.

'I'm curious, Lenny, is someone using drugs to control the kids? Are they getting them hooked, then bringing them down and feeding them all this neo-fundamentalist cult bullshit? It could be a deliberate ploy, a way of messing with the brain wiring of these kids. Can you see if Shahid is involved in drugs in some way?'

121

Wednesday
2 November 2005
1000 hours
The Trafalgar, King's Road, Chelsea

The pub was deserted. Jake had hoped it would be. Despite the unseasonably good weather, early on a Wednesday morning on the King's Road wasn't exactly peak pub hours. Jake had arrived early to make sure he'd see Zarshad. The poor bloke didn't know he wasn't going to get paid yet, but the opportunity of a free drink would entice him out of bed, at least, thought Jake.

Jake ordered a small Diet Coke and sat down on a black Chesterfield sofa by the window. The smell of day-old smoke seemed to ooze from every surface in the pub, making the air feel stale. There was a song playing in the background. Jake had heard it endlessly on the radio. Some Canadian band was singing about a photograph, but he couldn't make out the lyrics at this volume.

Zarshad swaggered in wearing torn jeans, flip-flops and a green T-shirt with the slogan 'In war, truth is the first casualty' emblazoned across the chest in dark blue lettering.

'You're drinking shorts already? It's a bit early, ain't it?' Zarshad said, eying Jake's small glass. He raised his eyebrows in mock surprise.

'It's just Coke. Grab yourself one and sit down, mate,' said Jake, motioning to the chair opposite him.

'Fuck that…' said Zarshad, as he walked toward the bar.

A few minutes later he returned with two pints of lager. He made himself comfortable in a brown wing-back chair opposite Jake.

'Coke's no good for men like us!' he said, as he pushed one of the pints toward Jake.

'I'm off the drink, Zarshad. I've indulged in one too many recently. I'm here because you mentioned your father was part of something. That's what I want to talk to you about.'

'My father? What the fuck? What's he been up to?'

'Tablighi Jamaat.'

'Tablighi Jamaat? You asked me to the pub to talk about TJ? Why?' asked Zarshad with a puzzled look on his face.

'You said that your father was a member of Tablighi Jamaat.'

'Yeah, he is. So what?'

'I wanted some background information on them, some work I'm involved in. It's just a chat, I can't pay you.' Jake grimaced involuntarily as he said it, remembering his dire financial situation.

'That don't sound good, Jake. I could do with some wonga at the moment.'

'Just drinks, Zarshad. That's all I can afford at the moment, mate. But let's just say I owe you some real work.'

'It's fine – I hate the TJ bastards anyway. Happy to help.' Zarshad gulped his pint quickly, determined now to get a few in as they spoke.

There was an awkward pause. Jake said nothing. His eyes had wandered to the lager in front of him on the table. His mouth began to water as he thought about drinking it.

'So what do you want to know, Jake? Jake?'

Jake looked up from his pint and snapped back to attention. 'Err... Anything... everything? Give me the full rundown.'

'Well, they're sort of like a missionary group, a sect. Unless you're Muslim you're unlikely ever to have heard of them. I'm really surprised to hear you mention their name, to be honest.

'The TJs love to talk about spiritual jihad, the inner fight between good and evil. Kind of like that fight you're having with yourself over whether you should drink that pint or not, Jake.' Zarshad broke into a smile and laughed.

Jake thought about his own inner turmoil. Zarshad was right. He was wondering whether he should really abstain from the lager. The past few weeks on the drugs and booze hadn't done him any favours. But something else was nagging him, something about the term 'spiritual jihad'. He'd heard it before. He waited for the penny to drop into the right machine in his head.

Samir Shafiq, the burka bomber, had said something similar to him when he'd been interviewed at Paddington Green police station. Perhaps Samir was also a TJ?

122

Jake smiled, picked up the pint of lager he'd been staring at and sipped it.

It was his first drink in nearly a week. He was just relieved that the chemical abuse he'd put himself through hadn't stopped the neurons firing. He swallowed a cold, fizzy mouthful. Sod the guilt, he thought. It tasted good.

'That's the Jake I know. Well done, mate!' Zarshad was laughing.

Jake took another mouthful. It was time to pick Zarshad's brain.

'I've done some basic research. I know the stuff anyone can find out, that they started in the 1920s in India. The aim was and still is to make better Muslims out of existing believers by going back to basics; they're an international group with millions of followers worldwide... I don't need to know that stuff. I'm looking for a more intimate understanding. What are they really about?'

'Well a lot of people believe it's character building. Many of us sort of inherit it from our dads. He once did it and so you have to do it. It used to be that some parents saw it as a rite of passage. You kaafir would say it's akin to doing something like VSO or an apprenticeship. Maybe like joining the Territorial Army or doing a gap year between school and uni.'

'VSO? What do you mean?' asked Jake.

'Voluntary Service Overseas. In the seventies and eighties you might serve your time in the TJs, do a load of good work, build a bit of character and then go back to normal life. But it's changed. It's changing.'

'How so?' asked Jake.

'A lot of Islam has traditionally been about academics and scholars. But to be a leader or a member of the TJ these days, you don't have to theorise on deep religious philosophy. You just need to know the right people, do the things that they want you to do, show the right commitment.

'It's not all bad, but it does sometimes attract the misfits who feel left out and alienated by mainstream Islam.'

'Why does it attract them?' asked Jake.

'Well, a lot of the stuff you'll find at a normal mosque is written in the language of our grandparents. It's heavy going. Kids today, they're not interested. They don't understand it. Their first language is more likely to be English. Some of the TJs know that. They make stuff simple. It's all word of mouth, anecdotes and urban myths.'

Zarshad continued, 'The Dawah missions to convert other Muslims, the pitching up at mosques, the door-to-door preaching and stuff – it's all about brotherhood and widening the net. It's not about the highest ethical standards.'

For the second time that morning, Jake had a creeping sense of déjà vu. 'Dawah'... Where had he heard that word before? Hadn't Shahid mentioned something? What was it? Something about important voluntary work in Bristol? Going door-knocking with his brother and their travelling group of preachers?

Zarshad was in full flow now. 'Drugs, alcohol and all that, mainstream Islam won't entertain it. The TJs are odd. I know people who've walked out of a nightclub and the same day they've walked into the bosom of the TJs just to make themselves feel better about their lives, and they are welcomed with open arms. It takes the piss out of Islam really. A lot of them join because it's more like a gang, with mates who do similar stuff. Some only do it because they've been feeling guilty about ignoring the faith, and feel they need to make an effort.'

'None of that seems so bad. They're making Islam more accessible?' interrupted Jake.

'Well, they are – but none of it is regulated properly. Anyone can get in, anyone can get to the top and anyone can preach whatever their version of the six principles it is they fancy… and that's where TJ and I have fallen out. I know some people are just there because it gives them power and influence over others.

'Some groups have become about controlling people, about cutting you off from the rest of your friends and family, simply isolating TJ followers from others, even from other Muslims! Sometimes they turn up uninvited at mosques and begin preaching their different views of Islam to those inside. They camp there, sleep there. I've heard tales that in some places they take over the mosque forever. They travel in groups for three, ten and forty days at a time, preaching to whoever will listen. They don't want contact with non-Muslims – it's all about converting existing believers. It's a bit like a cult, I suppose.'

'And what about your dad?'

'My father said it literally changed his life for the better when he found them and their work. But then thirty years later, the same lot he was involved with turned against him because he disagreed with some of the stuff they were doing and their interpretation of one of the Hadith. He was ostracised by them for a while. They made his name mud. Made life very difficult for him until he agreed to go back. They turned out to be wrong'uns, but he's still with them. I'm sure there are some good ones, but with my dad's lot there is a tendency to recruit the weak and the troubled and then assert power over them, so they don't have a voice to make decisions. There's an element of mind games played to keep you there. And you hear stories…'

'What sort of stories?' asked Jake

Zarshad's face clouded over for a moment. He looked troubled as he spoke quietly. 'On the internet forums. People who have left say that a lot of abuse goes on.'

123

'What, you mean a bit of bullying goes on?' replied Jake.

'No, it's more than that. You hear it time and again. People who've spent lengthy parts of their lives with the TJ. There are stories of abuse problems.'

'What, mental or physical?' Jake was all ears.

'Both, and it's not just by the new kids on the block. I've heard tales of established TJs that are meting out hard-core verbal and serious physical abuse. Some for decades, even. It's like there's a culture of bad behaviour in places. Some of the stuff you hear about beatings and protection rackets, all sorts of criminal activity. And no one is supposed to say anything because they might appear anti-Muslim. You never grass on your own kind. TJs are taught to stay away from you kaafirs and your police. It's a very separatist movement, but that just enables the bad apples to do what they want to do. The bad ones, they love the isolation of the TJ community from everyone and everything else. It gives them free reign to do what they want.'

'Is that why you've renounced your faith?' Jake asked, curious about Zarshad's leanings now.

'My father, he really believed in their stuff; preached it to me. I grew up in Fulham, not fucking Faisalabad. I didn't want those beliefs foisted on me. The TJs gave my father a choice – either I became part of TJ or he had to stop talking to me. He tried to leave. They got all heavy on him about it, threats and stuff. They ostracised him. Fucked up his business. Made him move out of his home. Stopped people talking to him. The pressure was too much and he went back to them. We've not spoken since. I renounced my faith altogether as a result of that. What kind of belief structure forbids you from seeing your own son?' Zarshad was looking into his now-empty pint glass as he finished his sentence. Jake thought that he could see him welling up.

'I'll get you another pint, mate...' Jake said as he stood up. 'Terrorism, are the TJs involved in that?'

'Terrorists? You mean are they political? Would they support an armed struggle against governments?'

'Yeah, is that what they're like?' Jake asked, still standing.

'Tablighlis will tell you that they aren't political – it's all complete bullshit. Their founder, Ilyas, started Tablighi Jamaat in India back in 1927 because he wanted to give Muslim communities more local influence and representation, more of a say in how things worked.

'Ilyas felt that local Muslims were not committed to their faith, some were being "Hindu-ised" or had turned to Christianity. Muslims weren't figuring on the census. They were losing representation and power in their own communities through decreasing numbers.

'Ilyas said he got some sort of divine inspiration to begin the TJs whilst on a pilgrimage to Mecca but, really, it was all about putting a stake in the ground for Muslim influence. They protest so much about being non-political. His whole game was politics. That's why he started it in the first place, to mobilise and motivate the community. Religious reaffirmation meant votes, votes meant Muslim influence, influence led to power and power led to money and land. That's what the TJs want – that's their game. I wouldn't say they were terrorists, but every movement has some sort of objective.'

Jake began to walk toward the bar.

'Numbers...' Zarshad said.

Jake stopped midway between the bar and where he'd been sitting. He turned and looked at Zarshad, who was staring into space, deep in thought, his eyes fixed on nothing.

Zarshad continued. 'Their power's in their numbers – the numbers of people they can get to do things in common. They slowly and gradually gain traction, become more powerful, win favour, wear people down.

'Tell me, Jake, which is stronger? A tiny drip of water or a slab of granite weighing thousands of tons?'

Jake stood motionless. He imagined a huge slab of granite with a drip of water on it.

'That drip of water will fall onto the slab of granite. It seems harmless at first, just sitting there. Until that drip is joined by others. Tens of others, a hundred others, thousands of others, millions of others, billions of others… drip, drip, drip, drip, drip. What happens then, Jake? What happens to the granite where the drips converge?'

'It wears a hole in the granite,' he replied.

'A hole so smooth that the big strong slab of granite looks like it was a block of cold butter cut with a red-hot knife. Eventually the drips will wear a smooth hole right through. The water goes where it wants; nothing can stop it then.

'It all starts with an annoying drip. No one notices it, not even the rock. No need to worry, it's just a drip. Numbers, it's all about numbers. That's why Ilyas started Tablighi Jamaat. That's what he wanted. People in larger numbers hold the balance of power. And every single number matters to the TJs. They want as many Muslims as possible following them, controlled by them.'

Jake continued to the bar. He returned with two more pints of cold lager and sat down opposite Zarshad.

'Why do the TJs want control of people? What can they achieve by it?'

'What do you see along the King's Road, Jake?'

'I see flash designer shops and swanky cars. What's that got to do with it?'

'Yeah, people are a commodity, Jake. People are money, they're power. They need places to live, cars to move around in, shops to shop in, beds to sleep in. Control them and you control their money. Simple. It's religious economics.

'If you can isolate an entire community, make them all think in the same way, make them all do the same sorts of things… If you and your friends rented them all places to live? If they shopped in your shops? If they voted for your friends in elections? Can you see the power that gives you?'

Jake thought about the East London mosque site. About the planning application Claire had placed inside Dusty's box. He said nothing to Zarshad in response.

Zarshad continued, 'Imagine how much that's worth? Hey, imagine you were a drug dealer and you could sell them drugs?'

'Drugs?'

'There's a huge number of young men who were previously drug addicts in TJ. They actively recruit people who have had drug or drink problems. I've often wondered how that can keep happening. It's obvious to me, to be honest – their people are just a mass market for anything and everything.'

'Are you saying TJ is just a front for a criminal enterprise?'

'Of course I'm not. There are people who do Dawah that really believe in it; think they're doing God's work. It's no better or worse than those American Mormons going off around the world and doing their missions, trying to convert people. Pretty harmless stuff really. What I'm saying is, there's also corruption, lots of it – it's human nature, isn't it? Muslims are no different; they still commit crime. Just like you have your bent coppers, MPs fiddling expenses, Catholic priests that have abused children, or the IRA and its money-laundering schemes. There are some people in TJ who exploit others for their own good. I call them "religious entrepreneurs". It suits them that many of their flock are poorly educated, can't speak English or can't speak the language of their grandparents, are unskilled, illegal immigrants, drug addicts or suffering from depression. These are by far the easiest sorts of people to con-trol, because they have nowhere else to turn.

'You can't separate religion from economy, Jake. And you know better than me, where there are questions of money and finance, power and control, there's always crime.'

124

'So what you got for me on Shahid, Len?' asked Jake in the middle of a mouthful of hash brown. 'You said you had big news from the National on the text?'

Jake was shouting Lenny to a heart attack on a plate by the roundabout on the old A-road near to Lenny's house. He was back on his legs again. He had stopped the drink fully now and the drugs. The suspension was still in force and he was still in limbo. Nothing could be properly dealt with until Claire was found, but he was back on full pay and his brain was once again in gear.

'OK. So you know we didn't pursue Shahid Bassam and the flat you found because the boss wanted him as a witness?'

'Oh, yes. What's the latest?' asked Jake eagerly. He was still gutted that he hadn't been allowed to continue with his line of enquiry and uncover more dirt on Shahid.

'Well, I've found out some more info, which may or may not be relevant. The National Crime Squad are looking at his brother.'

'His brother? Why?'

'It's in connection with drugs importation and money laundering. Get this, his brother is connected to a gang that the National reckon have made £19 million!'

'Jesus wept!' shouted Jake.

'I know!' Lenny exclaimed. 'There's something going on with drugs importation and money passing between Pakistan and the UK.'

'Blimey. If you were in any way connected to something like that, you might well be worried if you suddenly got a visit from the Met out of the blue. And his brother was supposedly quite devout? Do you remember? They were both going on some religious Tablighi Jamaat trip together. Dawah in Bristol or something?'

'So much for the brother being all religious,' said Lenny. 'How can you be religious and connected to a criminal gang like that?'

125

Jake shivered in the rusty old VW van that he'd bought with Stephanie's money. He hadn't noticed it until he was sat in the back but it smelled like something had died in there. Washing the inside of it out twice still hadn't gotten rid of the stench. A curtain with a small hole in it was rigged up across the bulkhead. It wasn't perfect, but it did the job of concealing him whilst he sat on a plastic garden chair in the back of the van and watched.

The place was busy, with men coming and going at all times. He'd not spotted a single woman since he'd been there. He was parked up behind a mesh-wire fence on an empty industrial unit adjacent to the mosque site. Just a collection of prefabricated buildings on an otherwise barren piece of wasteland, hemmed in by railway lines and a creek.

He had waited several days to see Mohammed Biaj. There were things he needed to know. Things that he thought he might glean from staking the place out. So far it had yielded nothing. He was no further forward than a week ago.

He'd half expected to see Claire. He was still wrestling with himself as to whether she was on his side or not or whether this was all an elaborate set-up for some reason. Yet all he'd seen was a lot of bearded men. The older ones looked impoverished. The rest were a younger flock — angry, boisterous and rebellious.

It felt like he'd been sat in the back of the freezing VW for weeks now. It was late afternoon; the light was failing. It would be dark soon.

His talk with Stephanie had hit him hard. He'd wanted to tell her everything, to share all the little confidences like they'd done once upon a time.

If he'd tried to explain to her that he was now no longer operating within the law, however, she would have told him that he was crazy. That he'd finally lost it. That she knew this day was coming.

He realised that he was now conducting his very own version of Operation Theseus. Perhaps he always had?

Sometimes he wondered if he was insane. Why couldn't he follow the rules like everyone else? Go with the flow. Maybe the stupid rice-packet actions from the MIR might have led somewhere if he had?

Jake had researched the owners of the piece of land he was now looking at. This was the land on which they were proposing to build the largest mosque in Europe, the 'mega-mosque'. The owners were a charitable trust, an arm of the Tablighi Jamaat sect, and the land had been purchased back in the mid-nineties.

A black VW Golf with tinted windows and shiny hubcaps flashed its lights toward a security booth at the gate, breaking Jake's train of thought. The site's entrance was protected by a security guard who inhabited a brick-built hut and operated a vehicle barrier. The guard stepped out of his hut and looked into the vehicle. It struck Jake as an unusual scene outside a place of worship.

The barrier was raised and the car wriggled its way down the muddy track toward a selection of Portakabins.

A few minutes later, Jake watched Mohammed Biaj emerge from behind the barrier on foot. He was wearing white kurta pyjamas and an off-white skullcap, but had thrown a green flying jacket with zip-pocket sleeves over the top.

There was a short conversation with the security guard manning the hut before Biaj walked up the road and past the old van that Jake was sat in.

Jake needed answers and he wasn't getting them sitting in the van.

He waited until the security guard in his high-visibility vest had returned to his cosy square-metre of office before he got out of the vehicle and followed Biaj up and around the bend in the road.

As Jake got to the apex, Biaj had disappeared. A short concrete ramp led down toward the creek; Jake assumed this was where Biaj must have gone.

As Jake walked down the ramp, the smell hit him. Sewage mixed with chemical effluent; the smell he thought had been coming from the van. It was the creek. It was black, a thick, oil-like film floating on top. Abstract shapes were breaking the surface at the water's edge. Jake thought he could make out the murky outline of an abandoned vehicle, but he couldn't be sure.

He found Biaj standing on a path by the stagnant creek's edge, his back to him. He was staring across the water toward an expanse of partially excavated wasteland.

The incandescent skyline of Canary Wharf was visible beyond. The setting sun reflected off the chrome and glass surfaces of the high-rise buildings; they glowed as if ablaze. Wasim's words from his martyrdom video rang in Jake's ears: '...Taste the punishment of the Burning Fire.'

Jake approached quietly and stood by the side of the bearded Middle Eastern-looking man who was lost in thought, gazing at the horizon.

'What do you want from me?' asked Biaj gruffly without turning to look at Jake. He spoke with an educated English accent that held just a faint hint of an Iraqi inflection.

Jake was surprised by the bluntness of the question. Biaj didn't even appear to have seen him approach.

'What do I want?' Jake asked. 'What do you think I want?'

'That van you got out of has been there for some days. You've obviously been watching the site for some reason. I assume it's me you want.'

Jake decided now was not the time to play games. 'I want to talk to you,' he said.

'Reporter? Security Service? Police officer? White supremacist?' Biaj barked back.

'Just someone who's interested in finding out the truth.'

'The truth about what?'

'The truth about your plans for the biggest mosque in Europe.'

Biaj narrowed his dark brown eyes. 'What do you mean "the truth"? It's hardly a secret.' He turned to face Jake fully. 'You look like a policeman,' he sneered.

Jake ignored the comment. 'There's more to this mosque than meets the eye though, isn't there?' he asked, fishing for a reaction, a loose thread.

'Like what?'

'It was a hefty investment back in the nineties. Seems odd that you've still not built your great big mosque here. Lack of money?'

'I could see the potential of this site. It was perfect. I sold them the vision of what we could really have. I wanted a seventy-thousand-capacity mosque...' Biaj pointed across the creek as he spoke.

The two of them stood looking at the barren industrial landscape that lay before them. The silence lasted too long. Biaj was waiting for Jake to speak, but Jake was thinking. There was something important in what he'd just heard this man say, but he couldn't quite grasp it there and then.

Biaj broke the silence. 'It's no secret; it's well known what I wanted here. Who are you? What's this about?'

Jake heard it again – the intonation in Biaj's voice, the way he moved his eyes as he said the word 'wanted'.

'You wanted it here? Past tense?' asked Jake as he stared intently at Biaj.

'Yes... *wanted*. Who are you and why do you need to know?'

'I'm Claire Richards' boyfriend...'

Biaj paused for a moment.

'The detective inspector who was suspended? Flannagan?'

Jake nodded.

A slight smile played across Biaj's face.

'I don't think you should be here, Mr Flannagan. You are going to be in even more trouble now.'

Biaj began to walk further on along the towpath and away from Jake.

'Claire was on to you,' Jake called after him, trying to grab his attention. 'I know about you and Lawrence Congerton-Jones.'

Biaj stopped and turned. 'You know nothing!'

'I know that you were both supplying drugs,' replied Jake, bolder now.

'So what?'

Jake wasn't getting the reaction he'd expected. He tried again.

'Claire knew the bigger picture – she knew you wanted more people to deal to. She'd cottoned on to the fact that a huge mosque meant a larger customer base… That's what this is all about, isn't it?' Jake asked.

Biaj broke into a smile. 'Is that all you've come here to ask me about?' He chuckled. 'A bit of drug dealing with a handler and a large mosque? Is that all you've got?' He began to laugh uproariously in Jake's face.

126

This was like a game of twenty questions, thought Jake. He didn't know all the answers, but he knew enough to realise when he hadn't got a bite. The drugs issue wasn't even rippling the surface. Biaj clearly thought it was some huge joke.

The stench seemed to be getting worse as the surrounding tidal rivers began to seep into the creek. Jake's nose wrinkled at the smell. Biaj noticed. 'That stink you can smell in the air. What do you think that is?'

Jake shrugged his shoulders blankly.

'It's shit! What you can smell is raw sewage. Sixteen million litres of raw, untreated overflow sewage passes through that creek every year. It's just the same as it was in Victorian times. The Thames is supposed to wash the sewage out to sea, but until the new tunnel is built, we are surrounded by shit. Can you see why no one wanted this land back in the nineties? That's why the TJs bought it. Cut off by railway lines and a shit-filled river; land contaminated by hazardous chemicals and highly toxic acids from the derelict factories. All these poor people wanted was their own place, in this toilet, and you bastards wouldn't even let them have that!'

'This is about Tablighi Jamaat, isn't it?' Jake pressed harder to see if he could get a reaction. He was running out of places to go with his questioning. Biaj ignored him and began to walk away, but Jake needed answers.

'Where's Claire?' he shouted after him.

Biaj was some feet in front of him now, his back turned as he walked away. 'I've no idea what you're talking about,' he called over his shoulder, waving the question away.

The time for being a shrinking violet had passed. Jake closed the space between them suddenly with an instant burst of speed, like in his old athletics days, go on the 'B' of the bang.

Biaj heard the footsteps. He spun around quickly, only for Jake to grab the collar of his jacket. His aim was to get in the Iraqi's face, to shout aggressively, scare him a little.

As Biaj twisted and pushed back, he lost his footing in the mud and slipped slightly from Jake's grasp. They were closer to the water's edge than Jake had realised. Biaj stumbled backwards, off balance, arms flailing wildly in the air as his feet missed the side. He plummeted downwards, landing almost waist-deep in the putrid smelling mud at the base of the creek.

Jake looked down at the bank below him. It was covered with sheet metal to stop erosion, creating a sheer drop. The other side, backing onto an ancient sewage works, was edged with crumbling Victorian red brick. The jagged shapes he'd seen emerging from the water earlier were gone now, as the tidal currents swiftly flowed in.

'Fucking get me out of here!' bellowed Biaj as he writhed and floundered around. The wild movement served only to make him sink further into the mire that lay beneath his feet.

Jake looked left and right. There was no one. His breath twirled up and into the evening gloom, descending quickly upon them now. It was almost dark. 'I need answers before I can help you,' replied Jake calmly, as he looked down from the creek's edge.

Biaj continued to try to free himself, this time forcing his hands down against the mud at his sides as if to push it off himself, but the sludge just wreathed its way further up his arms. He began to panic, thrashing about with his whole body, as if in a frantic struggle to free his legs and lower body from the mouth of some filthy, oily beast.

Jake looked on, saying nothing. Seeing the fear build. Listening to the cursing and hissing of anger as it turned into more scared cries for help.

Biaj realised he was just wasting his energy, that it was no use. He was truly stuck. He stopped thrashing about. He was panting, out of breath. The stinking water was just a foot or so away now. Biaj watched as it lapped against the bank of mud where he was trapped, the water like the tongue of the beast whose mouth he was now caught in. It moved slowly, silently, softly as it crept closer and closer, higher and higher.

'Fuck! Help me, the water…' Biaj screamed through frenzied intakes of breath. 'The tide, the water, it's…' Biaj began squirming around in the mud again, struggling ever harder to make the beast spit him out.

Jake watched as the panic took hold of Biaj; he'd seen panic many times before. It was no use trying to talk to him at the moment.

'… coming in… It's coming in, the tide, it's coming in, please help me… HELP ME!'

Jake knew that the planning forms that Claire had left him were somehow crucial. He thought back to Shahid and how his flat above the sandwich shop had been rented for use as a bomb factory by the bombers, how they'd all been involved with Tablighi Jamaat, how the planned mosque was going to be built and run by a charitable arm of the same sect. Yet what good was any of that information if he couldn't get the killer breakthrough, couldn't create a penny-falls machine payout?

Jake looked across the creek at the brownfield site opposite. 'You wanted a seventy-thousand-capacity mosque… here?' he said, repeating Biaj's earlier comment, thinking out loud now. It was a rhetorical statement spoken into the dusk air. 'You wanted… You "wanted" it – you can't have it now, can you? Why?' asked Jake.

'Get me out of here and I will answer every question you ask – I promise!' Biaj screamed, raising a mud-covered arm above his head.

'No. You talk now, and I'd talk fast if I were you. What do you mean by you "wanted"?' Jake asked, looking down at the now clearly terrified Biaj.

'Compulsory purchase order... Today. Get me out!' Biaj shouted as he began thrashing about again.

'Compulsory purchase order, why?'

The water was all around Biaj now, the muddy bank and weeds below its surface holding him firm in their grip as the levels rose around him.

'Those fucking idiots... they fucked it up – did it a fucking day late, that's why!'

Biaj was out of breath again. He began muttering dementedly to himself in a language that Jake didn't understand.

'A day late' – Jake played the words over in his head.

'A day late' was clearly important. More important to Biaj than any accusations of kidnapping, drug dealing or being in cahoots with his MI5 handler would ever be. Jake could feel he was getting close. What had happened a day late? What could possibly be more awful than the sum of those pretty serious misdemeanours? The penny-falls machine started whirring in Jake's head again. A twenty-four-hour delay. Something important had been put off, but what?

Delay.

Late.

Wait.

'Having major problem. Cannot make time. Will ring you when I get it sorted. Wait at home.'

Jake's brain was in overdrive. There had been another death on 7/7 – the very first death of 7/7. Salma Khan, Wasim's wife, had gone into hospital with complications and miscarried their unborn child. That had triggered a flurry of text messages from Wasim about a 'major problem'.

'Wait. Wait at home.'

The hospital visit meant he'd had to abandon the original schedule.

They'd carried out the bomb attacks twenty-four hours later than planned.

Jake remembered watching the CCTV footage from the supermarket. Wasim had been pottering round with his trolley full of ice at 0520 hours on the morning of the sixth, shortly after he'd sent his text message telling the rest of the gang to stay at home. Fifteen bags of ice to keep the improvised explosive devices cool for another day. Wasim wasn't rushing… he showed no panic… to him it was just a small detour, a minor diversion because his wife had gone to hospital and they couldn't travel to London that day.

The attacks being carried out a day late hadn't seemed the slightest bit important at any stage of their investigation, neither to Jake nor to the bombers themselves…

Until now.

127

Jake was suddenly transported back in time to the morning of 7 July, sat in his car on that West Yorkshire terraced street, listening to the BBC replaying the news over and over again.

The news from the previous day... the news from 6 July.

'And the host city for the 2012 Olympic Games... is... LONN-DONN!'

The pennies mounted up again and overlapped in Jake's head to form a perfect arc. They were beginning to flow out of the machine like a waterfall, a crescendo of coppers crashing down faster than Jake could catch them in his cup.

The attacks had been delayed on 6 July, a twenty-four-hour delay because of the complications with Wasim and Salma's unborn child.

Jake's head emptied of all the useless pieces of information that he had been storing, like water flowing out. He looked down at Biaj; the water was chest deep and climbing now.

'The delay. The sixth of July was the intended date for the bombings, wasn't it? The bombings were delayed, weren't they? How did we not see it? This was inspired by you?'

'Please help me... I will tell you everything, I promise.' Biaj's panic had given way to uncontrollable sobbing. Tears flowed down his cheeks. The fight had gone out of him. He had stopped moving. He remained motionless as the creek's wet tongue licked up his body.

'Keep talking,' said Jake, 'and I'll think about it.'

Biaj was clearly desperate now – he began babbling at high speed. 'No one knew. Not even the bombers themselves… They – they should have done it early on the morning of the sixth. But… but… but…'

'But what?'

'They didn't know!'

'Know what? They didn't know what?'

'They didn't know it was pointless on the seventh, the bombings were pointless… they fucked it all up by doing it a day late.'

Jake couldn't believe what he was hearing. 'Why should the bombings have happened early in the morning on the sixth? Tell me! Why?'

He remembered the note that Claire had left behind with the name Mohammed Biaj written on it. The note with the numbers two, zero, one and another two on it… Her handwriting had been sloppy, uneven and spread out. The numbers – he'd thought they were perhaps individual digits for a combination lock, but maybe they weren't? Maybe they were meant to represent something as a whole?

Biaj's eyes glinted as he growled back. 'London was a joke bid. Paris were the favourites. But London? It was a joke. Then they got serious. In – in 2003… I had to act.' Biaj was beginning to shiver now, from the cold water that was all around him.

'The Olympics? The bombings were supposed to happen before the Olympic vote took place?' Jake was incredulous. 'That was what you were targeting on the sixth? You didn't want London getting the Olympics?'

He thought back to the digits Claire had hastily scribbled on the piece of paper, two, zero, one, two. Of course! Claire's numbers were meant to represent a year – 2012. The London 2012 Olympics.

'International Olympic Committee. The report. Transport weak. London. Weak spot. That's what the IOC said.' Biaj was now talking in very short, sharp sentences. The freezing water was beginning to steal the oxygen from his body. 'Please. Get. Me. Out!'

The wet tongue of the tide was now lapping at Biaj's fingertips, which he had pulled into his chest. He wrenched one of his hands free of the water. It was wrapped in reeds and covered in lurid green slime.

Jake continued with his questions. 'The attacks were designed to affect the voting? The voting on London's bid. You did it to stop the Games coming here?'

Biaj was in full flow now, as if he knew that the truth was the only way out. 'Yes. The answer was simple. Fuck up the transport. Four bombs. 8.50 a.m. On 6 July. Three hours. Three hours before. Before voting. Before. Olympic votes. Before votes cast in Singapore.'

Jake stood there listening to this petrified voice. A man who'd helped to murder more than fifty people and disable, disfigure, traumatise and injure more than seven hundred.

'Stupid. Idiots. Couldn't even blow themselves up. On—' Biaj gasped in a lungful of air '—the right day!'

'So London won the vote when they shouldn't have? The bombs were supposed to dissuade the IOC members from voting for London and take the Olympics elsewhere?' Jake shouted.

'Yes! NOW HELP ME!'

Why, thought Jake. Why force the Olympics to move elsewhere? What could be important enough to Biaj?

128

As the light above them finally faded, the realisation dawned on Jake.

He felt the information flowing out of his head like a waterfall.

The rice packets, the Groom-Bates saga, the lump on the car... it was all nonsense. Nothing they'd done in the entire investigation would have brought them to this point. The creek continued to fill.

'You didn't want the Olympics here because... because... they need this land! The whole thing has put the kibosh on your mosque! It means your fucking great big mosque won't get built! The games are coming to London and you won't get your planning permission. The Olympics coming here has meant you've been served with your compulsory purchase order. They need this land to build on for the Games, and that's what's going to prevent your huge mosque!' Jake stared down at Biaj – disgusted with the man looking up at him. 'All those people died for planning permission for... for... your place of worship?'

The water was up to Biaj's neck and beginning to lap at his chin. 'Get me out...' he shouted.

Biaj was going to drown if Jake didn't help him. A couple of paces up the towpath, Jake could see a plank of wood, an old scaffold board. He ran to retrieve it. It looked about long enough to hook Biaj out of the water. He moved back to the spot where Biaj had fallen into the creek and leaned down, holding the wood. There was a sudden spark of life in Biaj. He held up his hands for the board.

'I will help you,' said Jake, 'but you finish it. You finish telling me now.'

Biaj realised he needed to keep talking, and fast. He began speaking at three times his normal speed. 'The mosque. Just one part of my Islamic city. The draw. A new enclave. Jamaatis, TJs. Thousands of them. Starts ball rolling. Money. Lots of money. Power. Control. Influence over the area. Influence over people in it.' Biaj paused, sucking in lungfuls of air again before continuing. 'A new headquarters, my new global HQ. My version of TJ. Houses, businesses, schools. People need goods and services.'

Jake nodded. 'You mean like slum accommodation, protection money, fake passports, dodgy visas, ropey insurance, drugs? And the vast riches that those things create come straight back to you? That's what this mosque is about?'

'Yes. Help me! Get me out! Please!' cried Biaj.

'No. You tell me it *all*, NOW! *Then* I get you out!'

Biaj was struggling to keep his head above the waterline. He was thrashing about with his hands, trying to reach for the board, which Jake had left frustratingly just out of reach. His skullcap had fallen off, his white robes were being held by an invisible vacuum, sucked down by the effluent and mud.

'The Tablighi Jamaat headquarters in India?' asked Jake. 'They never sanctioned this?'

'No! Elders believe in simplicity. We live life the way the Prophet did. Peace be upon him. We brush teeth with twigs. Cut beards to same length! I don't care what they want! This was to be my extravagant masterpiece!'

'This was a sect-wide plan?'

'No! It was me… Me! My friends. We duped everyone. *Now help, help!* HELP ME!' screamed Biaj at the top of his voice.

Biaj was still desperately trying to extricate himself from the bottom of the creek but he was taking in gulps of water now as the level rose around his chin.

'You duped everyone?'

'Yes… you police, the bombers, the trust, I even duped al-Qaeda!'

Jake pushed the scaffold board down to Biaj. Biaj grabbed it with both hands and started pulling himself up as Jake held onto the other end.

'Why here, why now?' asked Jake as he watched Biaj steady himself and gradually pull himself free from the mud. He began to slowly inch his way up the board. He craned his neck and looked up at Jake as he spoke. 'A global city like London with a prime location like our site? I could have taken power here. Created my own headquarters and my own walled city.'

Biaj crawled slowly on his belly, hauling himself further up the board like a caterpillar as he carried on muttering, 'Flash cars, watches, designer clothes and fancy lifestyles. I'm the man in the background that you can never touch. Friends in high places, friends with businesses, friends with money that make things happen. The people that will live near my mosque, they will rent their houses from my friends, but they will rent their souls from me.'

Jake looked into Biaj's eyes. The fear was gone. His words were boastful. He was talking about the future. This wasn't over for him.

Jake yanked the board as hard as he could, back up and toward him. Biaj lost his grip. As he did so, he was sucked back down into the water and back into the mud.

The water level was high now. Biaj's head went straight under the surface of the creek. All Jake could see were his arms flailing about wildly as they broke the murky surface.

With all his might, Jake tossed the board like a caber into the deepest part of the creek, way out of Biaj's reach.

A moment later, a face bobbed just above the surface, gasping for air. Biaj resurfaced again several times as if climbing an imaginary ladder, only to slip back down again below the gloopy black surface of the water, the weight of his Western jacket and Eastern robes sucking him down.

Jake stood there shaking, watching for what felt like an eternity, as the movements in the creek slowed. Bubbles began appearing from beneath the water as Biaj's thrashing arms eventually became still.

Jake thought about how alone he'd felt chasing Wasim down the M1 on the morning of the bombings; how desperate he had been for some help; how no one would listen to him throughout the investigation; how broken the families were that had lost people, both those of the victims and the bombers; how he'd felt so low that he had to seek solace with a different woman at the bottom of a bottle every night, when really it was Claire he missed, and his family. How the victims' families and even the bombers' families had become more important than his own. How, even now, he wanted answers to the bombings… stupidly forsaking questions about Claire to find out the solution to the puzzle that had dogged him for so long.

The putrid water was motionless. Nothing moved; it was dark and still.

There were no more thoughts. And his mind was made up.

He turned and walked away.

129

Jake walked briskly back to the van, backed out of his parking spot and made a rapid getaway. He didn't really know where he was going. He drove in a daze, the pennies still crashing down in his head. He pulled over onto some bumpy waste ground near to West Ham Tube station, put his head in his hands and wept.

Nothing they had done in the entire investigation would have brought them to this realisation – why the attacks had actually been perpetrated. Even the bombers themselves had believed their own personal motives were the reasons for the attacks. Jake still couldn't believe what he'd heard. This act of terrorism had been created by an entrepreneur who would stop at nothing to create and rule his very own kingdom on a toxic island of industrial wasteland in the very heart of London.

He grabbed his mobile; he needed to call Lenny.

'Hi, Jake, you OK? Where are you?' said Lenny on pick up.

'Lenny, listen – just trust me on this. Don't worry about how I know but… we missed it. It was staring us in the face this whole time and we missed something…' Jake was trying to get the words out as fast as he could.

'Lenny. The attacks. They were meant for 6 July but they lost their baby. It was to stop the Olympics coming here. They wanted to keep the land. It was all about the land. Biaj had his own special development planned.'

'Slow down. The Olympics? What do you mean? That happened the day before. The bombings took place on the seventh, Jake?'

'Remember the emergency hospital visit? The text messages? The CCTV showing Wasim buying the ice just after dawn on the sixth? It was supposed to happen on the sixth! It was delayed. But it had all been designed to affect the Olympic voting, to stop London getting the Olympics.'

'What the hell? So what was the point of going ahead with it then? Why not put a stop to it all after they knew they'd missed the deadline to influence the vote?' asked an incredulous Lenny.

'The bombers didn't know – they just thought they were there to martyr themselves, kill others and make a huge religious and political statement. Biaj made sure they knew nothing about his plans. They were totally unaware that it was the wrong day and too late to influence the Olympic vote. So what are you going to do with them? They were bent on martyring themselves. If he hadn't let them run with it, there was a risk to him in case they found out what he'd really used them for. You don't train an attack dog and then use it to fetch your fucking slippers, Lenny, do you?'

'But how did he get them to do it?'

'I guess they were just angry young men. Kids who couldn't stand the greyness of life. They needed absolutes. Their sect beliefs mean they regard this life as a "toilet", that the next life is far more important. He played on that. They were just a bunch of depressed and misguided drug addicts before the TJs and Biaj got their hands on them. They give up their addiction to drugs and become addicted to a misguided and warped religious sect instead. It's easy to fill young minds full of fanciful myths and visions at the crucial detox time. He harnessed their pain and anger. He used their utter belief in what they were doing, but he used it for his own entrepreneurial ends. It wasn't terrorism, it was economics.'

'Then why bother with a second wave of attacks on 21 July? What was the point?'

'I think the 21/7 lot were just the backup crew. They had a number of different team leaders for the same job. I'm pretty sure a lot of the hydrogen peroxide that the 21/7 guys purchased was bought on 5 July. People change their mind, get arrested, have accidents. I think they were the B team. They'd already had two youngsters who'd blown themselves up during their explosives training in Pakistan. The ones on 21/7 were just the understudies, but once they'd all been trained, albeit to a lesser degree, they were left to their own devices. They were the perfect decoy, weren't they? Tell them to go out and do it two weeks later, make it a copycat attack.'

'A second wave of attacks, designed simply to take everyone's eyes off the first?' asked Lenny.

'A stand-alone attack targeting the Olympic vote on the sixth – it would have looked too obvious, wouldn't it? But in the end they missed the vote anyway, so no one noticed.'

'It wasn't al-Qaeda at all, was it?' Lenny realised.

'No. I think someone paid in drug money to use their camps, their trainers and their explosives-training people. The videos were passed to al-Qaeda after the attacks. They slapped all the graphics on the martyrdom videos months after they'd been filmed. Al-Qaeda are just a bunch of out-of-work freedom fighters, but they still need to earn a living somehow.'

'But al-Qaeda claimed the attacks. They said they did it.'

'Yeah, they tried to claim some sort of vague responsibility. But, Len, it was months after the event when they finally got their hands on those videos. Yes al-Qaeda said that it came under their banner, but two other groups tried to claim the credit for it in the meantime too! I bet Biaj was quite happy for al-Qaeda to get their hands on those tapes and take the limelight. He didn't want anyone to tie him to the attacks. It was a cover-up so it couldn't be traced back to him...' Jake paused suddenly. 'Lenny, I have to go now. There's something I need to do.'

Jake put the van into gear and moved off. He was mesmerised by the rhythm of his own movements, changing gear, moving the rear-view mirror, moving the steering wheel; his mind a myriad of thoughts about what he had just heard as the dirty industrial backstreets of East Ham slipped past him.

'It was all about land and a fucking money-making enclave!' he shouted.

What was he supposed to do with what he had just been told? What he now knew? What he'd just done?

Biaj was dead.

He needed time to think. He was suspended from work. That had to run its course. Nothing he had just done would help that. He had to get back to work, had to keep his job. Jake admitting he'd been illegally watching the mosque, that he'd confronted Biaj, that Biaj had fallen into the shit-filled creek and drowned while Jake refused to help him – it would just make things worse. It changed nothing. Fifty-two people and four bombers were still dead.

Jake drove through Stratford town centre. The Olympics were coming. The mosque wasn't going to be built. Nothing had changed.

Claire must have known. How? He still had no clearer understanding of where she was, what she was...

Locard's theory. Every contact leaves a trace. Jake's fingerprints and DNA were all over the van. The van was the only thing that connected him to Biaj, to the mosque site.

Jake drove northwards and into the heavily industrialised area that was set to become the Olympic park. Right now it was just full of scrap-metal dealers and brickworks. He knew a car park that was concealed by railway sidings. Travellers regularly used the place to dump their rubbish.

A cold mist was the only occupant of the otherwise deserted place when he arrived. Jake got out of the van and left the key in the ignition. He rubbed down the exterior with his sleeve, paying particular attention to the mirrors, handles and paint-work around the driver's door.

Whilst camped out at the mosque site in the back of the van, Jake had spotted a can tucked under the Transporter's front passenger seat. It had previously been hidden by Paul's vintage mower, the one he'd disposed of at the dump. When he smelt it, Jake realised he'd struck lucky – it was petrol for the mower.

It was this petrol he now emptied over the van's interior, throwing the empty can into the passenger seat through the open driver's window. In Jake's experience, vehicles always burned better if you left the windows open. They sucked in oxygen to feed the flames.

He lit a match and dropped it into the van. There was a sudden whoosh as the petrol and its vapour ignited inside. Flames flew out through the open windows as the initial blaze struggled for breath and life. Jake watched as the fire fought for its existence, consuming everything just to stay alive.

He imagined Biaj fighting for breath below the waterline, trapped in the mud and scrabbling about in the freezing, putrid water of the creek. The burning and tearing of his lungs as the water rushed in and pushed out every last piece of air from them. The terror that he must have felt trying to draw breath from nothing, so close to the site of his dream venture, almost in the shadows of the gleaming tower blocks of Canary Wharf.

He stared into the flames as they licked at the roof and reached from the open window, the fire trying to grab hold of anything else that it could.

For the second time that day, a luminous sight triggered in Jake a memory of religious scripture, yet this time the numbers 8:50 were reversed.

Psalm 50:8 – I bring no charges against you concerning your sacrifices or concerning your burnt offerings, which are ever before me.

Jake walked slowly onto a patch of wasteland, down the hill, away from the burning van and toward Stratford.

He didn't look back.

Jake took the Tube from Stratford to London Bridge. His walk back to Whitechapel was filled with thoughts about what he should do next. His priority had to be finding Claire, but how? Maybe he could do some tracework on her missing iMac? The IP address of the computer might throw something up. But what if someone had already kicked over these tracks? Had the iMac even been used since she'd disappeared?

When he arrived home, Jake was surprised to see that the lights were still on in the sari shop. He was about to walk up the stairs when he heard a voice behind him.

'Hey, I think this is for you.' He turned to see the young girl from the sari shop standing behind him.

She was holding a postcard. 'It's got 26 Caroline Street as the address and not 26a, but it starts "Dear Jake", so I'm guessing it must be for you?'

'Thank you.' Jake took the single piece of card from her.

She smiled and returned to the shop's entrance, switching the lights off and pulling down the shutters.

Jake glanced at the small piece of card. It was the type of postcard you could get from any British seaside town, with a photo on the front and space for writing on the back.

The image on the front was a familiar one. It was of the harbour at St Austell. He flipped the card over. A message had been scrawled out in blue pen; it looked messy and rushed. He recognised the handwriting instantly – it was Claire's.

Dear Jake,

I'm fine. Will explain everything over some tea and scones with cream. Meet me in the place you waited for me that morning by the harbour.

X

Jake felt a sudden surge of emotion. She'd been watching him that morning while he waited.

She'd not tried to contact him in person – maybe she was aware that he might have been followed? She'd shunned using any electronic method to make contact. Whether because of family difficulties or work reasons, she'd been in hiding. The postcard had been deliberately sent to the sari shop so that it circumvented any trace and intercept that the Post Office had been asked to put on his address by the police or the Security Service.

Clever girl.

As Jake turned to close the door, Ted bolted in and began rubbing herself round his feet and legs. He picked her up and she purred loudly. He kissed her on the head and tickled her behind the ears.

'Come on, Ted, let's have cuddle on the sofa, just me and you.'

Tomorrow he would get the train to St Austell, eat scones and wait.

EPILOGUE: THE FACTS

(All times given as British Summer Time, BST)

Tablighi Jamaat

The Tablighi Jamaat movement has been banned in several countries, where it is viewed as an extremist, fundamentalist and separatist sect. It is known that Mohammed Sidique Khan and Shehzad Tanweer, two of the 7/7 bombers, had previously worshipped at Tablighi Jamaat's European headquarters in Savile Town, Dewsbury, West Yorkshire. Several other prominent extremists have been shown to have links to Tablighi Jamaat, including Muktar Said Ibrahim, leader of the failed 21/7 bomb plot in 2005; the failed shoe bomber, Richard Reid; several of those involved in the 2006 transatlantic-airline plots; John Walker Lindh known as 'the American Taliban'; and Kafeel Ahmed who died from burns whilst trying to set off a car bomb at Glasgow airport.

HISTORY

1865 Abbey Mills chemical works in the Lower Lea Valley is built to produce sulphuric acid. The site of chemical works for more than one hundred years, substances such as manure, animal fat for candles, oil and kerosene were also processed on the land.

1994 The Lower Lea Valley is included in the East Thames Corridor study area and earmarked for regeneration in a study entitled Regional Planning Guidance for the South East.

Also in 1994, a review of International Olympic Committee members shows that London is the only British city capable

419

of competing on an international stage and attracting enough votes to win an Olympic bid.

1995 Following three consecutive unsuccessful bids to host the summer Olympic Games (Birmingham tendered for 1992 and Manchester for the 1996 and 2000 games), the British Olympic Association decides that London is to be the site of the UK's next bid.

1996 An eighteen-acre piece of disused, brownfield land on the site of the former Abbey Mills chemical works in West Ham is obtained by the Anjuman-e-Islahul Muslimeen of London UK Trust, a charitable-trust arm of Tablighi Jamaat.

Cut off from the surrounding area by Abbey Creek and the Channelsea River to the east, the District Line Railway to the south and the Jubilee line to the west, the area can only be entered by a single access point, Canning Road, from the north. The site is purchased from RTZ Chemicals for a reported figure of £1.6 million. (On an unconnected note, RTZ goes on to become Rio Tinto and exclusively provides the metal to produce the 4,700 gold, silver and bronze medals at the London 2012 Olympic and Paralympic Games.)

May 1997 The British Olympic Association begins work on a fourth bid – this time for London 2012.

1999 The first of an ongoing series of applications to use the Abbey Mills site are lodged by the Tablighi Jamaat charitable trust, arousing intense opposition locally.

15 December 2000 A confidential report is submitted to the Government by the British Olympic Association about London's bid for the 2012 Olympic Games. East London versus West London options are assessed.

October 2001 Temporary permission is given for the Abbey Mills site to be used as a place of Tablighi Jamaat worship for five years. It is believed that plans for the proposed mosque are first agreed in principle in a deal between Newham Council and Anjuman-e-Islahul Muslimeen. Yet the Newham Unitary Development Plan also places the area within one of its 'major opportunity zones'.

November 2001 Four main potential Olympic Games 2012 sites in East London are analysed in a report.

January 2002 The Lower Lea Valley, East London, is assessed as the host site in a specially commissioned report. The plan for 2012 focuses on the regeneration of a five-hundred-acre swathe of land there, in one of the most deprived areas of the UK.

January 2003 London's 2012 Olympic bid is debated in Parliament. On 21 January 2003, the House of Commons Culture, Media and Sport Committee releases a report (entitled 'A London Olympic Bid for 2012') stating that due to the availability of land, a bid for the 2012 Games was London's (and therefore the UK's) only chance to host a Games for the foreseeable future, possibly ever.

May 2003 Tessa Jowell, Secretary of State for Culture, Media and Sport, announces that the Government would 'back London to the hilt' with £2.38 billion in funding.

11 July 2003 The International Olympic Committee is officially notified by the British Olympic Association that London will bid to host the 2012 Olympic Games.

January 2004 Planning applications for the proposed 2012 Olympic developments are submitted to the four relevant London boroughs affected by the Games. London officially launches its Olympic bid for 2012 on 16 January 2004. Tony Blair announces that the proposed East London base for the Olympics will be completely regenerated with new facilities for the Games.

1 October 2004 The four affected East London boroughs each grant planning permission for the 2012 Olympics.

14 November 2004 The London bid team flies to Lausanne, Switzerland, to hand in a six-hundred-page bid document to the International Olympic Committee (IOC). London's Olympic bid application states that the legacy of the 2012 games will be 'the regeneration of an entire community for the direct benefit of everyone who lives there'.

19 November 2004 *Just five days later*, the ringleader of the four 7/7 bombers, Mohammed Sidique Khan, along with another of the bombers, Shehzad Tanweer, both fly to Pakistan. There they spent four months at clandestine military training camps in Pakistan, learning how to make explosives and build bombs.

8 February 2005 Bombers Khan and Tanweer arrive back in the UK.

9 February 2005 *Just one day later*, the International Olympic Committee flies to the UK, to visit London for a week-long tour in order to audit the London bid.

22 March 2005 A subsequent IOC report following the February visit to London says that transport is the crucial limiting factor that impacts upon the strength of the London Olympic bid. Out of a total of eleven criteria, Britain's Olympic bid scores lowest for its 'transport concept' with a minimum score of 4.7 points and a maximum of 6.7 out of ten. The report calls for 'substantial improvement' of the London Underground system. Terrorism is also cited as a 'global concern' for the Olympic candidate cities.

Summer 2005 Plans for a Tablighi Jamaat mosque on the Abbey Mills site, to cater for forty thousand worshippers, are announced by acclaimed architect Ali Mangera of Mangera Yvars. The project for an International Islamic Centre with school, gardens, mosque and exhibition spaces is to cover a built area of 180,000 metres squared on a site one kilometre in length. The project is reportedly expected to cost around £100 million and include wind turbines and solar panels.

28 June 2005 The group of four 7/7 bombers carries out a full hostile reconnaissance mission and visits King's Cross station, London.

Tuesday, 5 July 2005 Mohammed Sidique Khan arrives with his pregnant partner at Dewsbury Hospital.

Wednesday, 6 July 2005

2 a.m. IOC members meet in Singapore to hear the final presentations for five host-city contenders: London, New York, Madrid, Moscow and Paris, in one of the most hotly contested bidding processes in Olympic history.

4.35 a.m. Bomb ringleader Mohammed Sidique Khan sends a hurried text message to co-bomber Shehzad Tanweer in connection with his partner's pregnancy complications: 'Having major problem. Cannot make time. Will ring you when I get it sorted. Wait at home.'

5.20 a.m. Khan and Tanweer are filmed arriving at the Asda superstore in Pudsey, driving a blue Nissan Micra hire car. They walk around the store leisurely and purchase fifteen bags of ice.

7.30 a.m. The London bid team, led by Lord Coe, takes to the stage to make its final presentation.

10 a.m. Conclusion of the host-city bid presentations.

11.26 a.m. IOC members vote in a secret electronic ballot. Moscow, New York City and Madrid are eliminated in the first three rounds.

11.45 a.m. Conclusion of the fourth round of voting, which is solely between the remaining contenders, London and Paris.

12.48 p.m. Announcement that London has won the bid over Paris by just four votes – and is named the official host city for the XXX Olympiad and XIV Paralympic Games.

Following the announcement, London's mayor, Ken Livingstone, says: 'This is an area with the poorest children, contaminated soil. Go and see the area as it is now and judge it after it is transformed.'

Thursday 7 July, 2005

4.30 a.m. In a carbon copy of the day before, the four bombers try again to set off for London, but this time without distraction or interruption. They take with them improvised explosive devices that have been constructed using materials purchased from garden centres and shops. The devices are packed into rucksacks using the ice purchased the previous morning, from the Pudsey branch of Asda, to keep them cool. The intention is to target Tube trains all departing from King's Cross station.

8.50 a.m. Three of the bombers detonate their bombs aboard underground trains. Hasib Hussain, the youngest of the four bombers, just eighteen years old, finds that his bomb fails to detonate in synchronisation with the rest. A faulty nine-volt battery used to send an electrical pulse into the detonator of the device is the cause. He returns to ground level from a very busy northbound platform of King's Cross station. He calmly goes into a WH Smith store.

8.59 a.m. Hasib purchases a new nine-volt battery for £4.49. He tries to make phone calls to his three friends, who by now are all dead, having martyred themselves, murdering thirty-nine people in the process. After failing to reach them on the phone, Hasib boards a number 30 double-decker bus and sits toward the rear on the upper deck.

9.47 a.m. As the bus passes the British Medical Association building at Tavistock Square, Hasib lets out a scream before connecting the newly purchased battery to his rucksack-based bomb. He dies instantly, murdering a further thirteen people in the process.

Fifty-two people had been murdered. The four bombers were dead and more than seven hundred people were injured.

25 October 2005 The mayor of London, Ken Livingstone, acknowledges that some of the venues for the 2012 Olympics might have to be moved, with increased security levels a priority, in light of the London bombings in July. He comments: 'Can we reconfigure some of those things so that we can all save money, that we can work with the local and neighbouring developments to integrate it all better?'

16 November 2005 A compulsory purchase order is issued for a part of the Abbey Mills mosque site under the London Development Agency (Lower Lea Valley, Olympic and Legacy) Compulsory Purchase Order 2005. It is stated that the CPO is for an area which links West Ham station to Greenway land, to enable the building of the West Ham ramp (footbridge and temporary walkway) which is cited will provide better pedestrian access for the 2012 Olympic Games, associated events and 'legacy uses'. The work is to be funded and undertaken directly by the Olympic Development Authority.

9 May 2006 A public enquiry is opened in relation to the application by the London Development Agency for confirmation of the London Development Agency (Lower Lea Valley, Olympic and Legacy) Compulsory Purchase Order 2005. The report states:

> During the Olympic Games some 80% of spectators are expected to arrive by rail, with West Ham station being one of the main arrival points. The above plots (Abbey Mills mosque site) are required for the construction of a ramp linking the

station to the Greenway, which will, in turn, provide access to the Olympic Park. After the Games the ramp will remain as part of the legacy of improved transport and pedestrian infrastructure with good accessibility to retained venues and to future development. On this basis... satisfied that there is a clear justification to secure the acquisition of these plots.

October 2006 The Tablighi Jamaat charitable trust's temporary permit expires before proper building work on the mosque can commence.

February 2007 Further details are revealed by the mosque's architect. It is reported that the mega-mosque will now house seventy thousand worshippers and incorporate a Muslim foundation, a mosque, an Islamic boarding school and accommodation to house travelling missionary groups. It is suggested that the development might serve as a reception centre for athletes and fans from Islamic countries during the 2012 games. The 'mega-mosque' development is reported to be Britain's largest religious building and expected to cost £300 million. At the time, the Tablighi Jamaat charitable trust Anjuman-e-Islahul Muslimeen had an average turnover of less than half a million pounds a year.

March 2007 A report by Waterman Environmental Services reveals that the Abbey Mills mosque site has medium to high levels of contamination. The report documents significant soil and groundwater impact (principally by mercury, lead, arsenic, oil and fuels), that asbestos fibres had been detected, that there is elevated soil contamination, and that there are methane and carbon dioxide land-gas readings.

February 2010 Newham Council orders Tablighi Jamaat to cease all public and religious activities on site.

February 2011 The Tablighi Jamaat trust begins a planning appeal against the decision.

23 May 2011 The Tablighi Jamaat trust overturns the enforcement notice and is granted a two-year extension within which to submit a master plan for the future of the site.

9 September 2012 The Paralympics closing ceremony takes place and concludes London's summer of Games.

19 September 2012 New plans for a ten-thousand-capacity mosque are submitted to Newham Council. New architects for the project tell the media that the scheme is the size of Battersea Power Station. The new development is expected to be at least four times the size of St Paul's Cathedral and is to include a library, dining hall, sports pitches and a visitor centre. (St Paul's Cathedral can house no more than 2,500 worshippers.)

October 2012 Just a month after the end of the London Olympic and Paralympic Games, a digger moves in to dig up the foundations of the West Ham ramp that had originally been installed at the far end of the District line platform to move a million stadium-bound spectators.

5 December 2012 Councillors consider at length new plans for a prayer hall for almost 7,500 men and a separate facility for about two thousand women. The planning application is rejected.

May 2013 The High Court orders the trust to clear the site and the Tablighi Jamaat trust makes an application to a judge to appeal the decision.

16 July 2013 The local council serves an enforcement notice on the charitable trust to remove those buildings without planning permission, stop using it as a place of worship, make the polluted grounds safe or appeal the notice.

June 2014 A public enquiry of the Planning Inspectorate opens at the ExCel Exhibition Centre to appeal the rejection of the plans for a 29,227-square-metre mosque and examine the expired permission granted to the site for the use of a temporary smaller mosque. A recommendation by the Planning Inspectorate is expected to be passed to the Communities Secretary for the final say on plans.

6 July 2015 At the tenth annual 7/7 Memorial Lecture, which took place at the British Medical Association in Tavistock Square, Tessa Jowell says, 'Empathy extends to the built environment – how new parts of our city are designed, how they fit with existing communities. So often "development" is seen as destructive of community. We need to keep a wide vision, looking at more than what immediately meets the eye, thinking empathically about how what is done affects the people all around. Just look at the way the Olympic park was developed. The idea was not just to transform the waterlogged and contaminated brownfield site into a glorious Olympic park but also to bind a community together, to help develop its capacity, to tighten and strengthen its bonds.'

7 July 2015 A tenth anniversary memorial service for the attacks is held at St Paul's Cathedral, conducted by the Bishop of London.

29 October 2015 The Secretary of State for Communities and Local Government, Greg Clark, dismisses the planning-permission appeal lodged by the Tablighi Jamaat trust and refuses planning permission for redevelopment of the derelict Abbey Mills site.

At the time of writing, temporary mosque buildings erected at the Abbey Mills site continue to be used and are reportedly attended by 2,500 to 3,000 Tablighi Jamaat worshippers each week – on an area of land in the heart of London, larger than six international rugby pitches in size.

Ten years on 7/7 remains the largest criminal investigation the UK has ever seen, costing £100 million. No direct convictions for involvement in 7/7 were ever made.

There remains no evidence to suggest that the bombers had any idea the Olympic vote was taking place on the morning of 6 July 2005.

There *is* evidence to suggest that someone was assisting them in their quest for martyrdom, which should have happened on the 6 July 2005 at 8.50 a.m., before the Olympic vote.

APPENDIX

Operation Theseus

Besides the 7/7 police investigation, which began in July 2005 and lasted five years, Operation Theseus was also the name for a failed World War II operation. During the Battle of Gazala, the Nazis had been heavily outnumbered, yet still triumphed when the Allies lost the city of Tobruk to German-led forces. Churchill called it a disgrace. After the defeat, the German general, Erwin Rommel, had allegedly said to a captured British officer, 'What difference does it make if you have two tanks to my one, when you spread them out and let me smash them in detail?'

The legend of Theseus

Theseus was the mythical Greek figure who journeyed to Crete in a black-sailed ship to slay the Minotaur in his labyrinthine lair using just a ball of string for guidance. On his return to Athens, Theseus had forgotten his promise to replace his black sails with white ones, to signal the success of the mission. On sighting the ship and thinking that his son had failed, Theseus's father, Aegeus, hurled himself off a cliff and drowned – resulting in the name for the Mediterranean between Greece and Turkey: the Aegean Sea.

The ship of Theseus paradox

After Theseus's ship had returned to dock in Athens, it was preserved in the harbour, for all to see, in memoriam.

Every time a plank decayed, it was replaced by a new timber. Eventually, it had been repaired so much and so often, that no one knew how much of the original vessel remained.

Philosophers argued over whether it was still the same ship or not, and the problem came to be known as the ship of Theseus paradox.

Identity and change

How many years had it taken before Jake's grandmother no longer thought of herself as Irish? If she lost that part of her heritage, was she still the same person? How many years before the girl in the sari shop no longer thought of herself as Indian? How long before you think of yourself as a British Muslim, rather than first and foremost Syrian, Iraqi, Somali? Is there a fear that our heritage will be consumed – replaced over time like the ship, plank by plank, by another culture – or does it remain steadfastly the same?

If we use the same old planks of wood each time to build an identical boat, generation after generation, and sail it to a new destination each time, expecting it to remain intact forever – is this realistic? Is this the Theseus paradox for religion?

Was the paradox of Operation Theseus the fact that it was set up to investigate a terrorist attack when all along it should have been concerned with the criminal motives behind it?

The Police Dependants' Trust

The Theseus Paradox supports the work of the Police Dependants' Trust, which includes development of the National Welfare Contingency Fund. The fund has been designed to assist with the mental-health needs of police officers following a major terrorist or other national incident.

Visit www.pdtrust.org for more details.

The 7/7 Memorial Trust

The Theseus Paradox supports the work of the 7/7 Memorial Trust as it continues to raise funds for a memorial in Tavistock Square gardens. The memorial will provide a fitting tribute to those who lost their lives on the Number 30 bus, and celebrate the courage and resilience of the survivors, the emergency services and those members of the public who did what they could to help. The Trust also stages the annual 7/7 Memorial Lecture, which was conceived to provide a lasting positive re-membrance to those who lost their lives across all four sites and to acknowledge the courage of survivors, victims' families and first responders, whose lives were changed forever on that day.

Visit www.tavistocksquarememorialtrust.org for more information.